If Only I Could Tell You

If Only I Could Tell You

Hannah Beckerman

wm

WILLIAM MORROW

An Imprint of Harper Collins*Publishers*

This is a work of fiction. Names, characters, places, and incidents are products of the author's imagination or are used fictitiously and are not to be construed as real. Any resemblance to actual events, locales, organizations, or persons, living or dead, is entirely coincidental.

HarperCollins books may be purchased for educational, business, or sales promotional use. For information, please email the Special Markets Department at SPsales@harpercollins.com.

Originally published as *If Only I Could Tell You* in Great Britain in 2019 by Orion Fiction, an imprint of The Orion Publishing Group LTD.

FIRST U.S. EDITION

Library of Congress Cataloging-in-Publication Data has been applied for.

ISBN 978-0-06-289054-2
ISBN 978-0-06-295218-9 (hardcover library edition)

19 20 21 22 23 LSC 10 9 8 7 6 5 4 3 2 1

For Aurelia:
from whom I promise never to keep secrets

Never to bid good-bye,
Or lip me the softest call,
Or utter a wish for a word, while I
Saw morning harden upon the wall,
Unmoved, unknowing
That your great going
Had place that moment, and altered all.

Thomas Hardy, "The Going"

Prologue

June 23, 1988

It is a Thursday morning and Jess is walking up the stairs even though she has no need; she has already brushed her teeth and pulled her hair into some semblance of a ponytail. Her schoolbag is leaning against the umbrella stand by the front door and, in a few minutes, she and Lily will meet in the hallway and begin making their way to school.

Later—many years later—Jess will speculate that somehow she knew, somehow she sensed what was happening: an inexplicable sisterly intuition compelling her to investigate.

As she reaches the top of the stairs, Lily is coming out of the spare bedroom. Her back is turned to Jess and she closes the door quietly, reverentially almost, her hands clasped around the handle. Jess watches her take in a long, deep breath that she seems to hold in her chest for an impossible length of time before letting it out slowly, steadily.

"What are you doing?"

Lily jumps around, her face flushed, eyes darting from left to right. "Why are you creeping up on me like that?" she hisses at Jess in an angry whisper that does not sound like her usual voice.

"We're not supposed to go in there this morning. We were told not to."

Jess hears plaintiveness in her own voice, bordering on a whine, and she winces at the sound of it.

"Do *not* tell Mum I was in there. I mean it, Jess. You don't want to be a telltale."

Lily's voice is quiet but firm, and there is a look in her eyes that Jess recognizes from all the times she has caught Lily using the telephone when their mum has told her not to, or the afternoons she has seen Lily smoking with her friends behind the children's playground in the park.

There is a moment of uncertainty, neither of them knowing what Jess's next move will be. Until her left foot joins her right on the top stair, Jess isn't sure what she's going to do next, either.

"I want to go in too."

The two sisters glare at one another and Jess feels something pass between them: something unknowable yet frightening that she can't, or daren't, articulate.

"You are *not* to go in there, Jess. Do you hear me?"

Lily's body blocks the door, her arm stretched behind her as if in the process of being arrested. Around the corner of Lily's body, Jess can see her sister's hand gripping the handle, a final barrier should Jess get that far.

"But I want to. If you've been in there, why shouldn't I?" Jess edges along the landing, emboldened by what she senses to be Lily's fragile hold over the situation.

"Stop it. I mean it, Jess. You must *not* go in."

The expression on Lily's face sends a cold draft tiptoeing along Jess's spine: her sister's flushed cheeks, narrowed eyes, pinched eyebrows. The panic trying to disguise itself as authority. It is unclear whether Lily is about to defend herself or launch an attack.

Fragments of memory play in Jess's head like conversational

earworms: things she has heard that she knows she shouldn't. All those murmured conversations behind closed doors, confessions whispered into telephones when the speaker thought no one was listening.

Jess's stomach somersaults beneath the elasticized waistband of her bottle-green skirt. She feels the blood pulsing at her wrists as if her body is urging her into action. She imagines taking a step forward and pushing Lily aside, a struggle in which she manages—against Lily's advanced years and superior strength—to emerge victorious. But thoughts of what might happen afterward—what she might see and what she might learn—cement her feet to the floor.

The alarm on Lily's digital watch beeps. Lily jerks her hand to turn it off and Jess feels herself flinch. She knows it is Lily's 8:30 a.m. alarm, the one her sister has set to ensure they leave for school on time now that their parents are too distracted to remind them. Lily holds Jess's gaze for a few seconds more until Jess is the first to turn her head away. Jess begins to make her way down the stairs, and only then does she realize that her legs are trembling. She hears Lily's footsteps close on her heels but does not turn around. She cannot bear to see that look on Lily's face again: a look that has told Jess something she does not want to know.

All the way down, Jess contemplates finding her mum, telling her where Lily has been, what she thinks has taken place inside that bedroom. But by the time she reaches the bottom stair, Jess knows she cannot. To tell her mum would be to voice suspicions Jess is not yet ready to assert, things she does not, at the age of ten, have the courage to say out loud.

Instead, she picks up her schoolbag and exits the front door, unsure whether it is the summer heat or Lily's breath she can feel prickling the skin on the back of her neck. She does not yet know it, but by the time she gets home this afternoon, the fabric of her family will have been altered irrevocably, and the morning's events will repeat in her mind like a record stuck under the groove of a needle for the next thirty years.

Part One

February 2016

Chapter 1
Audrey

Audrey Siskin sat on the bed, palms flat beside her on the duvet, arms locked, as if unsure whether she was coming or going, and cast her eyes around the room she was being encouraged to think of as her own. Familiar objects stood forlornly and ill at ease, like children in a classroom on the first day of school. There was the wrought-iron double bedstead that had served all the years of her marriage and beyond; the white-painted dressing table she'd dreamed of as a child but hadn't been able to afford until adulthood; the tall oak wardrobe she and Edward had bought when they'd first moved into the house in Barnsbury Square, newly married and five months pregnant.

Leaning forward, Audrey ripped at the packing tape on one of the two dozen cardboard boxes stacked up around the room but couldn't bring herself to flip open the lid. Once she'd unpacked, that was it: there was no going back.

It's not far, Mum. Only a few miles. Things won't be that different at all.

Both her daughters had said it, separately but equally persuasively. And technically—geographically—both Lily and Jess were right. It was barely seven miles, less as the crow flew. A simple exchange of north London for west. Islington for

Shepherd's Bush. Georgian for Victorian. And yet to Audrey it felt as though she'd swapped the Earth for the moon.

She knew how lucky she was, having two daughters vying for her to move in with them, knew that it was better to make the move now rather than in a year's time when she would likely find it even more difficult. But Audrey still couldn't help feeling that it was all wrong. Children shouldn't become responsible for their parents: it upset the natural order of things. But then, Audrey thought, images spooling through her mind of all the events she'd forget if forgetting were an option, so many episodes in her life had upset the natural order. So many of the defining moments—births, deaths, marriages—were not how they should have been had the world spun faithfully on its axis without ever tilting a few degrees out of kilter.

"Granny, how are you getting on? Do you need a hand with anything?"

Mia's voice drifted up the stairs and into the bedroom which had, until today, been hers. She would now be sleeping in the small bedroom on the top floor that had once been the attic. There was concern in her granddaughter's voice that had tried to reshape itself into something approaching normality.

"No thanks, darling. I'm just going to make a start on these boxes. I'll be down soon." Audrey pushed herself to her feet, the mattress springs creaking in sympathy. Looking around her new bedroom, she didn't know quite where to start. She'd organized the move in such a daze that she wasn't sure what she'd thrown out and what she'd kept or what she might find.

Ripping the tape off another cardboard box and pulling back the lid, she was greeted by a pile of carefully wrapped objects, neatly stacked. Unwrapping the first, she found a framed photograph, the color slightly faded. As she stared at the picture she was aware of the sands of time slipping back through the hourglass.

Her girls on a beach—Woolacombe Bay, was it?—running along the shore, their arms and legs out of focus where their limbs had swept too swiftly across the frame for the shutter speed to capture them. The sun high in a cloudless sky, indigo sea greeting the horizon, the small white triangle of a boat's sail visible in the distance. Her girls: holding hands, laughing, a shaft of light flaring across the frame to bathe them in an ethereal glow.

Audrey ran her fingers across the glass, over plaited hair, tanned limbs, and sun-kissed cheeks, and could almost feel the heat of that summer's day. She could hear the sound of her daughters' laughter, the waves undulating against the sand, the gulls calling across the sky. She could smell the salt on the breeze, feel the sand between her toes, taste her daughters' joy. She longed to stretch her arms into the photograph, wrap them around her children's shoulders, pull them close and never let them go.

Audrey gripped the photograph, her heart twisting beneath her ribs.

Sometimes, nowadays, only photographs reassured her that she hadn't made it all up, that it wasn't just a fantasy. That once upon a time her daughters had been friends.

She breathed slowly as she thought about all the years that had been lost. Even now it still seemed unreal to her that it had been almost three decades since Jess had turned against Lily. Audrey could picture Jess now, at ten years old, face hardened almost overnight by things no child should ever have to experience, as if those events had stolen Audrey's little girl and replaced her with a child she barely recognized. For months afterward, Audrey had hoped it was shock that had changed Jess's behavior, that soon she would revert to the happy little girl she had been before. She had spent years clinging to the belief that the events of their childhood would eventually bring Lily and Jess back together. Instead, they had torn Audrey's family apart.

Audrey's pulse quickened as she thought about all those family meals eaten in silence: Audrey, Lily, and Jess at a kitchen table too big for just the three of them, Audrey keeping her voice bright as she asked the girls about school, trying hard not to react to Jess's monosyllabic responses. She could picture her hand, knocking on Jess's bedroom door, asking if she wanted to come and watch TV, and hearing the same flat reply, night after night: *No, I just want to be on my own.* Audrey had asked herself repeatedly over the years what she might have missed and whether she could have done anything differently to change the course of her daughters' relationship. So many times since Jess had left home and cut Lily out of her life completely, Audrey had begged Jess to tell her the reason, but Jess had refused to confide in her. Now Audrey had two daughters who never spoke and two seventeen-year-old granddaughters, born just six weeks apart, who were not permitted to meet.

Her nails dug into her palms as she remembered the last time she had tried—and failed—to reconcile her family.

"Granny, is everything OK? Do you want me to come and help?"

"Thanks, darling, but I'm fine. I'm just pottering."

Fine. Audrey didn't know why she used a word they all knew to be so far from the truth.

Looking into the dressing table mirror there was no sign, nothing to give her away. Only the most modest lines around her eyes. Her hair, salon-dried yesterday, was artificially brown but still kicked up playfully from where it rested on her shoulders. Her makeup was faultless, applied that morning before she'd even got dressed.

People often told her they couldn't believe she was sixty-two. *You look at least a decade younger*, they'd exclaim and foolishly she'd allowed herself to believe there was some significance in it, that an outward appearance of well-being automatically filtered through to the inside. As though a perfectly appetizing apple couldn't be rotten when you bit into it.

It was only if you looked a little closer, as Audrey did now, that you might have detected the palest purple hue forming half-moons under her eyes, or the frequency with which the muscles across her forehead pulled into a frown. It was only watching her closely that you might have observed the shortness of breath, the small half-gasps as if some air had got left behind and was trying to catch up. But there was nothing really on her face to inform a casual observer that, inside her, cells were dividing and multiplying with unremitting speed. There was nothing to betray the truth that she was, in fact, dying.

Audrey turned away from the mirror and bent down toward the box at her feet. As she reached inside, a sharp pain sliced through the right half of her abdomen, causing her to ease herself back onto the bed. As she breathed slowly against the pain, Audrey understood why Jess had been so keen for her to move in sooner rather than later. Audrey had wanted to wait, to hold on to her house and her independence for as long as she could. She had hoped to live at home until her body made it clear that it could no longer cope. Now she felt grateful for Jess's counsel, grateful that she had sold the house and her furniture, keeping only the essentials—both practical and sentimental—before her health deteriorated even further. Sitting on the bed, willing the pain away, she realized that had she waited she might not have been able to organize the move herself, might have imposed an even greater burden on her daughters.

Pulling another framed photograph free of its wrapping, she was greeted by Edward and his parents staring back at her. In the center of the photograph, Lily lay swaddled in Edward's arms, his parents standing stiffly on either side of them in front of a Christmas tree. Turning over the frame, she found her handwriting scrawled across the back: *Barnsbury Square, Christmas 1972.* Her and Edward's first Christmas as a married couple, their first as parents, their first in their own home.

As her eyes roamed from one person to the next she searched, as she had so many times over the years, for any hint in those time-frozen expressions of what was to come. But all Audrey could see was her father-in-law's rigid social etiquette, her mother-in-law's sour grimace, and Edward's joy in the six-week bundle of perfection he held.

Looking at the photograph, Audrey wondered how Edward's parents would have coped with what happened sixteen years after that picture had been taken. The year her and Edward's lives had changed irreparably, the ground rupturing beneath them, sucking them deep into a sinkhole from which they would never truly emerge. She wondered how his parents would have borne the grief, the anger and the shame, how it had been a blessing, really, that neither of them had lived long enough to witness it. Sometimes Audrey envied them their ignorance, envied them being spared the guilt, the confusion, and the litany of unanswered questions that had plagued her all these years.

She tilted her head from side to side, trying to iron out her thoughts. She couldn't allow herself to think about Edward today when so many different feelings were already competing for attention. And yet, for the past five months, ever since a routine mammogram had detected a lump in her breast—a lump that had led to the discovery of secondary tumors in her liver and cancer in her lymph nodes—Audrey had become preoccupied with the past. Knowing she would most likely be dead in eighteen months' time had caused the floodgates to open on memories she had spent decades trying to forget.

She gripped the solid black finial at the end of the bed and ordered herself to stop thinking. But as she leaned forward and pulled the packing tape from the top of the next box, she remembered sitting around the kitchen table nearly three decades before, feeling the air thicken with a tension she could neither cut through nor explain, as Jess glared at Lily and refused to tell anyone why suddenly she couldn't bear to be in the same room as her sister.

Chapter 2
Jess

Standing in front of a small square monitor, watching actors repeat their lines for an eighth time, Jess rubbed the back of her neck where the muscles had compressed into tight knots. Halfway through his final speech, the male actor stumbled on words he'd already fluffed seven times, and Jess sensed a murmur of exasperation among the crew.

She'd known when she arrived on set at six o'clock that morning—before anyone else, as was her responsibility as senior location manager—that today would be one of those days. First-day shoots on new drama shows invariably were: the cast adjusting to performing outside the rehearsal room, crews reestablishing acquaintances from previous jobs or forming new alliances. There was always a tense anticipation, like the moments before the first guests arrive at a party you're hosting.

"Right, let's take it from the top again. Izzy, can we freshen up Lucia's powder, please?"

Justin, the director, started talking to the two lead actors about commitment to the scene while the makeup artist refreshed their powder. Jess pulled her thick padded coat tighter around herself, wishing she'd had the foresight to put tights on under her jeans and thermal socks inside her sneakers. The trouble with filming in listed buildings was that they were perennially cold, especially in late February. She'd warned the producer, when she'd first found this location a stone's throw from Spitalfields Market, that she feared it was one of those buildings that would be arctic no matter how many portable heaters they installed, but he'd wanted to go ahead with it anyway.

The director's assistant called for quiet and the cameras started rolling again before the two lead actors launched into the scene for the ninth time.

Jess sipped the sugary tea rapidly cooling inside a styrofoam cup corniced with the firm indentations of her teeth. She put the cup on the floor, undid the makeshift bun she'd wound her hair into at 5 a.m., and tied it back tightly into a ponytail, her hair protesting at the roots. Watching the monitor as the actors worked their way through the scene, she tried to quash her frustration that she was on set at all. Professionally she knew she had to be there today but that didn't stop her wishing she wasn't, didn't stop her resenting the fact that she wasn't at home helping her mum to unpack instead. Her mum had said that she understood, that she'd be fine and had lots to sort through, that she'd have Mia for company. But Jess knew how difficult it was for her to give up the house she'd lived in for forty-five years, the house which had seen all the defining moments of her mum's adult life.

"Excellent. That was great. Right, let's take a fifteen-minute break before we reset downstairs. Jess—where's Jess?"

Jess swallowed hard as she walked across the seventeenth-century mahogany floorboards into the first-floor drawing room, where Justin was sitting in a canvas-backed folding chair.

"Jess, Sam says there's a dodgy plug socket on the top floor where we're filming later. Could you check it out? I'd rather not electrocute the entire crew on the first day if we can possibly help it."

Justin laughed, and Jess fabricated a smile, mumbled a reply, and trudged up the stairs, her toes beginning to numb in her sneakers.

Locating the loose plug socket and covering it with black gaffer tape while cursing herself for not having spotted it sooner, she glanced back down the stairs to check that no one was on their way up before pulling her phone from her pocket and switching it on.

No messages, no emails, no missed calls.

She dialed Mia's number, the tips of her fingers stiff with cold, five rings trilling in her ear before she heard a breathless answer.

"Hi, Mum. What's up?"

"Nothing. I just wanted to check everything's OK with you and Granny?"

"Yep, we're fine. I'm doing my homework and Granny's unpacking."

Jess pulled at a loose piece of skin at the base of her thumbnail, felt a sharp skewer of pain as she tugged it free. "I'm hoping we won't wrap too late today. I'll ask Justin if Sacha can clear up for me and then I should be home in time to give Granny a hand."

"Honestly, don't worry about it. We're totally fine. *We're fine, aren't we, Granny?* Granny says yes. Seriously, it's not as if there's much you can do here anyway. Granny said she'd rather unpack by herself and I've already made a fish pie for dinner. If you're not home in time, Granny and I will eat, and we'll save you some for later."

Jess sucked at her thumb where a small speck of blood was seeping through. "OK, if you're sure. Just don't forget you've got that history essay to write this weekend. You don't want to be rushing it at the last minute."

"I won't, I promise. Have a good day and we'll see you later. Love you."

"I love you too."

As the call ended, Jess opened the address book on her phone and scrolled through the names, trying to find someone she might text to avoid the professional small talk downstairs. There were so many entries—school friends, university friends, former colleagues—and yet no one to whom she could send a chatty unsolicited message without it seeming strange. It was as if her address book were a directory of ghosts, a reminder of all the friendships she had allowed to lapse over the years.

She hesitated, felt temptation prickle the tips of her fingers. She watched her thumb hover over the internet icon, felt it goading her, enticing her, drawing her in.

Stop. Don't do it. You'll only regret it afterward.

The voice of reason spoke clearly in Jess's head but her hand now seemed to be working independently of common sense. She watched as she began typing in a name she had entered so many times before, and so frequently, that Google's search engine knew precisely what she was seeking after only the third letter.

Do not click on the links. It's not too late. You can still stop.

But it was too late. It was always too late once the seed had been sown. A moment's boredom, a sleepless night, a frustrating day. Jess could never stop herself once the thought had occurred.

Lily Goldsmith.

The sight of her sister's name caused a tightening of the muscles across Jess's stomach.

Jess scrolled down the list of results, hunting for an unread article. Three pages in and every item was something she'd seen before: Lily speaking at international conferences, Lily collecting awards, Lily in receipt of yet another promotion.

Jess clicked the news tab, hoping it might bear more fruit. But there was nothing there that she hadn't read before either. She didn't know whether to feel relieved or exasperated. Part of her was pleased her sister hadn't managed to garner any more press coverage in the forty-eight hours since she'd last checked but another part of her felt cheated.

Put the phone away, Jess. There's nothing new to see. Don't do it to yourself.

But it was too easy. All that information, all those photographs, just waiting for her to look at them. It wasn't really stalking. It wasn't as if she were checking the social media account of an ex-boyfriend. But Facebook hadn't been invented when Iain had walked out on her two weeks before Mia's first birthday, failing to give any explanation other than that he just couldn't handle the relationship any more. Google-searching your own sister was different. Jess was only finding out the facts of Lily's life that she'd already know if she ever let her mum talk about her. She knew it wasn't rational, knew that hunting for information about someone you'd refused to see for years didn't make sense. She knew that whatever she found would only burrow beneath her ribs and tap out a rhythm of envy for the rest of the day. But still she couldn't stop herself. She had a compulsion to know, even though the knowing would hurt her.

Jess clicked on a link that Google informed her she'd last visited five days ago: a magazine article with the headline "Having It All." As the piece opened, she stared, unblinking, at the lead photograph.

Lily, Daniel, Phoebe: the three of them sitting on a pale gray sofa against a backdrop of floor-to-ceiling bookshelves, multicolored spines providing wallpaper to a scene that spoke of confidence, culture, prosperity. It was the kind of room

Jess might have chosen as the location for a drama series about an affluent metropolitan family. Except this wasn't a TV set. This was Lily's perfect home. Lily's perfect life.

And in the center of the photograph sat Jess's sister, looking a decade younger than her forty-three years, with her neat dark chignon, cap-sleeve fitted dress, and minimalist makeup, as though she were a model in the pages of a fashion magazine.

Jess skim-read the article, text she was so familiar with she could have recited it verbatim, searching for something—anything—she might have missed before.

Lily Goldsmith has had what many regard to be a meteoric rise. Winning her first international award at the age of just twenty-three, she is now one of the most revered marketing professionals on either side of the Atlantic. She is, to many in the industry, a symbol of the penetrability of the glass ceiling.

Jess exhaled loudly, watched her warm breath condense in the cold air around her.

Married to millionaire entertainment lawyer Daniel Goldsmith, Lily has managed to achieve what so many women aspire to but few successfully accomplish: a happy work-life balance. The couple share their Holland Park home with their teenage daughter, Phoebe, currently a sixth-form pupil at an exclusive all-girls school in west London.

"If I knew the secret of success, I'd bottle it and sell it," Lily laughs. "What I do know is that I've worked incredibly hard and I've always set myself very clear goals. Sometimes the landscape changes and you can't always predict where you'll be in five years' time, but knowing where you'd like to be gives you a much better chance of getting there, I think. And I've been incredibly lucky in

having amazing support at home. I imagine it's nigh-on impossible doing a job like mine if your family aren't 100 percent behind you."

Jess studied the face of the brother-in-law she'd never met. He was exactly how she imagined a hot-shot entertainment lawyer to be: arrogantly handsome, oozing the kind of self-confidence that only extreme wealth and constant admiration could bring. Phoebe was pretty in the haughty, disinterested way that screamed of teenage entitlement, and there was something familiar about her that made Jess swipe through the other photographs, her finger jabbing at the right-hand arrow, propelling her through images she'd seen dozens of times before: the ebony grand piano gleaming in sunlight that streamed through floor-to-ceiling windows; the kitchen with its white bespoke units, shiny butler sink, white-painted floorboards, and wall of glass leading onto a manicured garden beyond; Lily's study, empty but for a stark metal desk, a MacBook, and a mobile phone. All so neat, all so clean and bright, as though Lily had whitewashed her past with a spotless designer home.

Jess thought about her own house in comparison: the tattered brown sofa she'd bought secondhand sixteen years ago and had never been able to replace. The cheap melamine kitchen cupboards sporting wonky hinges and peeling edges, their multiple chips like battle scars. The small round table that just about accommodated three people as long as you breathed in when someone wanted to pass behind you. The mortgage payments she feared, every month, she might not be able to meet.

She tried to imagine what her sister's life must be like: a carousel of dinner parties, cocktail parties, awards ceremonies, celebrity encounters. A diary filled months in advance with Saturday night plans, Sunday brunches, exotic holidays and, no doubt, an endless supply of friends to suit every occasion. Jess couldn't remember the last time she'd gone out on a Friday or Saturday night, couldn't remember the last time she'd had anyone around for dinner other than her mum. There always seemed to be more pressing things clamoring for her attention: washing and ironing, sourcing the next freelance job, preparing her accounts, helping Mia with her homework.

As Jess stared at the photograph of Lily sitting at her desk—the face so familiar yet so unknown—she was aware of her breath becoming shallow, of something lodging in her throat. She found herself thinking back to the day, almost three decades ago, when they had seen one another at their dad's grave on the first anniversary of his death. Jess had sneaked out of school in her lunch hour only to find Lily already kneeling by his headstone, crocodile tears streaking her cheeks. Jess had screamed at Lily that day, words she had forgotten the moment they'd erupted from her lips. She had been so filled with fury and bile that it hadn't been the words themselves that had mattered but the violence with which she'd delivered them. Now all she remembered about that gray September day was the feeling of ferocious certainty that Lily didn't deserve to be there. After what Lily had done, she had forfeited the right to weep at their father's grave.

"Jess! If you've fixed that socket, can you come back down? I want to check on something for Monday's shoot."

Jess stole one last glance at her sister's face, wondering how Lily managed to sail through life as though she had nothing to hide, nothing to feel guilty for, wondering whether her sister had managed to convince herself of her innocence or whether she was content living with the knowledge of the damage she had done.

A scene flashed into Jess's head, flickering in her mind like an old Super-8 film: standing outside the spare bedroom, looking into Lily's eyes and knowing what must have taken place behind that door, yet being too weak—too afraid, too overwhelmed—to raise the alarm.

"Jess! Can you come back down?"

Jess blinked away the image of Lily with her hands clasped around the door handle, breathed against the persistent memory of all that had happened later that day and all that had come after. Swallowing against the regret and the grief catching in her throat, she switched off her phone and traipsed back down the stairs.

Chapter 3
Lily

Laughter pealed from the far end of the table and Lily wondered what joke she'd missed. She passed the prosecco bottle to Pippa without filling her glass and sipped her mineral water, glancing at her phone for the second time in as many minutes, wondering how soon she might be able to escape.

"So, has Phoebe signed up for the China trip? Honestly, how lucky are our girls? In our day no one went further than France on a school trip. Clementine is *so* excited. She's done nothing but read up on Chinese history for the past two weeks. I've booked her a Mandarin tutor but I don't know how much she'll pick up in eight months."

Lily racked her brain for any mention of a school trip to China. She was sure she'd remember if Phoebe had told her but had no recollection of it. "Yes, it sounds amazing. I don't think Phoebe's decided yet. When's the deadline?"

"Monday, so she'd better get her skates on if she wants to go. It does sound marvelous. I said to Tom that perhaps he and I ought to go to China, but he said that if he's only got seven weeks' annual leave, he'd rather spend them in a place he knows and likes rather than risk ending up somewhere dreadful. Honestly, he's *so* unadventurous. Sometimes I think I should just pack up and head off somewhere exotic like that woman in *Eat, Pray, Love.*"

Lily tried to picture Pippa's husband, but men were so rarely expected to get involved in school-related social activities that they all morphed into one nebulous mass in her head. She glanced around the table at the group of mums she'd first met six years ago when Phoebe had started secondary school and with whom she'd dutifully been attending a termly get-together ever since. She knew some of the other mums met more regularly, that they had an encyclopedic knowledge of each other's lives, but then, some of these women hadn't worked for as long as Lily had known them.

"How's Daniel these days? Still hobnobbing with Hollywood celebrities?"

Lily turned toward Annabel and glanced briefly at her phone. "He's fine, thanks. Great. Busy, as always."

"We should organize a supper soon. I haven't seen Daniel for *ages* and he's such a great guy. I'll WhatsApp you some dates. Maybe I'll invite Anoushka and Pippa too—what do you think?"

Before she had a chance to reply, Lily's phone buzzed and her hand shot out toward it, knocking over Annabel's prosecco glass, its contents trickling across the wooden table in thin, determined rivulets. "God, I'm sorry. That was so clumsy of me. Here let me mop it up." A moment later, Lily handed the sopping napkins to a passing waiter and retrieved her phone, only to discover that it wasn't the message she'd been hoping for.

"Everything OK, Lily?"

"Yes, just my boss. Nothing urgent."

"They're sending you work emails on a Saturday? God, they really do squeeze every last drop out of you, don't they? But I've been meaning to ask, how's your mum getting on? Is she still living at home?"

Lily studied Annabel's face, wondering if somehow she'd found out the truth. "She is, yes. I wanted her to come and live with us but I can understand why she's keen to stay in her own home. I speak to her every day, she comes for lunch every Sunday, and I've got caregivers lined up to help look after her whenever she needs them."

Lily forced herself to stop gabbling, the lies pricking her tongue. But she'd learned over the years that the best lies were coated with a dusting of the truth. It was true that she spoke to her mum every day, true that Audrey came for lunch each Sunday. It was even true that she'd compiled a list of private nurses who could be dispatched to Jess's house when the time came, if Jess would let them through the door. But as for the rest of it, how could Lily possibly explain that her mum was living with her sister when she'd never told any of these women that her sister even existed?

Her jaw clenched at the thought of her mum, right now, unpacking at Jess's house. Lily still didn't understand her decision. Because what rational explanation could there be for her choosing to live with Jess, when Jess had single-handedly ruptured their family for the past twenty-eight years?

"Well, she's very lucky to have you. And at least you've got Daniel to share the burden with. I can't imagine having to deal with a sick parent on your own."

Lily nodded even as her head began to spin. Her fingers grabbed the hard edge of the table, her throat tightening as if invisible hands were pressed around her neck. She slid back her chair, pushed herself to her feet, picked up her coat. "I'm really sorry, I feel rather unwell all of a sudden. I think I just need some fresh air. I'm so sorry. Let me know how much I owe for drinks, won't you?"

She heard questions trailing after her as she negotiated

her way through the avenue of tables until she was out on Kensington High Street, the February chill numbing her cheeks. All around her people hurried to shops, bars, and restaurants as Lily stumbled forward, willing her pulse to slow down.

Turning a corner onto a quieter street, she wished she could teleport herself home and that, when she got there, things would have changed, decisions been reversed, life restored to some semblance of normality. But as she leaned against a wall and closed her eyes, it wasn't the hallway of the home she shared with Daniel and Phoebe that loomed into view. Instead, she was greeted by a scene she had tried so hard over the years to delete from her memory, a scene that occupied so many of her dreams in spite of her determination to erase it, as though the harder she willed it away the more fiercely it returned: following her sister down the stairs, praying that Jess would not suddenly find the courage to insist on going into the spare bedroom after all, willing Jess not to turn around and see the tears in her eyes.

Lily waited until the panic began to subside and then hailed a cab, stepped inside its warm blast of air and gave the driver her address.

All she wanted was to be at home.

Walking through the wide, glossy black front door, Lily was greeted by a sight she wasn't expecting to see. "Daniel? Where are you? What's going on?"

From Daniel's study farther down the hallway she heard the sound of a phone call ending and the squeak of his office chair. As he emerged and walked along the black-and-white tiled floor toward her, she registered the effort he was making to appear normal.

"You're back early. What happened to afternoon drinks with the school mums?"

"I didn't feel well so I didn't stay. Why are your bags in the hallway already? You're not leaving until tomorrow."

Daniel's eyes flicked from left to right before landing on the collection of suitcases gathered by the front door. "I had to change my flight. They've organized a partners' dinner for tomorrow night and it was going to be too tight if I didn't fly until the morning. I texted earlier to tell you, just after you left for the gym. I figured your phone must be out of battery."

Lily's fingers squeezed around the phone in her pocket which hadn't run out of battery until her cab journey home. "I didn't get a message from you. I'd have come straight home if I had. When are you leaving?"

A light rash stippled Daniel's cheeks as he glanced down at his watch. "The cab will be here in about ten minutes."

"Ten minutes? You were going to leave without saying goodbye?" Lily thought about the interminable hour of school-mum chat she'd just endured, all the time waiting to see if her phone would ring, to see if Daniel would call to tell her he'd changed his mind.

"I'm really sorry. Of course I didn't want to leave without saying goodbye. I did message you. But you've been out most of the day and I had to take this flight tonight."

"What about Phoebe? You can't leave without saying goodbye to her."

"I already have. She's in her room. She's fine, Lil, honestly."

Lily blanched at the thought of Phoebe upstairs having already said her goodbyes. "I'm worried about her, Daniel, you know I am. She's become so . . . secretive lately. I worry about the impact you being away will have on her."

Daniel sighed. "Please, Lil, let's not do this again. We've been through it a hundred times. I'd be mad to turn this opportunity down. It's only six months working out of the New York office and then I stand a really good chance of being made a managing partner. I thought that's what you wanted—what we both wanted."

Lily recalled all their conversations over the years about the milestones they planned to reach in their careers. She'd always supported Daniel's ambitions, just as he had hers. She'd just never envisaged that they would have to live on separate continents to achieve them. "It was. It is. It's just . . . A six-month assignment isn't insignificant. You're dismantling our lives and I'm allowed to feel ambivalent about that."

Lily folded her arms across her chest so that Daniel couldn't see how much her hands were shaking. In the tension between them she imagined him stepping forward, wrapping his arms around her, leaning his head against hers—his breath hot on her neck—and whispering into her ear that he didn't have to go.

"I'm not dismantling our lives. Let's be honest, we barely see each other during the week as it is because one of us is always working, so me moving abroad for a few months is hardly going to be a radical change. Don't look at me like that—you know it's true."

Lily glanced past Daniel, down the hallway, toward the new kitchen they'd finished installing only three months before. "I know we work hard and I know this is a great opportunity for you. I suppose . . . I just wish you found it a bit harder to leave all this—to leave us—behind."

Daniel took a step toward her, placed his hands gently on her shoulders. "Of course it's difficult to leave. But it's not forever. And I know our life is great in lots of ways, but that doesn't mean . . ." His voice was low and quiet before it trailed off altogether.

"Doesn't mean what?"

"I just think some space might do us good."

"In what way?"

There was a momentary pause during which it was almost possible to hear the scales balancing in Daniel's head, weighing up the pros and cons of saying what was on his mind. "You know what I'm talking about. You've never been able to let go of the past. I honestly don't know whether it's because you don't want to or that you can't, but it's always there between us. It's been like that for years. And I'm sorry, you know I am, but you're not the only one who's affected by it. It has an impact on all of us." He looked away, twisting the platinum band on his ring finger that Lily had placed there almost eighteen years before.

"You're bringing that up now? Daniel, that's so unfair."

They stared at one another and it was as if all the things they had never dared speak of were weeping silently in the space between them.

"For God's sake. Can you two stop arguing for *five minutes* before Dad leaves?"

Lily whipped her head up to where Phoebe was standing at the top of the stairs, glowering at them both, dark kohl framing her eyes, bright red burnishing her lips.

"You know I can hear every word you're saying? Do you ever think I might have had enough of listening to your arguments?"

"We're not arguing, darling. We're just—"

Daniel's phone bleeped loudly and Lily watched him glance down at it, grimace, return it to the pocket of his jeans. "My cab's here. I've got to go." He ran up the stairs, put his arms around Phoebe, and kissed the top of her head. "I'll come back for a weekend soon, OK, sweetheart? And, remember, I'm on email or Skype or WhatsApp or even the good old-fashioned telephone whenever you need me. I love you."

He kissed her again before racing back down the stairs, then took a deep breath and turned to Lily. "I'll message you when I get to the apartment, but it'll be late so I'll call you tomorrow. And, Lily, please let's see the positives in this. It might do us good, honestly."

His lips grazed her cheek, his fingers gently squeezing her arm just above the elbow. Then the front door was open and he was loading suitcases into the cab, turning to wave and smile one last time. And then he was gone.

Lily stood by the open front door, watching the cab until it reached the crossroads at the end, pulled out onto the main road, and disappeared.

"Can you close the door, Mum? It's bloody freezing in here." Phoebe was still standing at the top of the stairs, eyebrows raised, the sharp contours of her sleek dark bob jutting across her cheeks.

Pushing the door shut, Lily caught sight of her own reflection in the hallway mirror and was startled by how pale she looked. Footsteps stomped across the landing overhead and she heard the decisive slam of Phoebe's bedroom door.

She stood still in the silence, glancing down at her watch: a quarter to five. Hours until bedtime, yet she was overcome by a powerful urge to lie down and sleep. She thought about knocking on Phoebe's door, checking she was OK, seeing if she wanted a drink or a snack. But Lily knew that when Phoebe was angry, the best thing she could give her was space.

Walking up the stairs and into her bedroom, she closed the door and lay down on the bed. Curling onto her side, she pulled one of Daniel's pillows toward her and clutched it to her chest. And as she shut her eyes she found herself back there, in a bed she was never supposed to have slept in.

She is lying on her side, spooning her sister's body. They are not meant to share a bed, or even a bedroom, but sometimes Lily cannot help creeping in here after the television has been switched off, after the landing light has gone dark, after the soft murmurings of her parents' voices have fallen silent and the house is still save for the anxious beating of Lily's heart. Her sister breathes in deeply and when she exhales, Lily feels the warmth of her breath drifting across the soft down of her arm. It has been six months since it began and still Lily cannot persuade herself to accept it. It is as though her mind has been cleaved into two distinct parts: the knowing and the not-knowing, the acceptance and the denial. She can willingly tolerate the self-delusion if it means she is not forced to imagine a future that may have already begun to arrive. Lily tightens her arm around her sister's waist. Her body seems so small, like a baby bird alone in a nest, predators hovering overhead, with only Lily to protect her. She would, she knows, do anything to safeguard her little sister, to stop this happening to her. Her head hurts with the injustice of it and she leans in closer as though trying to divide the burden between them. She feels the warmth of her sister's feet against hers, imagines the pale half-moon of the toenails she has so often painted. As she lies in the darkness, she feels certain that she will never love anyone with the fierceness she feels right now.

Lily forced her eyes open and sat up, thrusting the pillow back against the white wooden headboard. She rubbed her fingers in concentric circles against her temples, trying to erase the image from her mind, but the memory was there in her muscles, her skin, in the feel of her sister's breath on her arm, and the gentle vibration of her heartbeat.

She thought about how she and her sister would curl up on the sofa together, watching movies under a duvet they'd dragged down the stairs, singing along to musicals at the tops of their voices, chocolate cornflake cakes balanced on their laps, mugs of steaming hot chocolate on the coffee table. She remembered running races in the park, slowing her own pace right at the end so that they always crossed the finish line together. She remembered her sister's laughter: such a rich, rounded, infectious sound that made you want to dive right in and float around inside.

The sense of loss burrowed deep inside Lily's chest. Sometimes she wasn't sure whether it was more painful to remember or if it would be more upsetting to forget.

The front door slammed and Lily called out Phoebe's name only to be greeted by silence.

She walked out of the bedroom, down the stairs, and into the kitchen, where she poured herself a glass of water, hoping to flush herself clean of memories. But as she stood alone, looking out of the window into the darkness, Lily acquiesced to the bitter regret that she had not known all those years ago, lying in bed just the two of them, that all her efforts to protect her little sister would be in vain.

Chapter 4
Audrey

Audrey sipped her cup of tea and drew the curtains against the faded light. She looked around the room: only half a dozen boxes to go. Tearing off packing tape from the box at her feet, she found her jewelry, perfumes, and various trinkets, none of which she felt inclined to unpack. She opened the packing crate next to it, wedged between the dressing table and the wardrobe. Inside were dozens of diaries in a rainbow of colors, their hardback spines cracked and fraying.

She had always kept a diary, ever since her tenth birthday. Audrey could picture it now, the bright blue journal her mum had given her the day she'd entered double figures, all those clean white pages waiting to be filled with her hopes, fears, disappointments, and dreams.

She picked one up at random.

1969. The year she'd turned sixteen.

As she flicked through the pages, nostalgia leaped out at her in sprawling blue ink. There was her unmistakable looped handwriting, plump and eager, as though the letters were yet to lose their childhood puppy fat. And then the sight of a particular date caused her to pause.

December 9, 1969. Her sixteenth birthday.

She smoothed her palm over the page and then held the

two corners between her fingers as if handling a prayer book, before allowing her eyes to cast down onto the writing below.

Had the best birthday. School was nothing special except Sandra and Val had clubbed together to get me a brooch we'd all been eyeing up in Woolworths last weekend, which I wanted to put on straight away, but I knew Mr. Gibbons would just confiscate it if I did.

When I got home, Mum and Dad were in the kitchen, waiting for me. I don't know how Dad managed to get out of the factory early because they never let you out early for anything, but when I asked him, Dad just winked and said he'd told his foreman it was a very special occasion. Mum had cooked a steak and kidney pie for tea and she'd bought some white paper doilies to put the plates on so it all looked really pretty. And then they gave me my present, which was the best present ever—Nina Simone's Silk & Soul. I've been listening to it loads round at Sandra's house, but I never thought I'd have a copy of my own. Then Mum brought out a gigantic Victoria sponge she'd made and Dad reminded me to make a wish when I blew out the candles. I wished I'd get good enough O-level results to stay on at school for A-levels, and that I'd get good enough A-level grades for university, even though you can count on one hand the people from our school who've gone to university, and Mr. Gibbons is always pointing out that not a single one of those has ever been a girl. And I wished that one day I might get to sing on a stage like Nina Simone or Aretha Franklin, and that when I'm older I'll go to America because New York is the city I most want to see.

After I'd eaten two slices of cake Mum said I didn't have to help clear up the dishes because it was my birthday, so Dad and I sat in the front room listening to Nina Simone and while I was singing along to "The Look of Love," Dad reached over and squeezed my hand and said I was every bit as good a singer as

Nina Simone. I laughed and told him he was being daft, but I couldn't help hoping that maybe there was a tiny bit of truth in it and that perhaps one day I might actually get to sing on a stage.

Now I'm lying on my bed, thinking about the fact that it's true what people say—you do feel different when you're sixteen. Before today I felt as though everything was fixed, as though my entire life had already been decided for me. But now I feel as though the whole world is out there waiting for me, just as long as I'm brave enough to go out and grab it.

Audrey read the extract three times, her hands shaking. She remembered writing that entry as if it were yesterday: lying on her bed, diary propped up on the pillow, pen in hand, and feet crossed at the ankles, the voices of contestants on *Call My Bluff* filtering through the flat's thin partition wall from the sitting room next door.

Where, she wondered, had that optimistic sixteen-year-old girl gone? What had happened to her hopes and dreams, her belief that anything was possible? When had her aspirations evaporated?

Audrey scanned the diary entry again, cataloguing the ways in which she'd let down her sixteen-year-old self. She had no university degree, nothing to service the promise of her A-level results. She'd never been to New York, hadn't managed any international travel beyond the occasional family camping holiday to France. She'd never sung on a stage, in America or anywhere else. Instead she'd spent her life as a wife, a mother, and a school librarian, and as much as she'd enjoyed her job, there was no deluding herself that her career had set the world alight.

Staring at the diary, Audrey felt as though somewhere in those pages were the answers to questions she wasn't yet able to articulate. There seemed to be such an immeasurable distance between the life she had imagined for herself and the life she had led.

How, Audrey thought, do you get to the end of your life and feel as though you've barely begun?

There were so many things Audrey would change were she afforded a second chance. But that wasn't how life worked, she knew that. She'd had her chances and now it was too late. The lump in her breast had made certain of that.

Perhaps, with treatment, she might have been able to extend the time her oncologist had predicted she had left. Perhaps she might survive twenty-two months, or twenty-four, rather than the eighteen months she had been given. But Audrey had her reasons for refusing chemotherapy and no amount of cajoling—by Lily, Jess, her granddaughters, or her oncologist—would persuade her to change her mind.

Audrey closed the diary and clutched it to her chest. It was too late to repair so many of the things in her life that had been broken: Edward's untimely death; the grief they had all suffered; the estrangement between Lily and Jess she had been unable to heal. Audrey no longer knew if she accepted her daughters' rift as the status quo or was wary of probing too deeply for fear of what she might discover at its root.

She picked up the photograph of her girls on Woolacombe Beach. She knew she couldn't wave a magic wand and bring back loved ones she had lost or undo anyone's pain. But as she looked again at her daughters' smiles—their happiness untainted by events that would devastate their lives less than two years after that picture had been taken—she was aware of her heartbeat accelerating, and a quiet determination slipping between her ribs.

If she had eighteen months left to live then she had eighteen months to uncover the cause of Jess's animosity toward Lily.

"Granny! Dinner's nearly ready. Mum says she'll be home in ten minutes."

Audrey placed the photograph on her bedside table, understanding for the first time why she had chosen to move in with Jess rather than Lily: this was her chance to get close to Jess, to find out the reason for her unhappiness. This was her chance to put her family back together.

As she walked out of the bedroom and onto the landing, Audrey called down the stairs to her granddaughter below. "OK, darling. I'm coming. I'm ready now."

Part Two

March

Chapter 5
Audrey

Audrey and Phoebe walked arm in arm down a narrow Notting Hill street until they arrived at a 1960s low-rise building that looked unprepossessing from the outside. It was grimy and architecturally at odds with the surrounding Georgian terraces.

"Are you sure this is the right address, Phoebe? It doesn't look very salubrious." Audrey stared at the peeling paint on the windowsills and the brown water marks streaking the walls like the tears of a giant.

"Oh, it's fine. Come on, stop stalling. We're probably the first ones here."

As they entered the building and followed the black-and-white signs up the stairs toward the second floor, Audrey wondered—not for the first time in the past two weeks—whether she was being brave and intrepid or simply foolish. She still couldn't believe she was actually going to go through with it.

It had been just under a month since she'd found her old diary. When she'd mentioned it to Phoebe a week later, during Sunday lunch at Lily's, her granddaughter's reaction had taken her by surprise: *But don't you see what finding that diary means, Gran? It means you've got a second chance to do all those things. You could sing. You could do a part-time university course. You could travel. This could be awesome.*

It was Phoebe who'd come up with the idea of Audrey joining a choir, Phoebe who'd gone online and searched for one that sounded perfect. And now it was Phoebe who was accompanying her to the audition, insisting she wanted to join the choir too, although Audrey found it hard to believe it was how any seventeen-year-old really wanted to spend their free time. But even with Phoebe for moral support, Audrey's heartbeat still stuttered each time she tried to imagine singing in front of a complete stranger.

As they walked along a dimly lit windowless corridor, Audrey recalled the online advertisment she'd read so many times she'd committed it to memory.

Choir members wanted for a one-off performance. No experience necessary—just passion, commitment, and a love of music. Gala concert at the Royal Albert Hall on Saturday 25 June in aid of Save the Children's Syria campaign. Concert to feature the Royal Philharmonic Orchestra, the London Symphony Orchestra, and further performers TBC. Open auditions: Wednesday 23 March and Thursday 24 March at West11 studios, 17.00–21.00. Nearest tube: Ladbroke Grove. For further information contact Ben Levine, Musical Director.

"Come on, Gran. Deep breaths. It'll be fine."

Audrey followed Phoebe into a large room where light fractured through metal bars to form splintered stripes across the floor. Orange plastic chairs lined the walls, only a few of which were unoccupied—at least thirty people were there already. Glancing around the room, she noticed a man of about her own age with thick-lensed spectacles that made his eyes seem to pop from his head like a cartoon character's; a woman in her early thirties, headphones clamped to her ears, drumming on her thighs with her fingers; and underneath the window, a woman in her late forties who glanced up from her book and smiled briefly before settling back into her story.

Audrey willed some confidence to rise up from where it had sunk into the pit of her stomach as Phoebe led her to the far end of the room where a young man was sitting behind a trestle table, beaming at them.

"Hello there! Are you here for the audition? It's super to see a younger face, although all ages welcome, of course. If you take a seat and fill out this form, Ben will be with you as soon as he can. There's quite a few ahead of you in the queue—we've had rather a better turnout than we expected—but hopefully it shouldn't be too long a wait."

As Audrey took a seat next to Phoebe and dug a pen out of her bag, she scanned the room once more, wondering whether anyone else was trying to rewrite the script of their life before it was too late.

"Audrey Siskin? Ben's ready for you now. Do you want to come up?"

Audrey's stomach lurched as if making its own bid for freedom as she lifted herself from the chair, urging her legs to stop trembling. She glanced at Phoebe before following an earnest-looking young woman up the stairs.

On the floor above, striding across the audition room, hand outstretched, was a tall, attractive man of about forty, his dark hair thick and shiny as though he'd just stepped out of a shampoo commercial. He was beaming at Audrey with a warmth she hadn't expected. "You must be Audrey? I'm Ben Levine. It's great to meet you. Thanks so much for coming along today."

His American accent took her by surprise. As Audrey shook his hand, her stomach nudging against the belt of her trousers, she tried not to think about the tumor in her liver making her tummy swell as though she were in the early stages of pregnancy in spite of all the weight she'd lost.

"Don't be nervous. This is all totally informal. All we want to do today is sing a song, have a quick chat, and figure out whether you'd be happy in this choir we're putting together. So what brings you here today?"

Audrey thought about her teenage diary, could taste a residue of that adolescent optimism. And then she thought about the future that was arriving far too soon and felt the truth dissolve under her tongue. "I always loved singing when I was young but . . . I don't know . . . I've barely sung at all since I was a child. And now . . . now I'm getting on a bit, so I thought it was time to put that right." The half-lie fizzed on her lips.

Ben hadn't seemed to notice her awkwardness and he sat down at the piano, smiled at her, gestured for her to stand next to him. "Well, that seems like a pretty good reason to me, though I don't think you're getting on a bit. The oldest person I've had audition so far today was ninety-two, so from where I'm sitting you're a veritable spring chicken. What are you going to sing?"

Audrey hesitated, still unconvinced of the answer to a question that had kept her awake for the past two weeks.

" 'Dream a Little Dream of Me' by the Mamas and the Papas. I've got a CD here of the backing track. My granddaughter downloaded it from YouTube—I hope that's all right?"

As soon as she'd spoken, the words tripping over one another, Audrey prepared to apologize, to say that she'd made a mistake, to tell this nice young American man that she couldn't possibly sing that song. It was a song she'd studiously avoided for almost three decades, one that had habitually prompted her to switch off the radio, flick television channels, beat a hasty retreat from shops, restaurants, cinemas. It was a song she hadn't dared listen to in full since they'd played it on a portable cassette recorder at the funeral almost thirty years before.

But before she had a chance to speak she heard the opening notes of an introduction that tugged at her heart in a way no other musical sequence ever could: a gentle lilting refrain that caught in the back of her throat and threatened never to leave.

"No need for a CD. I know it. G major should be good for you, I think. Does that sound about right? We can go half a tone lower if you like, but I think this should work."

Audrey nodded as Ben played, unwilling to tell him that she didn't know her G major from her A minor, that she'd never learned to read music, that there'd never been enough money for lessons. She'd always learned everything by ear, picking out melodies and harmonies instinctively, singing lower or higher depending on what her vocal cords required.

"I'll run through a four-bar introduction and then you come in, OK?"

He was smiling at her with an affability Audrey found disconcerting though she couldn't understand why. And then it dawned on her. Ben wanted her to do well. He was quietly urging her to succeed. And hard as she tried to remember as she waited for her cue to begin, Audrey couldn't recall the last time anyone had encouraged her to do well at anything.

Audrey filled her lungs and waited for the introduction to end.

Her first phrase was perfect, even a gentle vibrato that hadn't been distorted by nerves. But as she reached the middle of the second phrase, as she stretched up toward a minor third, her voice wavered, then split, and then dissolved altogether.

Ben's fingers halted across the keys, the room silent but for the thumping of Audrey's heart. As she stood next to the piano, staring at the floor and wishing it would open up and swallow her, she thought that perhaps there were simply too many miles between the dreams she'd had as a teenager and the person she was now. Perhaps the end of your life was just that: an ending. Not a chance to right wrongs, rectify mistakes or fulfill unspent ambitions. Maybe this wasn't the beginning of the final chapter of her life. Maybe she'd already reached the epilogue without even realizing.

"That too high, huh? No problem, my mistake. Let's try a tone lower, OK? Deep breaths. You can do it, I know you can."

The piano introduction began again and Audrey closed her eyes, allowing the music to envelop her. And this time when she sang, her voice didn't waver or fracture or dissolve. This time the notes rang out confidently as though there had never been any doubt that they would. And for three minutes, Audrey completely forgot herself. She forgot Ben at the piano and his assistant at the back of the room and the paint peeling on the walls. She forgot her cancer and the clock ticking loudly in her ears and the deep ruptures in her family. For the first time in years, Audrey managed not to think about her guilt and her disappointments and her catalogue of losses. She sang and all that existed was her and the music and the flood of memories that would forever be associated with that song.

When the music came to an end, Audrey opened her eyes to discover that she wasn't curled up with her daughters on the sofa, blinking back her tears, or standing at the front of a congregation in mourning, fixing her gaze firmly forward. Instead she was in an audition room in west London having sung a solo in front of strangers for the first time in her life.

Ben was staring at her and Audrey felt heat bleed into her cheeks.

I'm sorry, she wanted to say, *I shouldn't have come. It was all a dreadful mistake. I'm sorry to have wasted your time.* But her voice cowered inside her embarrassment and she couldn't coax it out.

"Well, I wasn't expecting *that*." Ben looked at her, eyebrows raised, and then glanced over her shoulder to his assistant. "Audrey Siskin—I can honestly say that you've made my day. That was incredible. You say you've never sung professionally before?"

Audrey shook her head, words still eluding her.

"Well, all I can say is that whatever brought you here today, I'm damn pleased that you came." He was standing up now, grinning at her.

"So . . . It was OK?"

"OK? God, if everyone auditioning today was half as good as you we'd be giving Gareth Malone a run for his money. It was fantastic. If you give your contact details to Caitlin, she'll keep you updated on everything. But the first rehearsal is two weeks from today and then we'll be rehearsing every Wednesday evening and Saturday afternoon—you can do that, right? And you know the concert is on June twenty-fifth? We have just over eleven weeks to turn all you auditionees into a professional choir."

Audrey nodded, her head feeling as though she'd just drunk two glasses of prosecco in quick succession. As she told her details to Caitlin, she tried not to think about her next appointment with the oncologist in three weeks' time, tried to reassure herself that there was no reason she wouldn't stay well enough for long enough to see this through.

Chapter 6
Lily

At the top of the white stucco steps leading to her front door, Lily cursed as her key jammed in the lock. It had been two days since she'd asked the housekeeper to get it fixed but clearly it hadn't been mended yet. She managed to wiggle her key at just the right angle to unlock the door before gesturing to the waiting cab that she'd only be ten minutes.

"Phoebe! It's me! Are you home?" The house was silent. She kicked off her shoes and ran up the stairs to Phoebe's room. "Phoebe, are you in there? I'm only popping back quickly. I've got a cab waiting outside."

Still nothing. Lily listened, her head pressed against the wood, then eased open the door, knowing the wrath she'd face if Phoebe were inside and she entered without explicit permission. But the room was empty.

Silence resounded through the deserted house, the stillness prickling the hairs on the back of her neck. Standing on the threshold to her daughter's bedroom, the quietness enveloping her, Lily found herself remembering all those nights she had lain awake in her childhood bed, hearing things she knew she shouldn't. A conversation from decades earlier began whispering in her ears, trying to draw her in, forcing her to remember: voices hissing into the silence after their owners had thought everyone had gone to sleep, Lily lying under her duvet, knowing she should put her fingers in her ears to shut them out but being unable to stop herself listening.

How could you? How could you have done that? I will never, ever be able to forgive you.

I'm sorry. I'm so, so sorry. I never meant to hurt you. The last thing I'd ever want is to hurt you or the girls. You must *know that.*

Lily snapped open her eyes, unfurled her clenched fists, and blinked against the memory. Hurrying across the landing into her bedroom, she swiped open her phone and tapped out a message to Phoebe.

> *Where are you? I've just popped home to get changed. I've got a last-minute work dinner tonight, but I shouldn't be too late.*

Heading into the small dressing room attached to her bedroom, Lily unzipped her dress as a message pinged on her phone.

> *I'm at the audition. With Gran. Not that you remember, obviously. Gran's supposed to be coming for dinner afterward and you're SUPPOSED to be picking us up. But I guess none of that's happening now and I'll just have to tell Gran that you've stood her up yet again.*

Lily frowned. She opened the calendar on her phone, scrolled through the day's appointments, could find no mention of her mum coming for dinner. She swiped through the rest of the week and there it was, under tomorrow's date, staring at her accusingly.

> *I'm so sorry, darling. I've put the wrong date in my diary. I thought it was tomorrow. Can you apologize to Gran for me and*

tell her we'll still see her for lunch on Sunday? I hope the audition goes well. Klaudia should have left some supper in the fridge so make sure you eat something when you get home.

Stepping into an almost identical black dress to the one she'd just put in the laundry basket and smoothing the material over her hips, worrying that perhaps it was a little tighter than it had been when she'd last worn it and making a mental note to add an extra weekly gym session to her diary, she turned toward the empty rail on the opposite side of the dressing room. Less than a month ago it had been filled with Daniel's suits and shirts, ties and T-shirts, sweaters and jeans. Now the hangers swayed on the rail as if unsure whether they'd been liberated from their burden or were bereft of purpose. She glanced down at her phone, opened her private email account, and reread the last message she'd sent Daniel the previous evening.

I know you're really busy and it's frantic there at the moment, but it would be really good to get dates in the diary for when you're coming home for the weekend. Phoebe misses you. We both do. I hope work's going well. Speak at the weekend. L xx

Lily checked the trash folder, in case Daniel's reply had somehow got mislaid, but the only messages in there were emails about marketing conferences and magazine subscriptions. She exited her Sent items, her eyes flicking down over the contents of her account. And there it was, staring at her: the folder containing all the emails she had written to Jess over the years, none of which had ever been answered.

Lily scrolled through them, page after page, and clicked on an email from January 1998, her hand tensing around the phone as she began to read.

Dear Jess,

I hope you got the card and flowers I sent. I was so thrilled to hear from Mum about the safe arrival of Mia. It's such a beautiful name and I've no doubt she's a beautiful baby. I hope you're OK and that motherhood is everything you thought it would be. I suspect these first few weeks will be tiring and probably a little overwhelming, but I'm sure you're doing a wonderful job.

As you probably know from Mum, my baby's due in just over six weeks—a little girl too. It's so strange to think of us both having our first child at the same time. Two little girls, two young cousins. Wouldn't it be nice if they could be friends?

It's been four years now, Jess. Longer if I think about how little you spoke to me when I was still living at home, or when I'd come home from uni in the holidays. I don't want us to be estranged forever. Haven't we both been through enough—been hurt enough—to let this continue? I miss you.

I can't pretend to know why you're so angry with me, though I understand that we've both got a lot to be angry about. But whatever the reason, I'm sorry, Jess. You were so young when everything happened, I can only imagine how confusing and upsetting it must have been for you. I don't know whether you're angry with me because I couldn't do anything to stop it or whether it's because I went to uni and left you alone with Mum when she was still having such a tough time. Sometimes I even wonder whether you're angry because you wish I was the one who wasn't here anymore. But whatever it is, I'm sorry. If only you'd tell me why you're so upset then perhaps we can start to put things right. After we've both lost so much, surely we don't want to lose each other too?

I love you,
Lily xxx

Lily closed the email, her fists curling into tight balls. She wished she hadn't looked, wished she'd had the self-discipline to delete them all. But since her mum's diagnosis six months ago, it was as though a sluice had opened up in her mind, releasing all the memories she had kept locked behind closed gates for years.

She shut her eyes, trying to avoid the scene she knew was sidling into her head, but there it was, waiting for her, as it always was.

The room is dark, only the faintest early morning light visible around the edge of the closed curtains. She can just make out the hummingbirds decorating the wallpaper around the window but everything else is in silhouette. The air is still and smells pungent—sharp and slightly sweet—like overripe fruit or an open bottle of vinegar. She hears the crying before her eyes have adjusted to the darkness, before they have found the figure sitting on the bed: the sobs are low and painful. It is a sound that causes Lily's heart to knock against her chest, gently at first and then more insistently until she fears that it might be heard. She knows she should not be there but now that she is—unnoticed, unheard—she is too scared to leave in case she accidentally reveals her presence. She allows only the smallest stream of air in and out of her mouth, the shallowest of breaths she hopes will not betray her. But the next thing she sees is so unexpected, so shocking, that she knows she will spend the rest of her life wishing she could un-see it. It takes so little time but the sight of it winds her. She stands motionless, her breath trapped in her lungs, watching, waiting, doing nothing to stop it. She swallows silently and she can taste it on her tongue: the bitter, metallic, unyielding taste of fear.

The phone rang, making Lily jump. Her boss's name flashed up on the screen.

"Ed, is everything OK?"

"Yes, fine. Just wanting to check your ETA? Tom and Dana have just arrived and you know they'll want you to walk them through the strategy, so it's just small talk until you get here."

Lily tucked her phone under her chin and crouched among the labeled shoeboxes, searching for the black velvet heels she wanted. "I'll be leaving in less than a minute. Cab shouldn't take more than fifteen to get there. I'll be with you as soon as I can."

As the call ended, Lily reached for the right shoebox, in a pile in the far corner of the dressing room. Pulling it free, a second box came tumbling down, and she remembered having failed to put it away properly the last time she had looked inside it two months earlier.

The box fell open at her feet and Lily knew she shouldn't look, knew she should slip the lid back on before her eyes had grazed something her heart didn't want to see. She thought about the cab driver outside, already kept waiting longer than she'd promised, instructed herself to close the box, put it back in the corner, walk away.

She knelt down, placed her hands on either side of the lid, heard her own silent order to slide it back in place. But it was as if her eyes were working independently of the rest of her, as if her hands no longer obeyed commands from her brain.

Looking inside, Lily stared at the grainy black-and-white images of a life not yet fully formed, of limbs not yet ready to stretch out into the world, of a future she had so desperately wanted to unfold.

Chapter 7
May 2009

Lily tugs the seat belt across her chest, pulls it a few inches loose at her stomach, then clicks it into the slot. She slips her right hand between her body and the belt. Beyond the muscle, the fat, the skin, and her clothes she wants there to be one last defense.

The flat of her palm rests against her gently convexing stomach. For eighteen weeks she has not dared take it for granted. She has divided her heart into two equal parts: hope and denial. Superstition demands denial for fear that complacency will be punished. But she cannot extinguish the tentative flame of hope: to do so would seem to be a different form of jinxing.

Next to her Daniel starts the car engine. He smiles, pleased that the weekend has been a success and that they have had something to celebrate.

"Are you sure you don't want me to drive? I really don't mind. The doctor said there's no reason I shouldn't."

Daniel shakes his head, strokes her knee. "Absolutely not. I just want you to relax. The weekend doesn't finish until we get home."

He eases his foot onto the clutch, slides the gearshift into first, and the car crunches across the gravel forecourt of the hotel, out into the Oxfordshire countryside. He switches on the radio and finds Classic FM. Lily prefers Radio 3 but Einaudi's "Il Giorni" is playing and she allows herself to sink into familiar music.

She barely dares admit it—that superstition again—but this time feels different: firmer, safer, more secure. And it can't be just her imagination. They have already passed their own personal danger zone. The last two babies have not made it this far. The first—two years after Phoebe had been born—made it to eleven weeks. The bleeding had started four days before they were due to have their twelve-week scan, a cruel fact that at the time had compounded Lily's grief. If only, she had silently wished, she had been able to see her baby once, even on a screen. But then the second baby, three years later, had made it to twelve weeks and Lily had seen it on the screen, had watched it stretch its legs and unfurl its fingers, had counted the vertebrae of its spine and seen the four chambers of its heart beating out a perfect rhythm of life. She had looked at the black-and-white video footage of her baby and had fallen in love. And when, two weeks later, that baby, too, had been scraped out of her uterus after the spotting had turned to bleeding and the bleeding had led her to the hospital, she had wondered whether the pain wasn't infinitely more acute having seen that tiny, perfectly formed creature on-screen. A baby who no longer existed beyond half a dozen grainy fetal photographs.

But this baby has already made it so much further. This baby—she can feel it—is a survivor. Five years since she last miscarried, Lily feels certain this pregnancy is different.

A piece of music begins to play on the radio: "Soave sia il vento" from Mozart's *Così fan tutte*. Lily automatically turns toward Daniel just as he turns to her. They smile, remembering their wedding, where a trio of operatic friends had performed the piece during the signing of the register.

Daniel's focus returns to the road but Lily gazes at his profile. Two days of stubble shadow his strong square jaw, long eyelashes frame his deep brown eyes. He is handsome, and she is grateful for his patience, his kindness, his understanding.

The weekend away had been his idea. He hadn't told her about it until Friday morning. *Pack a weekend bag, Lil. I'm collecting you from the office at four. It's all arranged with your PA. Your mum's looking after Phoebe until Monday*. Two nights away, just the two of them: a weekend to celebrate the baby who has given them cause for hope.

Lily turns to look out of the window at the miles of yellow rapeseed carpeting the fields. She rests her head against the glass, closes her eyes, feels the warmth of the sun on her face. She is not aware of drifting off to sleep, will not remember until later the dreams she had of a baby swimming underwater, its eyes open, gliding like a fish toward her, yet always out of reach.

It is not the dream that wakes her. It is the thump of two heavy objects colliding. The sound of tires screeching, metal crunching, Daniel swearing.

She feels her body thrust forward, feels the belt tighten across her stomach, feels her muscles tense in response. Before her eyes have sprung open, her hands move downward, tugging at the seat belt, pulling it loose.

On the other side of the windshield stands a tree: the wide, ancient trunk of an oak, so close as to be surreal. The hood of their Mercedes seems to have been compressed to half its former length, the front end now a mangled snarl of metal.

"Lil? Are you OK?"

She turns to Daniel. His cheeks have drained of color as though he has been put through the washing machine at too high a heat.

"Lil?"

She nods, even though she does not know whether it is true. Her neck aches and her mouth feels dry and her hand rubs gently across her stomach, trying to soothe the thirteen-centimeter baby within.

"I don't know what happened. It was just a really sharp corner. I only lost control for a second. I was barely even speeding." He is gabbling and she stretches out an arm, strokes the back of his neck.

"We should probably call the police, shouldn't we? Aren't you supposed to report damage to trees? I'm sure I read that somewhere."

Daniel shakes his head. "We can't. You know we can't. I had a few glasses of wine with lunch. I'm fine, I'm perfectly OK to drive. But you never know with Breathalyzers. You don't know how sensitive they might be."

There is fear in his voice. It is not something Lily is accustomed to hearing in him. "That's why I wanted to drive, Daniel. That's why I said I'd drive."

There is enough accusation in her voice—more than she'd intended—for Daniel to pull her hand from the back of his neck, for him to turn to her with an expression caught somewhere between hurt and anger. "For God's sake, I was trying to be nice. I didn't want you to have to drive all that way. I just wanted you to relax. And you know full well I'm absolutely fine driving after a couple of glasses. You *know* that." His voice is imploring: he needs to know she believes him.

Lily's head aches and she knows this is neither the time nor the place for an argument. All she wants now is to get home. "I know."

Relief washes across Daniel's face, prompting him into action.

She listens as he begins to make telephone calls, as he locates a local garage and persuades a mechanic—as only Daniel can—to bring a tow truck out on a Sunday afternoon and transport them back to London for an absurdly exorbitant fee. He does not call the AA, Lily knows, because there is a risk they will ask questions he would rather not answer.

All the time she listens to Daniel—on the phone, as they wait for the mechanic to arrive, throughout the journey home perched high up in a tow truck—Lily's palm does not leave her stomach.

The bleeding begins just after 3:00 a.m.

Lily wakes, opens her eyes, disoriented as to whether it is morning or still night. She blinks toward the clock and as she registers the time—3:06 a.m.—she becomes aware of what has woken her.

Pain grinds across her abdomen, grabbing at her, squeezing her. She is being dragged down into an abyss she does not wish to enter.

She knows this pain. It is hatefully familiar.

She swings her legs over the edge of the bed and lifts herself from the mattress, careful not to wake Daniel asleep next to her. If she is about to enter this circle of hell again, she would rather go there alone.

Her body doubles over as another wave of pain clenches her stomach. She stumbles out of the bedroom, past their en suite, along the landing, and into the guest bathroom at the end of the hall. She switches on the light, closes the door, lies on the floor, legs hugged to her chest, willing the pain to go away.

When the first trickle of blood comes, she feels it before she sees it. A violent tensing of the muscles above her pubic bone and then, abruptly, a release.

The insides of her thighs are warm and wet and she knows before she opens her eyes that she will be greeted by a dark red message spreading across the cream cotton of her pajamas.

Her eyes sting but before the first tear can surface there is another surge of pain. Her uterus contracts and she holds her breath until it passes. She knows there will be more blood, can feel it oozing out of her. But she cannot look. She will not allow herself to look.

She scrunches her eyes shut, awaits the next cycle of pain, tries to breathe through it, just as she knows she should, but it is too early to be breathing like this, four and a half months too early. She is only halfway through the pregnancy and her head does not want to comply with what her body is urging her to do.

More rounds of pain-and-release. Lily has no idea how much time has passed, how long she has been on the bathroom floor, bleeding. She knows that her head feels light and is swamped by a powerful desire to sleep. But she also knows that sleep is the one thing to which she must not, under any circumstances, succumb.

She forces open her eyes and when she raises her head to look down at her legs, her only instinct is to scream. She calls Daniel's name, over and over, until there he is, standing in the doorway. She sees immediately, from his expression, that it is worse even than she has registered.

"Shit, Lil. Shit. Just stay there, OK? I'll call an ambulance. You're going to be fine. Just stay there."

She knows he is not telling her the truth. But she also knows, as her mind floats away to some distant place, as her eyelids grow so heavy she can no longer keep them open, that she does not have the strength to think about it right now.

*

When Lily wakes she enjoys a few delirious seconds during which she believes she is emerging from a terrible dream. But before she is fully roused the sharp smell of antiseptic penetrates her nostrils and she knows she cannot pretend that the events of last night did not happen.

Her eyes scour the room, searching for something familiar amidst the foreign bedsheets, melamine wardrobe, white china washbasin.

Light is inching around the edge of the curtains but she has no idea of the time or how long she has been there. It is only when she shivers that she realizes how cold she is. Her body is shaking and she cannot imagine ever being warm again. She lifts her arm to pull the sheets higher over her chest and notices the small plastic cannula piercing the skin in the crook of her right arm, the attached tube rising up into a bag of ruby-red fluid hanging from a tall metal stand.

Blood. Foreign blood is being fed into her body through a tube in her veins. She experiences a moment of vertigo even though she is lying down.

She turns her head sideways, away from the transfusion she does not remember being administered. In the back of her left hand is another cannula, another tube, another drip, this time to a bag of clear fluid she assumes is saline.

She closes her eyes, tries to stop the swell of nausea surging into her throat. She does not need to be told what has happened. As the image of a future without this longed-for second child pulls itself reluctantly into view, a torrent of grief rises into her chest, squeezing through the narrowing of her throat, finding its way out in deep, guttural sobs.

Daniel sits on a brown plastic chair by the side of the bed, holding her hand which is now free of its cannula, just a small red mark and infant bruise the only evidence that it was ever there.

It is, Daniel has told her, almost seven hours since she arrived at the hospital, time of which Lily has little recollection. She does not know whether she ought to be grateful for this lapse of memory or mourn it.

Daniel is talking and she is trying very hard to focus on what he is saying. But it is as though her brain will let only certain words through, so that their meaning must be slotted together like a jigsaw puzzle in which half the pieces are missing.

Miscarriage, hemorrhage, emergency D and C.

She lets him talk, wondering why her mouth is so dry, hoping that soon he will tell her the only two pieces of information she wants to know.

Blood loss, transfusion, lucky to be alive.

Finally she can wait no longer. Her voice, when it emerges, is quiet and small, as though it has shrunk in the hours of lost consciousness.

"Do they know what caused it?"

Their eyes catch before he looks down, studies the back of her hand, shakes his head. "No. There'll have to be more tests. But given your history . . ." His voice trails off, leaving more questions than answers in its wake.

"Do they think it was caused by whatever happened with the other two?"

The doctors do not know the reason for her two previous miscarriages. The loss of those babies is a secret her body has thus far refused to divulge. Lily is hoping that perhaps this time the mystery will be solved and that, as a result, it can be overcome in the future.

Daniel shrugs. There is something noncommittal in the gesture which makes Lily want to pull her hand free from his but she hasn't the strength.

"So it could have been something different? It could have been something . . . specific?"

She cannot bring herself to voice the accusation. It is unfair, she knows, to apportion blame when they are both in mourning. But the unspoken allegation hangs between them, heavy and thick like winter fog, so that they are unable to reach out toward one another's grief.

"They don't know, Lil. They'll need to do more tests. They just don't know right now."

It is not the answer she wants but she hasn't the will to challenge him. Instead she turns her head away and blinks against the tears.

Daniel begins to speak again, his words tripping over each other in order to deliver quickly the news he knows she will not want to hear.

Pregnancy. Risks. Advised not to try again.

She hears the words but will not absorb their meaning. Turning to look at him, she cannot read his expression, cannot tell whether it is the frown or the smile he means her to see.

"We don't need to try again, do we, Lil? Three times, that's enough, surely? We have Phoebe. Shouldn't we just be grateful for her? Let's not put ourselves through all this again. I don't feel the need for another child to complete our family. We're fine just the way we are, aren't we?"

Lily neither dissents nor agrees.

Later, she thinks. Later she will be able to change his mind. It is not a conversation for now. She can wait. She can be patient.

She lays her head back on the pillow, closes her eyes, and invites in sleep. She just needs to give him time. He will, she feels sure, want to try for another baby eventually.

Chapter 8
Jess

Jess glanced at the clock on the dashboard as she edged over the speed limit along the Westway. Her jaw tightened as a queue of traffic ahead of her forced her to brake. Thirteen hours after arriving on set, all she wanted to do was head home, but instead she was having to clear up Lily's mess yet again.

Irritation needled her skin. Even when she had no direct contact with her, Lily still managed to inveigle her way into Jess's life, still managed to cause disruption. Even after all these years of avoiding her, Jess was still covering up Lily's mistakes.

Her mum had said she'd get a cab home from the audition, but Jess couldn't let her do that. Lily might be able to cancel arrangements at the last minute and leave their mum in the lurch, but Jess couldn't.

A dull throb pinched at Jess's temples as she thought about how different things might have been had her mum moved in with Lily instead of her. Lily had asked first—she had a habit of making grand gestures without any thought for the consequences—and in truth it hadn't occurred to Jess to offer until then. But as soon as her mum had said she was contemplating moving in with Lily, Jess had been forced to intervene. She couldn't have let her mum do that. She'd never have forgiven herself. The thought of it even now—even when the possibility no longer posed a threat—made Jess squeeze the steering wheel until her knuckles ached.

Stuck in stationary traffic as another minute ticked by, Jess silently cursed work for having made her so late. She thought about all the times when Mia was younger that her mum had collected her from school and taken her to ballet, gymnastics, or swimming classes because Jess had been at work. All the times she had fetched Mia from childcare, playdates, school outings, and delivered her home safely and on time.

Jess breathed deeply, an automatic barrier slamming down on the thought that one day, in the not-too-distant future, her mum would no longer be alive.

Turning her head sideways to look into the adjacent car, Jess's eyes sharpened their focus. The hairline, the jaw, the shape of the ears: the profile of the man in the driver's seat teased open the lid on a box of her memories.

"What's black and white and read all over?"

Jess is curled up on her father's lap, wrapped in an oversized bath towel, water dripping down her neck from her freshly washed hair. She squints with concentration, can feel her forehead creasing.

"I don't know, Daddy. That's too hard!"

"Come on, you can do this one, I know you can. What's black and white and read *all over?"*

Jess repeats the riddle in her head, determined to prove that her dad isn't mistaken in believing she can solve it, even though just thinking about it is beginning to hurt her five-year-old brain.

"That's easy. It's a newspaper." Her sister sashays into the bathroom only long enough to collect her hairbrush and answer the conundrum before swishing out.

Jess doesn't have time to compose an appropriate retort, but she feels humiliation bleed into her cheeks and buries her face in the towel.

"OK, how about a joke instead? How does a monkey make toast?"

Jess lifts her head and smiles. She knows there is no expectation to work out the answer to a joke. "I don't know, Daddy. How does a monkey make toast?"

"He puts it under the gorilla."

It takes a split second for the punchline to unfold in Jess's head and she collapses into satisfied giggles. "Tell me another one!"

"OK. Why did the lobster blush?"

Jess pretends to think, playing her role in a charade she knows makes the joke more fun for the teller. "I don't know. Why did the lobster blush?"

"Because the sea weed."

Jess's hand shoots up over her mouth, her eyes widening with delight that her dad has told her a joke her mum probably wouldn't approve of. She commits it to memory, ready to share with her classmates tomorrow.

"Come on, petal. Time to dry that hair and get you to bed."

He bundles the towel around her so that her body is cocooned in thick cotton, picks her up as if she were a baby, and carries her toward her bedroom, where her mum will blow-dry her hair and put her to bed.

Jess nuzzles against her father's neck, her nose filling with the familiar smell of grown-up offices, salted peanuts, and the last residue of aftershave her dad puts on every morning. On the short walk from the bathroom to her bedroom, she burrows into his shoulder and thinks—as she so often does—that when she's older she is going to live in the house next door so that she can always stay close to her mum and dad.

Jess blinked and shook her head, conscious that she was staring at the driver in the next car. As he turned toward her and smiled she saw that his eyes were too deep-set, his chin too large, his lips too full. Jess turned away, her cheeks hot, as though that man must know she did this all the time: that she was always seeing traces of her dad where there were none.

The traffic began to move and Jess eased her foot off the brake. Overtaking the car in front, she swerved into the outside lane and put her foot down hard on the accelerator, only slowing down each time a yellow speed camera loomed into view. When she finally pulled up outside the Notting Hill address her mum had given her, a sign informed her that it was residents' parking until 10:00 p.m. Jess peered up and down the street but could see neither meters nor traffic wardens. She wouldn't be more than a couple of minutes anyway.

Pulling down the sun visor, Jess looked at herself in the mirror, running a finger across her eyelid where the remnants of that morning's eyeliner had collected into small, soot-like particles. She turned her head sideways, studied her long nose—the one part of her body that made her understand why rich people resorted to plastic surgery—and practiced smiling at herself, wondering if it was true that you could alter your mood just by changing your expression. But the smile reflecting back at her was like a window onto the past through which Jess didn't want to look.

It was her sister's smile, always had been. For years, when she was little, Jess had taken such pride in her smile being a facsimile of her sister's. She had loved how strangers' heads had turned in the street to stare at the similarity between them, how she had felt the world to be a less frightening place with her sister by her side. And then, one day, the resemblance had disappeared, as though a wizard had slunk in during the night and cast a spell over them both. Jess had known—even then—that it hadn't really been that swift, that the change had occurred over days, weeks, months. But to her it had felt sudden, abrupt. Now she had no idea if she and her sister would still look similar if they stood side by side, no longer knew if strangers' heads would turn if they walked down the street together.

Jess stared at herself in the mirror and something about her reflection—perhaps the unkempt hair or the smudged makeup, or perhaps just the look of weary uncertainty—caused a shutter to open on a memory she rarely dared view.

Chapter 9
October 1987

Her hand is hot and clammy, squeezed tightly inside her mum's. They walk briskly, side by side, her mum's stride too wide for Jess to keep pace with, so that every other step she has to improvise a small half-skip, an unintended jauntiness she knows is inappropriate given the circumstances. Her mum looks down at her and smiles as if to say that everything will be OK and Jess tries to smile back but her attention is focused on the ward three floors above where the two of them are heading, just as they do almost every day after school.

It seems to Jess that they have been coming to the hospital forever even though she knows, really, that it is only a matter of months since these visits began. She can still remember when the time between the end of school and the beginning of dinner was filled with chocolate Nesquik and bourbon biscuits, *Hartbeat* and *The Really Wild Show*, games of Connect 4 and Guess Who?, which Jess would invariably have lost had her sister not occasionally let her win.

Now Jess no longer knows which is preferable: to be at home in a house filled with anxiety or to be here, where the collective fear is so great that she sometimes imagines it gobbling her up—head, shoulders, knees, and toes—until there is nothing left.

They hurry along the corridor toward the elevator, Jess unsure whether she wants to rush or not. She both wants to be there and yet wishes she weren't. It is a familiar feeling but one she still hasn't got used to: the wanting and not wanting at the same time.

The smell clings to the hairs in Jess's nose, a smell of counterfeit healthiness. Jess knows it to be a sham. There is no healthiness here. This is where people come when they are really sick. This is where some people come to die.

The thought knocks inside Jess's head, trying to get out, but she knows there is no escape.

They wait for the elevator to arrive, Jess watching the illuminated digits signal its slow descent. She glances up at her mum, who smiles at her again, the pad of her thumb running along the back of Jess's hand. Jess senses her mum's need to reassure her but can't decide whether it makes her feel better or worse.

The elevator doors open and Jess catches sight of them both in the mirror on the far wall. There are dark rings under her mum's eyes and strands of hair sticking out from Jess's two plaits: they look to Jess like a messy version of the people they once were, before this all began.

The elevator ascends and when the doors open at the third floor they are greeted by the sound of "Never Gonna Give You Up" drifting from the nurses' station along the corridor. The tune attaches itself to Jess's ears and she knows she will be unable to shake Rick Astley's voice from her head for the rest of the day.

Walking onto the ward, Jess feels hope burning in her chest, the same hope she has every time she comes to visit: that perhaps today they will discover that a full recovery has been made and that everything can go back to normal.

And then they are there, standing at the end of the bed, looking down at a body so familiar and yet so disturbingly changed that Jess has to fight the urge to scrunch her eyes shut: sallow skin, closed eyes, bones rising from hollow cheeks to greet them. Hope plummets in Jess's stomach, the muscles in her tummy shriveling to greet it.

It is the tubes that distress her every time. One tube in the nose, the very thought of which makes Jess want to gag. Another tube in the back of the hand, which makes Jess scratch herself as though it is her own flesh that is being pierced. A third tube emerges from underneath the sheets into a see-through bag of mustard-yellow liquid that Jess knows is darker than it ought to be and which she would rather not think about at all.

As Jess stands by the bed, trying to remember what the face in front of her looked like before the flesh began to melt away from the body, before the bones jutted out from beneath the skin, she thinks about all the weeks they have been going through this cycle of hospital admissions, temporary recoveries, discharges back home. This carousel of fear, limbo, and relief that has become the emotional rhythm by which they live their lives.

Mostly what Jess thinks, as she stands at the foot of the hospital bed, is that if only life can go back to normal she will never ask for anything again.

Then the sunken eyes flutter open and a face Jess loves more than any other in the world smiles at her and she feels, all at once, that her prayers are being answered.

Chapter 10
Jess

Jess snapped the sun visor shut, got out of the car, and ran into the building, following black-and-white signs up the stairs to a large square room that might have seemed welcoming were it not for the metal bars across the windows. Inside, her mum stood by a piano next to a tall, curly-haired man about the same age as Jess in the otherwise empty room.

"I'm sorry I'm so late, Mum. The shoot ran on forever and when we finally wrapped, the owner of the house accused us of scratching the floorboards in the hallway, which I knew for a fact we hadn't, but it took ages to find the photographs I'd taken on reconnaissance to prove him wrong. I'm really sorry." Her voice was breathless and she could hear herself rambling.

"Don't worry, darling. You should have let me get a cab. Anyway, Ben's been keeping me entertained with stories of his various travels. Ben, this is my younger daughter, Jess. Jess, this is Ben, who's running the choir."

Jess shook Ben's outstretched hand, only half reciprocating his broad smile.

"Hey, Jess. It's good to meet you."

"Yep, you too. So did it all go OK, Mum? Do you want to tell me about it in the car? I don't want to hurry you but I'm in a residents' parking bay and I don't want to get a ticket."

Her mum hesitated, and Jess glanced down at her watch, wondering whether Mia had eaten dinner already, wishing she'd had time to phone her before she'd left work.

"Yes, of course. But Ben was just telling me about his travels in South America. He's been to so many interesting places—Argentina, Chile, Bolivia, Brazil. You've always wanted to go to Patagonia, haven't you?"

Jess swiveled her key ring around her finger, felt it dig into her flesh. "Yes, but I don't think that's very likely in the near future. I'm sorry, I don't mean to be rude but I've still got a mountain of work to do for tomorrow's shoot and I do need to get back to the car. Do you think we could get going?"

"You know, Audrey, I could always run you home from rehearsals, if that's helpful? You're Shepherd's Bush, right? I'm Chiswick. It seems silly to drag your daughter here when I could easily drop you back."

"Oh, I couldn't possibly impose on you like that. It's really very kind, but I can easily get a cab."

"Honestly, it's no trouble at all. Saturdays would be tricky as I have private piano students straight after but Wednesday nights really aren't a problem. Seriously, it's crazy you paying for a cab or getting your family to collect you when I'm practically driving past your door."

"Mum, just say yes, for goodness' sake. He's obviously very happy to do it."

An echo of impatience lingered in the air. Jess noticed a tinge of pink heat her mum's cheeks, saw Ben look down at the piano keys as though he might have left something on top of them. She watched as her mum pulled a tissue from her handbag, coughed into it, and rolled it into a ball before slipping it back inside.

"Well, if you're sure, Ben, that really is very kind of you. Jess, I'm sorry to be a pain but I just need to use the bathroom quickly. You go ahead and I'll see you at the car."

Standing next to Jess's car, looking at her license plate, and tapping digits into a handheld device was a short, stout middle-aged man in a notorious bottle-green uniform.

"You've got to be *kidding* me. I've only been gone a couple of minutes."

The traffic warden glanced at Jess and then back at his machine, continuing to fill in the details of her parking ticket even as he replied. "You saw the sign? Then you shouldn't be surprised you got a ticket."

"I only left the car for a moment while I ran inside to collect my mum. Isn't there some rule about five minutes' grace?"

The warden pulled a small digital camera from his pocket, turned it on, and revealed a photograph of Jess's car. "See the time there, in the bottom left-hand corner? What does that say? Twenty-one thirteen. And what time is it now? Twenty one nineteen. By my calculation that's six minutes."

He jabbed a finger one last time at his machine and it whirred into life, a ticket rolling out of the top. He held it toward Jess, eyebrows raised as if daring her to challenge him.

"Really? You *really* want to give me a ticket? For God's sake, you people. How do you sleep at night?" She snatched the piece of paper from his hand and got into the car, slamming the door behind her before he had a chance to respond. She watched as he sauntered off down the street, glancing at each windshield he passed.

Her eyes skimmed over the ticket to assess the damage. Forty pounds. Or double that if she failed to pay within fourteen days.

Jess did a quick mental calculation. Her tax was due but she had the money set aside for that. Mia needed fifty pounds for a school theater trip to Stratford-upon-Avon, and the shower in the bathroom still needed fixing three months after it had been reduced to a light drizzle. And she was still paying off her credit card for the laptop she'd bought Mia for her birthday in January. Where another forty pounds would come from she had no idea.

Folding the ticket in two, she shoved it into the bottom of her bag. She couldn't face the awkward tussle that would ensue if her mum saw it: her mum would insist on paying it and Jess would refuse, both knowing that Jess couldn't afford it but that she would rather forgo breakfast and lunch for a month than accept charity. There'd been enough contention about money when her mum had agreed to move in. She'd wanted to contribute toward food, bills, and even the mortgage but Jess had refused. She'd told her then what she'd said repeatedly over the years: she had no intention of accepting handouts. Ever since Iain had walked out, just before Mia's first birthday, offering only minimal contributions since, Jess had supported herself and Mia. She hadn't been prepared to forgo her independence just because her mum was moving in with them.

Her phone bleeped and she retrieved it from her bag to find a message from Mia.

Are you nearly home? I was about to make some hot chocolate and I'll do some for you and Granny if you'll be back soon?

Jess checked the time. It was almost nine thirty. She'd left the house before it was light and hadn't seen Mia for almost twenty-four hours. She dialed Mia's number, picking at the skin around her thumbnail as she waited for an answer.

"Hi, Mum. Where are you?"

"Just collecting Granny from her choir audition. Is everything OK?"

"Yes. I just wondered when you were going to be home."

"We should be back in fifteen minutes. Why don't I pop to the Co-op and get some of that tortellini you like and we can have a late dinner together?"

"Thanks, but I've already eaten."

"What did you have?"

"Cheese on toast."

"That's not a proper dinner. Let me make you something when I get home. There might be some soup in the freezer—we could defrost it in the microwave."

"There's not. I already checked. There's nothing in the freezer except a bag of crumpets and some pastry."

Jess glanced out of the car window and back down the street, wondering what was taking her mum so long. "Well, I could still pick something up. You need to eat—cheese on toast isn't enough. Anyway, have you finished all your homework? Isn't your essay on *The Taming of the Shrew* due in on Friday?"

"I'm halfway through it. I'll finish it tomorrow night."

Jess thought about her work schedule for the next day. It was unlikely she'd be at home in time for dinner with Mia tomorrow either. "Wouldn't it be better to finish it tonight and then you can read it through fresh tomorrow?"

There was a moment's hesitation and Jess thought she could hear in the silence the cogs whirring in Mia's head.

"My art project's due on Friday as well and there's still loads I want to do on it."

Jess winced as she pulled the cuticle away from her thumbnail and watched a small drop of blood ooze out. "We've been through this before, Mia. The only reason I let you take art as a fifth A-level was because you insisted it wouldn't interfere with your other subjects. If you can't stick to that then we'll have to think again about whether you should be doing it at all."

"It's not interfering, I promise. I can easily finish my English essay tomorrow."

Jess sucked at her thumb, the blood metallic on her tongue. "You know what your teachers said. If you're going to get into Cambridge, you have to get straight A-stars in your four academic subjects."

There was another long silence and Jess wondered what Mia was doing, wished she could read her expression and work out what she was thinking.

"I know that, but it's just so unlikely. Only one person has gone to Cambridge or Oxford from my school in the last eight years so I don't know why you think I stand a chance."

"Because you're clever enough, Mia. If you work hard enough, I know you can do it. Just think how amazing it would be. I'd be so proud of you. And, believe me, if you don't give it your best shot and you end up just missing out, you'll be kicking yourself for the rest of your life."

An image flashed into Jess's head: standing in the school corridor, forming a circle with her three best friends, opening their brown A4 envelopes in unison, and pulling out the single sheet of white paper containing the results of their A-levels. Jess hearing her friends squeal with delight and relief as she watched her own future change before her eyes: not the straight As she needed for her place to read English at Cambridge but an A, a B, and a C—as though even her grades were showing her just how rudimentary her learning was—that might just scrape her through Clearing to somewhere half decent if she was lucky. She remembered feeling—as if she were back there now, standing in that corridor lined with photographs of the sixth formers' disco—that all her ambitions were swimming away from her toward a distant horizon she could never hope to reach. Ambitions to get to Cambridge, secure a role on the student newspaper, learn the journalistic ropes. Ambitions to forge connections, work hard, give herself the best chance possible of achieving her dream to edit a national newspaper one day. Jess had only just turned eighteen but she had understood, even then, that a place at Cambridge was a ticket not just to a first-rate education but to a first-rate contacts book that would service the rest of her career. A ticket she had torn up by failing to get the grades she needed.

"It's only fourteen months, Mia, that's all. Just get the A-level grades you need for Cambridge and you'll be set up for the rest of your life."

"Fine, Mum. I'll finish my English essay tonight. But I was thinking . . . I know I'm already doing art A-level but I honestly do find it really relaxing, and I've found this brilliant Saturday morning art class at the Royal College. It's only a couple of hours a week and they've still got a few places left for the summer term. I was thinking of putting my name down."

Jess heard a loud sigh and then realized it was hers. "Mia, haven't you been listening to a word I've been saying? You can't possibly take on something else when you're so overloaded. You're already doing an extra A-level and it sounds as though you're struggling to manage that. You'll have plenty of time for hobbies when you get to university."

There was the sound of a cupboard door opening and closing, water running into a glass, three long gulps. "But this course looks *really* good. And I can't study *every* second of the day. When I spoke to Dad about it he thought it was a great idea. He said I needed an antidote to exams, that it would do me good to relax a bit."

Jess felt her jaw lock, her back teeth grinding as if in a pre-emptive strike against saying something she might regret. She could hear Iain's voice in her head, his infuriating nonchalance unpicking all the maternal work she had done over the past seventeen years. It had been the same ever since he'd left: him charging in on a white horse to play the parental savior whenever Mia felt irked about something. Taking Mia for fun days out a couple of times a month, flitting in to whisk her away for the occasional weekend during the long summer holiday without any consideration for how Jess would manage the remaining weeks while she was at work, leaving her to create a military-style schedule of friends, babysitters and, most often, her mum to fill the breach. He behaved more like an irresponsible avuncular family friend than a father. And yet, in spite of all that, to Mia he could do no wrong: she would return from days out with him questioning why Jess wasn't as easygoing and fun as he was. Sometimes Jess couldn't help wishing that Iain had abandoned them completely rather than offering this occasional malign interference, that he'd disappeared to the other side of the world and had never been heard of or seen again.

Iain's face morphed into her head like an image emerging onto photographic paper. The apologetic furrow of his brow, the narrow edges of his eyes, the pinched corners of his mouth as he'd told her he was leaving: *I just can't handle it, Jess. I can't handle your moods and your insecurities and the sheer bloody unpredictability of living with you. One minute you're needy and affectionate, the next you're blocking me out as if you don't want me anywhere near you. It's like there's a part of you that's permanently shut away, under lock and key, and you won't let*

anyone get close. It's impossible, Jess. Life with you is impossible. You don't want a partner. You don't want an equal. You want someone to take care of you when you feel vulnerable and someone to lash out at when you don't. Well, I can't handle it anymore. I just can't do it.

Even now, all these years later, the memory of Iain's criticisms pained her, although Jess was never sure whether that was because they were unfair or because she feared they might be true.

"Sweetheart, I know it's hard—please don't think I don't understand how you feel—but it's not forever. Don't jeopardize everything you've worked so hard for at the eleventh hour for the sake of a hobby. You'll thank me for it in the long run, trust me."

"But if Dad can see it's a good idea, why can't you?"

"Because your father hasn't been raising you single-handedly since you were one, that's why. Perhaps if he had, he might have earned a say in what you do with your life."

The second the words spilled out, Jess wished she could scoop them back in. "I'm sorry, Mia, I didn't mean that. I'm sorry. I'm just tired, that's all. And I don't think it's helpful your dad giving advice when he doesn't understand how much pressure you're under. So, please, can we just agree that another art class is something you can do later, but that right now you just need to focus on your A-levels?"

Mia was silent and Jess took a moment to wrap a conciliatory tone around her voice. "Mia? Can we agree on that, please? Promise you'll get your head down on your school work?"

"Fine. But if I'm going to finish this essay tonight I need to get off the phone. I'll see you when you get back."

"OK, sweetheart. We shouldn't be too long. I love you."

"Yep, love you too."

The phone went dead as the passenger door opened and Jess watched her mum lower herself into the car. There was something slow and painstaking in her movements as if the manipulation of every muscle, tendon, and bone had to be silently negotiated.

"Sorry I took so long. All OK with the car?"

Jess nodded, noticing how her mum's knees protruded under the thin material of her trousers, how dark rings hung under her eyes. She saw her mum every day, yet somehow hadn't noticed how much she had changed physically over the past few weeks. But now that she had, it was as though a future Jess wasn't yet ready to greet was hurrying toward her and there was nothing she could do to slow it down. "Yes, all fine. So the audition went well, I'm guessing."

"Really well. Ben's wonderful—a really interesting man. It's a shame you couldn't chat to him for longer. The audition was packed, and there's another one tomorrow night. I can't imagine how he's going to make us sound any good in less than three months though."

Audrey smiled but Jess noticed that her eyes were bloodshot, and she saw a tiny globule of something white and viscous stuck to the corner of her lips. "Mum, are you OK? What took you so long in the bathroom?"

Audrey reached for her seat belt, but didn't meet Jess's gaze as she clicked it into place. "Oh, you know. Everything seems to take me a long time these days."

Jess studied her mum's profile. She suspected she knew what might really have happened, feared her mum hadn't just been going to the toilet or powdering her nose all that time. "Mum? You would tell me if you were starting to feel worse, wouldn't you?"

Chapter 11
Audrey

Audrey nodded, wondering if somehow Jess knew. She'd been so careful to hide it, had tried so hard to be quiet when it had happened at home. She'd take herself off to the bathroom, run the taps when the sound began to reverberate around the toilet bowl, always make sure to wipe her lips and brush her teeth afterward to expunge any trace. It was ironic, really. There was barely anything in her stomach to be purged and yet, several times each day, her muscles heaved with a determination so much more dramatic than the results.

"Honestly, darling, I'm fine. But you look exhausted. Are you all right? It's madness, you working such long hours. Is it really necessary for you to be on set for so long every day?"

Jess started the engine, a weary half-smile shadowed in the glow of the streetlights. "It is what it is. That's my job. Anyway, tell me about this concert. What's it going to involve?"

As Jess pulled out of the parking space and headed toward Ladbroke Grove, Audrey told her about the audition, the choir, and the organizers' plans for a charity concert that involved professionals and amateurs from all over the country.

"Are you sure it's a good idea for you to be in this choir, Mum? I do understand why you want to do it but I'm still worried it'll be too much for you. Rehearsals twice a week

sounds like a big commitment. Don't you think you should be taking it easy?"

There was concern in Jess's voice that Audrey felt she ought to be used to by now, given that it had infused every conversation with her family since her diagnosis. But they'd had this conversation already, when Audrey had first mentioned her plan to audition, and nothing had changed since then. If anything, having met Ben and heard about the concert, she was more determined than ever to join the choir.

"I know it's only because you care, but there's no need to worry. The choir will help take my mind off things. Give me something else to focus on."

As they turned onto Ladbroke Grove, Jess's sigh seemed to fill the car with fatigue.

"What is it, Jess? Really, there's nothing to worry about. The choir will be good for me."

Jess looked straight ahead, eyes fixed on the road. "It's not that."

Audrey detected an almost imperceptible twitch at the corner of Jess's mouth, invisible to anyone who wasn't attuned to it. "What is it, then? Come on. Something's wrong, I can tell."

"Nothing, honestly. It's just . . . I've been thinking about Dad, that's all."

Audrey waited for Jess to say more, could hear the ambivalence in the silence, was unsure whether to press further. She allowed a few moments to pass, waiting to see if Jess might volunteer anything else, but they'd stopped at a traffic light and Jess was staring out of the window in the opposite direction. "What have you been thinking?" Audrey's stomach swirled and she could taste the acidic residue of vomit despite the Trebor Extra Strong Mint she'd sucked on her way to the car.

"Nothing specific, really. Just little things."

Audrey watched Jess's mouth open again, as if she was preparing to say more, but then her lips closed. As the light turned to green and the car moved forward, Audrey studied her daughter's face. Jess had always complained that her looks were unattractive, nondescript, but Audrey had always seen a quiet beauty in them: eyes that seemed to change color, from gray to green to hazel, depending on the light; lashes so long people often assumed they were false; lips neither too full nor too thin that Audrey had often joked, when Jess was little, were perfect for kissing.

"What kind of things?" Audrey was aware of the air stiffening as the muscles in Jess's jaw twitched. It was always a risk pushing Jess—however gently—to talk about Edward, but she opened the door so infrequently that Audrey couldn't afford to ignore it.

"Like I said, nothing specific. Just random things from when I was little."

"Nice things?"

"For God's sake, Mum. Yes, nice things. Things that mean what happened later makes no sense. Things that mean I still don't understand what he did or why he did it. Is that what you want to hear? Is that what you want me to say? God, I wish I'd never mentioned it."

Audrey clasped her hands together, her rings jabbing into her fingers. "I'm sorry. I didn't mean to upset you. I know it's hard. I'm sure, in a way, it always will be. Dad was never the same after what happened with your sister."

Jess whipped her head around, eyes ablaze. "I *know* that, Mum. Don't you think I already know that?"

She hissed the words with a ferocity that still had the power to shock Audrey even though she'd heard it many times before.

The miscalculation rattled in Audrey's chest, berating her for having failed, yet again, to help Jess speak about events she had kept to herself all these years. She had an urge to reach out and squeeze the top of Jess's arm but she curled her hands into balls, her fingernails digging into her skin. "I'm sorry, Jess. I know you don't like to talk about it."

Audrey stared at Jess's profile, silently willing her daughter to turn her head, to offer even the smallest sign of forgiveness, but Jess didn't look at her, didn't smile, didn't speak.

They drove on in silence, Audrey replaying the conversation in her head, wondering what she could have said differently to change the outcome. But she realized that her only alternative was to have said nothing at all.

Staring out of the window as they turned onto Holland Park Avenue, she counted down the roads until they arrived at the junction with Lily's street. Her eyes darted left to right even though she knew a chance encounter was unlikely. Lily would already be at the work dinner that had caused her to cancel their supper.

It was the same every time she drove down this road with Jess, whatever time of day or night, whatever day of the week: the hope that somehow fate would bring her daughters together on the streets of west London. But even though Lily and Jess had lived in the same city, three miles apart, for fifteen years, not once had they met by chance.

Peering out of the window into Lily's street, Audrey felt the question niggling her. She turned to Jess, knowing there would never be a perfect time, that she couldn't put it off much longer. She'd been living with Jess for nearly a month now and every day she'd searched for a good opportunity to broach the subject, but none had arisen. She could hear the clock ticking loudly in her ears, knew she didn't have the

luxury of time, and took a deep breath, trying to remember the phrasing she'd been rehearsing for weeks.

"Jess, I need to ask you something, but I want you to listen before flying off the handle. Can you do that for me?"

The tension thickened as Jess's forehead puckered into a frown. "Why? What is it?"

Audrey tried to swallow but her mouth was dry. "I don't want to get maudlin, and I know you don't like talking about it, but I can't just sit by, knowing I'm ill, and do nothing while you and Lily are still estranged—"

"Mum, I—"

"Please, Jess. Please hear me out—"

"But there's no point. This conversation's going nowhere."

"There *is* a point, of course there is. I don't want the first time you and Lily see each other in years to be at my funeral. I can't bear the thought of it. Surely you can understand that? And what about Mia and Phoebe? Do you really want them having to contend with all that tension on the day you bury me? Please, Jess, please just meet her, talk to her. I can be there or not, whatever you want. Just please agree to see her."

Audrey's voice began to crack and she pinched her lips together. She didn't want emotional blackmail to force Jess into agreeing. She wanted Jess to see for herself that this decades-long feud was pointless, that it did no one any good, least of all Jess.

She kept her eyes trained on her daughter, searching for any sign of a softening, but when Jess began to speak her voice was so eerily calm that a chill inched down Audrey's spine.

"I don't know how many times I can say it, Mum. I know it's hard for you, but this isn't about you. It's about me and Lily. And I'm an adult so you have to let me manage my

relationships as I see fit. I don't want Lily in my life and I never will, and there's nothing anyone can do about that."

"But if only I knew the reason, if only you'd tell me why you won't speak to her, perhaps I'd understand. Perhaps I'd be able to help. I just don't believe we can't sort this out, whatever it is. I have to try, you must understand that."

Jess thumped hard on the steering wheel. "I am *not* telling you. How many times do I have to say it? I don't want to see Lily and that's that. I don't want you and me falling out about this, Mum, but if you mention it again then I can promise you we will."

Jess glared at her, and Audrey resisted the temptation to try to bridge the gap between them with words of reassurance. She knew, from decades of experience, that there were times when her attempts to appease Jess only exacerbated her anger.

Neither of them spoke until Audrey heard Jess sigh, then swallow.

"I'm sorry, Mum. I'm sorry for getting so angry. I know this is hard for you, really I do. And if there was any way I could make things better, I would, honestly. But I can't. I just can't."

Their eyes met fleetingly before Jess turned back to the road. Audrey looked out of the window to see a throng of shoppers emerging from Westfield—friends, families, couples, laughing, chatting, sharing stories of their day—the knowledge settling in her head like a thick winter fog that, nearly a month after moving in with Jess, she was still no closer to effecting a reconciliation between her daughters.

Part Three

April

Chapter 12
Audrey

"I'm so sorry it's not better news. I know it's a lot to take in. Can I get you a glass of water?"

Audrey moved to shake her head but she felt as if it were no longer attached to her body. "Thank you, no. I'm fine."

I'm fine. She almost apologized to the doctor for the absurdity of it.

She'd known, as soon as she'd walked into the doctor's room and seen the home-care nurse sitting in a high-backed chair upholstered in standard NHS blue vinyl, that today was going to be a Bad News Day. They only ever brought in the home-care nurses when there was heavy emotional lifting to be done.

"I know it's really difficult news to hear. I wish I could be telling you something different. But from your latest scan and blood tests, it does seem to be spreading more aggressively than we'd originally thought. And this fourth tumor we've found on your lung—as I say, it's small, but of course we'd rather it wasn't there at all."

Audrey felt the room shrink as though each of the four walls was slowly advancing toward her. "How does this change the prognosis? How long have I got?"

Dr. Sharma shifted in her seat and swept some invisible dust from the surface of her desk before raising her head and

looking directly at Audrey. "As I've said before, it can be really unhelpful to talk in terms of timelines. There's no reliable means of predicting how cancers are going to behave. Every case is unique. What I will say is that now might be a good time to reconsider whether you'd like to undergo any treatment. I know you were against it before, but this latest diagnosis does change the outlook. I have to be honest with you: given the way your cancer has spread in the last few weeks, treatment options are limited. But chemotherapy may help slow the growth of the tumors and minimize the risk of the cancer spreading. You don't have to decide anything now. I'm going to give you all the leaflets again, just so that you have the information to hand. Maybe you'd like to discuss it with your family over the weekend."

Audrey reached out and took the same collection of leaflets she'd first been given nearly seven months before, filled with advice and information she could have recited verbatim if tested. "But assuming I still don't want treatment, how long do you think I've got?"

An almost imperceptible flicker of something skittered behind the doctor's eyes: impatience or pity, uncertainty or apology, Audrey wasn't sure which.

"Honestly, Audrey, I really don't think it's helpful to talk in those terms."

"It will help me. Please. There are things I want to do. Things I need to do . . ." Her voice trailed off, the words trapped in her throat. She breathed slowly, tried to compose her face into that of someone who was prepared for the answer, however difficult.

The doctor eyed her silently, glanced over at the home-care nurse, and leaned forward in her chair. "As I say, Audrey, there's no accurate means of prediction. And every case really is unique. But on average, patients with cancer like

yours—cancer that's spread in a similar way, with a similar alacrity—might be looking at a life expectancy of somewhere around four to six months."

Audrey felt all the air escape from her lungs. Her limbs loosened, as if she were about to topple forward out of the chair. She tried to focus on a fixed point—the cardboard calendar on the windowsill—like a seasick sailor gluing their eyes to the safe line of the horizon.

Four to six months.

She'd arrived at the appointment believing she had at least a year left to live. Now she had just half of that, possibly a third. She sat completely still and thought about all the events she might not live to witness.

Her sixty-third birthday. Mia and Phoebe's eighteenths. The girls' A-level results.

Christmas, New Year, Easter: all those milestones she'd experienced for the last time without knowing it.

"I know it's *really* hard to hear. That's why we try not to give timeframes unless someone's determined to know. This isn't a precise science—we can't know exactly how your cancer's going to behave. It could be that you have longer. As I say, I can only give you averages."

Audrey nodded, wanting to remove any doubt on the doctor's part that perhaps she'd made a mistake in telling the truth. But now that she had the facts, Audrey didn't know what to do with them. They felt hot in her mouth, loud in her ears, tight in her chest.

She blinked and swallowed, trying to reteach herself the simple task of breathing in and then out again. Such minor victories over her body: controlling her breathing, holding back her tears. Such small battles won when they all knew she'd already lost the war.

She felt a hand on her arm, looked up to see the home-care nurse crouched next to her, saw such compassion in her eyes that she wondered how anyone had the strength to do that job: offering comfort where there was none to be had.

"Can we call someone for you? We'd really rather you didn't go home on your own. Was no one free to come with you today?"

Audrey shook her head, thinking of the people who'd asked to accompany her: Lily, Jess, Mia, Phoebe. But she'd insisted on coming alone, and now she was relieved that she had. Having to cope with someone else's shock was more than she could have borne.

"Well, there's no rush to leave. We can sit outside in the waiting room for as long as you like. I might even be able to rustle up a cup of tea."

The home-care nurse smiled and Audrey felt herself try to reciprocate but it was as if the muscles around her mouth had slackened and couldn't quite pull themselves up. "That's very kind but there's no need. I'll call a taxi."

"I can do that for you."

There was a moment's silence, as though all three of them were paying respects to an event they knew was coming far too soon. Then Dr. Sharma glanced at her computer screen, and leaned back in her chair. "Audrey, we don't have to make any decisions about your treatment today. Go home, discuss things with your family, think it all through. Let's make an appointment for next week. That gives you the weekend to mull it over. How does that sound?"

Audrey nodded, thinking back to the discussions she'd had seven months ago, when she'd first announced her decision to refuse treatment: Lily's pleading, Jess's frustration, Dr. Sharma's patient explanation of the options, as though

perhaps a repetition of the facts might somehow change her mind. But Audrey had been resolute. She knew the doctors were offering her nothing more than palliative care. There had been no conversations then about possible remission, no hope of a reprieve. Just chemotherapy to try to slow the growth of something nobody denied would kill her. Audrey had imagined a day room filled with a dozen patients sitting in high-backed cushioned chairs, silent and immobile as drugs were pumped intravenously through cannulas in the back of their hands, medication seeping into their bloodstream and charging toward an enemy it was destined not to defeat. Seconds, minutes, hours ticking away, accompanied by nothing more than the hope of a brief stay of execution, with no guarantee that those faulty days would ever be refunded.

Audrey knew all too well the effects of those therapies. Once upon a time she had been told they might work miracles. Sometimes, in her darker moments and against her rational judgment, she found herself wondering whether perhaps, given time, they might have done.

It was more than that, though. Audrey might not allow the admission to hover on the surface of her thoughts for too long but it was always there. She didn't deserve treatment. Whatever help the doctors might be able to offer, whatever temporary miracles they might be able to perform, Audrey felt she was the last person in the world who actually deserved them.

"Thank you. But I won't change my mind about the treatment. I'm sure of that."

"Well, there's no rush. Let the news settle and we'll discuss it again next week."

Audrey rose and shook Dr. Sharma's outstretched hand, felt the doctor's soft, youthful skin beneath her fingers. She felt an arm around her shoulders as the home-care nurse guided

her through to the waiting room and lowered her into a chair as though the muscles in Audrey's legs might not be able to negotiate the maneuver, then left to order a taxi.

Audrey leaned her head against the wall, her temples throbbing.

Four to six months. She pulled out her diary and began leafing through the pages, counting down the weeks and months until her time might run out. And the act of looking at dates, willing them to tell her a different story, took her back to a scene from years before, when she had similarly wished that time could be more on her side.

Chapter 13
April 1972

Audrey sits on the edge of her bed beneath a poster of Aretha Franklin, frantically turning the pages of her diary, urging them to give her a different answer. She flicks back through the weeks—one week, then two, a third, and then a fourth. A fifth whips past her fingers and still she has to press on. Past the sixth until there it is, seven weeks previously. Practically a lifetime ago.

She stares at her own unintelligible scribble, the shorthand her mum has taught her to mark this monthly event, unreadable to anyone else who may chance upon her diary.

Seven weeks and somehow she hasn't realized until now.

She continues to stare at the open page in front of her, as though the strength of her gaze might have the power to alter history. She notices that her hands are shaking and tries to hold them steady, but it is as if they are a separate entity over which she has no control. She is eighteen, and it seems surreal to her that only a few minutes ago she could have described how her life might pan out over the next three years yet now she is unsure how to manage the next three minutes.

She lifts her head and looks toward the net curtains, notices the tired gray tinge to the thin white material. She remembers she had promised her mum she would take them down

and wash them during the school holidays, a promise she has failed to keep.

Perhaps, Audrey thinks, if she washes them now, her parents won't be quite so disappointed in her when she tells them. Just imagining the dismay on their faces—the realization that she is no longer a little girl, that she has not behaved how they would expect her to—causes her to scrunch her eyes shut.

Audrey swallows the rising tide of bile at the back of her throat and drops her head into her hands. She has no idea what she's going to do next.

Simon and Garfunkel's "Bridge Over Troubled Water" plays on the jukebox. Audrey has to strain her ears to hear the lyrics because the machine is on the far side of the bar and she has deliberately chosen the quietest table, tucked away in a corner far from eavesdropping ears, even though she is not expecting to see anyone she knows in this Holborn pub.

She sits waiting for Edward to return from the toilet, unsure whether she wants him to come quickly or not. But after more than two weeks of holding on to the news, she no longer feels able to bear the weight of it alone.

The table rattles and she leans over, wedging a coaster underneath the leg. As she sits up, the palm of her hand instinctively finds the flat of her stomach.

There is no sign yet, nothing to give her away. Nothing to indicate what is taking place inside her and has been for nine weeks now, according to the doctor: the cells dividing and multiplying, a brand-new person slowly morphing into life. This strikes Audrey as remarkable. That it is possible for another human to be growing inside her with no external evidence to communicate this fact to the rest of the world:

no change in the color of her skin, no readable message on her face, no visible aura of protection around her.

Audrey sips gingerly at the white wine Edward has bought for her but it tastes strange—bitter—and she puts the glass back on the table.

And then there he is, striding around the bar toward her, smiling: his tall, dependable frame; his expression a question in need of an answer; his walk toeing an invisible line.

Can a walk, Audrey wonders, be sensible?

"That's better. So how's the revision going? First exam in six weeks? You're going to do brilliantly, I just know it." He takes a long, thirsty gulp from his pint of bitter before letting his fingers rest on hers.

His touch is light, but Audrey feels as though her hand is pinned flat to the table like a butterfly in a lepidopterist's display case. "It's OK. But you never know, do you? Not until you get in the exam room and read the questions. You could find out you've prepared completely the wrong topics." She listens to her preemptive excuses, a preparation for the disappointment she feels sure will greet her results in four months' time even though she is yet to sit her first paper.

She has done no A-level revision for the past two weeks. Every time she has opened a book the words have dissolved in front of her eyes. She has sat on her bed, hour after hour, imagining the A grades she has been predicted in English, History, and French flipping like letters on a train station noticeboard, replaced by Bs and then Cs, until they land, decisively, on Ds. She has felt her future sliding from her grasp: all her ambitions slipping through her fingers, like grains of sand on a windswept beach.

"You'll be fine, Auds. This time next year you'll be two terms into an English degree at UCL and all this worry

about your exams will be a distant memory. Trust me, I've been there. I wouldn't be able to tell you a single question I answered in my A-levels now." Edward continues to talk, presenting her with platitudes of support and encouragement she hasn't requested but feels she should be grateful for nonetheless.

His voice fades in her ears, as if a sound engineer has remixed the volumes so that she can no longer hear him above the white noise of a busy pub on a Saturday night.

This time next year.

She tries to imagine it, but can't. She cannot visualize herself with a baby, cannot imagine where she might be living, or with whom. She cannot picture a version of her life that doesn't involve Senate House library, lectures on the Bloomsbury Group, tutorials in Chaucer, Shakespeare, Austen, Dickens, Eliot, Hardy, Waugh.

"I need to talk to you about something." She has interrupted him without realizing he was still speaking.

A microscopic twitch hovers at the corner of Edward's mouth. At first she thinks it is irritation. They have only been going out for eleven months and she has not yet learned the full repertoire of his facial expressions. But then he frowns and she sees that she is mistaken: it is not irritation but fear. She realizes that he thinks she's about to end their relationship and is surprised by how distraught he seems.

Words scramble from her mouth, like unruly children piling out of a classroom as the bell rings. "There's no easy way to say this so I'm just going to come out and say it. I'm pregnant. About nine weeks, the doctor thinks. I'm sorry, I know it's the last thing either of us wants."

Her lips part in preparation for another apology but she forces herself to close them. It is true that she is sorry, but it

should not be her apologizing. It has been his responsibility, after all. She has trusted him to buy them, put them on properly, withdraw ensuring that nothing escapes.

Edward is shaking his head and Audrey cannot tell whether it is in disbelief, horror, or denial.

"Say something. I need you to say something." She does not know what she wants him to say, only that his silence is suffocating.

"Sorry. It's just a lot to take in. How are you feeling? I mean, are you OK?"

Audrey nods but she cannot find the words to articulate how she is feeling. She fears that if she tries, all that will emerge will be a persistent, fearful howl.

"Look, I don't want you to worry about anything. I'll go to the town hall in the morning, inquire about marriage licenses. I think you can get them pretty quickly these days. And then we'll tell our parents. You haven't told yours yet, have you? OK, well, I'll come with you. We'll tell them together. It'll be much easier for them to accept if they know we're getting married."

Audrey listens to him talking and envies him his clarity, his certainty, his unambiguous sense of purpose. It is a decisiveness, she knows, that should reassure her. She has a sense that in a parallel world there is a version of herself whose lungs are inflating with relief and gratitude. But the Audrey sitting here, opposite Edward right now, feels his words slip into her chest and clatter against her ribs, demanding to be let out.

"But what about my university place?" Her voice sounds small and she wonders whether she has managed to say the words out loud. But then he turns over her hand, squeezes her fingers, and she cannot discern whether the clamminess between their flesh belongs to him or to her.

"Audrey, we're having a baby. And I want to be with you—with both of you. Maybe you can go to university later, when the baby's gone to school?"

Audrey stares down at their hands, notices how neat his clipped fingernails are in contrast to hers, bitten to the quick.

Edward is six years older than Audrey—six years wiser, she has always believed—and there is a kindness about him she finds reassuring. He is steady and reliable: a junior aviation strategist for the British Overseas Airways Corporation who has enjoyed a quiet, unblemished journey through private school and university. He is not maverick or spontaneous in the way that Audrey's friends' boyfriends usually are. But then, those boys always break girls' hearts. And one thing Audrey is sure of is that Edward would never break anyone's heart.

Audrey loves Edward, she is in no doubt about that. She has just never imagined spending the rest of her life with him. She has never, in truth, imagined spending the rest of her life with anyone. While most of her friends daydream about weddings and motherhood, Audrey saves her dreams for a dark mahogany desk in a university English department, library books stretching from the floor to the ceiling and lecture halls filled with students taking notes from her meticulously prepared lessons. For years she has secretly harbored the fantasy that if she works hard enough, and believes in herself, a future in academia may await her. It is a dream, she knows, that stretches her imagination to its limits, yet one which, in moments of fortitude, she dares to believe might come true.

Now, suddenly, that dream seems to be little more than a childish fantasy.

"I love you, Audrey, you know I do. And I will always, *always* look after you and the baby, I promise. Will you marry me, please?"

He is waiting, she knows, for her to lift her head and meet his gaze. But it feels like a gargantuan task, to heave this great weight from her shoulders. She hears the seconds tick by, feels him stroke the back of her hand, senses the anticipation thicken between them.

She is aware of the points shifting, hears the grinding of gears as she reaches the base of the V where two lines diverge, watches herself hurtle along this new route. She glances sideways out of the window to where the other branch is receding, the distance growing ever greater until there is nothing more than a memory of where her alternative future had once been.

And then she is nodding. Her head is moving independently of her ambivalence. She feels his fingers encase her hand, can sense his happiness radiating from his touch. His words echo in her ears—*I will always,* always *look after you and the baby*—and she tries to hold on to them, to take comfort from the reassurance and stability he is offering.

Chapter 14
Lily

Lily sat at her desk, staring out of the glass wall onto the Thames beyond. Steel clouds hung low in the sky, the river leaden and unmoving. A tourist boat drifted across the water, camera flashes blinking into the gray air, its passengers keen to take home a more enviable image of the city.

She forced her eyes back down to the computer screen, the cursor blinking on an empty document. Her fingers moved across the keys, typing out a sentence she read back and then deleted.

The phone on her desk rang, startling her. She glanced down to see her assistant's name flashing on the LCD screen. "Sophie, I said I didn't want to be disturbed. What is it?"

She heard her assistant clear her throat, could feel the girl's anxiety filtering through the handset. "Um, I just had a call from reception. They said your mum's down there wanting to see you. I couldn't see anything in the diary."

Heat rose into Lily's cheeks and she picked up the glass of water from her desk, gulped down its contents. "Could you go and collect her?"

Replacing the phone in its cradle, Lily stood up and glanced out into the busy open-plan office, her thoughts leapfrogging each another as to why her mum should be paying her an impromptu visit.

The door opened and Sophie showed her mum in.

"Can I get you both a cup of tea or coffee?"

Her mum glanced in Lily's direction, hands clasped together as if in prayer, before turning back to Sophie. "Thank you, that's very kind, but I'm fine."

"Yes, me too, Sophie. Can you check my four o'clock meeting's still happening?"

As the door closed there was a moment's silence. Lily gestured to the sofa, her arm extended stiffly, her body reacting against a clash of worlds she usually kept separate. "Sit down, Mum, please. Is everything OK?"

Her mum sat on the edge of the sofa, handbag clutched on her lap, coat still done up. Lily noticed the buttons were in the wrong holes, the collar jutting out at an awkward angle.

"Yes, I was just passing and I thought it's been ages—years—since I've seen you at work. I'm sorry, I should have telephoned. I didn't think." She opened her handbag and fiddled with something inside, then zipped it closed again.

"Don't be silly, it's lovely to see you. I've probably only got about fifteen minutes, though. The diary's crammed with meetings until seven. How are you?" Lily's mobile pinged with a trio of successive bleeps. "Sorry—I'd just better check those. There's a board meeting tomorrow and I've been waiting for some info. Just bear with me a second." She retrieved her phone from the desk, swiped open the screen, and scanned three emails. Opening her electronic calendar to check on an appointment, she noticed a small note at the top of today's date. "God, I'm so sorry, Mum. You had your doctor's appointment today. How was it? Nothing bad's happened, has it?"

Her mum looked up at her, blinking as though some dust was trapped under her eyelid. She coughed, lightly at first, and

then vigorously, her hand flat on her chest. "I couldn't get a glass of water, could I? I seem to have a tickle in my throat."

Lily popped outside her office door, filled a glass with water from the dispenser, and headed back in. Her mum was exactly where she'd left her: sitting on the edge of the sofa as if uncertain how long she wanted to stay. "There you go. Are you sure you're OK? That cough sounds like it's getting worse."

Her mum nodded without looking up. "I just had something caught in my throat, that's all."

"So what did the doctor say?" Lily sat down opposite her mum, smoothed her dress over her thighs.

"Everything's fine. Just a routine appointment, nothing to report."

The phone on Lily's desk rang and she peered through the glass wall to where Sophie was waving an apologetic hand at her before the ringing stopped.

"Are you sure? How were your blood counts?"

"Honestly, darling, it was all the same as before. No change. But how are you? You've been working so hard since Daniel left and I'm worried about you. Has he said when he's coming home for the weekend? You must be missing each other terribly."

Her mum smiled and Lily tried to hold her gaze, tried not to let her expression betray her. "Not yet—he's pretty frantic out there. He'll come back as soon as he can. I know it's not ideal but it's only for six months and you can't expect to have careers like ours without making a few sacrifices." The half-truths tumbled out of Lily's mouth.

"I'm not criticizing you, darling. You know how proud I am of both of you. I honestly don't know how you keep all the plates spinning. It makes me tired just watching you."

Her mum stretched out an arm and took Lily's hand. Before Lily knew it was going to happen, there was a lump in her throat, tears in her eyes. She felt the truth rise into her mouth and sit readily on her tongue, felt the preemptive relief of disclosure: the strain her marriage had been under, Daniel's suggestion that some space might do them good, her fears that she would not be able to fix whatever was wrong in their relationship when they were living thousands of miles apart. She could feel it all, ready to be divulged, ready to find a sympathetic listener and wise counsel in her mum.

The shrill beeping of her mum's phone broke the silence.

"Oh, I'm sorry—I don't know why the volume's so loud. You need to show me how to turn it down. Let me switch it off. Oh . . . hang on a second."

Lily blinked against her tears, her hand hanging limply by her side where her mum had let it go to read the message.

"Darling, I'm really sorry but I'm going to have to dash. You need to get on now anyway, don't you?"

Something in her mum's voice made Lily's shoulders stiffen. "Why? What is it? What's wrong?"

She watched the questions skim across her mum's eyes, watched the two sides of a dilemma being weighed up in her mind.

"Nothing. Nothing bad, it's just . . . Well, Jess forgot to tell me that a plumber's coming to look at the shower and neither she nor Mia will be at home, so she's asked if I could let him in." Apprehension twitched between her mum's eyebrows.

Lily got up, went to her desk, and bent down toward her computer, swiping the mouse to bring her screen back to life. "That's fine, Mum. You go. I need to get this presentation done anyway." Her tone was brusquer than she'd intended.

She kept her head down, eyes on the screen, as she heard the rustle of her mum standing up to leave.

"I'm sorry, it's just bad timing. But are you sure everything's OK? Was there something you wanted to tell me?"

Lily shook her head, still staring at the screen. "No. Nothing." She forced herself to stand upright and smile, trying to dissolve the tension. "It's fine, Mum, you go. I'll see you on Sunday for lunch."

There was a brief hesitation before her mum stepped around the desk, folded her arms around Lily like a pair of giant wings, and hugged her gently.

Stay, Lily wanted to say. *Please don't go.*

But instead she loosened herself from her mum's embrace and took a step back. "You'd better get going. You don't want to be late."

Her mum looked at her, and Lily felt a succession of unspoken questions congeal between them. She walked over to the door, found Sophie at her desk, and asked her to accompany her mum back downstairs.

"Don't work too late, will you, darling? And I'll see you at the weekend."

They kissed goodbye, and as her mum headed toward the elevator with Sophie, Lily watched them go, noticing how much narrower her mum's shoulders were than they had been just six months ago.

Back inside her office, Lily sank into the chair at her desk and spun it around to face the window. Fat raindrops hit the glass, sliding down to collect in small pools on the black metal ledge. She breathed slowly and methodically, silently repeating the line her therapist had been schooling her in for years: *You can't change others' behavior. You can only control your own reaction to it.*

Lily closed her eyes, thinking about all the times over the years that Jess's behavior had tested her reactions. All the times her mum had canceled arrangements because of some eleventh-hour emergency of Jess's. All the extra help her mum had given Jess because she was a single parent who'd messed up her life. And not once had her mum acknowledged the irony that Jess—who had torn their family apart—was awarded the lion's share of maternal time and attention.

She thought about her mum, just a few minutes earlier, sitting on the sofa holding her hand, and suddenly found herself imagining the gaping absence her death would leave behind. It was as though something were pressing down hard on her windpipe: an assault, a compression, panic inhaled with each breath.

She was forty-three years old, she told herself. She must have known this day would come eventually, that there would likely be years—decades—when she would be alive and her mum would not. She knew that most children, at some point, became orphans.

Opening her eyes, she looked out of the rain-streaked window to the street ten floors below: miniature figures hurried along the pavement beneath a canopy of umbrellas; car headlights illuminated the glistening tarmac; farther down the river the London Eye continued its almost imperceptible rotation.

Lily knew there was only one person in the world who might understand how she felt about the prospect of losing her mum, just one person who might comprehend how great a loss it would be. But that particular conversation was impossible. These days, she couldn't even imagine how it might feel.

Lily swung her chair around and pulled it close to her desk, tucking her legs neatly underneath. Focusing on the empty

presentation in front of her she began to type, but as her fingers tapped at the keyboard she couldn't help noticing that her hands were shaking.

Eleven hours later Lily woke with a jolt and sat bolt upright in bed, her heart pounding, beads of sweat gathered at her temples. She looked around the darkened room and glanced at the clock beside her bed—3:04 a.m.—a voice in her head reminding her that it was just a dream.

Switching on the bedside light, she reached across for a glass of water and wrapped her clammy palms around it, sipping gently, her mouth desert-dry. She was desperate to lie down and sleep but every time she blinked, they were there: those tiny blue hummingbirds.

The dream was always the same. She is standing in a darkened room, silent save for the gentle rhythm of flapping wings. In front of her there are thousands of tiny blue hummingbirds: small, fragile, beautiful. She studies them, unsure whether she is unable to move or simply unwilling to disturb them. They flutter in the tentative light of early morning, their tiny bodies a miracle of nature, the speed of their wings too fast for the eye to follow. There is something meditative in watching them, their miniature movements hypnotic. But suddenly they are swarming toward her, beating their wings against her cheeks, her hair, her neck. She raises her hands to protect her face, but the birds are so small they inch around the gaps, their long beaks pecking at her flesh. She closes her eyes, tries to bat them away, but there are too many, all flapping and pecking, and she feels the first sting of a beak piercing her skin, followed by another, and then another: the bridge of her nose, her forehead, her scalp. And then they are pecking at her eyes and she is flailing her arms, trying to escape their assault, but

there are too many and there is nothing she can do to stop them. She feels the blood trickle down her cheeks, tastes its metallic flavor on her tongue, hears their wings beating in her ears. And then she wakes up.

Lily gulped at the water, willing the images to release her now she was awake. She'd been having this dream for years yet still she woke every time panicked, sweating, scrabbling for air.

She lay down again and stared up at the shadow of the chandelier on the ceiling. It had been Daniel's anniversary present to her last year: bespoke hand-blown Italian glass, a thousand separate clear pendants hanging from a central stem like an exotic crystal tree, the kind of chandelier you might find in the lobby of a boutique hotel or a Michelin-starred restaurant. Lily had seen the receipt lying on the desk in Daniel's study, had balked at the cost, but Daniel had needed to give her something extravagant to assuage his guilt at being abroad on their anniversary for the third year in a row.

Lily stared up at the chandelier, imagining that perhaps the two men who'd come to install it hadn't done the job properly, that it might come crashing down on her head one night as she lay sleeping.

Reaching over and switching off her bedside lamp, she curled her limbs into a fetal ball, held herself tight, and implored herself to go to sleep.

Chapter 15
Jess

Just over two miles west of where Lily lay awake, Jess raised her head from the pillow and looked at the clock.

3:22 a.m.

From the room next door she could hear the rustle of a duvet. There had been so many nights since her mum moved in that Jess had been aware of her restlessness in the early hours of the morning. So many nights she had sensed them both lying awake in adjacent rooms, barely fifteen feet apart, separated only by a line of bricks, two thin layers of plaster, and three decades of unspoken conversations. On many occasions she had listened to her mum tossing and turning, knowing she should get out of bed, put her head around the door, and offer to make her some cocoa. But she hadn't, not once. And Jess didn't know whether what stopped her was the fear of discovering the reason for her mum's insomnia or the anxiety that she might disclose her own.

Jess heard her mum attempt to stifle a cough. She lay completely still, hardly daring to breathe, remembering all those childhood nights curled up alone in bed. All those nights she had listened to her mum sobbing in the bedroom across the landing. All those nights she had heard hissed conversations from the floors below. She remembered sitting at the top of the

stairs, hearing Lily's voice from behind closed doors, knowing she should not have been eavesdropping but being unable to tear herself away as she listened to her sister's pleading: *Please, Dad. Please stop it. You* have *to. Please.*

Light glared into the room from the gap between the wall and the curtains, and Jess pulled the duvet high over her head, her breath circulating hot and damp in the confined space, but still the images kept coming. She scrunched her eyes until her forehead ached, but instead of forcing the memories from her mind, it sharpened their focus until she was back in her childhood home on the day it had happened.

Chapter 16

September 1988

Jess opens the shed door and peers around in the darkness, her eyes accustoming to the gloom. She steps inside, wary of spiders and their webs, but decides she would rather not see them even if they are there. Reaching toward the flowerpot on the middle shelf, she pulls it toward her and hears the key rattle before her fingers find it. She grabs it and backs out of the door, heads across the garden and through the side gate, around to the front of the house.

When her after-school netball practice had been canceled, it had crossed Jess's mind that her mum would expect her to find Lily, tell her that she was finishing early and wait until her sister was free to bring her home. But as she had hovered at the bottom of the stairs that led up to the fifth-form classrooms, something had stopped her. She had thought perhaps it had been her newness at secondary school that had made her fearful of entering the fifth-formers' territory: just two weeks since her first day, her August birthday making her one of the youngest pupils in a thousand-strong school. But she had known, deep down, that it was really because she did not want to be at home alone with Lily.

Throughout the summer holidays, Jess had craved an escape from the tears, the tension, the hushed conversations behind

closed doors. For months she has not accepted invitations to friends' houses in case they look at her in the way they had at the end of last term when everyone found out what had happened: those looks of curiosity, pity, sympathy, and horror that had made her want to shout into their faces: *It's not my fault. I didn't want this to happen. I didn't know how to stop it.* She has not wanted to invite friends home in case they discover the truth about how her family are living now: her mum's tear-stained cheeks emerging only rarely from under the duvet in the spare bedroom; her dad bookending his ever-lengthening days at the office with a quiet restlessness, as though he cannot sit still but does not know where he wants to go; Lily disappearing before Jess is up, often staying out all day as though the house is contaminated and she fears infection, although Jess has no idea where her sister goes, whether she sees anyone, what she does.

Jess cannot seek refuge in her friends for fear they will ask questions she is unable to answer.

She slides the key into the front door, thinking about the Oreos and mug of hot chocolate she will get from the kitchen before settling down in front of *Grange Hill*. Closing the door behind her, she feels a shiver tiptoe down her spine and fears momentarily the reprisals when her mum discovers her transgression. Having only recently celebrated her eleventh birthday, she is not supposed to be in the house alone.

It is only when she turns and sees what is at the top of the stairs that the cold trail along her spine spreads toward her ribs, her neck, her head, until her whole body is ice cold from her scalp to her toes.

Jess stares, unblinking, knowing what she is seeing yet unable to comprehend it.

It is her dad, but also not her dad. He is not standing on the landing, waving and smiling, calling her *petal* and asking about her

day at school. Her dad is swinging from a beam on the ceiling, the cord of her mum's navy blue dressing gown around his neck, his head slumped forward, his legs dangling beneath him.

Jess stares, cannot take her eyes off him, even as she feels the nausea swirl in her stomach. She stares at his suit and tie, his freshly polished shoes, waiting for him to raise his head, smile at her, tell her it's all some terrible joke. But he does not move.

She does not move her eyes from him, yet somehow she absorbs the rest of the scene: the broken dining chair lying at the bottom of the stairs; the fat double knot under his chin; the deafening silence that seems to be pressing down on her until she fears it will crush her on the hallway floor.

Jess does not move, her body remote, distinct, as though it no longer belongs to her.

And then, all of a sudden, a sound is ringing in her ears and vibrating across her skin, but it is only when she hears a key in the front door, only when Mrs. Sheppard, their neighbor, bursts into the hall and gasps, that Jess realizes the sound she can hear is screaming and that the screams are her own.

She is aware of Mrs. Sheppard's arm around her shoulders, of being led into the sitting room and lowered onto the sofa, of Mrs. Sheppard speaking but the words feel gluey in Jess's ears. She sits on the sofa, her whole body trembling, and she knows there is nothing she can do to stop it. She hears Mrs. Sheppard whispering in the hallway, and for a split second she thinks she has got it all wrong, that Mrs. Sheppard is chatting to her dad, that it has all been some terrible misunderstanding. But above the noise of the blood pounding in her ears she hears the words *police, dead,* and *body* and they sound strange, unreal, as though they have drifted accidentally into her house from some other time and place.

Mrs. Sheppard returns and sits down next to her, holds her hand, says the same words over and over: *You poor girl. You*

poor, poor girl. It's all going to be OK. Jess can hear the horror in her voice, knows that what she is saying is not true. All Jess wants is her mum to be there, to hold her and stroke her hair. And with each passing second that she is absent, the panic grips tighter around Jess's throat that perhaps something has happened to her too, perhaps her mum will never come to rescue her.

And then there are two police officers in the room—a man and a woman—though Jess has no recollection of them arriving. They are asking her questions but she cannot get their words to stick in her ears so she stares silently at her hands, watching them tremble, wishing that everyone would stop talking, that they would all go away. She senses Mrs. Sheppard buzzing around the room, sees the policeman scribbling into his miniature notebook, hears the policewoman speaking into the walkie-talkie attached to her shoulder. She wants them all to leave but knows she could not bear to be left alone with what is at the top of the stairs.

And then suddenly her mum is there, holding her tight as if fusing their bodies together. Jess feels the first hot tears burn her cheeks, feels the heat of her breath pressed against her mum's chest, feels the air scorch her throat and char her lungs. She buries herself in her mum's cotton blouse, not knowing whether she feels relief at her presence or dread in their collective horror.

She does not know how long they stand there, her and her mum, locked inside their shock and grief. She hears more people bustling in and out of the house but will not listen to their explanations of who they are and what they are doing because then she would have to acknowledge that this is actually happening. Instead, she clings to her mum, feeling as though she is adrift in a vast ocean and that tethering herself to someone else is her only chance of survival.

She senses Lily's presence before she sees her.

And then her sister is standing next to them, and her mum is explaining what has happened, and Jess wants to clamp her hands over her ears, wants someone to take the words away and with them the pain. And when she hears Lily's sharp intake of breath, when she hears it exhumed in loud, potent sobs, all she wants to do is scream into Lily's face: *This is all your fault. If you hadn't said what you said, if you hadn't done what you did, Dad would still be alive.*

Fury weaves through Jess's ribs and encircles her heart. She had thought she couldn't hate Lily any more than she had at the beginning of the summer but it is as though her anger three months ago was nothing more than a dress rehearsal for the enmity now coursing through her veins.

Now, she thinks. Now is the time to tell her mum the truth about what happened. Her mum needs to know that this is all Lily's fault.

She prepares to speak, to say the words that have been eluding her all summer. But her mum begins to cry so loudly that the sound fills Jess's ears, swims inside her head, slips down, and lodges in her throat. And she knows she cannot say anything, that she does not have the courage or the cruelty—she is not sure which—to tell her mum the truth. Instead Jess cleaves to her mum and closes her eyes. But all that greets her is the image of her dad's body looming over her like a grotesque version of the stick men she used to draw in a game of Hangman. As Jess clings to her mum, grief and fury simmering in her chest, a single thought hammers inside her head: Lily is the reason that her dad is swinging from a noose at the top of the stairs. If it weren't for Lily, the man Jess loves most in the world would still be alive.

Chapter 17
Audrey

The illuminated digits on the bedside alarm clock flicked listlessly from one number to the next.

3:57 a.m.

Audrey turned onto her side, experiencing a breathlessness that had been bothering her for weeks, but until now she hadn't dared question its cause.

3:58 a.m.

Almost fifteen hours had passed since she'd seen the oncologist. More than twelve hours since she had arrived at Lily's office, fully intending to confide in her. The desire not to be left alone with the news had been overwhelming as she'd waited in reception for Lily's assistant to collect her. But then Lily had asked about the hospital appointment and there had been such concern in her voice that Audrey had known she couldn't do it.

She had kept up the pretense all afternoon and evening, during anxious phone calls first from Jess and then Phoebe. By the time Mia had arrived home from the library, Audrey was so well rehearsed in the lie she almost believed it herself.

Yes, all OK, thanks . . . Nothing much to report . . . No change.

OK: that catchall word signifying everything and nothing.

Audrey closed her eyes and tried to sleep, but for months—

ever since her original diagnosis back in September—her brain had been busy stoking memories she'd spent years trying to suppress. Scenes from family history now hummed in her head like Muzak in an elevator from which there was no escape. It was as though her mind, knowing it had so little future, had become obsessed with the past. Except there was no solace in looking back; she knew that. But sometimes it seemed to Audrey that she had forgotten all the things she wanted to remember, and remembered everything she wished she could forget.

For months now she had been haunted by memories of Edward: Edward on their wedding day, strong and handsome in his charcoal gray suit and royal blue tie. How happy they had been at the service in Islington Town Hall, just their parents as guests and witnesses, her wedding dress a long cream halter-neck that flowed seamlessly over her five-month bump. How Edward's enthusiasm at impending parenthood had been infectious, his careful research into everything they needed to buy, everything they needed to be, making her fall in love with him in ways she had never expected. Edward holding Lily the day she'd been born, cradling her in his arms, tears in his eyes, telling Audrey he had never been happier. Edward arriving home from work and kissing Audrey on the lips before seeking out the girls to bathe them, read to them, put them to bed. Edward planning trips to the cinema, holidays by the seaside, excursions chosen to ensure everyone was happy. Their lives, for so many years, lived to a soundtrack of laughter.

Miracles do happen.

Edward's voice rang in her ears as clearly as if he were lying in bed next to her. She knew that was what he'd say if he were there now. He'd said it so often, trying to reassure

her, to be strong enough for both of them. And later he'd said it again, but by then with such rage and disbelief it was as though a different man had inhabited his body and taken over his voice.

If Edward were there now, he would hold her hands in his and look directly into her eyes, determined to convince her that, in spite of the oncologist's diagnosis, there was still a chance of recovery. This time, Audrey wondered, might she believe him?

4:09 a.m.

Audrey breathed silently into the darkness, thinking about Jess in the room next door and how there never seemed to be the space or time for the two of them to talk. When she had moved in, she had imagined them chatting late into the night over bottles of red wine and squares of dark chocolate, the drawbridge finally lowering, Jess at last confiding in Audrey what had troubled her all these years. In truth, she felt no closer to Jess now than she had two months ago.

A car door slammed and Audrey felt her body tense.

She rolled over, a sharp pain needling beneath her ribs that caused her to inhale short, staccato breaths. She thought about her conversation with Jess a few weeks ago, recalling the fury that had greeted her suggestion that Jess meet Lily after all these years. And before she knew it, a memory was edging into her thoughts: the memory of how, once before, she had got it all so horribly wrong.

Chapter 18
July 2003

Two little girls squeal as bubbles float through the air, popping on their hands as they reach out to catch them. "More, more!"

Audrey twists the stick in the plastic bottle, pulls it out, and blows gently, watching the bubbles drift off into the garden. Some glide over the fence, others land on waxy magnolia leaves, bee-laden lavender bushes, the multicolored petals of sweet peas, geraniums, begonias, fuchsias. The late afternoon sunshine illuminates the bubbles as they hover in the air, their rims glistening like the decisive moment of an annular eclipse.

"More, Granny, do some more!"

Audrey smiles as the girls jump and giggle, feeling the warmth of their camaraderie. She had known this would happen: that they would be friends, given the chance. For five years she has waited to test her belief and now her only regret is that she has left it so long.

Phoebe grabs Mia's hand and they race to the far corner of the garden, stopping under the apple tree. Phoebe whispers something into her cousin's ear before they grin at one another with wide-eyed wonder. Audrey can only speculate as to her granddaughters' secret. It is long overdue, she thinks, the girls finally meeting. It is time they were allowed secrets of their own.

"Gran, we're thirsty! Mia says she saw *lemonade* in the fridge!"

They stare at her, smiling and impish, and Audrey cannot help but laugh. "I may have some. But only for girls who promise to be really good for the rest of the afternoon."

They nod in unison, staring at her with round, earnest eyes.

"Come on then. I'll get you both a glass."

The girls clutch one another's hands and skip toward her, bare knees lifting at right angles beneath Mia's floral dress and Phoebe's navy shorts. They sit down next to each other at Audrey's kitchen table, legs swinging, faces flushed from the midsummer heat, and for a split second it is as though time has reversed and her own little girls are sitting in the kitchen, grinning at one another with collusive smiles.

Audrey studies them while trying not to stare. She does not want to unnerve them, not when they are so relaxed in one another's company. But it is strange seeing them together for the first time. For so long she has imagined what it might be like to have her two grandchildren in the same room, but until today it has been nothing more than a fantasy.

Phoebe gurgles the last of her lemonade through her straw and Mia copies her, the two of them eyeing one another and giggling, their smiles so similar it is as though one has been molded from the other. Audrey had known, before the girls met today, that their resemblance was uncanny, but it is only now seeing them side by side that she truly appreciates the similarities: the same sleek dark hair; the same questioning green eyes; the same porcelain skin. A stranger in the street would mistake them for twins, not cousins.

Audrey glances down at her watch—5:50 p.m.—trying not to think about how the coming minutes may unfold.

"Right, ladies, would you like to go outside for a last play? Your mums will be here soon."

Mia and Phoebe hop off the wooden chairs and grab each other's hands. They run out of the back door and onto the lawn, bending down on all fours to prowl through the grass like lions, occasionally roaring at each other or stopping to nuzzle with an easy affection that tugs at Audrey's heart.

She looks down at her watch again. She does not know who will arrive first—Lily or Jess—but if she had to hazard a guess she would assume Lily. Even though Jess is the more protective, and Lily has the higher-profile career, it is Lily who is punctual and precise. In all the years Audrey has been taking care of Mia—after school, during the holidays, at weekends—she can think of few occasions when Jess hasn't been late to collect her.

Audrey clears away the girls' lemonade glasses and throws the straws into the bin, wondering when Mia and Phoebe might next sit together at her kitchen table. It is the summer holidays and she does not have to return to work at the school library until the week before Mia and Phoebe return to their respective schools in September. Feasibly she could look after them both every day. She already has Mia throughout the school holidays—one more grandchild would be no problem. It would, in fact, be a delight. She begins to imagine all the things the three of them could do together: trips to London Zoo, the Natural History Museum, the National Gallery; picnics at the seaside, the park, Kew Gardens; exploring the wide open spaces of Cliveden, Polesden Lacey, Hatchlands Park, all the National Trust properties Audrey rarely visits because there is too much melancholy in going alone. A fantasy about how the summer might unfold plays out in Audrey's head, accompanied by visions of her granddaughters laughing, the sun gleaming against their dark hair, their years of separation melting away.

Audrey brings the dustcloth to a halt on the kitchen table. She is getting ahead of herself. First, she must navigate the

next few minutes. Only then will she know what the rest of the summer—what her family's future—may hold.

She checks the time again: 5:55 p.m. Her pulse quickens at the thought of Lily and Jess's arrival. She imagines their faces when they find out what she has done, when they discover that she has engineered a playdate between their daughters despite Jess's insistence that the girls should never meet and Lily's acceptance that it would never happen.

She looks out into the garden to where Mia and Phoebe are climbing inside a hula hoop together, trying to spin it around them both, collapsing onto the lawn in a heap of hot, tangled limbs and infectious giggles. Surely, Audrey reasons, when Jess and Lily see how beautifully they're playing together, not even Jess will be able to argue that Mia and Phoebe—who understand nothing of the sibling estrangement which began long before they were born—should not be friends. Surely Jess will see they are innocent casualties in a family war of which not even Audrey knows the cause.

The doorbell rings and Audrey jumps. She glances once more into the garden at a sight she has waited so long to see, before walking up the basement stairs and into the hallway, taking a deep breath as she opens the door.

"Hi, Mum." Lily smiles and there is such trust in her expression that Audrey experiences a few seconds of panic. But as she ushers her daughter along the hall, down the stairs, and into the kitchen, she reminds herself—with all the fervor of a religious mantra—of why she has done this: Mia and Phoebe should not have to suffer for their mothers' mistakes. Children should not be punished for the sins of their parents.

As they walk into the kitchen, to where double doors open onto the sunken patio and the raised lawn beyond, Audrey does not take her eyes off Lily. She watches Lily's tender

smile at seeing her daughter, watches her glance toward the second girl—so similar to her own yet so unknown—watches the question hover behind her eyes as she turns to Audrey.

"I don't understand . . . What's going on? Is that who I think it is?"

Lily has seen plenty of photographs and Audrey knows the question is rhetorical. But she nods and watches as Lily turns back toward the garden, as she gazes at Phoebe and Mia taking it in turns to jump up and reach for the unripe apples on the tree. Lily drinks it all in: the first time she has seen her niece.

The doorbell rings again and goose bumps stipple Audrey's arms. As she turns away, she senses Lily's head pivot toward her but she does not look back. Her legs, as she ascends the stairs, are unsteady and she clings to the banister, trying to remind herself that she has done this for the right reasons. She has acted not out of control or punishment but out of love. She opens the front door and there is Jess, head down, fumbling inside her bag.

"Sorry I'm a bit late. One day a shoot will end on time and I might actually turn up without needing to apologize." She looks at Audrey and tries to smile but something seems to stop her.

"Not to worry. Mia's fine." The deception scratches at Audrey's throat and she looks away, fearful the duplicity may be etched on her face.

She hears Jess close the door behind her, hears her daughter's footsteps follow her across the wooden floorboards and down the stairs, Audrey's heart thudding with every step.

All she has to do, she thinks, is get Jess into the kitchen, allow her to view the scene in the garden, and there is a chance everything will be OK.

As they reach the bottom of the stairs, Audrey hears a sharp intake of breath behind her.

"What the hell is she doing here, Mum? Where's Mia?"

There is venom in Jess's voice which burrows under Audrey's skin. Lily's head whips around and Audrey sees the anxiety shadowing her eyes. When Audrey begins to speak, her voice is strained, high-pitched, as though it is being squeezed through the holes of a sieve. "Mia's in the garden. She's fine. She's having a lovely time."

Audrey feels a rush of air as Jess brushes past her, ignoring Lily, storming toward the patio doors. "Stop! Jess, please. Just listen to me. Mia's with Phoebe. They've been having such a nice time. If only you'd watch them just for a minute . . ."

Audrey's words dissolve in the face of Jess's fury. "You've had them both here? Together? How dare you, Mum? How *dare* you?"

Audrey tries to speak but all the moisture seems to have evaporated from her mouth. When she hears a voice it is not hers but Lily's.

"Don't speak to Mum like that."

Audrey watches, paralyzed, as Jess turns to Lily for the first time. "Then don't agree to have your child anywhere near my daughter."

"I didn't. I didn't know anything about it."

Jess turns toward the garden, her sneakers already over the threshold to the patio when Audrey finally finds her voice again. "Don't go out there, Jess, please. Lily didn't know until a few minutes ago. Neither of you knew. It was my idea—"

"I don't care, Mum. I don't care who knew what or when. When will you *finally* get it? I don't want anything to do with her and I don't want her anywhere near my daughter. How many times do I have to tell you?"

Audrey feels the error of her judgment coiling into a fierce knot in her stomach. "I didn't think you'd be this angry. I thought . . . I thought if you could see them together—"

"You thought what? That we'd all play happy families? That I'd forgive and forget? That is never going to happen. *Never*. And as for you . . ."

Audrey watches as Jess turns toward Lily. There is such hatred in her expression that Audrey can hardly bear to see it but neither can she tear her eyes away, like a voyeur at a car crash.

". . . standing there so holier-than-thou. Don't you *ever* go near my daughter again, do you hear me? You don't deserve to be a parent. You shouldn't be allowed anywhere near children."

Audrey sees the color drain from Lily's cheeks. She feels the sharp stab of Jess's words, knows the force with which the attack will land. It is less than three months since Lily was in the hospital grieving for her second miscarried baby. Jess does not know about it but that does not make her words any less hurtful.

"*I* shouldn't be allowed near children. That's a bit rich coming from you. You've already driven away the father of your child by being so bloody needy and moody and angry all the time. Now you cling to your daughter as though she's some kind of possession, not a child in her own right, because she's all you've got left, because you've pushed everyone else away. Don't you dare lecture me about who's deserving of being a parent and who's not."

Audrey senses Jess's eyes dart toward her but cannot meet her daughter's gaze. She feels the heat of disloyalty in her cheeks, silently curses Lily for having betrayed confidences about Jess's broken relationship that Audrey had shared in the belief they would never find their way back.

There is a moment's silence during which an entire spectrum of possibilities plays out in Audrey's head: scenes of apology and explanation, tears and reconciliation, of the broken pieces of her

family being glued back together so that the joins are barely visible.

"Don't ever try something like this again, Mum. I will *not* have Mia exposed to this shit. If you ever pull another stunt like this, I will never let you see Mia again. I mean it. Do you understand?"

Behind the force of Jess's fury, something catches Audrey's eye and she glances into the garden.

Standing on the edge of the lawn, looking down into the kitchen, their jaws slack, eyes wide with confusion, stand Mia and Phoebe hand in hand.

Audrey is aware of Jess and Lily following her gaze. Then time seems to speed up, as if someone has pressed a fast-forward button and everything that follows is a blur.

She watches as Jess runs into the garden, scoops Mia into her arms, rushes back through the kitchen and up the stairs without another word, the front door slamming behind her. She watches Lily retrieve Phoebe, hears her daughter's words only foggily—*I'd better get her home. I'll call you later. I know you were just trying to help but you can't help someone that unhinged. She's completely deranged.* She feels the soft brush of Lily's lips on her cheek, feels her face pulling itself into a smile as Phoebe hugs her and whispers goodbye.

And then she is standing in the kitchen, alone, silence throbbing in her ears. She looks out of the patio doors and it is as if the garden is still wearing an imprint of the day's events, as if she can still see two little girls holding hands, laughing, playing, dancing, while the sun glints against their hair.

She does not know how long she stands there, staring into that empty space, but it is only as her eyes begin to tire that she wipes her fingers across her face and discovers the tears streaking her cheeks.

Chapter 19
Audrey

Audrey pulled the duvet tight around her shoulders, wishing she could erase the memory of Jess's hatred. For thirteen years, every time she had been tempted to plan another family reunion, she had remembered the wrath with which Jess had issued her warning: *If you ever pull another stunt like this, I will never let you see Mia again. I mean it.*

Her memory wound back to the day she had run across Barnsbury Square, past police cars and curious neighbors, into the sitting room to find shock and grief printed indelibly on Jess's face, to discover that her husband was dead and that it had been her eleven-year-old-daughter who had found him. She remembered how, throughout that bewildering afternoon—Lily's arrival home, the questions from the police, the explanations of a procedure over which Audrey had no control—a single thought had gone around and around in her mind: *Nothing bad shall ever happen to my children again.*

Audrey's head felt heavy with the knowledge of her own failure. She had not been able to protect them, then or now.

She pulled the duvet up to her chin as she remembered the day nearly seven months ago when she'd been given her original diagnosis. Ever since, only one thing had been guaranteed to send panic pulsing through her veins: the thought

of leaving Lily and Jess behind. It was not life Audrey was terrified of losing but her family.

Nothing bad shall ever happen to my children again.

Audrey opened her eyes, sat up in bed, turned on the bedside light, and blinked into its glow.

She wouldn't tell them. She couldn't. She wouldn't tell any of them about the new prognosis or how little time she had left. She would spare them the sound of the clock ticking loudly in their ears for the next few months.

Reaching for the pillows on the empty side of the bed, she put them behind her head and leaned back. She thought again about the day her granddaughters had played together in her garden, how brief their enjoyment had been yet how deep, how satisfying. And then she pictured again—as she had so many times before—the scene of her funeral: Lily and Jess standing on opposite sides of the grave, avoiding one another, the atmosphere thick with animosity. Her granddaughters eyeing each other warily, wanting to speak but knowing it was forbidden.

As the first dawn light began to creep around the edge of the curtains, Audrey pulled her dressing gown around her narrow shoulders and, pushing aside the memory of the last time she had attempted to reconcile her family, began to think of all the ways in which she might bring them back together before it was too late.

Part Four

May

Chapter 20
Audrey

Audrey glanced up at the naked man in front of her, heat pinching her cheeks.

He was young, tall, muscular, his skin the color of caramel, with a sheen that made you want to reach out and stroke it. There was no readable expression on his face, nothing to indicate what he was thinking. His eyes were raised, staring up at the skylight through which the sun was streaming, bathing him in a celestial glow.

Audrey shrugged off the cardigan draped over her shoulders and prepared to begin.

Picking up her pencil, she made the first tentative strokes on the paper in front of her, just the lightest impression of an outline. Around the room, gathered in a semicircle, seven other life-drawing students stood at their easels. And walking behind them, offering advice and encouragement, was their tutor, Virginia.

Audrey stared at the hesitant sketch marks she'd made. She needed to be bolder, more decisive—Virginia had been telling her so for the past two weeks since she'd started the class. Follow the shapes you see, not the shapes you think you see. Teach your brain to unthink what it knows about the way an arm hangs from the shoulders, the way a head emerges from

a neck, the way a rib cage narrows into the waist. Discard your preconceptions about the human body and think purely in terms of shape, form, and lines.

Audrey leaned back on her stool, surveying her work in progress. No amount of self-delusion could persuade her that she had a natural talent for this, but that wasn't the point.

Glancing sideways, Audrey looked at Mia's drawing: it was in a different league. It wasn't just a case of grandparental pride. You could hear it in Virginia's approbation every time she walked around the class appraising their efforts.

Looking at Mia's work, Audrey reassured herself that she'd made the right decision. She didn't like deceiving Jess but Mia had been so passionate, so persuasive. And it had seemed such a small thing to ask: just the loan of the course fees for a weekly Saturday morning class at the Royal College of Art. *Mum wouldn't lend me the money even if she could afford it, you know she wouldn't. She thinks even the smallest distraction from studying is a disaster. But I won't let it affect my coursework, I promise. I just* really *want to do it, Granny. And I promise I'll pay you back. I'll get a holiday job and pay back every penny, I swear.*

Money wasn't the issue, they both knew that. It was the duplicity. Audrey didn't allow herself to imagine Jess's fury if she ever found out they'd gone behind her back. But as far as Audrey was concerned, attending weekly art classes was hardly the pinnacle of teenage rebellion or the stuff of parental nightmares.

It had been Audrey's idea to accompany Mia. It wasn't that she had a burning desire to test her own artistic abilities. It was simply the fact of having Mia to herself for one whole morning a week when her granddaughter wasn't squirreled away in her bedroom studying. Although now she was here, Audrey was finding the class calming in ways she hadn't expected.

There was something meditative in the gentle scratch of pencil against paper, in shapes emerging where once there had been nothing, in the collective sound made by eight students each at their own easel.

Leaning to one side to pick up a different pencil, Audrey felt a grinding pain slice through her right shoulder, causing her to inhale sharply.

"What's wrong, Granny? Do you need me to get you something?"

Audrey shook her head, molding her grimace into a smile. "No thanks, darling. It's just a little twinge, that's all. It's better now, honestly."

The pain continued to jab at her shoulder, like a clamorous child demanding attention. She knew it was referred pain from the tumor in her liver, had been tolerating it for weeks, but still its intensity took her by surprise.

"OK, everyone. Shall we have a fifteen-minute break? Back here at quarter past?"

Pencils clattered against trays. Mia looped her arm through Audrey's and together they walked down the single flight of stairs to the canteen. In two weeks it had already become a habit: Audrey taking a seat at a corner table by the window, Mia joining her a couple of minutes later balancing a cup of tea, a hot chocolate, and a heavily iced cupcake on a tray.

As Mia sat down opposite, Audrey noticed the dark rings beneath her granddaughter's eyes.

"Are you getting enough sleep, Mia? You look exhausted. Are you sure this class isn't too much for you?"

Mia shook her head. "Definitely not. It's the highlight of my week. I'm not even exaggerating." She tried to offer Audrey a reassuring smile but it got lost somewhere between her lips and her eyes.

"I just don't want it to add to your stress when I know how much pressure you're under. Only a week until your first AS exam. Just think, in a month it will all be over." Audrey picked up her tea but before she'd managed the first sip, tears had begun to well up in Mia's eyes. "What is it, Mia? What's wrong?"

"I'm going to mess them up, I know I am. And then Mum'll be furious and I can't cope with her disappointment."

Audrey took Mia's hand, rubbing the back of it gently. "You're going to be fine. You work so hard and you're so bright. I know you're under a huge amount of pressure, but it'll be over soon."

Mia sniffed, the skin marbling around her eyes. "It won't. These are only my AS exams. There's a whole year before my A-levels. And I'm not going to be fine, Granny. There's no way I'm going to get an A-star in history."

"That doesn't matter, Mia. Nobody can get top marks in everything."

"It *does* matter. It matters to Mum. You *know* it does."

Audrey wiped her granddaughter's tears with the pad of her thumb. "Mum will be proud of you whatever you get."

"No she won't. You know that's not true. If I don't get four A-stars next year she's going to think I've failed. She's only ever happy when I get top marks. You've seen her, you know what she's like."

Audrey wanted to say that Mia was exaggerating but she'd witnessed too many fraught exchanges between her daughter and granddaughter to contradict her. "Mum only wants the best for you. She's going to love you whatever grades you get. Would you like me to talk to her, tell her how you're feeling?"

Mia rooted around in the pocket of her jeans, found a tissue, blew her nose, and shook her head. "Definitely not. It would just annoy her, knowing I'd been moaning to you about it. I just have to get on with it."

Neither of them said anything for a moment as Mia wiped her eyes and took a deep breath. "Granny, can I ask you something?"

"Of course you can. Anything."

"What happened when Grandad died? And why won't Mum talk about it? I mean, I know she really loved him and I know it must have been horrible for her but . . . I don't know . . . She seems really angry about it too. I've stopped asking her because she never answers me."

Mia's questions hummed in Audrey's head, peeling back the layers of memory until she was back there, running past the police car and into her house to discover the cause of Helen Sheppard's hysterical phone call.

When the young policeman had told her what had happened, Audrey had thought there must have been some mistake. It could not have been Edward who had done this. Edward was strong and sensible, the one upon whom they all depended to be the voice of reason.

But as the policeman had stated the facts again, slower this time, Audrey had known deep in the pit of her stomach that it was true. She had not needed the policewoman to tell her that he had left no note because she had already known why Edward had chosen to take his own life. She had been the only person who knew, and the knowledge had felt like a shroud of loneliness wrapping itself around her.

She remembered holding on to Jess, remembered how quiet the house had been, how still. How there had been no sound

bar a duet of sorrow and heartbreak, and how it had taken a little while for her to realize that one of the voices chanting the lament was her own.

She had stood in the sitting room, police officers bustling around her, and thought about the last time she had seen Edward as she had walked out of their bedroom that morning, him still cocooned under the duvet. She had asked whether he should start getting ready for work, the pretense at normality straining her voice. He had kept his back to her, told her he was taking the day off, his voice the distant monotone that in recent weeks had become his only alternative to rage. That cold, distant behavior was so unlike the man she had married, so unlike the man he had been just three months before. She had promised to keep the girls quiet, told him that a day off would probably do him good, trying to find in her voice something to dissolve the animosity that had wedged itself between them.

Holding on to Jess, not yet able to comprehend that she would never see Edward again, Audrey had wondered why she hadn't been more vigilant. Why she hadn't thought it odd that Edward—whose sick days in seventeen years she could count on one hand—should suddenly grant himself a day off. Her cheeks had burned with self-reproach that, after everything they had been through, she had not been more alert to changes in his routine, however slight. As the clock in the hall had chimed, Audrey had known that she was to blame. Edward might have tied the noose around his neck, but she had handed him the rope.

Audrey had not known it at the time, but her guilt was to be a storm that would rage for years to come, that would rise and fall with her moods, with the seasons, with the notable dates in the calendar that whipped it back into a frenzy.

Later that day—Audrey could never remember when exactly—she had gone downstairs to the kitchen with the policeman and policewoman and they had asked her questions she had discovered only later constituted her statement. She had given them only the bare facts—the usual timings of departures and arrivals, place of work, age, and health—but she had not dared tell them everything. It was too tortuous a tale and the repercussions had been too momentous, not just for her but for the girls too. But as soon as she had informed the police of what had happened in June—the parts she could divulge without any further incrimination—she had sensed them concluding that they had found their motive, had watched them close their notebooks on the case.

When the police had finally finished asking questions, she remembered unfurling her fingers to find deep indentations in her palms where her nails had dug into the flesh. As anonymous figures had bustled in and out of her house, Audrey had been aware of a gnawing dread that this was an experience from which her girls would never recover. She had not known it then but in the following years, as she had watched her family implode, she had suspected there had to be a link between Jess's trauma at having discovered her father's body and her decision to cut Lily out of her life. But Audrey had never been able to uncover what that link was or why Lily had borne the brunt of Jess's rage.

Audrey looked out of the window onto the street below. She could feel Mia watching her, but however she rewrote the story of Edward's death, there seemed to be no way to craft it into a meaningful synopsis. "It was a very hard time. That summer had already been so difficult and then losing Edward . . . I think it probably hit your mum worst of all."

Audrey thought about how Jess had changed that summer: from an affectionate, carefree ten-year-old at the beginning to a watchful, angry eleven-year-old by the end.

"But before that, before Grandad . . . before he died, were you happy?"

Happy. Audrey repeated the word in her head, wondering if there were as many definitions of it as there were people on the planet.

She and Edward had argued so much in the months leading up to his suicide, arguments of such quiet ferocity that they had shifted the foundations on which their marriage had been built. So many times since, Audrey had imagined a parallel life, one in which she had chosen never to tell the truth. Because through whichever prism she viewed it, she could not escape the possibility that had she never told anyone what had happened, Edward might still be alive now.

"Yes, we had been happy. For a long time we were very happy. But sometimes life has a habit of throwing things at you that are too big even for the strongest relationship to withstand. What makes you ask?"

"I've just always wondered whether you were angry with Grandad about not going to university. I've never understood why you didn't go later, after you'd got married and had children. You got straight As in your A-levels and you're easily one of the cleverest people I know. From what you've always said it sounded like you really wanted to go, so I wondered what stopped you, whether it was Grandad."

Audrey thought about how to answer honestly without betraying the life she had lived and the choices she had made. "No, it wasn't Grandad. If anything, it was my own cowardice. I couldn't imagine how people might have reacted if I'd said I wanted to go to university in my mid-twenties." Audrey's

mouth felt dry and she sipped the cup of tea cooling between the palms of her hands. "Sometimes, in those months between finding out I was pregnant and marrying Edward, I'd imagine myself sitting down and typing a letter to the university, asking if I could defer for a year. I had it all worked out: I'd get someone to look after the baby while I was at lectures and I'd study in the evenings and at weekends when Edward wasn't at work. The plan was so clear and simple in my head, yet whenever I thought about actually writing the letter, I felt completely paralyzed. When I look back now, all I can think is, What on earth stopped me? Why didn't I at least try? And however many times I ask myself that question, there's only ever one answer I can offer in response. Because I was scared. It's as simple as that."

Audrey's voice began to splinter and she drank the last of her tea, noticing the small brown spots decorating the bottom of the mug where it hadn't been washed properly.

"What were you scared of?"

"That I couldn't do it, I suppose. I was worried that I'd cause all that fuss, make all those arrangements, only to discover I couldn't cope. It was a failure of courage, nothing more complicated than that. It's the greatest trick people play on themselves, allowing their fears to destroy their ambitions." Audrey looked out of the window, where the sun was fighting its way through the clouds.

"I'm sorry, Granny. I shouldn't have asked. I didn't mean to upset you."

Audrey shook her head. "Don't be sorry. I'm pleased you're interested. Honestly." She reached for a tissue from her handbag, coughed into it, knew without checking what she'd find if she dared look. She crumpled it into a tight ball and tucked it into her pocket.

"Do you regret it now? Not going to university, I mean. Getting married, having children. Do you wish you'd done things differently?"

Mia's questions circled inside Audrey's head.

Regret. It was such a powerful word, a word that implied the desire for an undoing. And that wasn't how Audrey felt about her marriage, her children, the family to whom she'd devoted the best part of her life. So many times she'd imagined parallel versions of herself: an Audrey who'd written that letter, got a deferred place, started university a year later, and completed her degree in spite of the odds stacked against her. An Audrey who might have fulfillled that teenage ambition to sit behind a mahogany desk in a university English department, preparing the next lecture for her enthusiastic students.

But each of those scenarios demanded an impossible unraveling of her life. Because there would be no Jess at home, no Mia sitting opposite her. None of the past forty-four years as she'd known them would exist. And that was unthinkable: the untangling of a life back to a moment of critical decision. Audrey could never know where that other track might have led her, could never know what kind of a journey it might have taken her on. All she could know was the family she'd have needed to give up in order to find out.

"I don't regret it, no. It's not regret so much as melancholy, maybe. A mourning for alternative lives you can never know. Do you remember those choose-your-own-adventure books you used to read when you were little? Life is a bit like one of those, except in real life you can't go back to the beginning and start again."

Mia let out a heavy sigh, her eyes still blotchy.

"What is it, Mia? What's wrong?"

"Nothing. Just what you said. It's got me thinking, that's all."

Audrey squeezed Mia's hand, studied her granddaughter's smooth, elastic flesh in contrast to the delta of veins rising up beneath her own skin. "Mia, if you can get to the end of your life without having accumulated too many regrets—your regrets, no one else's—I think you'll be happy with the life you've led. It's easier said than done, I know. Just try not to get to my age burdened by too many if onlys."

Mia smiled but it was as if something was trapped behind her eyes that Audrey couldn't reach. "Look, Granny, everyone else is heading back to class. We ought to go too."

"Are you still free afterward, for our trip to the Tate? We can have lunch there before my choir rehearsal this afternoon."

Mia nodded. As Audrey slid back her chair and pushed herself to her feet, there it was again: the sharp stabbing sensation in her shoulder. She ground her back teeth against the pain, breathing slowly and counting the seconds until, she hoped, it would subside.

As they headed out of the canteen and back up to the art room, the pain in her shoulder still needling inside the joint, Audrey thought about what she'd planned for their trip to the Tate and couldn't be sure whether the violent knocking against her ribs was a feeling of fear or hope.

Chapter 21
Audrey

Walking into the Turbine Hall at Tate Modern, Audrey scanned the length of the vast, cavernous space.

"Right, Granny, where shall we start? How about the Rothko room? We always love it in there. Or do you want an early lunch first?"

Audrey's eyes continued to sweep the hall.

"Are you OK? You seem a bit distracted."

Audrey turned to Mia and smiled, trying to ignore the pounding of her heart. "I'm fine. I'm just always surprised by how busy it is in here." The little white lie was hot on her tongue.

It had been three weeks since her latest diagnosis, when the idea had begun to formulate. She knew it was risky, knew the jeopardy involved should she be caught, but in spite of the possible repercussions, she hadn't been able to stop herself.

"Shall we go up, then?"

"Let's just stand here a moment, shall we? Even when there's no exhibition in here, I still love this space."

They both looked up at the steel joists running from floor to ceiling, at the viewing windows jutting out from the floors above like enormous bird boxes, at the strip of skylights running the length of the room beneath intersecting metal

beams. Audrey felt the clamminess between her palms, tried to reassure herself that this time things would be different. She had deliberately planned it as far away from home as she could without arousing suspicion, had chosen the one place she had felt sure they wouldn't be caught. But as she looked up at the light streaming through the glass ceiling, she couldn't erase memories of the last time she had attempted this.

Over Mia's shoulder, she spotted a familiar figure walking toward her, their face breaking into a wide, trusting smile.

And then she sensed Mia turn and follow her gaze, felt the crackle of tentative recognition as Mia's eyes locked onto the young woman heading toward them.

"What the . . . ? Granny, what's going on?"

And then Phoebe was there, standing in front of them, just inches away from the cousin she hadn't seen for twelve years.

The two young women stared at one another and Audrey watched them, aware that time had slowed down, that all around them parents hurried children toward escalators, friends rushed to greet one another, first dates were met with disappointment or relief, and tourists rotated gallery maps from left to right, while in the center of the ramp, standing on the fossil-gray concrete floor as though the clocks had stopped, Audrey's granddaughters looked into each other's eyes for the first time in more than a decade.

Audrey felt the muscles in her chest pull taut. It was only now, seeing the two of them together, that she understood how deeply she had wanted to witness this encounter and how long she had waited for it to happen.

She watched as looks of confusion passed between her granddaughters and then words began to fall from her lips before she had a chance to collect them in the right order. "I'm

sorry, I didn't want to fib to you both. But I thought that this way neither of you had to lie to your mums about where you were going and no one could accuse you of duplicity. I just wanted you to have a chance to meet and get to know each other. It's absurd, you being kept apart all these years. I'm sorry, I probably shouldn't have done it in secret. It must be a terrible shock . . ."

Audrey's explanation dissolved as Mia and Phoebe collapsed into fits of laughter. "What is it? What's funny? I don't understand."

Her head felt foggy as she watched the girls laughing, tears in their eyes.

"Oh, Gran, I'm sorry. We shouldn't laugh really. It's sweet of you. Please don't think we don't appreciate it." Phoebe glanced at Mia and they both started laughing again.

"I don't understand. What's going on?"

And then she saw the look exchanged between them: a look of knowledge and recognition, of friendship and intimacy, and all at once she understood. And as the realization spread, it was as if someone had placed a hot-water bottle in the center of her chest that was warming her from the inside out. "What . . . ? When . . . ? How did it happen?"

Questions scrambled from her lips, and then Mia and Phoebe were answering, their sentences leapfrogging one another, picking up a part of the story the other had missed: a tale told by two voices that could have been one. The story of how, two years previously, Phoebe had tracked down Mia on Facebook, sent her a message, and begun a correspondence. How, soon after, they had begun meeting in secret, after school or on Saturday mornings. How they had seen each other every week since, a clandestine friendship that had soon become closer than any other, transcending the family

politics they had never understood but which had kept them apart for years.

"You're not angry with us, are you, Granny? We honestly did think about telling you—didn't we, Phoebe?—but we thought if you knew, you might have felt you had to tell our mums and it just seemed easier this way. We never meant to lie to you, really we didn't."

Audrey took each girl by the hand, holding them with all she wanted to say but couldn't find the words to express, hoping they might understand just a fraction of how happy they had made her.

And then all three of them were laughing. Standing in the center of the Turbine Hall, there was a split second when Audrey looked outside their unexpected trio, catching the glances of passersby, and it took her a few seconds to interpret their curious expressions. But as she turned back to her granddaughters, she understood what people were staring at: the sight of these two beautiful young women whose similarities were so striking they could easily be mistaken for twins. As she held on tight to their hands, her heart swelled with pride and relief but most of all with love.

Chapter 22
Audrey

"Right, if I can have everyone's attention, please."

Audrey's head turned, along with dozens of others, to where Ben was leaning on the upright piano, his assistant by his side. She caught Phoebe's eye and they exchanged a wry smile. It was just over an hour since they'd left Mia at Tate Modern and it felt to Audrey as though the three of them were now linked by the knowledge that, even amid familial chaos, something good and unexpected could emerge from the rubble.

"It's fantastic to see such a great turnout again this afternoon. Caitlin's just told me that ninety-three of you have signed in, which is incredible. We assumed you'd be dropping like flies by the fifth week, so perhaps I'm not working you hard enough."

There was a low murmur of laughter as Ben grinned, his eyes roaming across the room. It was similar to the one in which the auditions had been held—wooden floor, white-washed walls, wide rectangular windows on one side—but at least double the size.

"Seriously, putting together something like this is a bit like sending out party invites. You only expect about half the people to turn up, so I really am grateful that so many

of you are still here after nine rehearsals. It may sound like an obvious thing to say, but a choir doesn't exist without singers. It doesn't exist without *you*. And given how well you guys have started coming together already, I'm confident that when we step onto the stage at the Albert Hall on June twenty-fifth, the audience are going to believe we've been singing together for years."

Audrey savored Ben's confidence, wondering what it was that made someone like him able to pull a disparate group of people into a choir in such a short space of time. He had an infectious, boyish enthusiasm that made you want to succeed, not just for yourself but for him too. She thought back to the first time she'd met him at the audition just over six weeks before, how relaxed he had made her feel in spite of her nerves. It was as though he looked past the surface to something underneath, something hidden, that you hadn't yet discovered yourself.

"So far we've been focused on getting you to sing in unison—we wanted you to start feeling like a group, like a choir. Now the hard work begins. Today we're going to start singing in harmony. Don't look so worried—I know most of you have never done that before and I promise we're going to take it one step at a time. If I'm totally honest, I suspect there'll be moments over the next few weeks when it feels like this thing is never going to come together. But I want you to trust that it will. Because, believe me, I wouldn't have started it if I didn't think we could pull it off. So let's get going, shall we?"

As Ben began dividing them into sopranos, altos, tenors, and basses—Phoebe to sopranos and Audrey to altos—Audrey glanced around the room, smiling at some of her fellow choir members as she caught their eye: Isabel, thirty-eight, recently

separated from her alcoholic husband and locked in a custody battle over their two young children; Binti, twenty-four, the daughter of Somali immigrants who fled the civil war twenty-five years previously; Tim, forty-six, whose story of his fourteen-year-old daughter having recently entered remission after two years' battling leukemia had reduced Audrey to tears. As she looked around the room, she realized that many of the people she'd got to know over the past few weeks had some painful truth from which they were escaping, some demons they were laying to rest, or perhaps some unfulfilled dream they were trying, in some small way, to achieve.

"OK, as you know, we'll be singing just one song in the concert, so we need to make sure it has real impact. I've spent a lot of time thinking about what it should be and I hope you're going to approve of my choice. It's Nina Simone's 'I Wish I Knew How It Would Feel to Be Free.' Caitlin's handing around song sheets now, but I expect most of you know it anyway. If you read through the lyrics, I hope you'll agree they're pretty fitting for this concert."

Audrey smiled as she remembered the first time she'd heard the song, sitting on the mustard-yellow rug in Sandra Bailey's front room nearly fifty years before, Sandra's eyes luminous with anticipation: *Just you wait, Auds. Just you wait till you hear this album. You've never heard anything like it.* Sandra pulling the vinyl from its paper sleeve and lowering it onto the record player as carefully as a mother placing her baby in a crib. Lifting the stylus, balancing it delicately on her forefinger, gliding it through the air, and lowering the needle into one of the shiny grooves. The familiar crackle of static, the expectant whirring of near-silence before it began: that mournfully optimistic piano introduction, just the lightest accompaniment of brushes from the drums before the decisive finger-clicking. And then

the voice, Nina's voice, inviting you into a musical world of hope and regret, longing and ambition. The lyrics touching Audrey in a way no song ever had before, with its impassioned advocacy of freedom, opportunity, choice. There being a feeling of certainty in that moment, a feeling that anything was possible. And when Nina's voice had faded away, Audrey and Sandra had turned to one another and, without either of them speaking, Sandra had lifted the record player's arm and moved it back half an inch, setting it down at the beginning of the song. And the two of them had listened again. They had listened in silence, five, six, seven times, until Sandra's mum had burst through the living-room door and told them to turn the record off before they wore it out.

Audrey had only been fifteen, but she had known songs like that were rare: songs that made you understand something you couldn't otherwise articulate, something you could only feel and were a better person for having felt it.

Now, almost five decades later, Audrey heard that piano introduction again, and as her diaphragm expanded and she joined in with the opening line, she felt the physical pleasure of singing with nearly a hundred other voices. As they sang through the whole song Audrey wondered why on earth she had left it so long to do something that gave her such joy.

They reached the end and Ben grabbed at the air with his fist, ninety-three voices coming to a standstill, only the echo of the final note hovering in the air as though it wasn't quite ready to leave. "Wow, guys, that was really good. A genuinely impressive start. Keep that up and you're going to be great."

Audrey turned to smile at Phoebe, grateful to be spending this precious time with her granddaughters—at choir rehearsals and art classes—that might never have happened had she not known she was ill.

"Right, given you've made such a fantastic start today, there's something I want to tell you all. I was going to wait until the end of the rehearsal, but I figure you'd probably like to hear it now. I had a call from the organizers of the concert last night. It looks like you lot are going to be on TV."

A wave of excitement rippled around the room as Ben filled in the details: plans for the concert to be broadcast live on BBC 2 and about a telethon being organized to boost the money raised from ticket sales. But, hard as Audrey tried to concentrate on them, Ben's words were hazy in her ears.

A mental calendar flipped through the weeks in her head. Seven weeks until the concert. That was all she had to manage, just seven weeks. And if the doctor was right, she should still have at least three months ahead of her. As Ben returned to the piano and started to play through the various harmonies he'd arranged, Audrey tried to reassure herself that it was going to be OK. She'd have to be horribly unlucky not to make it.

Chapter 23
Lily

Lily glanced around her boss's office. The desk was empty except for a laptop and a pair of mobile phones side by side. The glass wall had a more expansive view of the Thames than Lily's office, and the shelf of industry awards held more than Lily's but only two more: Lily had counted.

She looked down at her phone and put it on silent just as Nisha came back into the room.

"Sorry to keep you waiting. And I'm sorry to drag you into the office on a Saturday afternoon. I hope I haven't disrupted too many plans."

Lily crossed her legs and shook her head, thinking of the empty house she'd left behind. An image flashed in her mind of Daniel strolling through Central Park, takeout coffee in one hand and phone in the other, reading her latest email and not finding time to respond.

"It's fine. I need to do some work on the strategy paper this weekend anyway, so I might as well do it here." She tucked a stray lock of hair behind her ear, could feel it trying to edge loose again.

"So, the reason I wanted to have a quick chat, face-to-face, is to give you a heads-up. The US office is planning to make some changes—streamlining operations, merging some

roles—all part of the drive to make the company more efficient. It's likely that marketing is going to be one of the affected departments. They're keen to centralize it in the States, which doesn't mean there won't be any department here in London, but they're looking to keep a skeleton staff, possibly just junior roles. Nothing's fixed in stone yet so there's always room for discussion, but obviously I wanted to let you know before the announcement. There's going to be an all-staff conference call with the US office on Monday afternoon."

A heavy silence slipped into Lily's ears, and she felt untethered, as though she might tip forward out of her chair onto the gray-carpeted floor. She was aware of a need to fill the silence, aware that it was her turn to speak, but she couldn't grab hold of the words spiraling in her head, couldn't navigate them toward her mouth and out through her lips.

"I do realize this creates a lot of uncertainty but let's not jump to too many conclusions until we've had this call with the US office."

Nisha smiled with unnerving warmth and Lily looked at the floor, not wanting Nisha to see the heat she could feel in her cheeks. She waited for Nisha to say more, but when she looked up, her boss was standing by the office door, poised to open it, glancing at her watch.

"We'll catch up again on Monday, OK?"

Lily managed to nod, understanding that the meeting was over and it was time for her to leave, but for a few disconcerting seconds she wasn't able to communicate those facts to her legs. She sat pinned to the pale blue sofa wishing that she could somehow be spirited back to the privacy of her own office without needing to move a muscle.

"Lily?"

"Yes, of course. I . . . I'll see you on Monday."

Humiliation throbbed in her cheeks and she managed to push herself to her feet, walk toward the door, and glance only briefly at Nisha before heading out into the open-plan office where banks of desks sat empty, computer screens blank, telephones silent. All the way through the maze of desks, Lily kept her eyes fixed firmly forward until she reached her own office, stepped inside and closed the door behind her.

Blinking away the tears, Lily looked around the space that had been her second home for the past eight years. The room seemed to sway in front of her and she grabbed at the back of the sofa to steady herself, needing to hold on to something solid while her future spun out of reach.

She tried to order her thoughts, tried to imagine how her life might look in six months' time, but couldn't. Slumping into the chair at her desk and burying her head in her hands, Lily felt her life begin to unravel, like a loose thread on an old sweater, a feeling she had first experienced almost thirty years before and which she had spent the next three decades trying to ensure she would never feel again.

Chapter 24
Christmas Day 1988

"Will you two be OK while I make a start on lunch?"

Her mum sips the lemon and ginger tea that she has been drinking all morning, trying to fend off the winter cold that is threatening to ruin a Christmas Day already in jeopardy.

Lily nods and tries to smile in response but it is a question, all three of them know, that cannot be answered neatly.

She glances at Jess, but her little sister is sitting cross-legged next to the fire in the living room, looking at her new *Jackie* annual, and does not raise her head to reply.

"OK. Well, if either of you want to come downstairs and give me a hand peeling potatoes or preparing the sprouts, you know where I'll be."

Her mum's voice sounds strange, as though someone has flattened it with an iron and put it in a box for safekeeping. She glances between Lily and Jess as if searching for something, before turning and leaving the room, her slippered feet padding down to the basement kitchen.

Lily grabs a bin liner and starts tidying up the wrapping paper that litters the sitting room floor. From downstairs she hears the opening bars of "Hark! The Herald Angels Sing" on the radio and her eyes smart with her mum's efforts to

pretend that this Christmas is like any other, even though they all know it bears no resemblance to normality.

It is thirteen weeks and five days since her dad committed suicide. Sometimes Lily still wakes in the morning to a brief spell of amnesia before remembering what has happened, and the realization is like someone scooping out her insides and dumping them unceremoniously on the floor all over again.

"Are you going to help tidy up, Jess?"

Her sister's eyes remain glued to the magazine resting on her knees.

"Jess, will you help? Or you could go downstairs and give Mum a hand?"

Jess says nothing, does not even turn to look at Lily. It is as though Lily has not spoken, does not exist.

Jess has been like this ever since it happened. For months she has been cold, abrupt, aloof, as though she cannot stand being in the same room as Lily. Lily understands that her little sister is grieving but she cannot help feeling resentful that Jess doesn't seem to care that she is not the only one in mourning. Every time Lily enters a room, Jess becomes tense, rude, monosyllabic, and Lily doesn't know what she has done to warrant Jess's hatred, but she knows that it seems trivial to make a fuss about it. Ever since the events of the summer, Lily has felt as though her family is held together by spider silk and that one strong gust of wind will blow them all apart forever.

She hears the whisper of a page turning and stands behind her little sister, looking down at her slim shoulders hunched over the magazine. She cannot imagine what Jess has been through, cannot adequately put herself in her little sister's shoes to know how the events of the summer have affected her. The thought of all that has happened melts her irritation and

she crouches beside Jess, feels her voice molding into something warm and comforting. "Jess, I know it's hard today. I know it doesn't really feel like Christmas, but it'll get easier in time, I promise."

Lily doesn't know if she believes the platitude about time healing—she has only just turned sixteen and sometimes feels as though she doesn't really know anything at all—but people have said it to her so frequently and with such conviction that she is hoping if she repeats it often enough it may come true.

Still Jess says nothing. Impatience inches toward the surface of Lily's skin.

"Jess, come on. I know you're upset, but you're not the only one. It's hard for all of us, today especially."

Jess turns to her and there is such fury in her expression that Lily feels it sting her cheeks as fiercely as if she has been hit. The same cold dread she has been feeling for months creeps down her spine. She knows that Jess blames her for everything that has befallen their family over the past six months but every time she feels close to asking the question directly—every time she is on the verge of pressing Jess for an answer—she finds her courage abandoning her.

The music on the radio downstairs changes and Lily hears the first verse of "In the Bleak Midwinter." She leans forward, wanting to find some way of soothing Jess's anger, not just for her own sake but for their mum's. She reaches out and places a hand gently on her sister's elbow.

"Jess, please—"

"*Don't* touch me! Don't *ever* touch me. I don't want you *anywhere* near me! I *hate* you."

Jess pulls back her arm with such force that her hand swings through the air, clipping Lily's chin. Lily staggers to her feet, steps back, and touches her face where the skin is hot. Then

she turns and flees. She closes the sitting room door behind her, slumps onto the bottom step of the stairs, and buries her head in her hands.

Plenty of times, in the heat of the moment, she and Jess have said that they hate each other but Lily has never believed either of them actually means it. She has never believed it until now. Lily cannot help feeling that if Jess were given a choice as to which of her family members would no longer be alive this Christmas, it would be Lily she'd willingly sacrifice, a feeling that compounds Lily's grief. After they have already lost so much, Lily misses Jess and craves being close to her, a need Jess has repeatedly rejected. Now Lily can only hope that when Jess's grief begins to fade, so too will her rage, and that Lily will eventually be permitted back into her sister's life.

What are you up to for Christmas?

Lily hears the echo of a question that had been asked again and again during the final week of term. It was all anyone had talked about at school. All the endless chatter about family get-togethers, parties, presents. Lily had tried to avoid it but when someone had asked her directly, the lie had tripped off her tongue before she'd even known it was inside her head: a story about a parallel fantasy Christmas. A big house in the countryside—the Cotswolds, she'd said, even though she'd never actually been there—with a large extended family who existed only in her imagination.

Lily presses her palms to her head, wondering what people would say if they found out the truth. But she knows the chances of anyone asking about her holidays when she returns to school in January are remote. Over the past term she has managed to distance herself from everyone with whom she used to be friends. It has been easier than she imagined to cut herself off: after the reports in the local newspaper and the

rumors on the grapevine, Lily's friends have been only too glad to steer clear of her, as though her family's adversities might be a contagious disease they are in danger of catching. Lily has buried herself in her studies, not just because schoolwork is the only activity that allows her to forget, but because she knows that studying is her only route out: away to university and toward the possibility of becoming someone new, someone different, someone better.

Lily turns her head and looks up the stairs. She can't imagine ever going up there again without the ghost of her father dangling from the rafters, daring her to walk past him. She can't imagine ever tiptoeing across the landing without remembering what she saw in the bedroom that morning, three months before her father's suicide: the hummingbirds on the wallpaper, the figures on the bed, the bittersweet smell she had never known before and hopes never to know again. The sound of crying that still rings in her ears if she does not make a conscious effort to block it out.

From the kitchen below Lily hears a muffled cry. She clamps her hands over her ears, knowing she should go downstairs and comfort her mum, but she does not move. She fears that, faced with the intensity of her mum's grief, she will reveal things she knows must be kept hidden. Instead she sits alone, palms pressed to her head, aware of the huge empty cavern that the events of the summer have left behind, an abyss she fears may never be filled.

Chapter 25
Audrey

"Are you sure you don't mind giving me a lift today, Ben? It's more than enough you driving me home after Wednesday rehearsals. I'm not going to make you late for any plans, am I?" Audrey watched as Ben shuffled some sheets of music on top of the piano and threw a stack of discarded plastic cups into the bin.

"Honestly, it's fine. The student I teach on Saturday is away this week so I'm totally free. Just let me get this lot cleared up and then we'll be good to go."

There was laughter from the far side of the rehearsal room and Audrey turned to see Phoebe chatting with some of the younger choir members she'd befriended over the past month. One of them—Harry—seemed to laugh louder than the others at her jokes, reaching out a hand to touch her arm, training his gaze on her long after she'd finished speaking.

As Audrey caught Phoebe's eye and returned her granddaughter's smile, she realized that she looked forward to these choir rehearsals—and her art classes with Mia—more than she had looked forward to anything for years. "Ben, it really is a wonderful thing you're doing here. Not many people would give up their evenings and weekends voluntarily to put something like this together."

Ben half smiled and shrugged his shoulders. "Well, I guess we all have to atone for our sins somehow." He laughed, but the sound was thin and reedy.

"I can't imagine you having any sins to atone for."

"Don't you believe it. We've all got skeletons in our closet, haven't we?"

Audrey turned around and bent down to pick up a discarded chocolate wrapper from the floor, and felt a pain pull across her chest. She breathed deeply against it but it continued to slice between her ribs, a lightning flash of heat every time she inhaled. Clamping her jaw shut, her back teeth grinding, she forced herself upright. As she stood up, her head felt fuzzy and light, as though it might just roll away. She grabbed the lid of the piano, reminding herself that this was to be expected, that there was nothing to be alarmed about, that it would pass as long as she didn't panic.

She waited a few seconds until her body was vaguely under control, and when she turned back to Ben she saw that he was sorting through folders of music balanced on the piano stool and was relieved he hadn't noticed. During their car journeys over the past few weeks, Audrey had told Ben many things about her life, but never that she was ill. She hadn't felt he needed to know, hadn't wanted to see the look of sympathy, surprise or pity in his eyes when she said the words out loud.

Now, looking at him, she realized that Ben had told her next to nothing about himself. Recalling their conversations, she was sure she'd asked about his life outside the choir but, now she came to think of it, she couldn't remember him ever giving her any answers.

"So what are you up to tonight, Ben? Anything special?" Audrey leaned against the piano, her head still woozy.

"Nothing much. Just a good book and a decent glass of

red wine. I'm afraid my Saturday night partying days were over a long time ago."

He smiled but Audrey caught a flicker of hesitation.

"Do you not have any family? No Mrs. Levine? No children of your own?"

"I do, actually, yes. Two kids, Zach and Erin."

A stiffness in Ben's tone made Audrey glance up. She saw something in his expression she thought she recognized though she couldn't identify what it was. "They're beautiful names. Do they like living in London or would they rather be in America?"

Ben began shuffling pieces of paper he'd already tidied just a few moments before. "Erin's back home in New York, with my wife. My ex-wife. I'm divorced. I haven't seen them in a while."

The shuffling continued, Ben removing song sheets from plastic folders before slipping them back in again.

"I'm really sorry to hear that. It must be very difficult, for all of you. And what about your son? Is he here with you?"

There was a heavy silence in which Audrey sensed she had asked a question Ben didn't want to answer.

She watched as Ben's paper-shuffling stopped and his body came to a standstill. She watched the slow rise and fall of his Adam's apple as he swallowed, the gentle elevation of his rib cage as he breathed in and then out. It was as though the world had paused, neither of them knowing quite what might follow.

"No, he's not. Zach, he . . . Well, he . . . he died a few years ago."

Ben turned toward her, deep creases lining his forehead, and Audrey could feel the distress spreading across her face. She was conscious of an echo in her ears, and she readied herself

to reply, hoping the right response might emerge before she gave herself away. But instead of the sound of her own voice, Audrey heard only a rush of air around her ears and the dull thud of flesh against wood.

And then everything went black.

Chapter 26
Jess

Jess stood in the middle of a field in the far reaches of west London, watching the director talk to the two lead actors, their heads bent together like children conspiring in a playground.

The crew reset and the director's assistant called for quiet. The camera turned over and the scene began again.

Jess looked at her watch, wondering how much longer she'd be at work today, thinking about the pile of washing that had to be done, the carpets that needed vacuuming and the bathroom that required a long-overdue clean. Sometimes when she was on location Jess couldn't help feeling that somewhere out there, real life was happening while she watched pretend life repeat itself again and again.

Her mind began wandering into fantasies of how different her life might be had she not got pregnant years before she was ready and spent the last months of university battling morning sickness instead of studying for finals; had Iain not asked her to move in with him immediately after she graduated and had she not mistakenly believed that his maturity—twenty-one years her senior—meant he would provide the security she craved; had she understood, at the time, that her fear of returning to Barnsbury Square was fueling a decision that would determine the rest of her life.

She thought back to that day, standing in the kitchen at Barnsbury Square, an overnight bag at her feet, waiting to hear her mum's reaction. On the radio next to the microwave, All Saints had been singing "Never Ever," and Jess had turned down the volume even though it was one of her favorite songs.

She remembered her mum standing opposite, hands gripping the back of a kitchen chair as though needing to steady herself in the face of Jess's news.

I can see how disappointed in me you are, Mum, but I'm not going to change my mind. I'm having this baby whether you like it or not. Jess recalled the defiance in her voice, alongside the conviction and the confidence. Even now she didn't know how she had managed to sound so certain when it had been such a long way from what she'd felt. So many times prior to that conversation she had pictured her mum's response: had imagined her smiling, folding her in her arms, giving her the answer to a dilemma she didn't know how to resolve. In each imagined scene, Jess had felt the tension between them dissolve, had felt the news sweep aside all the years of caution and mistrust, narrowing the distance between them. It was a fantasy she hadn't even known existed until she'd become pregnant. But as soon as she had learned she was having a baby, she had wanted more than anything—more, even, than Iain's promises to stand by her—to feel close to her mum again. But instead, as they had stood opposite one another in the kitchen, Jess had been aware of the chasm between them widening.

Iain loves me and I love him. And we can make this work. I'll only need to take a year off after I graduate and then I'll get a job. Iain will be able to support us in the meantime, and then when I start work we'll get someone to look after the baby. So please don't think we haven't thought this through.

She could hear, even all these years later, the confrontation in her voice but also, underneath it, the fear. She remembered hoping that the more she talked, the more she might come to believe the things she was saying. It had been true that she and Iain had discussed it, true that they had a plan which, on paper at least, seemed entirely achievable. It was true that she loved Iain. And yet, even as she had stood there, challenging her mum to contradict her, she had not been able to turn off the anxiety, flickering like a faulty lightbulb at the back of her mind, that history was repeating itself: that, just like her mum, she was giving up on her ambitions because of an unplanned pregnancy.

But you're so young, Jess. And Iain . . . I know you think you love him, but the age difference . . . When you're forty, he's going to be on the brink of retirement. What's that going to be like for you? What will it be like for the baby?

Her mum's questions had reverberated in Jess's head but she had been unable to produce any answers. *Why can't you just be happy for me? You've never liked Iain—why can't you just admit it? You've never given him a chance.*

That's not true, Jess. It's not that I don't like him. I just worry—you must be able to understand why. He's old enough to be your father.

Jess had experienced then a feeling that defied a single adjective, that seemed to compound all the anger and resentment, fear, and grief that had simmered inside of her for more than a decade. *I'm almost twenty-one, for God's sake. I know what I'm doing. It's not as if I'm a child.*

There had been another, unspoken, sentence that Jess had allowed to hover in silent parentheses, knowing it would be a cheap shot. But in the end she hadn't been able to stop herself.

It's not as if I'm as young as you were when you got pregnant with Lily.

She remembered how her mum had looked at her with such sadness, regret, and longing, and how Jess had known instinctively that this was another of those moments when the ties that bound them slackened and pulled in different directions, to which they must both, gradually, become accustomed. But each time it had happened before, Jess had not been consciously aware of the adjustment until after it had been made. This time, it was as though she was watching it happen and there was nothing she could do to stop it.

The director called something to the lead camera operator and Jess looked around the crew, thinking about the career she had fallen into through necessity rather than choice, a career other people seemed to imagine was glamorous, ignoring the unsociable hours, the disruptive travel, the egos she worked with. All these years later, she still couldn't resist the fantasy that perhaps, had she never got pregnant and moved in with Iain, she might now be sitting in the office of a major newspaper, commissioning articles about artists, scientists, politicians, or captains of industry, rather than standing in a muddy field worrying about parking permits and traffic noise.

Sometimes Jess felt as though she'd exited, stage left, from her own life many years ago, but no one in the audience had noticed.

"Right, everyone, let's take a break. Back on set in fifteen. Charlie and Lucia, can I have a word?"

As Justin swung his arms around the shoulders of his lead actors and steered them deeper into the field, the crew melted away.

"Are you coming for a drink tonight, Jess? There's a pub Steve spotted nearby that looks half decent so a few of us are going for a couple of pints when we finally wrap."

Jess shook her head as she and Paul—a cameraman she'd

known for ten years and one of the few colleagues she'd describe as a friend—set off toward the catering truck. "Thanks for asking but I've got loads to do this evening."

"It's Saturday night, you can't just go home. Come on, loads of us are going—me, Steve, Ray, John, Milly, Lexi. It'll be a laugh."

Jess thought about sitting around a pub table, having a drink and a packet of crisps, gossiping about the day's events with people who would be her colleagues for another four weeks, and suddenly she was answering before she could stop herself. "OK, then. Just a quick one. That'd be nice, thanks."

"Great. It doesn't have to be a late night. Wait there—I'll go and get us both a cup of tea and a couple of pastries if there are any left."

Paul wandered off while Jess pulled her mobile phone from her pocket and switched it on. As it blinked into life, a series of notifications pinged onto the screen.

Four missed calls, four new voice messages, all from Mia. Jess didn't need to listen to them to know something was wrong.

She pressed down hard on Mia's name to return the call. There was less than one complete ring before it was answered.

"Mum, why haven't you been answering your phone? I've been calling you for ages. You need to come now. It's Granny."

Chapter 27
Audrey

Audrey slid her eyes from left to right, a simple enough movement yet one that sent a sharp pain shooting across her forehead.

"How are you feeling now, Mum? You gave us such a scare."

Sitting on one side of the hospital bed holding her hand, Lily was looking unusually harried: a faint smudge of mascara bruised the skin under one eye and strands of hair poked out from a makeshift bun. Phoebe stood on the other side of the bed, both of them smiling with a forced cheerfulness that made Audrey nervous. From the busy ER corridor outside the cubicle, she could hear machines beeping, phones ringing, doctors calling out names of medicines, nurses issuing instructions to orderlies.

Hospital. It was the very last place she wanted to be.

"Can I get you anything, Gran? A glass of water? Something to eat? I could pop to the shop and see if there's any of that salted caramel chocolate you like?"

Audrey shook her head. It felt as though someone must have filled it with lead while she was unconscious.

"You need to eat something, Mum. I know it's hard when you feel nauseous, but you'll get terribly weak if your blood sugar's too low."

Audrey's hand moved instinctively to her stomach. It felt permanently bloated in spite of its emptiness, as though someone had blown up a balloon and put it inside her when she wasn't looking. The last thing she wanted was food.

"Come on—we must be able to get you something."

Audrey remained silent, knowing that the only thing she wanted was the one thing no one could give her. She thought about all those hours she had wasted over the years: the boring TV shows she'd watched, the depressing newspaper articles she'd read, the friendships she'd allowed to run miles beyond their course. All those days she'd pottered through life as though she had all the time in the world.

"You have to eat, Mum. Come on. There must be something you fancy."

Audrey shook her head again. As she lay under the stiff white hospital sheets, beneath the fluorescent glare of strip lighting and the watchful gaze of her family, she suddenly realized that she'd become the very thing she dreaded: a patient, not a person.

Lily squeezed her hand as if Audrey were a child in need of gentle encouragement, and Audrey suddenly understood that it wasn't death she feared so much as the process of dying.

"I should let Jess know I'm here. She'll be worried if she gets home and I'm not there."

At the mention of Jess's name, Audrey felt the atmosphere thicken. Lily stood up and began tucking in sheets that hadn't come loose, then rearranged the jug of water and plastic cup on the bedside cabinet that were in no need of tidying. Audrey glanced at Phoebe in time to catch her granddaughter's raised eyebrows and almost imperceptible nod.

Audrey's thoughts scrambled toward an understanding. Of course Phoebe would have told Mia, and Mia would have

told Jess. Which meant that Jess might be on her way to the hospital right now.

Audrey pulled herself up to a sitting position, her head sluggish, her pulse throbbing. For years she had hoped for another meeting between her daughters but not in these circumstances, not in this location. As she tried to imagine the scene that might unfold should Jess arrive, she was hit by a new wave of nausea that rose up through her chest and hung, suspended, in her throat.

"Why don't I find a doctor, Mum, and ask when they might have the results of your tests?"

Audrey was about to agree when the cubicle curtain swished back and there, standing on the threshold, was Mia.

Chapter 28
Lily

The cubicle curtain opened to reveal a young woman so strikingly like Phoebe that, for a terrible, dislocating second, Lily thought that somehow she must have given birth to her without even knowing it.

Lily stared at Mia, at a face she had seen many times in photographs at her mum's house but which she had begun to believe she might never see again in the flesh. So many times she had imagined chance encounters on the tube, in the park, trapped in an elevator together. On so many nights she had lain awake envisaging circumstances that would lead her to turn up at Jess's house and hope that Mia answered the door so she could introduce herself. But none of those scenarios had prepared her for what she would feel when she stood two feet away from a young woman to whom she had always felt indelibly linked even though they had never properly met.

She tried to think of all she wanted to say, tried to remember all the speeches she had prepared over the years in case they met accidentally. But now Mia was standing in front of her, Lily wanted nothing more than to look at her. She felt an immediate sense of attachment to her niece, as though a double helix of DNA stretched between them like an invisible bridge, anchoring them together.

She was aware of needing to do something, say something. But having waited all these years for precisely this moment, she now wasn't sure what to do with it. She felt like a child on Christmas morning who, after weeks of feverish anticipation, could not bear to open her presents because, once she had, it would all be over.

Lily swallowed hard and willed herself to find the right words. "I can't tell you how wonderful it is to meet you at last. You're . . . It's just so strange seeing you and Phoebe in the same room. Not strange, I don't mean that—it's lovely. It's lovely to finally meet you. And is Jess . . . is your mum here too?" Lily heard the tremor in her voice and smiled in the hope of smothering it.

"Not yet. But she's on her way."

Chapter 29
Jess

The soles of her sneakers squeaked against the rubber floor as she ran past a sea of anonymous faces, past blue plastic chairs and an empty water dispenser, her forehead pleated in a frown, her cheeks pink with exertion.

At ER reception, Jess waited at the desk while the receptionist stared at a computer screen, her long red nails tapping percussively at the keyboard.

"Excuse me? I'm looking for my mother, Audrey Siskin. She was brought in a couple of hours ago in an ambulance. My daughter's here already, I think." Anxiety hung on the sharp edges of Jess's consonants.

"If you take a seat I'll find out where she is."

"Can't I just go through? My daughter must be in there with her. I keep trying to call her mobile but it just goes straight to voicemail."

"Jess? Can I help with anything?"

Jess spun around and saw a face she half recognized though for a moment she couldn't think where from. "Ben, isn't it? What are you doing here?"

"Your mum was at choir rehearsal when she collapsed. I was the one who called the paramedics. I just wanted to see how she was, make sure everything was OK."

Jess thrust her hand into her jacket pocket, pulled out her phone, and scowled at its empty screen. "Do you know where she is? My daughter texted ten minutes ago to say she was with her and she's OK, but the woman on reception isn't exactly forthcoming with information."

"I don't know—I'm sorry. But I'm sure she's fine. She had a brief blackout but only for a few seconds. She'd come around long before the ambulance arrived. She tried very hard to persuade us that she was fine, but both Phoebe and I thought she ought to get checked out."

Jess's eyes narrowed. "Phoebe's here? What the hell was she doing at the choir rehearsal?"

"Rehearsing. She's in the choir too. Didn't you know?"

Ben's words scrambled in Jess's head, trying to form a meaningful explanation. But however she replayed them, they told the same story: her mum had been heading off to choir rehearsals twice a week for the past five weeks and had not seen fit to tell Jess that Phoebe was going with her.

"So where is she now? Phoebe? Is she still here?"

"I'm not sure. I guess so. She came in the ambulance with your mum and I haven't seen her since so I'm assuming they're still together. And another young woman turned up a little while ago—looks a lot like Phoebe but with longer hair. I figured she might be your daughter. She's through there now as well."

A cold skein of dread pulled tight in Jess's stomach. "My daughter's through there? With Phoebe? For God's sake, next you'll be telling me my sister's here too."

Jess watched as Ben shifted his weight from one foot to the other and cast his eyes around the waiting rooms where people were beginning to glance in their direction.

"Well, I don't know for sure, but I do know Phoebe phoned her mum just after the paramedics arrived and told her to meet us here. But I couldn't honestly tell you whether she's arrived or not. I don't understand. What's wrong with your sister and your niece being here?"

Jess stared at him, unblinking. "Jesus Christ. As if today wasn't bad enough already." Without saying goodbye, she turned around and rushed through the double swing doors toward the emergency treatment rooms, ignoring the receptionist's instructions for her to stop.

As she hurried down the corridor, the smell hit her: the unmistakable stench of unspoken fear and tentative hope. It was a smell that flung open the door on memories Jess had tried so hard to keep closed: memories of men and women in white coats and blue scrubs, pretending they could make everything better, only for Jess to discover that it was a lie, that they were no more able to safeguard her family than she was.

It was years ago, Jess told herself, as she rushed past curtained cubicles and carts, past blood pressure machines and computer screens, past medicine cabinets and an empty wheelchair. The medical profession had come a long way since then.

Halfway along the corridor there was a nurses' station, and after a few polite inquiries, Jess was directed toward a cubicle two bays from the end. Without pausing to think about what she was going to say or what she might find, she swept back the curtain. And all at once she felt the past rushing toward her.

Her mum was sitting up in bed, flanked on one side by a teenager Jess knew from countless Google searches was her niece, and on the other side by the daughter she'd have given

her life to protect. And there, in the middle, as if this were a stage and Lily was in the starring role, stood the sister Jess had cut out of her life more than two decades before.

"Get up, Mia. We're going."

Jess's voice was hard and sharp as four pairs of eyes turned toward her and four smiles flattened into horizontal lines.

Chapter 30
Lily

Lily stepped forward, though whether in greeting or defense she wasn't quite sure. She opened her mouth to speak but nothing emerged. Instead she stared at her sister, wondering how someone could look so changed and yet so unmistakably familiar: the same warm cream skin, now lightly etched with age; the same fire in her eyes, serving both as a statement and a warning; the same determined expression. For a second it was as though their years of separation evaporated and standing in front of her was the little sister Lily had only ever wanted to protect.

Her legs tensed as if preparing to move, to walk the single step that would place her within touching distance of Jess. Repressed affection seeped into her muscles from where it had lain dormant for decades. As Lily looked at Jess, it was as if she could see the gap narrowing, as if the distance between them was nothing more than one small step across a hospital cubicle.

But then Jess's eyes caught hers and Lily felt the heat of her sister's rage, was reminded of the day thirteen years ago when they had last seen one another: *Don't you* ever *go near my daughter again, do you hear me? You don't deserve to be a parent. You shouldn't be allowed anywhere near children.*

The memory throbbed like a bruise on Lily's heart. So many times over the years she had replayed that conversation,

wondering whether anything could have been said to alter the outcome. So many times she had seethed at the recollection of Jess's tone. But mostly, whenever she had allowed the memory to creep into her thoughts, Lily had been left with only a litany of silent questions. Except now that Jess was standing in front of her, Lily realized she didn't know where to begin. She didn't know whether she wanted to shout at Jess or turn and flee, whether she wanted to assault her sister with questions or wrap her arms around her and hope that somehow the space between them might shrink until they could feel it no longer. It was as though the passage of time and the enormity of the absence were so great that Lily no longer knew where this story started, couldn't find her way back to the point at which their paths had diverged, like a child in a fairy tale whose trail of bread crumbs has long since vanished.

Chapter 31

Audrey

It was the moment she had been hoping for all these years: her whole family in the same room together. All this time Audrey had been imagining family reunions played out to a soundtrack of tearful apologies and biblical forgiveness. But now, instead of feeling relief or pleasure, she was aware of her breath hiding in her lungs, her fingers curling into tight balls.

Seeing her daughters together was like peeling back the layers of an onion, stripping back the years to when they had been two little girls in the midst of a squabble. Audrey wished she could find the words to make Lily walk toward Jess with open arms, that would allow Jess to accept the embrace. But each time her lips parted, her voice dissolved inside the fear that if she got this moment wrong she might never have a chance to put it right.

Her eyes darted from one daughter to the other—Lily staring at Jess, Jess staring at Mia. It was as though they were figures in a tableau: Jess's face locked in an expression of horror, Lily's in a frame of uncertainty.

"I'm sorry I took so long. Saturday evenings are never the best time to visit the ER, but I've finally got all your test results."

A young female doctor swished the curtain closed behind her, scanning the notes in her hand as she entered. She glanced around the cubicle long enough to clock the excessive number

of visitors, raised an eyebrow, then appeared to decide that, of all the battles she'd have to fight that night, a few additional visitors weren't worth her energy.

"OK, Mrs. Siskin. You'll be pleased to know that your collapse was the result of nothing more sinister than low blood sugar. I know it's difficult to eat when you're feeling nauseous, but even just a few mouthfuls—little and often—will help prevent this happening again. I can see from your oncologist's notes that you've refused chemotherapy, and of course that's entirely your decision. The only thing I would say is that the discovery of the fourth tumor on your lung and the results of your latest blood counts do mean that we're likely to see an increase in episodes like this. I don't want to pressure you, and I'm sure you're being well advised by your oncologist, but given the aggressiveness of your cancer and what's happened today, you may want to reconsider. Anyway, I'm sure you can discuss all that with your doctor at your next appointment. For now, we're going to move you up to the ward as soon as we can find you a bed, so we can keep an eye on you overnight. I'll get the orderlies to come by when there's a ward ready to take you."

The doctor waited for Audrey to acknowledge that she'd understood, offered a weary smile, and then left the cubicle, her words lingering behind like an unwelcome party guest refusing to leave.

Fourth tumor on your lung. Latest blood counts. Aggressiveness of your cancer.

Audrey felt the weight of her deception pressing down on her shoulders. But then she saw the fear on Lily's face, the disbelief on Jess's, the shock in Phoebe's eyes, and the tears in Mia's, and all at once she understood that this was why she had chosen not to tell them.

Chapter 32
Jess

"What on earth was she talking about, Mum? Why didn't you tell her she'd got it wrong? She must have had someone else's notes. I'll call her back."

As Jess turned to walk out of the cubicle she heard an intake of breath behind her, a single word trailing after her.

"No."

She looked back, saw her mum sitting up in bed, saw the expression on her face: a plea or an instruction, fear or an apology, she couldn't tell which. Jess was aware of a pause, as though for a fraction of a moment, like the final seconds before the sun dips below the horizon, everything in the world appears to have stopped moving.

"Don't call her back. She didn't have the wrong notes."

"What do you mean? What was she talking about?" Jess watched distress burrow into the lines around her mum's eyes, into the crevices at the edges of her lips, deep into her pores until her whole face was awash with it.

"I didn't want to worry you. I didn't want it to be a burden . . ."

Her mum's voice trailed off and even though Jess was scared of where the conversation was heading, the questions lining up in her head forced her to follow it. "You didn't want to

worry us? So all that stuff she said—about the tumors, about your blood counts—all that was right? Why on earth didn't you tell me? Did you think I wouldn't find out?"

"I don't know. I just thought it would be for the best. I just . . . I didn't want to put you through it all. Please don't be so angry, Jess."

Jess opened her mouth and then closed it again, frustration catching in her throat.

"So what's the prognosis? Is there anything they can do?" It was Lily's voice, softer than Jess's had been, but Jess kept her eyes fixed on her mum, watched her shake her head.

"Nothing beyond palliative chemo but I don't want that, you know I don't."

"For God's sake, Mum, *why* won't you accept help? I didn't understand it when you first said it months ago and I don't understand it now. It's like you *want* to die. It's as if you don't care what happens to you. I don't understand why you'd reject whatever treatment's available to you."

"Mum, stop it. Come on, you can see Granny's upset."

Jess turned to where Mia was standing, so close to Phoebe as if their bodies might fuse together, and she couldn't be sure whether the anger pulsing at her temples was directed toward her mother or her daughter. "We're all upset, Mia."

"I know. But flying off the handle isn't going to help. I get why Granny doesn't want treatment and you do too, don't you, Phoebe?"

Something about the ease with which Mia said Phoebe's name, something about the way Phoebe turned to Mia and fired a look of panic, sent a cold trickle of sweat down Jess's spine. "How do you know what Phoebe thinks?"

It was the most fleeting of glances: had Jess blinked she might have missed it. A transitory look of caution that passed

between Mia and Phoebe: a silent note of warning, like a tell in a badly played game of poker.

"I asked you a question, Mia. How do you know what Phoebe thinks?"

Guilt flared in Mia's eyes and it was all the confirmation Jess needed.

"Don't be too hard on her, Jess. What did you expect? They're seventeen-year-old girls, with social media at their disposal. Did you really imagine they wouldn't be able to find each other?"

Her mum's voice was soft, imploring, but all Jess heard was complicity.

"Are you saying you knew? Are you telling me you knew they were in contact and you didn't see fit to tell me?"

"I only found out earlier today."

Words began to erupt from Jess's mouth and she couldn't have stopped them even if she'd wanted to. "I don't care, Mum. You should have told me. You *know* how I feel about this. I couldn't have made it any clearer. Mia, get your bag, we'll talk about this at home. Mum, let me know when you're ready to leave tomorrow and I'll come and pick you up."

"Darling, please . . ."

Ignoring her mum, ignoring Lily and Phoebe, Jess grabbed hold of Mia's hand, gripped it tightly, and walked out of the cubicle without looking back.

Chapter 33
Audrey

Nobody spoke. Outside the cubicle, pagers bleeped, phones rang, a child cried, a doctor called for help.

Audrey looked at the open curtain, hoping that if she stared at it long enough, Jess and Mia might reappear, like magician's assistants in a stage trick.

"Mum, are you OK?"

Audrey nodded, her chest hollow as if someone had opened the cage of her ribs and scooped everything out. The mattress creaked as Lily sat down on the bed, her fingers tracing the veins on the back of Audrey's hand.

"Mum, whatever you want to do, it's your decision. But please, help me understand. Why won't you accept treatment, even now?"

Audrey glanced at Lily, then up at Phoebe standing behind her. *Because I don't deserve it*, she wanted to say. *Because I know it won't work. Because I feel as though I've been waiting almost three decades for something like this to happen and now that it has, I don't have the strength to fight it.*

Audrey reached for the water beside her bed and sipped it, but her mouth still felt dry. "Can we talk about this tomorrow? I know it's a shock and I'm genuinely very sorry I didn't tell you before. I'd never upset any of you intentionally, you know

that. I honestly thought it was for the best. But I'm exhausted now and I'm not sure I have the words in me to explain."

Concern twitched between Lily's eyebrows before she pulled her face into a facsimile of reassurance. "Of course. Whatever you want."

Audrey kissed Lily and Phoebe goodbye, felt the weight of their expectation linger long after they'd left.

She rolled onto her side, coughing against the fluid in her lungs she knew couldn't be cleared. Her limbs sank into the mattress, heavy and leaden, the noises outside in the corridor—nurses, telephones, carts—muddy in her ears. She thought again of the horror on Jess's face when she had first come in and seen them all together, and the fury in her voice as she'd instructed Mia to leave.

Audrey closed her eyes, and felt the past begin to claw at the edges of her memory.

Perhaps she had been naïve to hope that Lily and Jess might recover from the events of that summer. Perhaps the grief was too deep, the injustice too great. Perhaps there was no way to repair the heartbreak they'd endured after the losses they had suffered.

Because once upon a time there had been three little girls: Lily, Jess, and Zoe.

Chapter 34

June 1988

She sits on the side of the bed, watching her daughter sleep. It should, she knows, be a moment of maternal quietude, but it cannot be peaceful when carts are clattering outside in the corridor, when another child is wailing in the midst of injections two beds away, when the noxious combination of illness and bleach pollutes the air like a fateful specter.

It cannot be tranquil when her little girl is lying in a bed that is not her own, punctured by tubes.

Audrey chokes back her tears and commands herself to be strong. Zoe could wake at any moment.

She looks down at the pale, almost translucent skin stretched across her daughter's cheekbones. Sometimes she fears that one day she will arrive at the hospital and the skin will have thinned so much that she will be able to watch the blood pulse through Zoe's veins.

It has been fourteen months since Zoe was diagnosed with leukemia. They have been through more than a year of treatments no one has ever promised will be successful. For months, Audrey has oscillated between hope and despair, never knowing which will take the lead on any given day.

She brushes her fingers lightly over the back of her daughter's hand, careful not to disturb the cannula piercing her skin.

Every afternoon when she arrives the nurses remind her that Zoe needs rest, as though Audrey might have forgotten it during the previous twenty-four hours. If rest could cure her, Audrey would happily let her sleep for a year, for ten years, for however long it might take, like a princess in a fairy tale.

She sits beside Zoe's bed, wishing she could lift up the stiff hospital sheets and climb in beside her, wrap her arms around her and hold her close until the warmth of their bodies has dissolved the space between them. She wants to feel Zoe's skin against her cheek, feel her breath hot against her neck, sing her favorite songs—"Edelweiss," "Castle on a Cloud," "Dream a Little Dream of Me"—just as she has done for the past ten years.

Audrey's throat narrows and her hand tightens around Zoe's fingers.

Ten years she has had to love her little girl; to protect her, comfort her, laugh with her, take pride in her. Ten years to wipe away her tears, sing her to sleep, kiss her scraped knees, bathe her fevered brow. Ten years to teach her to walk, talk, run, jump, paint, draw, sing, skip, read, write. But now a rogue collection of blood cells over which Audrey has no control is stealing her away.

Ten years: a lifetime and yet the blink of an eye.

Zoe's eyelids flutter and the muscles pull taut across Audrey's chest, a feeling she once thought might have been hope but which she now understands is simply love.

She remembers how, when Zoe was younger, she had always wanted to climb trees that were too tall for her. *I can do it, Mummy, I know I can.* Audrey had always capitulated eventually, letting Zoe climb a little way up, hovering underneath, her hands outstretched ready to catch her should she fall. And then, when the girls were older, it was always Zoe—not Lily or Jess—who climbed the highest: fearless, athletic, nimble Zoe. The child Audrey had once believed to be invincible.

Audrey glances at the clock on the wall: a quarter past six. She has promised to collect Jess from Emily's house before seven and she is already at risk of being late. But she does not want to leave before Zoe has woken up.

Audrey is grateful to be here alone today. Most days Jess accompanies her and sits by the bed of her twin sister, reading to her or relating anecdotes from school, the resemblance between the once-identical girls now just a faint echo. It has become a strange after-school ritual the three of them share, one that Audrey worries may not be good for Jess, but the girls have been inseparable for a decade and it is painful enough that they no longer share their days, their nights, their hopes, and dreams without denying them this hour each afternoon too.

All three sisters had been so close, once upon a time, before Zoe's frequent spells in the hospital cut short their childhood. Her three musketeers, Audrey had called them. On Sunday afternoons they would perform musicals for her and Edward—*Annie, The Sound of Music, Bugsy Malone*—all under Lily's careful direction, seeking out costumes from the dress-up box or the back of Audrey's wardrobe, outfits she hadn't worn for years and couldn't remember buying. Jess would invariably forget the words or the choreography and Lily would get cross with her until Zoe would leap to her twin's defense, point out that it was supposed to be fun, tell Lily to stop being mean. But to Audrey it was perfect whether or not they were in tune or in time.

Had Audrey known what would happen later, she'd have recorded every single minute of it on film.

Audrey looks down at her daughter lying under anonymous hospital sheets and wonders, not for the first time, how it is that the fate of a life—the fate of a family—should swing on an imperfect collection of blood cells, invisible to the naked eye.

The parcel rustles in her lap and Audrey looks at the present wrapped in shiny silver paper decorated with tiny stars. Zoe has been fascinated by stars ever since she was little. Whenever she has been asked what she wants to be when she grows up, she has always replied that she plans to be an astronomer, to uncover the mysteries of the universe, as though such an ambition is entirely within her grasp. Now people no longer ask Zoe the question.

Audrey wonders about putting the gift on the chest of drawers next to the Walkman that gets less and less use as the days go by. The present is a double cassette of *Now That's What I Call Music! 11* and Audrey hopes it will help turn up the brightness behind Zoe's eyes.

She thinks back to the previous week, to how brave Zoe had been as the nurses had hooked a bag of medicine to the tall metal stand, as drugs had dripped through the transparent plastic tube into her vein to engage in yet another battle against Zoe's defective bone marrow. Audrey thinks about the dozens of times Zoe has had to endure this process: all the times she has vomited into disposable cardboard bowls, all the times she has been unable to lift her head from the pillow because it makes her stomach churn, all the times she has looked down at her arms, her legs, her jutting hip bones, and questioned the bruises that seem to materialize overnight. She thinks about all that Zoe has had to withstand and her heart strains with the injustice of it and with the guilt that she is unable to take away Zoe's pain. Keeping your child safe, keeping her free from harm: these are a mother's primary tasks and Audrey has failed to fulfill them.

How many more times do I have to have that done, Mummy?

Zoe's words haunt Audrey as she remembers how, at the end of last week's chemotherapy session—as Audrey had wiped traces of vomit from her daughter's lips, shortly before Zoe had begun

to throw up again—Zoe had looked up, her expression fixed with a determination not to complain, and asked Audrey the question.

Not too many more, my love. Not too many more.

The ambiguity of her reassurance had grasped at Audrey's throat.

She runs her fingers gently across Zoe's scalp where once her hair had been. An image slips into her head that she feels should belong to another era but which she knows belongs only to the recent past. An image of Zoe, twelve months ago, soon after her second chemotherapy session, scratching her head and pulling back her hand to discover a clump of her beautiful dark, wavy hair in it. The confusion on her face, and then the horror, before the tears had welled up and tipped over onto her cheeks. The strength Audrey had needed in order to hold back her own tears, to clasp Zoe in her arms, to whisper into her ear that it was all going to be OK, that Mummy was there, that she would take care of her.

She thinks about how she has watched Zoe accept this most ignominious of side effects. She has observed the stoic resignation that has followed the flash of panic as Zoe has raised her head from her pillow in the morning to find it covered with hair no longer attached to her head. She has seen, through a gap in the bathroom door, Zoe run a brush through her hair and stare with disbelief and distress at the contents in the bristles after each stroke. On better days, during better weeks, Audrey has accompanied Zoe through the fabric department at John Lewis, picking out material to fashion into headscarves, watching Zoe smile reassuringly at shop assistants in response to their expressions of shocked, uncomfortable sympathy.

Now only a few stubborn tufts of Zoe's hair remain.

Audrey has an envelope of Zoe's hair at home, tucked away in a wooden box at the bottom of her wardrobe. She cannot let Edward know it is there: he thinks it ghoulish, macabre.

There have been days when Audrey has felt chastened by Zoe's courage, days when she has watched her laughing at a nurse's jokes even as a needle pierces her skin, days when Zoe has smiled to greet the doctor who will be prodding her for the next half an hour, days when she has nodded to reassure Audrey that she is OK as she lies down on a gurney for yet another biopsy. There have been days during which Audrey has watched the suffering, pain, indignity and distress of her little girl and felt an impotent fury that she is unable to stop it. There have been many days when Audrey has silently raged against her own powerlessness.

She places the star-wrapped present on the beige chest of drawers next to the Walkman and a selection of Zoe's favorite cassettes: audiobooks of *I Capture the Castle, Little Women,* Roald Dahl, and Shirley Hughes. On top lies the tattered copy of *Ballet Shoes* that Jess often reads aloud when they arrive to find Zoe awake. The twins know the story of Pauline, Petrova, and Posy almost off by heart and they seem to find an unspoken comfort in it, as though time has reversed to the Christmas three years ago when Audrey first gave it to Zoe. Reading Noel Streatfeild, it is as if time has been paused in 1985 and they do not have to acknowledge what the future will bring.

Over the past few weeks, Audrey has watched Zoe grow weaker day by day. She has witnessed the tiny portions of food and water shrink even further, felt the heaviness of Zoe's head as she has lifted it to plump her damp pillow. She has watched the life begin to seep from Zoe's body, watched the light dim behind her eyes. Some days she feels as though she is watching her daughter slowly disappear, like some terrible, long-drawn-out magic trick, and there is nothing she can do to stop it.

She thinks about the doctor's kindness when she and Edward had sat in his office six days ago: a compassionate elderly man

who seemed to have the loss of every patient etched into the lines around his eyes. She remembers his gentle tone—almost a whisper, as if he knew the world wasn't yet ready for what he had to say—as he had told them there was nothing more to be done. Recalling the conversation now, Audrey can feel the air leaking out of her, like a badly tied balloon, just as it had as she'd sat on a high-backed melamine chair, wishing her legs would carry her out of his office so that she didn't have to listen to what he was saying. She hears his voice in her head, talking through their options: keep Zoe in the hospital; move her to a hospice; take her home. Three separate options, each with the same outcome: Zoe is going to die.

Audrey blanches as she thinks about all the arguments she and Edward have had in the past six days: more rows than in the past sixteen years. Audrey still cannot believe that he does not want to bring Zoe home, that he thinks she will be better cared for by professionals. *They know what they're doing, Audrey. They know best how to look after her. She'll be more comfortable with them, I promise you.* Sitting now beside Zoe's bed, thinking of Edward's rationale, disbelief rises again into Audrey's chest, filling her lungs with a quiet fury. Her fists curl into tight balls, recalling her response: *I'm the best person to look after my daughter. She's coming home. There's nothing more to say.* She still cannot believe that Edward is prepared to forgo a single second of however long they have left with Zoe.

They have not told the twins the reason Zoe will be coming home later this week. She and Edward have discussed it and it is the one thing upon which they are agreed: Lily, at fifteen, is old enough to know the truth; Zoe and Jess are not. Audrey cannot bear the thought of the twins spending Zoe's last few weeks under the cloud of knowledge that they are to be permanently separated. If it is not within her gift to

ensure that her girls can spend their whole lives together, she can, at the very least, give them time together unencumbered by the awareness of what is to come. She does not want Jess's overriding memories of her sister to be the crippling apprehension of Zoe's imminent death. Audrey already feels certain that Jess will never recover from the loss. The twins' closeness is something beyond language, beyond understanding, a bond formed in a place preceding memory. Audrey cannot imagine how any of them will cope with the loss of Zoe. But it is Jess, she knows, who will feel it most profoundly.

Zoe's eyelids flicker, and then open slowly, as if uncertain where they might find themselves. "Mummy."

One word, two syllables: enough to break Audrey's heart.

She leans over and kisses Zoe on the lips. They are dry, the skin unyielding, as if coated in a thin film of plastic. Audrey raises her head, painting an expression of reassurance on her face. "Hello, angel. How are you feeling?"

Zoe smiles but with an effort that causes the muscles to contract inside Audrey's chest. "A bit tired. Where's Jess?" It is always the first question Zoe asks on the days her twin is absent.

"She's at Emily's today, sweetheart. She'll be here tomorrow."

Zoe closes her eyes and Audrey thinks that perhaps she has gone back to sleep. But then they open again and Zoe's voice, when it emerges, is low and small as if she has drunk a potion in Wonderland and it has shrunk to a fraction of its normal size. "When can I come home, Mummy?"

Audrey squeezes her daughter's hand, the reply lodging in her throat. She blinks against her tears, forces her lips into a smile. "Soon, my love. I promise." The declaration tastes bitter on her tongue, not because it is untrue but because it is a half-truth so painful she is not yet ready to say it out loud.

Holding Zoe's hand, she remembers the first day she cradled her in her arms, just seconds after Zoe had taken her first breath. She remembers promising always to protect her, to look after her, to shield her from harm. They are promises she is painfully aware of having failed to keep.

Zoe smiles again before closing her eyes and drifting back to sleep.

Audrey looks at her daughter, her heart aching with love. Where, she thinks, will all that love go when Zoe is no longer able to receive it?

Audrey stays for a few minutes more, watching, waiting, wishing that the sheer strength of her love could make her daughter well again. She leans over and kisses Zoe's forehead, strokes her cheek, and is filled with a panicked disbelief at the thought that there will come a time, very soon, when she will never be able to do this again. A time when she will never again be able to caress her daughter's skin, kiss her lips, hold her hand. It is baffling to Audrey: how can Zoe be here now and yet soon she will not? How can that possibly happen? It is incomprehensible, yet Audrey knows it to be true: a knowing and a wishing not to know that sears her heart as she gazes down at her daughter, yearning to fuse their bodies together so that she would never have to leave her side.

She kisses Zoe again—twice, three times—knowing there will never be enough time for all the kisses she aches to give. Grief stings her eyes with the loss she knows is to come. She hesitates beside Zoe's bed, aware that it is time to leave yet longing to stay. The ticking of each precious second chimes loudly in her ears and she knows that in just a few days' time she will leave the hospital for the last time, carrying in her arms the little girl she had once thought invincible, the little girl for whom she would give her life to shield from harm.

Part Five

June

Chapter 35
Audrey

The babble of conversation filled Audrey's ears as she looked around the room at her fellow choir members and then down at her watch.

In just over an hour and a half, all ninety-three of them would step onto the stage of the Royal Albert Hall and, with Ben conducting, perform a song in front of a five-thousand-strong audience, half a dozen TV cameras, and potentially millions of television viewers.

Something caught in the back of Audrey's throat and when she coughed it was like glass shattering in her chest. It could just be nerves but in all likelihood wasn't. The breathlessness and the coughing had escalated in recent weeks, just as her doctor had warned they would. She'd breathe in only to find that her chest cavity seemed to have shrunk, as though her lungs had begun to give up the fight long before Audrey was ready.

She leaned against the dressing-room door, thinking about all she'd done in the past few weeks, all the researching, planning, and booking. The idea had come to her as she'd lain in the hospital on the night of her collapse, unable to sleep because of the woman snoring in the bed next to her and the whirring of her own memories. But as soon as the

thought had nudged its way into her head, Audrey's only surprise was that it hadn't occurred to her sooner. It seemed so obvious: the one thing, surely, that neither daughter could refuse. And yet, although decisions had been made, tickets paid for and reservations confirmed, Audrey's confidence still plummeted every time she imagined telling Lily and Jess what she'd done and asking them to come with her.

A group of female musicians walked along the corridor, carrying instruments and chatting to one another without any sign of nerves. They were all in their late thirties, the same age Jess was now, the same age Zoe would have been. Audrey studied each of them in turn, wondering whether Zoe might have smiled as generously as the violinist or laughed as unselfconsciously as the clarinetist; whether her hands would have moved as expressively as the flautist's or whether she'd have listened as attentively as the oboist. Perhaps, Audrey thought, Zoe would have been all those things and more. Or perhaps she would have been none. Perhaps she would have been completely different in ways Audrey couldn't even begin to imagine. And the thought of it—the thought of the impossibility of ever knowing what kind of an adult her little girl might have become—made Audrey reach out and grab the edge of the door to steady herself.

"Are you OK, Gran? Do you need to sit down?"

Audrey shook her head in spite of the dizziness, as Phoebe looped arms with her. "Just a bit of nerves, that's all. How are you feeling—excited?"

Phoebe nodded with half-hearted commitment.

"What is it? What's the matter?"

"Nothing. I don't know. I've just been thinking about stuff recently. I've been wondering about you and Grandad . . . about how you knew that you wanted to be with him forever?"

A light flush, the color of strawberries and cream, dappled Phoebe's cheeks.

Audrey suppressed a smile. She glanced across the room to where Harry was laughing with some of the other choir members. She'd thought there might be something between them, but things had clearly moved faster than she'd realized. "Forever can be an awfully long time, Phoebe. You've got your whole life ahead of you. Don't feel you have to commit to anything—anyone—until you're sure you're ready."

"I know that. But you weren't much older than me when you got married. I just want to understand how you knew that Grandad was the person you wanted to spend the rest of your life with, especially when his parents didn't like you very much."

Audrey swiveled her plain gold wedding band around her finger. "There'll always be someone who disapproves of the choices you make. But as long as *you* understand the reasons for them, as long as you're happy with them and no one's unduly hurt by them, you need to be strong enough—brave enough—to make your own decisions."

Audrey flinched at the irony of her counsel: she had lost track of the number of times she had failed to follow her own advice.

"But what if you *know* your parents are going to disapprove? What if you *know* your choices will make them unhappy? What do you do then? What if they never forgive you?"

Phoebe's anxiety made Audrey wonder what on earth could be so dreadful about Harry—who seemed very nice to her—that could possibly cause Phoebe such concern about Lily and Daniel's reaction. "Most parents will forgive their children almost anything. It's part of the job description: unconditional love. I know Mum can be quite particular about things but

I also know that she loves you very much. She only wants you to be happy."

"No, Gran, that's not true, and you know it. What Mum wants is for everyone to *think* we're happy. It's not the same thing. As long as she can convince the rest of the world that we're a perfect happy family and that she's some kind of superwoman, she doesn't actually care what's *really* going on. She's never around long enough to find out anyway."

There was a fragility beneath Phoebe's contempt, her words skating on thin ice. She blinked hard and then swallowed, winding a strand of hair from the nape of her neck tightly around her finger.

Audrey took Phoebe's free hand, stroked the back of it where the skin was softest, wishing she could tell her granddaughter that she'd got it all wrong. But the truth was that Lily had missed so much of Phoebe's childhood: the school plays, sports days, music recitals, tennis matches. On so many occasions both Lily and Daniel had been too busy with work to attend, so Audrey had filled in for them, parental pride one step removed. And as much as Audrey had loved watching Phoebe run races, sing songs, hit a ball over a net, her enjoyment had always been marred by the guilt that Lily was missing those moments and that Phoebe was having to accept second best. So many times Audrey had wanted to say to Lily: Your children have only one childhood. The years in which they need you—in which they really need you—flash by like a star shooting through the sky. A blink of an eye and they go from babies to toddlers. Another blink and they're starting school. A third blink and they're teenagers, stretching their wings and preparing for life without you. And then, one day, when you're certain it can't have been more than a few months since you first held them in your arms—bloodied

and mucus-coated, their hungry mouths reaching for your breast—they're gone.

"No parent gets it right all the time. I know Mum's got her flaws—we all have—but that doesn't mean she doesn't love you or isn't interested in you. And it certainly doesn't mean she'd ever disapprove of you, not really. Most parents can recover from pretty much anything their children throw at them."

Audrey thought about Lily and Jess, about how, even when your children act in ways that break your heart, you still find it in yourself to forgive them.

"So what's your advice? Just do whatever I want and to hell with the parental consequences?"

Audrey allowed herself a wry smile. "I'm not sure I'd put it quite like that. But without getting maudlin, you do have only one life and it's only yours to live. All any parent can do is try to equip you as best they can—dig the foundations and give you the tools to build the kind of life you want to lead. The rest is down to you and your courage. And I think you've got bags of courage, Phoebe. I think you've got it in spades."

Phoebe smiled and for the first time Audrey saw a trace of Zoe in her: the verve, the energy and the sheer unassailable chutzpah.

"Thank you, Gran. Really. You've no idea how much that means. I don't know what I'd do without you."

There was a moment's hesitation—discomfort at a truth neither wanted to acknowledge—before Audrey put her arms around Phoebe's shoulders, hoping that her granddaughter would feel able to confide whatever was on her mind while she was still in a position to help her. "Now, you're all set for later, aren't you? You and Mia have got the timings agreed?"

The thought of what the three of them had planned caused fresh nausea to churn in Audrey's stomach.

"Yes, it's all fine. Don't worry. We're doing the right thing. You know we are."

Audrey nodded even as her head swam with uncertainty. She hadn't told Mia and Phoebe everything, just enough to elicit their help. Now, as she stood backstage listening to singers warm up their voices, stage managers issue instructions, and PA announcements from inside the auditorium, she couldn't tell whether her agitation related to singing in the concert or to what she had planned for afterward.

Chapter 36
Lily

Sitting in the vast empty auditorium of the Royal Albert Hall, Lily berated herself for having arrived so early.

She glanced at her watch: forty minutes to go. Most sensible people wouldn't take their seats for another half an hour. An usher at one of the entrances caught her eye and smiled, and Lily forced herself to reciprocate before looking down at her phone and jabbing a finger at its screen.

She contemplated going to the bar, buying herself a glass of white wine, pretending she was the kind of person for whom that would be easy. But she knew she wouldn't. She could comfortably stand on a podium in front of hundreds of people and deliver speeches but the prospect of sitting alone in a bar filled her with dread.

Her phone rang—loud and shrill—and she scrabbled to answer it. "Daniel, hi—I was just thinking about you."

Lily slipped out of her seat and scurried out of the auditorium, into the corridor, where groups of people stood together, sharing bags of crisps and stories of their days.

"Hey, Lil. How are you? Everything OK?"

"Yes, fine. I'm already here, miles too early, of course." Lily laughed but it rang hollow in her ears.

"Where?"

"The Albert Hall. For Phoebe and Mum's concert. You hadn't forgotten, had you?"

There was a momentary pause. Next to Lily, a man cupped his hands around a woman's face and kissed her gently on the lips. Lily turned away and pressed her palm against her free ear to hear Daniel better.

"I thought that was next Saturday. Shit, sorry, I'm all over the place—it's been one of those weeks. Wish Phoebe luck from me, won't you? And your mum, of course."

"They're backstage already. Why don't you call Phoebe, or message her?"

Lily heard impatience in her voice and rushed to fill the silence. "Anyway, how's work? The redundancy stuff on my end is a nightmare. I wish they'd just be honest and say they're getting rid of me instead of making me go through this ridiculous charade."

"It's shitty, the way they're treating you. I'm sorry. But you'll find something else, something better. You know you will. You're too good at your job not to."

Lily thought about the meetings she'd already had with headhunters and how, at each one, she couldn't muster any excitement about the prospect of marketing airlines or clothes or one brand of beer over another. "I've been thinking. You were right in what you said, before you left. It's ridiculous that we spend so little time together. We give far too much time to our jobs and not enough to each other. And it's not as if anyone's genuinely grateful for all the hours we put in. So how about we carve out some proper time for each other? Why don't I come out there for a week or two? I've got plenty of leave owing. We could act like proper tourists for a few days together. And then, when you get back, we should institute a proper date night: once a week, nonnegotiable,

whatever's going on at work. Start putting ourselves—and each other—first, instead of always being slaves to our jobs. I think it could be just what we need."

Her words tripped over each other, eager to escape before he had a chance to interrupt her.

Daniel was silent and Lily pressed the phone harder against her ear.

"Are you still there? Did you hear all that?"

"Yes, I heard. Look, it's clearly not a good time to talk. You go and enjoy the concert and let's speak another time."

Something in Daniel's tone made Lily grip the phone more tightly. "No, it's fine. Like I said, it's ages before the concert starts. You sound strange. What's up?"

There was a pause.

"Honestly, it's nothing we need to talk about now. It's just . . . Well, there's an option for me to extend for another six months, that's all."

That's all. Daniel's unsentimental delivery hummed in Lily's ears.

"You're thinking of staying there? For a whole year? What about us? What about Phoebe?"

Her voice began to fracture and she swallowed, trying to meld it back together.

"Nothing's been decided yet. I did say this wasn't a good time to talk about it."

The hairs on Lily's arms bristled. She tried to imagine Daniel in an apartment she'd never seen, in a city she wasn't living in, and was aware of fears she didn't want to acknowledge needling her, demanding to be noticed. "This *is* just about work, isn't it?"

"What do you mean?"

Lily hesitated, wishing she'd bought herself a glass of wine, that she could take a few gulps before answering. "This isn't . . . It's not about us, is it?"

If the clamor of conversation in the corridor hadn't been so loud—if there hadn't been so much laughter, so many greetings, so much chatter—Lily might have been certain she'd heard a sigh at the other end of the line.

"Of course it's not. It's about me trying to get made managing partner, just like we've always discussed, and which I've got a much better chance of achieving by working out here for a while."

Lily tried to settle Daniel's words in her head, tried to get them to sit down in a straight, orderly line, but they were jumping over one another like recalcitrant children. "I know that's always been the plan. But still . . . when you left . . ." She faltered, felt her courage turn around and start walking away. She knew that if she didn't ask the question it would haunt her for days. She took a deep breath and forced the words out before her resolve disappeared. "There's not someone else, is there?"

Her words were muted in her ears so that for a second she couldn't be sure whether she'd said them out loud.

"Of course not. Don't be silly. It's just work. Are you telling me that if you got an opportunity like this you wouldn't jump at it?"

Lily tried to imagine herself upping sticks, moving to another continent, leaving Daniel and Phoebe at home by themselves, but it was so unlikely—absurd, almost—that she couldn't begin to envisage it.

"Lil, this clearly isn't the time to discuss it. I'll email later. It's probably easier to lay out the details if I write it all down. It'll give us time to think it through. I'll call again tomorrow."

"But, Daniel—"

"There's someone at the door—I'd better go. Give Phoebe my love, won't you? I hope it goes really well."

"Daniel—"

Lily pulled the phone from her ear, glanced at its screen, and saw the red icon informing her that the call was over. She leaned against the wall, her arms folded across her chest.

An extra six months. A year of living apart. The weeks flipped forward in her head. If Daniel stayed on he wouldn't be home permanently until well into next year. Phoebe would have submitted her university applications. Lily would be in a new job. And she would almost certainly be an orphan.

Behind her, the kissing couple were discussing their honeymoon plans—South Africa, Botswana, Rwanda—and Lily headed farther along the corridor, away from them.

The sound of children laughing made her look back. Two little girls were skipping toward her, holding hands, plaits bouncing over their shoulders. The way one of them smiled and ran ahead dragging the other behind her caused Lily to stare at them with an uncanny sense of recognition.

She was reminded of sitting on a beach more than thirty years ago, the sand itching between her toes. From somewhere along the crowded shore music had crackled through the static of a transistor radio, Madonna singing about getting into the groove. Lily had been reading *The Catcher in the Rye*, unsure whether she was enjoying the novel or simply that it was contraband reading: her English teacher had refused to let her borrow it from the school library, had told her it was too grown-up for her, so she had gone to the public library and borrowed it from there instead.

She remembered how her sisters' laughter had rung out across the beach as if taunting her, how she had glanced above her sunglasses, watched Zoe and Jess throwing seaweed at each other, bowing her head back to her book before they caught her watching them, beads of sweat dripping from her forehead onto the page.

Why don't you go and play with them, Lily? You've been reading all morning. You must be in need of stretching your legs?

Her mum had been sitting on a portable green camping chair surrounded by coolers filled with foil-wrapped sandwiches, apples, and bottles of fruit drinks. She had been reading *Enormous Changes at the Last Minute* by an author Lily had never heard of. Next to her, Lily's dad had been sitting in an identical chair with a copy of *The Times,* which he had been reading—one column inch at a time—since they had arrived at the beach nearly two hours before.

Lily remembered looking over her shoulder to where the twins had resumed work on their sandcastle, an ambitious triple-story construction with towers, moats, and flags, the kind of project which Lily might once have attempted with help from her dad. She remembered shaking her head even as a part of her craved involvement.

Oh, do join in, Lily. It won't be a proper summer holiday if my three musketeers don't build the biggest sand palace on the beach.

She could hear now—as if the clocks had rewound and her mum was standing right next to her—the good humor in her voice. But back then Lily's fingers had curled around the corners of her book.

My three musketeers. Her mum had called them that for years and Lily had often wondered whether it had once been an accurate description or whether it was something she'd said because she wanted it to be true.

I'm fine reading my book. I don't want to build stupid sandcastles. It's babyish.

Even all these years later Lily could hear the despondency in her voice, could sense the confusion that she didn't know where her sadness had come from or why it had sneaked up on her like that.

There's no need to be rude, Lily. Mum's only offering a suggestion.

Her dad's voice had been firm, unyielding. It was a voice he had only ever used on Lily, never on Zoe or Jess, a fact Lily had pointed out many times, only to be told she was imagining things.

Lying on the beach that day, Lily had thought about all the years she had wished for a sister to play with, all those weeks when her mum's swollen stomach had offered such promise, before the news that there were to be two babies, not one. Lily had understood, even then, that after all that time together in her mum's tummy, those twin babies would be close in a way Lily could never hope to be a part of.

Abandoning their sandcastle, Zoe and Jess had begun acting out Rapunzel: Jess the helpless princess, Zoe—as always—the handsome woodcutter come to rescue her.

Hey, Lily. We need someone to play the evil witch and cast horrible spells. Want to come and join in?

Zoe had grinned, fearless and defiant, as Lily had glared at her. She remembered her eyes stinging behind her sunglasses as Zoe had flung an arm around Jess's shoulders, the two of them giggling with an intimate camaraderie. She remembered how a single thought had circulated in her head that day as she had lain on the beach at Woolacombe Bay, the smell of chips and vinegar and suntan lotion filling her nose, listening to the sound of other people's happiness: she had wished they could turn back the clock to the time before the twins had been born, and discover that there was only one baby, not two, waiting inside her mum's tummy to be her little sister.

An announcement over the PA hauled Lily back into the present. She allowed herself one last glance along the corridor to where the little girls had been playing but they had disappeared, replaced by couples, families, parents, and children who now crowded the passageway in both directions as far as Lily could see.

Chapter 37
Audrey

From somewhere along the corridor, Audrey could hear the sound of instruments being tuned; the glide of a bow along strings, the triple-octave span of a flute, the deep growl of a tuba.

She glanced down at her watch for the second time in as many minutes. It was almost half past six: thirty minutes until the concert began, nearly an hour until Audrey and the choir were due onstage. They were third on the bill, after the cast of *Les Misérables* had opened with a rousing medley that had caused the hairs on the back of Audrey's neck to stand on end during rehearsals that afternoon, followed by the BBC Symphony Orchestra and Chorus performing the fourth movement of Beethoven's 9th Symphony: the Ode to Joy.

"Everything OK there, Audrey? You look as though you've lost something."

Audrey turned to see Ben standing next to her, almost unrecognizable in a dinner jacket and black bow tie rather than his usual jeans and T-shirt.

"Not something. Someone. Phoebe popped to the bathroom ages ago and I'm worried she's got lost."

"Don't worry. We've still got heaps of time. She'll find her way back. How are you feeling anyway?"

Audrey was so used to the question being asked in relation to her health that it took her a few moments to remember that Ben didn't know she was ill. "A little nervous, I suppose. But that's only natural, isn't it?"

"Absolutely. There are rock stars and concert pianists who throw up before every performance. A little bit of nerves does you good—gets the adrenaline pumping, gives the performance that extra edge."

A voice came over the backstage PA announcing thirty minutes to curtain up.

"But are you OK, Audrey? I haven't wanted to pry, but is everything all right after your trip to the hospital?"

Audrey thought about the half-truth she'd told Ben at the first rehearsal after her collapse: about the low blood sugar and the blackout, but nothing about the cancer. She was about to repeat herself, felt the little white lies line up in her mouth like foot soldiers intent on protecting her. But then she saw something behind Ben's eyes—a glimmer of light struggling to break through a thick, dark cloud—and suddenly the words were tumbling out before she was sure she wanted to set them free.

"Not really, no. I've got cancer. Stage four: breast, liver, lymph nodes, lung. The doctors think I've got about three months left. I haven't wanted to make it public—I'm sure you can appreciate why."

She might have said more but horror was spreading across Ben's face like ink on blotting paper.

"God, Audrey, I'm *so* sorry. I had no idea. I don't know what to say. Should you really be here? Shouldn't you be—I don't know—at home resting or something?"

Audrey couldn't help smiling. "I joined the choir to escape unnecessary fussing. I'm more than well enough to take part

this evening so please don't worry. I wouldn't miss it for the world."

It was only as she spoke that Audrey realized the truth of it. Waiting to go onstage, she finally allowed herself to acknowledge how much she'd been looking forward to the concert, how much she'd been holding on to it with both hands, determined not to let the opportunity slip from her grasp. There had been so many times over the past three months when she'd thought she might not make it, when she'd feared the cancer would beat her to the finish line. But here she was, about to head out onto one of the most famous stages in the world, and there was nothing she'd let get in her way.

"Well, I'm very glad to hear it. We wouldn't want to do it without you. But I really am very sorry. If there's anything I can do to help—not just tonight, but whenever—you will let me know, won't you?"

Audrey nodded, and as they exchanged a rueful smile, she had an uncanny feeling that she would know Ben for the rest of her life, however fleeting that might be.

"But what about you? That day at rehearsal before I fainted, you were in the middle of telling me about your family and I feel bad we haven't had a chance to talk about it since. I wanted to say how sorry I am about your son. I don't think there's anything worse for a parent than losing a child." Audrey was conscious of her airways narrowing, of a struggle between her desire to say more and her fear that she simply couldn't.

Ben stared at her, unblinking, and Audrey felt sure he was going to turn around and walk away. But then he took a deep breath and began to speak. "There's no need to apologize. I haven't wanted to talk about it for five years so there's no reason anyone else should."

Something in Ben's voice—a thin shard of light edging around the frame of a closed door—emboldened Audrey to continue. "Well, if ever you did want to talk about it, I don't think I'd be the world's worst listener."

Ben glanced at her, then down at the floor, his body quite still, and it seemed to Audrey that she could see the grief leaking out of him, a vapor rising from his skin like a plume of gas from the surface of a distant moon.

"Your daughter—Erin, isn't it? How old is she?"

He took a deep breath, as if something in the air might provide him with the fortitude he needed. "She just turned sixteen. I . . . I haven't seen her in a while. I've been traveling. After Zach . . . it was just . . . it was just too . . ."

His voice faded and Audrey watched the steady rise and fall of his chest, the clenching and unclenching of his jaw, the pinching of the skin at the bridge of his nose. She could almost feel the heat of his grief. She thought about placing her hand on his back, wondering whether there was any way of telling him that she understood without either of them having to say anything at all.

"Mr. Levine? I'm sorry to interrupt but one of the stage managers needs to have a quick word with you. Would you mind coming with me?"

Ben looked up, eyes glazed, as though he'd just woken from a deep winter sleep. He shook his head as if trying to free his thoughts before looking up and nodding at the young man wearing a headset, carrying a clipboard, and fidgeting from one foot to the other as though precious seconds were being unnecessarily wasted. "Will you excuse me, Audrey? I'll be back soon. I want to get the choir together for a pep talk before we go onstage so don't let anyone wander off, OK?"

He smiled at her, all traces of distress wiped from his face, and headed down the corridor with the young man.

Audrey watched him until he'd rounded the corner. She leaned against the wall, her shoulders lighter now that she'd told him the truth. It was as though her diagnosis had lost a little of its power now she had entrusted it to someone outside the family.

She turned around and walked into the dressing room where her fellow choir members were waiting to go onstage, hoping that Phoebe would find her way back soon.

"OK, folks, can you all gather around? Can you guys hear me at the back? Harry, Siobhan—can I have some quiet, please?"

Audrey shuffled forward with the rest of the choir to where Ben was standing on a wooden crate, head and shoulders above them all. She looked back toward the door just as Phoebe rushed in.

"God, Gran, this place is a rabbit warren. I thought I'd never find you. What have I missed—anything important?"

"No, you're just in time. Ben's only just called us together."

Audrey squeezed Phoebe's hand and looked up at the clock on the wall—five minutes until the concert began, thirty-five minutes until they were due onstage—before turning her attention back to Ben.

"I just wanted to say a few words. First off, I want to thank you all. It's been a crazy three months and I know some of you doubted at the outset that it was possible to whip a hundred random strangers into a choir in such a short space of time. To be honest, I doubted it myself once or twice . . ."

A light wave of laughter rippled around the room.

"But the thing I've been constantly impressed by is the commitment you've all shown to making this thing work.

When you step out onto that stage tonight, I want you to feel proud of what you've achieved. Because I'm proud of you. I know you're going to do a fantastic job out there. And this song we're singing—just think about the power of that title: 'I Wish I Knew How It Would Feel to Be Free.' I want you to feel every single word of it, just like Nina Simone did back in the day—feel it, sing it, communicate it, and let's help raise a ton of money for charity."

An almost imperceptible crack in Ben's voice caused him to pause, swallow, breathe. He caught Audrey's eye and she smiled at him.

"Now, I know it's late notice and I don't want anyone to freak out but I want to make a tiny change to our song tonight."

Panic bristled around the choir. Ben raised both his hands, palms flat toward the group, as if preemptively seeking forgiveness. "Just hear me out, OK? It's not a huge change. I want to start the song as a solo—just the first verse, nothing more—and then we'll pick it up as a group exactly as we've done throughout rehearsals. And I'd like you, Audrey, to take that solo."

Audrey felt ninety-two pairs of eyes pivot toward her, felt their collective gaze burn into her cheeks.

Ben grinned at her, eyebrows raised. "What do you say? Will you do that? Just the first four lines, that's all. I think it'll be so much more powerful as a solo. And you can do it, I know you can."

"Oh, go on, Gran, you *must*. It'll be awesome. You have to say yes."

Audrey was aware of Phoebe's arm around her shoulders, of nearly a hundred faces gazing at her expectantly, of Ben waiting for a response.

She felt words begin to morph into recognizable shapes in her head. Words that felt familiar, safe, reliable. Words that began to make their way toward her mouth as if knowing through decades of experience that they were the right ones.

No, I can't. Don't be silly. Of course I can't.

Audrey readied herself to reply. And then a snapshot of memory flashed into her head.

She is lying on her bed, feet crossed at the ankles, the voices of contestants on *Call My Bluff* filtering through the partition wall from the sitting room next door. Her diary is propped up on her pillow, a pen in her hand. She writes. As she pours her hopes and dreams into her diary on the evening of her sixteenth birthday, she experiences an unbridled sense of optimism: that the whole world is out there waiting for her, just as long as she is brave enough to go out and grab it.

Audrey looked around the room at the faces of her fellow choir members, strangers three months ago and yet now part of a group to which she felt deeply attached. She raised her head to look at Ben. And then, without affording herself an opportunity to change her mind, she heard herself reply, loudly and clearly, "OK. If you really think I can, I'll do it."

In the hubbub that followed—Phoebe hugging her, the choir applauding, Ben calling them to order to explain exactly how it was going to work—Audrey could see out of the corner of her eye the ghost of her sixteen-year-old self, leaning against the wall and smiling at her.

Chapter 38
Audrey

Audrey stood listening to the last few resounding chords of Beethoven's 9th, the entrance to the auditorium within touching distance ahead of her. As the sound of applause crashed through the closed doors, she breathed in through her nose and let the air out slowly through a tiny circle in the center of her lips.

"Right, that's your cue. Good luck—and enjoy it!"

The stage manager ushered them forward, Ben first, Audrey fourth in line. She cast a glance over her shoulder to see if she could spot Phoebe but her granddaughter was too far behind.

And then, suddenly, she was through the doors and the glare of lights was hot on her face. She squinted into the brightness, her eyes taking a moment to adjust.

She walked onto the stage, toward the front row of tiered platforms. Behind her five rows of the choir filed in, the stage set up in front of them for a full orchestra but empty of players now save for a pianist, a drummer, and a double bassist.

As Audrey looked out into the auditorium, from the tiny figures standing high up in the gallery to those seated in the orchestra, she couldn't believe how different it looked—how different it felt—from when they'd rehearsed there that

afternoon. Then it had seemed bare, cavernous, uninviting almost. Now it felt as though half of London must be in attendance.

Her right leg trembled and she tried to restrain it but realized it was operating on a network beyond her control. She instructed herself to ignore it, hoped it wouldn't be noticeable to any TV viewers watching at home. She felt someone squeeze her shoulder but didn't dare turn around for fear that if she looked anyone in the eye she might realize the enormity of what she was about to do, and how many people were depending on her to do it well. Then the shuffling of feet behind her stopped and the purest silence fell like a blanket over the auditorium.

And there was Ben, standing in front of them on a small square podium, grinning and nodding. He gave a thumbs-up that made Audrey want to giggle but she held it tight behind her lips because she knew it was just nerves playing tricks on her, and she feared that if she began to laugh now she might not be able to stop.

Ben caught her eye, raised his eyebrows in a silent question, and she nodded in reply.

She watched as Ben lifted his arms and conducted a single bar of silent time-setting before the pianist placed his fingers on the keys and the drummer poised his brushes in midair. Together they began to play the first notes of a sixteen-bar introduction that Audrey knew so well it was as if it had soaked into her skin and now flowed through her veins. Her heart clenched and unclenched like an impatient fist and she tried to swallow but there was nothing there.

It was too late anyway. Ben was looking at her, that broad, encouraging smile reassuring her that he believed in her, that

she could do this, that all she had to do was believe in herself and she could pull it off.

Audrey managed to prize her dry lips apart, felt her diaphragm expand, and then she heard the sound of her voice singing into the microphone clipped to her daffodil-yellow blouse. And there was a split second of shock at its volume, how all-encompassing it was, her ears full of the sound of her own voice.

She sang note-perfect, her voice so much more confident than she had ever imagined it could be, and it was as though her sixteen-year-old self were holding her hand, singing alongside her, reminding her of all the things she had once hoped her life might be. There, in her voice, was the optimism she had once felt for the future, the plans she had once dared to make, the courage she had lost sight of for so many years and only now regained. Wrapped inside Audrey's singing was all the love, the loss, the grief, and the guilt that she had been carrying inside her for almost thirty years.

Chapter 39
Jess

Jess leaned forward in her seat, oblivious to the fact that she was blocking the view of the person behind. Her hands gripped the armrests, her knuckles the color of chalk.

That was her mum. *Her mum.* And yet it was someone else entirely: someone who was wearing the same black trousers and yellow blouse as the woman who'd left her house earlier today, but who was doing something Jess could never have imagined her doing. This woman was standing onstage and singing a solo in front of five thousand people as though she'd been doing it all her life.

Her mum's singing was rich and deep and resonant, a sound that awakened in Jess a sequence of memories that had been long forgotten: a sound that had, once upon a time, sent her to sleep every night accompanied by the gentle sweep of fingers through her hair and kisses across her forehead. A sound that had been whispered into Jess's ear—warm and comforting—as she had lain awake through the night, encased in her mum's arms, while her twin sister occupied a hospital bed two miles away. A sound that spoke of refuge from bee stings, bullying classmates, grazed knees, and bad dreams. It was a sound of love and hope, encouragement and comfort.

As Jess stared unblinking at the stage, listening to her mum

sing for the first time in decades, her scalp tightened as a cold, unwanted knowledge crept into her head. It was knowledge Jess had kept locked away—not daring to look at it, not daring to admit its presence—ever since she had been told nine months ago. Now, for the first time, the thought opened up in her mind that her mum would not be around forever. That there would come a time, very soon, when she would no longer be there to listen to the story of Jess's terrible day at work or to answer prosaic questions Jess had asked countless times before but always needed to ask again: how long to roast a whole chicken, when best to have her flu shot, which month she should plant her bulbs. There would come a time all too soon when her mum would no longer be there to provide all the support and reassurance Jess had spent a lifetime taking for granted.

It was only now, sitting in the Royal Albert Hall, that Jess realized her mum was the only adult with whom she'd maintained a relationship for the past fifteen years. That in spite of all that remained unsaid between them—all the tales Jess had never dared tell, all the times she had pushed her mum away to protect them both—her mum had always been there, unwavering in her love. And soon she would be gone. And the acknowledgment of it clutched at Jess's heart as if it might never let her go.

Someone clasped her hand, and she turned to see Mia beaming at her. As their fingers interlocked, Jess realized that she couldn't remember the last time her daughter had willingly held her hand.

Jess watched her mum sing, knowing that the realization of how much she would miss her had come almost too late. And it was only when Mia handed her a tissue that Jess understood the reason her face felt hot and damp was because of the tears streaming down her cheeks.

Chapter 40
Lily

Lily had heard her mum sing hundreds of times during her childhood but never quite like this, never with a voice that filled every corner of a concert hall, seeming to burrow under your skin and anchor itself to your heart. Sitting in the ninth row of the orchestra, staring up at the choir onstage in their black trousers and rainbow of colored shirts, she felt as though she were watching her mum transform into someone new, someone different, someone confident, poised, extraordinary.

Glancing sideways along her row of seats, Lily saw the face of every audience member break into a wide, surprised smile. She turned back to the stage, her chest swelling with pride.

Her eyes flicked above her mum's head to where Phoebe was standing two rows behind, looking down at her grandmother and grinning as though there was not enough room on her face to contain all her admiration.

Lily experienced a flash of anger that Daniel wasn't there. He should have been sitting beside her, watching his daughter onstage. He should have been there to see his mother-in-law in this moment of unexpected triumph, not just because Lily wanted him there but because her mum deserved to have everyone hear for themselves how incredible she was.

As Lily watched and listened, a sense of unreality washed

over her: the perverse truth that at this moment her mum could not have seemed more alive, more full of vitality, or have had more reason to want to go on living.

Lily kept her eyes glued to the stage, determined not to miss a single second of her mum's performance. Because she knew, even without consciously acknowledging it, that in the months and years ahead, this would be a memory to treasure.

Chapter 41
Audrey

As Audrey reached the end of her solo she realized that this was it: this was how it felt to be free.

She sang her final line and then her solo was over and the rest of the choir were joining in. Her head felt light, her legs weak and her palms damp, as though her body was only now recognizing the magnitude of what she'd done. But now that she had, all Audrey could think was that she wanted to do it again. She wanted to turn back the clock sixty seconds to the moment the pianist had struck those first two iconic chords, to relive every single note in the knowledge of how quickly they would pass.

Singing along with the rest of the choir, Audrey looked out into the audience. She could see people smiling in the front rows, could hear a note of optimism reverberate around the hall.

Then the song came to an end and there was a fragment of silence, a splinter of time in which anything seemed possible. And then the silence was shattered by a sound so thunderous Audrey almost clamped her hands over her ears. Not just the noise but the feel of it: an eruption of applause that vibrated through the soles of her feet.

Audrey turned to see Phoebe two rows behind her, flushed and beaming. And then she felt someone taking hold of her

hand and she turned to find Ben leading her toward the front of the stage, gesturing for her to stand there, alone.

Hands clasped behind her back, Audrey stood listening to the applause before bending her head in an unrehearsed bow. When she straightened up again, it took her a few seconds to understand why the audience looked different: closer, bigger. They were on their feet, not just clapping but cheering.

She turned around, in need of a cue from Ben as to what she should do next, but when she looked behind her, Ben and the rest of the chorus were applauding her too.

Audrey beamed at the audience, savoring every second.

And in that moment she didn't think about the fact that her life was going to end so much sooner than she wished. She didn't think about the grains of sand slipping through the hourglass, nor that she had had to wait so long to experience something like this. What mattered to Audrey as she took her fourth and final bow was the incontrovertible knowledge that even at her age—even this close to the end—life still had the capacity to surprise her.

Chapter 42
Jess

"Did you know Granny could sing like that?"

Jess looked at Mia over the top of her menu. Around them, waiters delivered pizzas, salads, bottles of wine, and jugs of water to neighboring tables, the restaurant noisy with Saturday night concertgoers.

She closed the menu, not feeling hungry. She had known she wouldn't be at ten o'clock on a Saturday night, but Mia had been so keen for them to have dinner together that they were seated in one of the restaurants inside the Royal Albert Hall, waiting for her mum to join them.

"Not really. Having heard her tonight, I remember her singing to us when I was little, but I don't think I've heard her sing since I was a child." Jess thought back to all those lonely nights she had lain on the bottom bunk, Zoe having moved into the spare room next door as soon as she'd got ill, listening through the wall to her mum singing "Dream a Little Dream of Me" or "Somewhere Over the Rainbow." On days when Zoe was well enough, in the weeks she was allowed home from the hospital during the fourteen months of her illness, their dad would carry her downstairs and they would make up a bed for her on the sofa. Jess would slip

under the far end of the duvet, careful not to take up too much space or sit on her twin's spindly legs, and together they would watch *The Wizard of Oz* for the eighteenth, nineteenth, twentieth time. Zoe would laugh at the Tin Man, shout at the Cowardly Lion, and tell Jess not to be silly when she got scared of the Wicked Witch of the West and her flying monkeys. And no matter how many times the two of them watched it together, the same thought always went through Jess's mind: that perhaps somewhere at the end of a rainbow was a pot of gold that could make her sister well again.

A thought skittered through Jess's head, a thought so familiar it ought not to have hurt as much as it did: the question of what Zoe might have done with her life had she lived. And the same answer was waiting for her as it always was: that funny, fearless, spirited Zoe would have achieved so much more than Jess ever had. Sometimes Jess couldn't help feeling that when the egg had divided in two, the wrong half had been given the faulty cells.

"I can't wait to watch the whole concert back on TV. I hope they did a close-up of Granny during her solo. They probably did, didn't they?"

Jess was about to reply when, over Mia's shoulder, she saw her mum walk through the doorway to the restaurant. She was about to stand and wave when she registered two figures following closely behind, a sight that caused her stomach to twist into knots.

"For God's sake, what are they doing here? What's Mum playing at? Mia, get your things, we can't stay."

Jess rose to her feet and grabbed her jacket from the back of the chair as her mum, Lily, and Phoebe crossed the room toward them. She turned to Mia in preparation to leave. "Mia,

didn't you hear me? We're leaving. I can't believe Mum has done this. What on earth is she thinking?"

Mia stood up. But instead of picking up her bag and edging away from the table, she turned to the trio walking toward them and waved. And all at once Jess realized she'd been duped.

Chapter 43
Lily

It was too late to turn back. Lily glanced at her mum and saw in her face a quiet determination. She looked across the restaurant to where Jess was grabbing her bag from underneath the table, felt time stretch as though it knew, before the next second struck, that she had to make a decision.

She looked again at her mum, saw the naked desire to fix what was broken. And then she was following her mum and Phoebe through the thoroughfare of tables to where Jess was standing with her jacket draped over her arm, her face stony with rage or hatred, Lily wasn't sure which.

"Why are you doing this, Mum?"

It was strange how one forgot. How time or self-preservation eroded the memory of Jess's brusqueness: the accusatory tone and the clipped consonants.

Lily looked at Jess, unsure whether she wanted her sister to meet her gaze or not. She remembered all those times after Zoe's death that Jess had left the room whenever Lily had entered, when her questions had been met with monosyllabic answers. She thought about all the occasions she had apologized to Jess without knowing what she was supposed to have done wrong. All the times she had wished—for their mum's sake, if no one else's—that Jess could cast off her anger, like

a caterpillar shedding its skin. Mostly what Lily thought as she stood opposite her sister, feeling the heat of Jess's rage, was that she wished she could turn back the clock twenty-eight years to the morning she had stood on the landing with her hand on the doorknob to the spare bedroom, and choose not to go inside.

"I'm just doing what I should have done years ago, Jess. I'm trying to make things better."

Chapter 44
Audrey

As she waited to see how Lily and Jess might react, Audrey imagined what the scene might look like now if there were three daughters standing opposite her rather than two. Whether all three might be smiling, rather than one looking thunderous and the other wary. Whether there might be more grandchildren to join Mia and Phoebe, chatting among themselves, rather than looking on anxiously to see how the adults might next choose to make a mess of their family.

So often, in the space where Audrey's third daughter should have been, was an imagined scene of how life might have been unfolding if Zoe were still alive.

"Mum, I don't know how many times I have to tell you: this fantasy reconciliation of yours is never going to happen. Why can't you leave it alone? Why can't you just be happy with the relationships you've got?"

The exasperation in Jess's voice was sharp, piercing. Audrey glanced between Lily and Jess, wondering whether there was anything she could have done to put an end to this sooner. "I love you both. You know I do. And I can't bear to see you estranged like this. Can you imagine what it's like when the two people you love most in the world refuse to be in the same room?"

She turned to Jess but her daughter looked away, her expression glacial.

Audrey felt her heart bend out of shape. Part of her wanted to retreat, to accept defeat. But even as Jess glared at her, words began to tumble out of her mouth. "For goodness' sake, Jess, you must understand how this is for me. I've got one daughter who refuses to speak to the other and two granddaughters I'm not allowed to see together. And I don't have time to wait around for a reconciliation. Whatever it is you think Lily's done, I'm asking you to put an end to it. Please, Jess, I'm begging you. Forgive her, please."

Chapter 45
Jess

Jess said nothing as her mum sank into a chair and rested her head on her hands. She didn't move as Mia and Phoebe flanked their grandmother, their arms around her shoulders. All around her people were eating, drinking, and celebrating together, perfect examples of the family her mum wished theirs could be.

A familiar irony drummed inside Jess's head: that only by incurring her mum's wrath could she protect her from a story she wouldn't want to hear.

She looked up to where Lily was gazing at her with an expression of hurt and confusion that made Jess want to scream: *What is it you want from me? What more could you possibly want other than my silence?*

Seeing that look on Lily's face made Jess shut her eyes to try to escape it. But it was still there. It was always there.

Whatever it is you think Lily's done, forgive her, please.

But Jess could never forgive Lily. Jess didn't want to forgive her. Because if it hadn't been for Lily, her dad and Zoe would still be alive today.

Chapter 46
June 1988

It is a Thursday afternoon. Years later, Jess will remember this detail because of the dampness of her hair against the back of her neck, the smell of chlorine clinging to her skin, the residue of that afternoon's swimming lesson still sore in her eyes.

She is supposed to be doing her homework, has promised her mum that she will have it done by the time her parents return, so that the five of them can spend their first evening together in more than two months.

Zoe is coming home from the hospital today. Jess cannot concentrate on her school work, is too distracted by thoughts of all the things she will do with Zoe once she's home. Her sister has been at Great Ormond Street Hospital for almost nine weeks this time, and Jess cannot wait to have her sleep in the room next door again, cannot wait to watch films beside her, read stories with her, tell jokes to her. She has a conviction—a certainty she has shared with no one—that this will be the last time Zoe will ever have to go to the hospital, that this time she is coming home for good.

She looks down at her exercise book—religious studies, her least favorite subject—and cannot muster the motivation she needs to answer ten questions about the Good Samaritan. At ten years old, homework is the last thing Jess wants to do

when she gets home from school. Instead she emerges from her bedroom, thighs sticky with the early June heat, convinced that a chocolate Hobnob cookie—perhaps two—will help provide the enthusiasm she needs.

She hears Lily's voice before she reaches the top of the stairs, before Lily has a chance to see her. Her sister is on the phone in the hallway to one of her friends, whose identity Jess will never know.

"Yeah, she's coming home today. Mum and Dad are collecting her now . . . No, neither of them asked—I don't think they even remembered they were happening."

Jess crouches behind the banisters on the landing, her breath shallow in her chest.

It is rude to eavesdrop, Jess knows this, but it is a habit she seems unable to break. It is something Lily complains about frequently, causing the ridges across their mum's forehead to deepen, like a paper napkin folded back and forth in the making of a fan. It is this sight—her mum's weariness at having to mediate their squabbles—that provokes the feeling Jess has had ever since Zoe first became ill fourteen months ago: the feeling that someone has taken a pin and punctured her lungs so that all the air is slowly escaping.

"Yeah, I know they're only end-of-year exams, but still . . ." Lily's voice sounds strange, as though anger and sadness are performing a complicated dance in her mouth. "Sometimes it just feels like they've forgotten they've still got two other children. It's like we don't exist anymore . . . I don't know, I can't really explain it . . . No, that's fine, you get off . . . Yep, I'll see you tomorrow . . . Bye."

Jess unpeels her thighs and scrambles to her feet, tiptoeing silently into her bedroom, not daring to close the door for fear that the sound of it scraping against the carpet will betray her.

She slips back onto the chair at her desk and resolves to stay there until her parents get home.

Three days later, Jess is walking down the stairs to the basement kitchen when she is stopped by the sound of crying.

It is a quarter to seven on Sunday morning and she has woken earlier than usual, hunger growling in her stomach. She had assumed everyone else in the house would still be asleep, but there are three voices coming from the kitchen and Jess sits silently on the top stair, listening.

"It's not fair, Mum. Why is this happening to Zoe? Why can't it happen to someone else instead of her? It's just not fair."

Lily is crying: loud, convulsive sobs that make the hairs on Jess's arms stand on end.

"I know how hard this is, sweetheart. I know it's . . . horrific."

Her mum's voice wavers but Jess can tell she is trying to make herself sound calm.

"We just have to be strong for her, Lily. We just have to make sure she knows we love her and we're here for her."

Her dad is speaking now and for a few lonely seconds, Jess feels left out, as though the grown-ups and Lily are deliberately excluding her from a conversation she ought to be a part of. She imagines the three of them creeping down the stairs so as not to wake her or Zoe, imagines them having planned this secret rendezvous down in the farthest reaches of the house where they are unlikely to be heard.

"But she's in so much pain. It's horrible. No one should have to be in that much pain. I *hate* seeing her like this. We can't just sit by and watch her suffer and do *nothing*."

Lily is sobbing and Jess feels a frown pucker her forehead. It is news to her that Zoe is in pain. She has known, since

Zoe came home from the hospital three days ago, that her sister is very tired and needs lots of rest. She knows that she needs to be quiet so as not to disturb her, has perfected the art of tiptoeing up the stairs and across the landing as silently as a mouse. But no one has told her that Zoe is in pain. And the revelation makes her feel cold inside, as though someone has packed ice cubes around her heart.

"I'm sorry, Mum. I'm sorry for all those times I was jealous. I didn't mean it. I didn't mean any of it."

"Shh, stop that. You're a lovely sister to Zoe, to both of them. I know it's always been difficult, that you've always felt a bit left out, but you mustn't start thinking like that."

Jess rubs her fingers over the bridge of her nose. There is too much new information fighting for space in her head and it is beginning to ache.

"I don't understand why the doctors can't do more for her. It's inhumane. For goodness' sake, people do more for sick pets than they do for people. There must be *something* we can do. Please, Mum. Please, Dad. Please stop it. You *have* to. Please."

Lily is still crying—loud, heaving sobs—and Jess imagines her mum folding Lily into her arms, stroking her hair, kissing her forehead.

"I wish it could all be over."

"Don't you *dare* say that, Lily. Don't ever let me hear you say that again." Her dad's voice is sharp, as though you might cut yourself on it if you dared say more. It is a voice he uses only rarely—not a voice Jess remembers him using at all before Zoe got ill—and the sound of it reduces Lily's sobs to a gentle whimper. Jess does not know why but something in Lily's voice has caused the muscles in her tummy to coil like snakes. She replays Lily's lines over in her head but cannot

make sense of her feelings: Jess also wants Zoe's illness to be over, wishes more than anything that her sister could get better, yet something about the way Lily said it, and her dad's furious reply, will not sit comfortably in her head.

And then Jess hears the click of the kitchen door. She jumps to her feet, skitters noiselessly across the hall to the sitting room, and picks up a copy of *Anne of Green Gables*, ready to pretend she has been reading all along.

She does not yet know it but what she has just heard is a conversation she will remember verbatim for the rest of her life, the words replaying in her head on a never-ending loop.

It is eleven days since Jess overheard Lily crying with her mum and dad, wishing they could do something to stop Zoe's suffering, wishing it could all be over.

She doesn't know on this otherwise innocuous Thursday morning—unremarkable except that it is now exactly two weeks since Zoe came home from the hospital—what compels her to walk up the stairs. There is no need for her to do anything except put on her shoes and wait for Lily to come down. She has already brushed her teeth, pulled her hair into some semblance of a ponytail, packed her schoolbag. And yet she continues putting one foot higher than the other, climbing toward a future she cannot possibly predict.

Many years later she will come to believe that somehow she knew, somehow she guessed what was about to happen—what had already happened, too late for an intervention—an inexplicable sisterly intuition compelling her to investigate.

As she reaches the top of the stairs, Lily is coming out of Zoe's bedroom. Her back is turned to Jess and she closes the door quietly, reverentially almost, her hands clasped around the handle. Jess watches her take in a long, deep breath that

she seems to keep in her chest for an impossible length of time, as though perhaps if her lungs hold on to it for long enough, eventually she will be elevated like a balloon and fly away to some happier place.

"What are you doing?"

Lily jumps around, her face flushed, eyes darting from left to right as if scrabbling to get her bearings. "Why are you creeping up on me like that?" she hisses at Jess in an angry whisper that does not sound like her usual voice.

"We're not supposed to go in there this morning. We were told not to."

It is true. Less than forty minutes earlier, over breakfast, Jess had asked if she could say goodbye to Zoe before she left for school, but her dad's response had been one of those sighs that had gone on so long it had made Jess wish she'd never asked the question.

No, Zoe's resting this morning. You had a lovely time reading to her last night, didn't you? Just leave her be this morning, OK?

The way her dad had said it, Jess had known that, in spite of the upward inflection at the end of his sentence, he wasn't really asking a question at all.

It was true that the previous evening Jess had spent a lovely time with Zoe. She had curled up in the double bed in the spare room where Zoe now slept, and read aloud the collections of poems they used to recite as little children—*When We Were Very Young, Now We Are Six*—poems about beetles and bears and buttercup days that seemed to belong to a different, kinder world. Zoe had drifted in and out of sleep—she had done that a lot since she'd come home from the hospital—so Jess hadn't been sure how much she'd actually heard, but that hadn't mattered. She didn't mind that Zoe's room smelled a bit strange: a thick, sticky, sweet smell that clung to the hairs

inside Jess's nose and refused to be sniffed away. She just liked being close to her twin, cuddling up in bed together, just as they'd done every night before Zoe got ill.

"Do *not* tell Mum I was in there. I mean it, Jess. You don't want to be a telltale."

Lily's voice is quiet but firm, full of anger and warning, and there is a look in her eyes that Jess recognizes from all the times she has caught Lily using the telephone when their mum has told her not to, or the afternoons she has seen Lily smoking with her friends behind the children's playground in the park.

There is a moment of uncertainty, neither of them knowing what Jess's next move will be. Until her left foot joins her right on the top stair, Jess isn't sure what she's going to do next either.

"I want to go in too."

The two sisters glare at one another and Jess feels something pass between them: something unknowable yet frightening that she can't, or daren't, articulate.

"You are *not* to go in there, Jess. Do you hear me?"

Lily's body blocks the door, her arm stretched behind her as if in the process of being arrested. Around the corner of Lily's body, Jess can see her sister's hand gripping the handle, a final barrier should Jess get that far.

"But I want to. If you've been in there, why shouldn't I?" Jess edges along the landing, emboldened by what she senses to be Lily's fragile hold over the situation.

"Stop it. I mean it, Jess. You must *not* go in."

The expression on Lily's face sends a cold chill tiptoeing along Jess's spine: her sister's flushed cheeks, narrowed eyes, pinched eyebrows. The panic trying to disguise itself as authority. It is unclear whether Lily is about to defend herself

or launch an attack. Jess knows there is only one emotion that pulls her sister's face into that expression: guilt. Except this guilt is unlike anything Jess has seen before. It is so powerful that it saturates the empty space on the landing until Jess can feel it filling her lungs.

Fragments of Lily's telephone conversation from two weeks before begin to repeat in Jess's head like a musical refrain she is unable to silence. *Sometimes it just feels like they've forgotten they've still got two other children. It's like we don't exist anymore.* And then the memory of Lily sobbing to their mum and dad a few days later: *No one should have to be in that much pain. For goodness' sake, people do more for sick pets than they do for people. There must be* something *we can do. I wish it could all be over.* She remembers the strange voice with which Lily had spoken, and their dad's angry reply, a response Jess hadn't understood at the time. But now, all of a sudden, Jess feels as though she understands everything, all those conversations she was never meant to hear. And now that she does understand, she wishes with all her heart that she didn't.

Jess's stomach somersaults beneath the elasticized waistband of her bottle-green skirt. She feels the blood pulsing at her wrists, trying to force her to confront the possibility of what has taken place inside that bedroom. Her heart pounds as if her body is urging her into action. She imagines taking a step forward and pushing Lily aside, a struggle in which she manages—against Lily's advanced years and superior strength—to emerge victorious. But thoughts of what might happen afterward—what she might see and what she might learn—cement her feet to the floor.

The alarm on Lily's digital watch beeps. Lily jerks her hand to turn it off and Jess feels herself flinch. She knows it is Lily's 8:30 a.m. alarm, the one her sister has set to ensure they leave

for school on time now that their parents are too distracted to remind them. Lily holds Jess's gaze for a few seconds more until Jess is the first to turn her head away. Jess begins to make her way down the stairs, and only then does she realize that her legs are trembling. She hears Lily's footsteps close on her heels but does not turn around. She cannot bear to see that look on Lily's face again: a look that has told Jess something she does not want to know.

All the way down, Jess contemplates finding her mum, telling her where Lily has been, what she thinks has taken place inside that bedroom. But by the time Jess reaches the bottom stair, she knows she cannot. To tell her mum would be to voice suspicions Jess is not yet ready to assert, things she does not, at the age of ten, have the courage to say out loud.

Jess can barely breathe as she opens the front door. She has passed the day in a trance, the fear of what she might discover when she gets home churning in her stomach. As she walks through the door, anxiety scratches at her skin.

Stepping into the hallway, there is a stillness, as though her entry has disrupted the most delicate of equilibriums. She stops and listens, and it is then that she hears the noise that causes her heart to drum in her chest.

It is the sound of her mum crying. Not the quiet, muffled sobs Jess has become accustomed to in recent months, but noisy, uninhibited, primitive cries.

And in those few, potent seconds between entering the house and her dad opening the sitting room door and ushering her inside, Jess experiences a moment of clarity she has never known before.

She knows, immediately, that Zoe is dead. She knows that what she saw this morning—Lily standing outside Zoe's

door, face flushed with guilt, hands clutching the door handle, refusing Jess entry as if her innocence depended on it—was the aftermath of something so awful that to think about it makes Jess feel as though her heart is being clamped in a vise. She knows, as she enters the sitting room and falls into her mum's arms, that in spite of the way her mum holds her tightly, rocks her back and forth, says *I'm sorry, I'm so sorry*, over and over again, it is not her mum or her dad or even leukemia that is to blame for Zoe's death. It is Lily.

What Jess understands as she cocoons herself inside her mum's embrace—as hot, fat tears stream down her cheeks—is that she has lost not one sister today but two. She has lost the twin with whom her life has been inextricably linked since before they were born. Without her, Jess knows she will never feel complete again. But as grief squeezes her throat and blood pounds in her ears, she understands that Zoe is not the only sister she has lost today. She knows that she will never forgive Lily for what she has done. As of today, she is not one of three siblings but an only child.

The remainder of the afternoon passes in a blur and yet, in years to come, Jess will remember fragments of it in such microscopic detail it is as though her brain had been set on automatic timer, capturing individual frames at regular intervals: sitting next to Lily on the dusky pink sofa in the sitting room, flinching every time Lily tries to touch her, speak to her, catch her eye; the sound of murmured voices from the kitchen below rising up through the floorboards like audible phantoms, conversations Jess wants to be neither a part of nor excluded from; the front door opening and closing, anonymous footsteps padding along the hallway, some heading upstairs, others down; Mrs. Sheppard popping her permed head around the sitting room door, exchanging silent communications with

Lily that Jess is on the verge of being able to decipher but cannot yet decode; Lily trying to comfort her when all Jess wants is to shout at her: *I know what you did and I will never, ever forgive you.*

Shortly before the time they would normally have dinner, her mum comes into the sitting room and Lily leaves, saying she needs the bathroom. Jess knows that this is her chance to disclose what she saw, perhaps the only opportunity she will have all day.

She feels the revelation scorch her tongue, knows she must tell her mum what Lily has done. Her lips part, the accusation fizzing impatiently in her mouth.

But then, next to her, she hears her mum's chest heaving, followed by the most terrible, keening howl Jess has ever heard. Her mum holds Jess tight in her arms, and sobs ferociously until Jess's dad comes in to rescue them both.

Jess feels her lips close against an unspeakable truth.

She will tell her mum later, she thinks, when there are not so many people around, when the stillness is no longer punctured by grief and her mum's face has reverted to its normal shape.

Later, Jess thinks. Later she will be able to unburden herself of this terrible knowledge.

Two and a half weeks have passed since Zoe's death. The funeral has been and gone. The four remaining members of Jess's family move among one another like ghosts, unable—or unwilling—to acknowledge each other's grief.

Their mum has not yet returned to work and Jess has begun to speculate that perhaps she never will. Perhaps she will spend every day, forevermore, in her bedroom crying into the

duvet, as though the muffled sound does not travel through doors and walls, into Jess's bedroom with its redundant bunk beds where Jess has got used to plugging her fingers in her ears every night.

Today Jess sits cross-legged on the sofa watching *Blue Peter*. The presenters are in Russia, a country which seems so far away that it might as well be a foreign planet, but Jess likes the look of its grand palaces and deep blue rivers, and wonders whether she might, one day, see it for herself. She scratches at a gnat bite on her bare leg: she is wearing shorts and a T-shirt in honor of sports day earlier at school, Jess the only pupil without either parent to cheer her on. Her hand digs into the biscuit packet for her fourth chocolate digestive of the afternoon.

The door opens and as Lily walks into the room, Jess feels her stomach whirl like the drum of a washing machine.

"What are you watching, Jess?"

Jess ignores her and stares straight ahead at the TV.

"Jess? Did you hear me?"

Jess feels her heart thumping and hopes Lily cannot hear it. She does not want to give herself away, does not want Lily to guess what she knows, not before Jess has found the right time to tell their mum. But this is what happens now, whenever she and Lily are alone in a room together: Jess's body threatens to betray her. She does not know whether it is because she is scared she may say something she shouldn't, or because she knows what her sister is capable of.

Lily flops down on the sofa next to her and Jess instinctively shifts a few inches to the left.

"Are you OK, Jess? Look, I know how hard this is—especially with Mum being how she is right now—but things will get easier, I promise."

Lily's voice sounds different, as though she is trying on grown-up reassurance for size and discovering that it doesn't quite fit.

"Jess, please talk to me. I know how you feel. We're all grieving. We're all going through the same thing. I know it's worse for you because you two were so close, but you might feel better if you talk about it."

Jess does not know what it is that finally provokes her to ask the question that has been burning her tongue for eighteen days, but suddenly there it is between them before she has a chance to stop it.

"What happened in Zoe's bedroom that day?" Her voice sounds bolder than she had imagined it would.

"What day? What are you talking about?"

"The day Zoe died."

Panic skitters across Lily's face like marbles across cobblestones. "What do you mean, what happened? You know what happened."

There is such force in Lily's response that Jess's confidence begins to falter. But the look on Lily's face—the same expression she'd worn as she'd barricaded herself in front of Zoe's bedroom door—gives her the courage to continue. "No, I don't. And I want to know."

In the few hesitant seconds of silence, something more than fear or panic flares in Lily's eyes. There is guilt. And it is all the confirmation Jess needs.

Lily gets up from the sofa and storms toward the door, her voice trailing behind her. "You're being completely impossible, Jess. You're making everything harder for everyone. Just stop asking questions, OK? Just *stop it.*"

Lily charges out of the room and there is a part of Jess that wants to run after her, challenge her, finish a conversation that

has only just begun. But when she thinks about following Lily, when she thinks about saying what is really on her mind, her determination flounders. The accusation is so big and frightening, Jess can still not imagine saying it out loud. To say it aloud would be to give it a permanence she is not yet ready to accept.

Instead, she turns back to *Blue Peter*, to stories of a Russian world far enough away from her own to distract her from truths she does not know how to manage.

Almost exactly three months later, with the secret still burning in her chest, Jess's netball practice is canceled and she decides—on a whim she will never fully understand—to take herself home to an empty house. She plans to retrieve the spare front door key from the flowerpot in the garden shed and let herself in, to spend the next hour at home alone with a hot chocolate, Oreos, and *Grange Hill*. And it is there that she discovers her dad swinging from a beam at the top of the stairs, the cord of her mum's navy blue dressing gown knotted unambiguously around his neck.

What creeps across every inch of her skin—before the shock hits her brain, before the adrenaline floods her bloodstream, before the first screams erupt from her throat—is a white-hot fury like nothing she has ever experienced before. As she stands in the hallway of the only home she has ever known, looking up at her dad's body suspended from a makeshift noose, Jess experiences a febrile certainty that this is all Lily's fault.

As her first screams emerge, a single thought pounds inside Jess's head: Lily now has blood on her hands for the death of not one person but two.

For the next twenty-eight years, people will assume that the worst fate ever to befall Jess is to have discovered her father's

body at the top of the stairs. Jess will choose never to contradict them. She will tell no one the truth. She will never confess that in fact the worst thing that has ever happened to her is not her father taking his own life, but Lily taking Zoe's. She will never explain to anyone that, over the course of a single summer, she lost her entire family: the deaths of her twin sister and her dad; her older sister never to be trusted again; her mum forever at arm's length, Jess's determination to shield her from the truth creating an impenetrable barrier of tension and mistrust between them.

Zoe's death becomes, over the years, an all-consuming absence. It is an absence that leaves Jess feeling as though someone has sliced away a piece of her heart that she knows will never be returned and can never be replaced. And beyond Zoe's absence are the concentric circles of loss that ripple out from that kernel of grief: the adults Jess no longer trusts for their failure to prevent so heinous a crime; the friends and boyfriends she rejects for fear that intimacy may lead to disclosure; the family from whom she is estranged. It is knowledge that isolates Jess from the rest of the world, like a patient in quarantine who fears infecting others with the truth.

At times the loneliness devours her. There are moments when she has a burning need to confide in someone—therapists, telephone helplines, the police—but each time her courage fails her. She is too fearful of the evil spirits that may emerge if she opens that Pandora's box. Every time she imagines it, all she can picture is the horror on her mum's face: the shock, the pain, and the renewed grief.

Instead, Jess remains silent, conscious of her own impotence, the secret slowly strangling her every day of her life.

Chapter 47
Jess

A waiter brushed past Jess and she looked around the restaurant, the white noise of diners' conversations slowly filtering into her ears as though someone was turning up the volume and pulling her back into the present.

"Please sit down, both of you. Just for five minutes, that's all I'm asking."

There was desperation in her mum's voice and Jess didn't know whether to resent it or give in to it.

She watched Lily sit, sensed her mum silently urging her to do the same. Seconds passed, then half a minute, Jess's body tensing, urging her to leave. But then she thought about her mum singing onstage less than two hours before, the triumph on her face as she'd taken her fourth and final bow, and suddenly she found herself stepping forward, pulling out a chair at the end of the table, and sitting down.

Allowing her eyes to flick briefly to where Mia and Phoebe were sandwiching their grandmother, Jess fixed her gaze firmly forward as her mum took in a deep breath.

"I don't want to get maudlin but sometimes I can't help feeling that in the year Zoe and your dad died, someone pressed the emergency stop button on my life and I just stopped moving. It's as though I've spent the past thirty years

treading water and it's taken me all this time to see how static my life has been."

"Don't be silly, Mum, your life hasn't been static. You've done a brilliant, important job all these years—think of all those thousands of children you've encouraged to read. That's no small achievement. And what about us? You're an amazing mum, a wonderful grandmother. Your life hasn't been that bad, has it?"

Something familiar in Lily's voice—the need to be the first to dive in with proof that she was the kinder of the two sisters—caused Jess's back teeth to grind together.

"Of course it hasn't. I know I've been lucky in lots of different ways. But that doesn't mean there aren't other things I'd like to have done. Take tonight. Would I ever have joined a choir if I hadn't known I was dying? It's silly, really. We all know it's going to happen to us eventually and yet it's as though we don't want to accept that our time is limited until we're issued with a specific sell-by date."

There was a pause in which Jess sensed her mum biding her time.

"So that's why I've booked three first-class tickets to New York and five nights at the Plaza Hotel. It's over a weekend, so you'll only have to miss a couple of days' work. All I'm asking is that the two of you come away with me—together—to New York. Can you do that? Can you put your differences aside, just for five days?"

No one spoke. Around her, Jess could hear the ambient hum of other people's lives, but inside her head the prospect played itself out like a movie she wasn't sure she wanted to see: Jess, Lily, and their mum playing happy families in New York as if the last twenty-eight years had never happened; the three of them walking through Central Park, watching boaters on the lake, and stepping out of the path of speeding

skaters; drinking coffee on the High Line and looking out across the Hudson to New Jersey; navigating their way around the labyrinthine rooms of the Met and marveling at the views from Top of the Rock. Her mum smiling and laughing, one final wish granted.

The fantasy tugged at Jess's heart. It would be so easy to let out a single word that would make her mum happy. But then a memory crept into her head: lying in bed with Zoe that final night, reading her poems, watching her eyelids flutter, wishing she could share whatever deep sleep her sister was in, not knowing then that it would be the last time she would ever see her. Not knowing that the next morning she would spy Lily emerging from the spare room, see her barricade herself against the door, and watch the guilt, fear, and panic burn in her eyes.

"I can't. I'm sorry, I just can't."

"You *have* to, Mum! First-class tickets to New York? You can't say no. I'll go with Granny if you don't want to."

Jess shook her head, confirming a decision she knew to be right.

"Why not, Mum? It's *five days*, that's all. Stop being so selfish. It's not all about you, you know." Mia's voice was laced with frustration.

Jess looked at her daughter, wishing there was some way to explain the past without having to tell her anything at all. "Mia, please. There are lots of things you don't understand."

"Oh, I know. You've been telling me my whole life there are things I don't understand: that I'm too young or they're too complicated. But don't you think you owe it to Granny, to Aunt Lily, to tell *them* at least why you won't go?"

Aunt Lily. Three short, clipped syllables and yet enough to cause all the moisture to evaporate from Jess's mouth.

She looked at the four of them, watching her, waiting for an explanation they thought they wanted to hear, an explanation that, once heard, could never be unheard. A story that would haunt them just as it had haunted Jess all these years. She knew she couldn't do it to them. She wouldn't do it to her mum. "I can't. It's complicated. I just can't." Jess looked down, picked at the skin around the base of her thumbnail, tore at the cuticle until the first drop of blood oozed through.

"Please reconsider, Jess. It's only five days. Just five days with both of you—that's all I'm asking."

Jess watched as her mum reached across the table, as familiar fingers enfolded her hand and a sequence of memories flickered into view.

Waiting outside the classroom with Zoe, her collar rubbing against her neck, the line of pegs hanging with coats, bags, and cardigans: so many, how would she ever find out who they all belonged to? Something invisible bouncing around her stomach, like jumping beans. And then the squeeze of her mum's hand reassuring her that her first day at school was going to be OK.

Perched on a stool in the kitchen, hot tears soaking her cheeks, her left forefinger bent at an angle that even a seven-year-old could see wasn't right, her discarded bike lying on the kitchen floor, wheels still spinning. Her mum grabbing the car keys, calling to Lily to look after Zoe, mentions of hospitals and breakages and emergency departments. And then the clutch of her mum's hand telling her there was nothing that couldn't be fixed.

Queuing to enter the graduation hall, conscious of curious eyes flitting from her face to her tummy, its gentle curve concealed by the generous cut of her gown. Self-consciousness pinching her cheeks while the palm of her hand rested over the place

where six inches of life was just beginning to swallow, suck its thumb, hear Jess's voice. And then the clasp of her mum's hand telling her she was proud of her, whatever the circumstances.

Lying on the sofa, Mia curled up on her chest, at eight days old still preferring the fetal position she had been accustomed to inside Jess's womb. Jess's head heavy with fatigue, her breasts aching with the milk Mia was not yet able to drink despite repeated, frustrating attempts to help her latch on. And then the gentle fingers of her mum's hand telling her she could do this, she could be a good mother.

Sitting in an armchair, legs hugged tightly against her chest where panic knocked at a door she was too scared to open, Mia at her feet, pulling at threads on a rug Jess could not imagine ever being able to replace now that she was a single parent. *Single parent.* The phrase throbbing in her head, too new to feel real, less than three days since Iain had left her. And then the encircling of her mum's hand around hers telling her that this was not the end, just a different beginning, one she was capable of surviving.

A lifetime of love, reassurance, and pride expressed through the gentle containment of one hand inside another.

And then a more recent memory: sitting in the concert hall just a few hours earlier, watching her mum sing, feeling Mia's hand inside hers and knowing there would never be anything at once so simple and yet so complicated, so straightforward and yet so profound, as a child's hand held inside their mother's. A gesture which she had, for so many years, taken for granted.

As Jess glanced between her mum and her daughter she had an image of a future she hoped never to encounter: of sitting where her mum was now, Mia opposite, Jess asking her daughter for something so small—so undemanding—and Mia refusing.

"OK, Mum, I'll come. I'll come to New York."

Part Six

July

Chapter 48
Jess

A deep sigh emerged from the back seat of the car, and Jess glanced in the rearview mirror to where Mia was staring out of the window, chewing her thumbnail. She seemed distracted—anxious, almost—as though she cared more than anyone about whether or not Jess got on the plane. Jess still didn't understand why Mia had insisted on accompanying them to the airport but it had been too early in the morning for an argument.

In the passenger seat next to Jess, Audrey was fiddling with something in her bag. Jess had first heard her pottering around at half past five this morning and had already watched her unpack and repack her hand luggage at least half a dozen times.

There had been so many moments during the past four weeks that Jess had wanted to sit next to her mum at the kitchen table, clear her throat, and tell her that she was sorry, she'd spoken precipitately, she should never have agreed to the trip. So many nights since the concert at the Albert Hall Jess had lain awake in bed wondering how five days in New York with her mum and Lily could be anything other than disastrous.

Mia sighed again, and Jess's patience stretched like a rubber band on the brink of snapping. "What is it, Mia? You've been sighing in the back of the car ever since we left. I did say it

was too early for you to come with us. You're wasting the best part of a morning when you could be in the library."

Out of the corner of her eye Jess saw her mum turn to look at Mia, glimpsed a silent communication pass between them. "Mia, what is it? Whatever it is, just tell me."

Mia paused, and Jess detected another undecipherable look pass between them as her daughter fiddled with the silver stud in her ear.

"OK. Well, the thing is . . . there's something I haven't been entirely honest with you about. You know those Saturday mornings I said I was going to the library or studying at a friend's or whatever? Well, that wasn't exactly true. Granny and I . . . We've been going to that art class at the Royal College together, the one I told you about . . ."

As Mia's voice trailed off, the words took a few seconds to find form in Jess's head, like numbers in a color vision test emerging from a mass of dots. "You've been going to that art class together *behind my back*? I can't believe you've been colluding in this, Mum. What on earth were you thinking?"

"Don't be cross with Granny. She really didn't want me to lie to you, but she didn't understand any more than I did why you were so adamant I couldn't do it. It's just one morning a week."

"Please don't get angry, Jess. I know it was wrong of us to go behind your back but you can see how passionate Mia is about art. I honestly didn't think that one Saturday morning a week was going to be such a big issue."

"You and Mia both lying to me *is* a big issue. You know Mia doesn't have time for hobbies this year. How can she expect to get into Cambridge if she doesn't apply herself?"

Jess turned her head in time to see another surreptitious glance pass between her mum and her daughter: if she hadn't

had to look back at the road, she'd have sworn her mum had nodded at Mia.

"Well, that's the other thing, Mum. You know I love art—I've always loved it—and this course . . . Well, the tutor seems to think I'm pretty good. Really good, actually. She thinks that if I got a portfolio together I'd have a really strong chance of getting on an art foundation course after my A-levels. And when I spoke to my art teacher at school, he said the same thing. They've even said they'll write me references. So, the thing is . . . I don't think I want to go to Cambridge."

Jess was aware of words forming sentences but when she tried to replay them in her head she couldn't seem to structure them into meaning. "What are you talking about, Mia? Of course you're applying to Cambridge. You want to study English. That's been your plan for as long as I can remember."

"No, that's been *your* plan. *You're* the one who's always wanted me to go to Cambridge. *You're* the one who's been talking about it for as long as I can remember. Have you ever even asked me what I want?"

"What's got into you, Mia? Where's all this come from?" Jess pressed her foot down hard on the accelerator, watched the speedometer edge over the speed limit.

"Slow down, Jess. Please. Just listen to Mia. Let her explain."

Jess swerved into the outside lane, felt the pressure in her knuckles as her hands gripped the steering wheel. "Please don't tell me how to behave with my own daughter. You've clearly been party to all this, and for some inexplicable reason have chosen not to tell me, so I'm not really in the mood for maternal advice from you."

She pulled back into the middle lane, eased her foot off the accelerator, and glanced again in the rearview mirror. As she watched Mia undo her ponytail and retie it, it became

perfectly clear to Jess where the idea had come from. "It's Phoebe, isn't it? She's put you up to this. I *knew* I shouldn't have let that family anywhere near us. They're toxic. This is all her idea, isn't it?"

She sensed the tension in the car thickening, as though an invisible wall were being erected down the middle with Jess on one side, and her mother and daughter on the other.

"For goodness' sake, Mum, can't you even credit me with making my own decisions? This has got nothing whatsoever to do with Phoebe. If anything, it's Granny who's made me realize that it would be madness to spend my whole life doing something I don't want to do. I want to make you happy and proud of me, but can't you just let me do it in my own way?"

There was a heaviness in Jess's head, like the metal shutters of a migraine being drawn over her eyes. She felt oppressively tired, an overwhelming desire for the world to stop and let her off. "I don't know what you've been saying to Mia, Mum, but whatever it is, please can you tell her that you didn't mean it, that she's got it wrong. Please tell her that she needs to apply to Cambridge, just like she's always planned, even if she's having a bit of a wobble."

"I'm *not* having a wobble. Why can't you listen to what I'm saying? It's not my dream to go to Cambridge. It's yours. *You're* the one who's jealous of the fact that Aunt Lily went to Oxford when you didn't get the grades for Cambridge. *You're* the one who was pregnant by the time you sat your finals and who's spent the rest of your life regretting it as far as I can see."

"That's not true and you know it. Of course I don't regret it. How could I possibly regret having you? I love you. You're the best thing I've ever done with my life."

"It *is* true. You want to live your life through me. You want me to do all the things you failed to do when you were

younger. You want me to have all the same ambitions you used to have, just because you never got to fulfill them. And that's just not fair."

Jess drove as though her body had taken control of the car with no input from her brain. This was one of those rare moments when she dared to imagine how different her life might have been were she not always having these parental conversations alone.

As she pulled into the mid-stay car park at Heathrow's Terminal 5, Jess let Mia's words settle in her head. She could sense her mum staring at her but was too angry to turn and meet her gaze. "Mia, I know you're passionate about art, but that doesn't mean I should stand by and let you make mistakes I think you'll regret for the rest of your life. It's my job, as your mum, to protect you as much as I can, sometimes even from your own decisions."

"But I don't want your protection. If I'm going to have regrets, I want them to be mine, not yours. I've spent my whole life trying to be what you want me to be. I've never got into trouble, I've always got straight As, I've never set a foot wrong because it felt like you only loved me when I was doing everything right—"

"Come on, Mia, that's not fair. I'm sorry if—"

"Yes, it is, Mum. That's what it's always felt like. Can't you just let me do this one thing I want to do without making me feel as though somehow I'm letting you down?"

In the seconds that followed it seemed to Jess that every possible response ran through her mind. As she wended her way up the narrow ramps of the car park in search of a free space, it struck her that this was one of those moments when the stitches of her relationship with Mia eased loose and there was no way of knowing what pattern they would form when

they finally knitted back together. She knew, deep down, that it was only a matter of time: that she would, in the end, give her blessing, grant Mia the autonomy she craved if only so as not to lose her. But now, without understanding why, she couldn't seem to find the words to communicate any of that to Mia.

"I only want what's best for you."

"Fine. So stop going on about Cambridge and let me go to art college. I'm going anyway, whether you want me to or not."

As Jess nudged the car into a parking space she imagined getting out, folding her arms around Mia, holding her close, and blanketing their conflict in an embrace. She imagined reassuring Mia that she could never disappoint her, not really, because even the greatest maternal disappointments were shrouded in love.

But before Jess had a chance to do any of that—before she had found in the gap that had opened up between them the words to tell Mia that of course she would support her, whatever she wanted to do—Mia was getting out of the car, wishing her grandmother a good trip, slamming the door, and storming off toward the exit.

Jess yanked at her seat belt, the buckle sticking. She thrust her fingers down on the release button until she'd managed to free herself, clicked open the driver's door and scrambled out, an apology forming on her lips. But her words dissolved into the ether as Mia strode away, already halfway across the car park. Jess hesitated, contemplated following her, but then she glanced back into the car to see her mum looking at the clock on the dashboard, anxiety pinching the skin between her eyebrows. Jess looked up again and watched Mia go, watched her little girl get smaller and smaller until she had jumped through the elevator doors and disappeared altogether.

Chapter 49
Lily

There was a bleeping from Phoebe's phone and Lily watched—her skin prickling with irritation or heat, she wasn't sure which—as Phoebe read a message and tapped out a reply.

"For goodness' sake, Phoebe, do you have to be glued to your phone? Gran will be here soon and then I'll be leaving. I'm not sure why you insisted on coming if you were just going to be on your phone the whole time."

Around them on the airport concourse, taxis fought for prime drop-off positions as the humid July heat seeped into Lily's skin. It was early still but she could feel tiny beads of sweat gathering in the pores above her lips.

"Jesus, you can talk. You're never *off* your phone. I already told you, I want to see Gran off. This is quite a big deal for her, in case you hadn't realized. And I'm meeting Mia so we can head back into town and go to the film festival together."

Lily locked her jaw to stop herself replying. She knew Phoebe was baiting her. Ever since the truth had emerged about her daughter's friendship with Mia, it was as if Phoebe couldn't stop mentioning her cousin, pointing out that she had a relationship with her extended family even if Lily didn't.

"Phoebe, can't we wait inside? It's so muggy out here. I honestly don't understand why you've got such a hatred of air

conditioning, especially on days like this." There was a note of unintended impatience in Lily's voice. She didn't know why she felt so irritable. Perhaps it wasn't irritability so much as anxiety, or excitement even. It wasn't every day that you got on a plane to New York where your husband had been living for more than four months to pay him a surprise visit.

She'd told Daniel nothing about the trip, nothing about her mum arranging it all without her knowledge or the mock truce between her and Jess that felt like nothing more than a box-ticking exercise. Daniel would assume she was spending the weekend at home, seeing friends or catching up on work. But Lily had it all figured out. After dropping her bags at the hotel she'd head straight for his apartment. Even allowing for delays here and there, she should be at his front door by lunchtime. They'd have the rest of the day alone together.

"The thing is, there's something I want to talk to you about. Are you even listening?"

Lily had been miles away but she nodded anyway.

"There's something I need to tell you. And if you don't like it, that's your problem, there's nothing I can do about it. But you need to hear me out before you start going mental, OK?"

Lily felt the color drain from her cheeks. "What is it? What do you need to tell me?" Her voice had emerged a couple of tones higher than usual.

"OK, so here's the thing. I've been seeing someone for a while now. Just over a year, in fact. Sam. Their name's Sam. What I mean to say is . . . *her* name is Sam. She's a girl. The person I'm seeing is a girl. The thing I'm trying to tell you is that I'm gay."

Stories began rewriting themselves in Lily's head, scenes from Phoebe's adolescence slotting into place like in a game of Tetris.

"Are you going to say something or are you just going to stand there, staring at me?"

Lily understood that she had to speak, that she needed to find the right words and deliver them in the right order, and scrabbled frantically for an appropriate response. "You're sure?"

The moment she asked the question, Lily knew it was the wrong one. She prepared herself to apologize, to blame her crass response on the unexpectedness of it all, but Phoebe was already talking.

"Yes, I'm *sure*. Do you really think I'd be telling you if I wasn't? What do you think this is? Some kind of passing fad I'll recover from with the right vitamins? For God's sake, I've just told you I'm gay and all you can do is ask me if I'm sure."

"I'm sorry, darling, I'm really sorry. That came out all wrong. I didn't mean it like that." If in doubt, apologize. It was the only useful lesson Lily had taught herself since Phoebe had hit adolescence.

"So what *did* you mean?"

Lily needed time to think, to rehearse the words before she released them into the world, but Phoebe was glaring at her. "I just meant . . . I just want you to have a happy life, that's all."

"*Happy*? What's that supposed to mean? Can't gay people be happy? What is this—the nineteenth bloody century?"

"I didn't mean that, you know I didn't. Don't put words in my mouth."

"So what *did* you mean? What 'happy life' are you talking about?"

Lily paused. Sometimes in conversations with Phoebe she could feel her daughter pulling her toward a flaming pyre of disagreement and however hard she tried to rein them both back to safety, Phoebe's grasp was always stronger. "You know what I mean. You're being deliberately obtuse."

"No, I'm not. It's not like I'm *choosing* to be gay as some kind of lifestyle statement. What exactly do you mean by being 'happy' anyway? Do you mean happy like our family?"

"There's no need to take that tone, Phoebe. But yes, if you want to put it like that."

Phoebe began to laugh, not the kind of laughter that invited participation but the kind that made it clear Lily had said something incredibly stupid.

"What's funny?"

"If you think our family's happy then I'd hate to see your definition of unhappy. Dad lives three and a half thousand miles away and we haven't seen him in over four months. Your sister can't bear to be in the same room as you and wouldn't even let me meet my cousin for seventeen years because she hates you so much. And now you're heading off on this transatlantic trip with Gran based on a half-baked fantasy that you're all going to come home gloriously reunited. And you call *that* happy?"

Phoebe laughed again—high-pitched, grating—and Lily felt as though she'd been deposited on top of a mountain at an unfeasibly high altitude. "Phoebe, I know you're upset, but that's no excuse to speak to me like that. I'm sorry I didn't realize about you being gay, but you must know I wouldn't have a problem with it. You *must* know that. I'm sorry I didn't guess without you having to tell me. You're my daughter and I probably should have intuited it but I didn't, I had no idea, and I'm sorry."

"Of course you had no idea. How can you have any idea about anything when you're never around?"

"That's not fair. I'm not never around. You're the one who's barely at home these days, and that's fine—you're a teenager, I expect you to be out and about with your friends. But please don't attack me for it."

"So it's all my fault you work every waking hour? It's because I'm never home? So what's your excuse for never being at home when I was little? What's the reason you missed practically every sports day, every nativity play, every school concert? What's the reason you turned up late to every parents' evening, as though somehow you were more special than everyone else and all the teachers should have to wait for your arrival, like you were the Queen of bloody Sheba? Do you know something? When I was little I thought I must have done something really naughty because you were never at home. Because it was the nanny who took me to school, who collected me afterward, who listened to stories about what I'd been doing all day. Because she was the one who spent every afternoon painting pictures with me and acting out *The Lion King* or *Sleeping Beauty*, who cooked my dinner and sat next to me while I ate it, who played games with me at bath time and read books before bed. I spent years thinking there must be something wrong with me because you weren't one of the mums who ever picked up their child from school. So was that my fault too? Was that my fault for being so stupid when I was five years old?"

Phoebe glared at her and Lily felt something shift between them, something she wouldn't have been able to articulate even if she'd dared to try.

"I'm sorry you think I got it so wrong. I thought I was doing the best for everyone, for you and for me. I wanted to be a strong role model for you. I wanted you to know that you had choices, that anything was possible."

"I know that, I get it. But when you're little you don't want a role model. You just want a mum."

There was a hairline fracture in Phoebe's voice that made Lily want to reach out, enfold her daughter in her arms, let

her know that everything was going to be OK. But something stopped her. Because it was only in preparing to hug Phoebe that Lily realized she couldn't remember the last time she had.

Her phone bleeped in her hand. She looked down, saw an email from her boss flash up, felt herself hesitate.

"Oh yes, Mum, you'd better look at that. Let me guess—work? You couldn't possibly keep them waiting while you actually have a conversation with your daughter, could you?"

Lily flushed, felt her fingers itch with temptation, and then shoved the phone into her pocket. "I don't know what to say, Phoebe. I did the best that I could. I'm sorry if it wasn't enough."

"*Do not* say you're sorry. I'm *sick* of hearing it. You seem to think it's a get-out-of-jail-free card but it's not and I've had enough of it. I've had enough of pretending everything's perfect when it's not. I've had it with the pretense and the lies and the sham of it all. You go off to America, have a good trip, and when you come home you can act like none of this ever happened, just like you always do."

Phoebe's invective fired at Lily like bullets from a machine gun. Lily wanted to say something, to find whatever words would mend a relationship she hadn't realized was so broken. But it was as though things she had thought were solid had begun to melt, and she was watching them leak away from her.

She felt her phone vibrate again in her pocket—once and then a second time—and the thought of those messages from work demanding an immediate response, even as they were in the process of discarding her, caused her fingers to find the phone's power button and press down hard to turn it off.

Phoebe was still staring at her, waiting for a reply. *I'm sorry,* Lily wanted to say. *I'm sorry I got it all so wrong. I've given all my time to a job that doesn't even want me anymore and now there's no way I can turn back the clock and do things differently.*

A thought slid into her head: maybe it wasn't too late to do things differently. Maybe she should embrace the redundancy, spend some quality time with Phoebe. Perhaps they could both spend the summer in New York with Daniel. And maybe, when she got back, she could look for a job that might give her more purpose, more meaning. Perhaps it might not be too late to rectify her mistakes after all.

"I'm sorry, Phoebe. Perhaps if we—"

"I *don't* want to hear it, Mum. Your apologies are meaningless. You're never going to change, *never.* And I've had enough of it."

Phoebe turned and ran into the airport terminal. Lily's hand reached out toward her just a fraction too late, the rest of her explanation shriveling on her tongue. She moved to follow, to tell Phoebe there was still time, there was still a chance for them to have the relationship Phoebe wanted—that Lily wanted too—her heart suddenly aching with love as though a dam had burst after years of restraint. But by the time she had hauled her suitcase through the revolving doors and into the terminal, Phoebe had vanished.

Chapter 50
Audrey

Nine hours later, a yellow taxi snaked through the midday Manhattan traffic, horns blaring, sunlight glinting on buildings that stretched up as if to touch the sky. Audrey gazed out of the cab window at a view that looked less like a city and more like a movie set. She couldn't believe she was actually here.

It was only now that she could see the pinnacle of the Chrysler Building gleaming in the sunshine that she realized how deep her fear had been that she might not make it. She watched the steam rising from manhole covers and smelled the perversely delicious mix of car fumes, hot tarmac, and burning ambition all cooked together in the sweltering July heat. So many times over the past month she had imagined all the things that might have stopped her making this trip: Jess announcing she'd changed her mind; Lily deciding she couldn't possibly leave work, even for a few days; her doctor prohibiting long-haul travel. So many obstacles, both real and imagined. But now she was here.

Inside the handbag clasped tightly on her lap, next to the Trebor Extra Strong Mints, a half-used packet of tissues, and her anti-nausea medication, nestled Audrey's diary from 1969. It had felt only right to bring it with her. Without it, she might never have remembered how much her sixteen-year-old self had wanted to come.

Audrey glanced sideways, at Lily next to her and Jess in the front passenger seat, both of them staring out of the window. They'd barely uttered a word since they'd left London. Jess was clearly still furious with her and had watched movies back-to-back throughout the journey, while Lily had spent most of the flight under her eye mask, complaining of a headache. Any attempt to engage either of them in conversation had been met with monosyllabic responses until Audrey had swallowed her disappointment and instructed herself to be patient. She couldn't expect decades of estrangement to be resolved during the course of one flight across the Atlantic.

But now, driving through the streets of Manhattan, Audrey felt irritated that her daughters couldn't put aside their differences just for a few minutes so she could enjoy her first glimpses of a city she had waited so long to see. She turned to look out of the window—at the New York Public Library, Rockefeller Center, Radio City Music Hall—trying not to let the atmosphere spoil the moment completely.

Leaning forward to retrieve a bottle of water from her hand luggage, a sharp pain stabbed behind her sternum. She tried not to wince, tried to stop the discomfort writing itself onto her face. She couldn't let them know how much pain she was in. For weeks she'd been falsely reassuring them that her symptoms were stabilizing, that she was plateauing rather than declining. She'd insisted, time and again, that she was definitely well enough to go on this trip. If they knew how much her health had deteriorated over the past three weeks, they'd never have agreed to get on the plane with her.

Looking up, expecting to see her own anxiety reflected back at her in her daughters' faces, she was instead met by the backs of their heads. She rubbed a hand against the bony wall of her chest, breathed slowly, and turned to look out of the window.

Ahead of her she saw the trees of Central Park but before she'd had a chance to absorb the sight, the cab swerved into the main entrance of the Plaza Hotel, the car door opened, and a man in a navy blue uniform—complete with peaked cap—welcomed her to New York. As Audrey stepped out of the cab and onto the checkerboard concourse, she tried to focus on all the things she might be able to say and do over the next few days to bring her daughters back together.

Fixing her family: it was the only thing that mattered. And Audrey had five days in which to achieve it.

Chapter 51
Lily

Eighteen blocks and fifteen minutes later, on a road running perpendicular to Central Park, Lily stepped out of a cab. Humidity enveloped her like a thermal blanket she was unable to shrug off. Her mum had tried to persuade her against going straight to Daniel's apartment—had suggested she settle in at the hotel and freshen up first—but Lily hadn't wanted to waste any time.

The house in front of her looked just like the photo Daniel had sent: steps climbing up to a wide front door, black railings on either side, a redbrick building nestled between two elegant cream town houses.

Lily pulled out her compact, pressed some powder onto her nose, reapplied her dark red lipstick. She felt girlish almost, like a teenager arriving for a first date. She instructed herself not to be silly, reminded herself that this was Daniel, her husband of eighteen years, and she was turning up in New York to surprise him. It was, she thought, exactly what their relationship needed: spontaneity, excitement, a reordering of priorities.

She walked up the steps, reached the glass door, looked at the list of names next to the buzzers—Cohen, Harris, Garcia, Perez. Goldsmith was about halfway down, innocuously typed, nothing to suggest that Daniel was a temporary guest of the city.

Later Lily would not be able to explain what had made her finger hover above the buzzer, would not know what had caused her to hesitate as though the scene had been paused by an invisible third party. She would not know what had prompted her to press her face to the glass door, cup her hands around her eyes to shut out the light and peer into the building's lobby like a Peeping Tom. None of these things Lily would ever be able to explain beyond the slippery answer that somewhere, deep down, she must have known.

Lily pressed her face to the glass and it was as if the world had stopped turning on its axis.

On the other side of the door, Daniel stepped out of the elevator, laughing. As he took another step into the small lobby, Lily saw that his arm was outstretched around someone's shoulders, that the shoulders belonged to a young, flame-haired woman wearing a cream silk blouse and scarlet lipstick, that the two of them were laughing, heads bent together, as if sharing the most delicious joke in the world.

Time seemed to slacken as Daniel and the redhead turned toward the door. Lily saw the woman's eyes widen in surprise, watched her lipsticked mouth form into a perfect shocked circle, caught a glimpse of Daniel's startled expression.

Lily felt herself back away from the door but then it opened and there he was, standing in front of her. And Daniel's first words were not *It's great to see you* or *What a lovely surprise* or *I'm so pleased you're here.* Lily's husband stood and stared at her as if he didn't quite recognize her.

"Lily, what on earth are you doing here?"

Chapter 52
Audrey

Lying on the super-king-sized bed, three goose-down pillows under her head, Audrey understood why the rich always wanted to get richer: once you'd had a taste of this, you'd never want to give it up.

There was a gentle knock at her hotel room door. She moved to lift herself onto her elbows but her limbs felt impossibly heavy. Parts of her body she hadn't consciously registered before were making themselves known to her, clamoring for attention, trying to prove that each could ache more than the last.

"Mum? Are you in there?" Jess's voice drifted through the locked door.

"Yes, I'm just coming." Audrey tried to swing her legs over the edge of the bed but they seemed glued to the duvet. She rolled onto her side, felt a sharp skewer of pain dig into her right shoulder, managed to stifle a cry before it escaped her lips.

All she had to do was get off the bed. How hard could it be? She must have done it thousands of times before. And yet now it seemed that her limbs wouldn't comply with a task she'd spent sixty-two years taking for granted.

"Mum? What are you doing?"

Jess's voice oozed concern and Audrey knew she needed to nip it in the bud before the trip was declared over before it

had barely begun. Sucking air through her lips and clamping her jaw shut, she hoisted herself onto her elbows and forced her legs over the side of the bed. Breathing out slowly, she willed the heaviness to drain from her body.

Why had no one warned her that, at some point during her illness, even the simplest of tasks would denude her of all energy?

Pushing herself to her feet and ignoring the pain griping in her shoulder, Audrey walked toward the door, remembering just in time to pull her face into a smile.

"Is everything all right? You took ages to answer."

Audrey nodded, trying to look reassuring. "I was just enjoying the view. I didn't realize we'd be quite so high up. How's your room?"

"It's absolutely amazing. Thank you so much."

Jess pulled her into an embrace and breathed a kiss into her hair before walking into Audrey's room toward the two armchairs by the window overlooking Central Park.

"So what's on our itinerary this afternoon, Mum? We could try getting up the Empire State Building or Top of the Rock? Though maybe we should do those early one morning when they're less busy. I know you want to walk the High Line but it's a bit of a schlep from here and we might be pushed for time. Is there anything you're really desperate to do? It is our first afternoon, after all."

Audrey fought the desire to close her eyes, to let her chin rest on her chest, to sink into whatever temporary oblivion her body was craving. Out of the window, cars circled the park and in the shadow of skyscrapers people scurried through the streets like ants in a colony, keeping the city moving. This was a city teeming with life. And that was why she'd wanted to come: to drink its elixir the way others might swallow holy water from Lourdes.

"The park. Let's go to the park. It seems silly not to when we're so close and it's such a glorious afternoon. At least there'll be shade."

At least, Audrey thought, there'll be benches.

As she leaned forward to pull on her shoes, another surge of pain jabbed at her shoulder: fiercer, sharper, more insistent than before. Audrey ground her teeth, pulled her body up straight, and hauled herself to her feet.

Chapter 53
Lily

On the steps of Daniel's apartment block, Lily's husband was staring at her, waiting for her to speak. There had been a question but Lily couldn't remember now what it had been. The only thing she could remember was the sight of Daniel with his arm around the young redhead, who was now standing at his shoulder, frowning. "What . . . I don't . . . What's going on, Daniel?" Lily's voice felt small, as though her lungs had been pierced and all the air she breathed in leaked straight out again.

"Sweetheart, could you give us a few minutes?"

Lily looked up at Daniel, wondering where he meant her to wait, what he expected her to do. But Daniel wasn't looking at her. He was looking at the redhead. He was looking at the redhead and calling her sweetheart and directing her back upstairs to his apartment.

Something crumpled in her chest, her breath trapped beneath the rubble. Her legs, as she turned and ran back down the stone steps, felt weak as though her bones had been removed and only some strange force of momentum was keeping the muscles and the flesh moving.

"Lily! Wait! For God's sake, just wait!"

Lily kept on running, each step pounding into her ankles through the high heels of her shoes.

"Lily! What are you doing? Where are you going?"

Ahead of her Lily saw the main road and beyond it the green trees of the park. All she had to do was get to the park. If she could just get to the trees she might be able to breathe.

She felt a hand grab the top of her arm, felt Daniel's fingers sink into her flesh, and imagined the quintet of small red circles they'd leave behind. "For God's sake, Lil. You can't just run away—we need to talk. You need to let me explain."

His voice was raised, exasperated. Lily shook herself free and ran across the road, car horns trailing behind her. She stumbled forward into the park, Daniel close on her heels, calling her name.

Not sweetheart. Not darling. Just Lily.

She kept on running: past joggers, dog walkers, men in suits on mobile phones, women pushing strollers. She kept on running because while she ran, the world was a blur and she wasn't yet ready to pull it into focus.

Ahead of her in the middle of the park was Belvedere Castle, like something out of a fairy tale. Lily ran toward it, up the steps, onto the terrace overlooking a lake, and found herself trapped with nowhere to run.

"I'm sorry, Lil. I'm sorry."

She could feel the heat of Daniel's breath on her cheek but didn't turn to look at him.

"I didn't want you to find out like this. I didn't mean to hurt you. Please believe that. It's the last thing I wanted to do."

His words were muffled, as though her head were deep underwater and he was speaking to her from high above its surface.

"Shit, this is all such a mess. I was going to tell you, honestly. I was going to tell you soon."

Lily wanted him to stop talking, wanted to tell him that she couldn't bear to hear his voice because with every word he eroded any hope that this was all some dreadful misunderstanding.

"Say something, Lil. Please."

She was aware of her nails digging into her palms: a sensation, not a feeling. There was no pain, just an understanding that it ought to hurt but didn't, like the tugging of stitches under a local anesthetic. "How long?" She heard his hesitation in the silence, heard the clanking of scales as he weighed the pros and cons of telling her the truth.

"A year. Just over."

Lily heard herself gasp, felt the shock rattle between her ribs. But still she felt nothing: just fractals of ice creeping up from her stomach and crystalizing around her heart. "But I asked you. I asked you explicitly on the phone *three weeks* ago. And you categorically denied it. You told me I was being silly."

"I'm sorry. You caught me off guard. And I couldn't tell you on the phone. But I don't want to lie to you anymore."

"You don't want to lie to me? What do you think you've been doing for the past year? Our whole family—our whole life—is a lie."

Her voice was thin and shrill, a voice she didn't recognize.

Scenes from their marriage began to tug at her memory. The restaurant receipts she had thought unlikely venues for client dinners. The weekends he'd ventured to the office when he could have worked from home. The last-minute trips to film sets that had never been necessary before. All those nights—dozens of them—when he'd been working late and then showered as soon as he'd returned, saying he needed to wash the day off his skin. He had covered the tracks of his infidelity with little white lies he had known she was too busy to question, and she had walked behind him, blindly smothering the evidence.

"That's not true, Lil. Of course it isn't. I didn't plan for this to happen, it just did. Please don't make this any harder than it already is."

His voice was imploring, as though he had the right to ask anything of her.

"You don't want this to be hard? You think this should be easy? You detonate our lives and you think we're all going to walk away unscathed? That's not how this works, Daniel." She had wanted her voice to remain calm and controlled but anger rumbled beneath it like distant thunder. "Who is she?"

Daniel groaned and a ripple of impatience skimmed across the surface of Lily's fury.

"Who is she, Daniel? I want to know." She sounded convincing, no trace of the fear of his answer.

"She's a lawyer, from a different firm. We met at a conference."

So factual, so unsentimental. Lily almost felt like punching him.

"What's she doing here? Is that why you haven't come home at all? Has she been coming here instead? For God's sake, Daniel, you haven't seen our daughter except on Skype in over four months and for what? So you can have your mistress come and visit you instead?"

An almost imperceptible twitch flickered at the corner of Daniel's left eye. Lily had seen it countless times over the year: an unmistakable tell. "What is it? What aren't you telling me?"

He raised his head, catching her gaze before evading it, like a moth fluttering too close to a flame. "She lives here. Amy. She lives in New York. She's American."

The words took a few seconds to attach themselves to meaning. "You moved here *for her*? I don't believe I'm hearing this. I can't believe you could be so duplicitous, so devious. You moved your career—your life—here for *her*?" A sharp acidity bubbled in the back of Lily's throat. So many lies, so much deceit. And then she remembered.

Sweetheart, could you give us a few minutes? The way he'd said it, the way he'd directed her back upstairs.

"You're living with her, aren't you? You're actually bloody living together. I'm right, aren't I?"

Daniel dropped his eyes to the ground and Lily heard the deafening slam of one door closing and the palpable silence where another failed to open.

I've had it with the pretense and the lies and the sham of it all.

Phoebe's words echoed in Lily's ears. "Phoebe doesn't know, does she? There's no way she could have found out?"

Daniel looked up and frowned. "Of course not. How could she? I've been really careful."

He spoke with such earnest reassurance, as though Lily should find comfort in his vigilance.

"But Phoebe gets it, Lil. Before I left, we talked . . . She could tell things weren't right."

He said it as though it were a fact of which they should both be proud: that their seventeen-year-old daughter had seen the writing of their marriage on the wall long before Lily had.

She thought about her conversation with Phoebe earlier, about her fantasy that the three of them might spend the summer together in New York. Humiliation scorched her cheeks at the memory of such a recent delusion.

Lily glanced at Daniel and felt the distance open up between them. She had an urge to walk away, to get a cab to the airport and fly back to London on the next available plane, to hold Phoebe in her arms and begin to rebuild their fragile relationship. But first she needed to hear the rest of Daniel's story, like a self-harmer slicing a razor blade across raw flesh.

"So what was your plan? When were you going to tell me? Or were you just going to stay here, living your double life indefinitely, hoping I might throw in the towel first?"

They looked at one another directly for the first time and

she saw it immediately: not just the sadness but the fear. The tangible fear of a secret yet to be confessed.

"What is it, Daniel? Just tell me. Whatever else there is, just bloody tell me."

There was a heartbeat of silence in which a thousand permutations spun through Lily's head. But when Daniel finally spoke—when he finally gave her the missing piece of the puzzle—it was too awful for her even to have imagined it.

"Soon. I was going to tell you soon. I'm . . . We're . . . Amy's three months pregnant."

And with those four short words, Lily heard the decisive sound of her marriage ending.

She stared at the whiteness of her knuckles gripping the castle's stone wall. She couldn't look at Daniel, couldn't bear to see whatever counterfeit expression he'd painted on his face.

He'd been adamant, immovable. She could hear him now, during those endless, cyclical arguments they'd had in the months after her third and final miscarriage.

I don't want another baby, Lil. To be honest, I never understood this automatic need to have more than one child.

I like our family the way it is.

We tried—three times we tried—because that was what you wanted to do. And it didn't work out.

Please let's just be happy with what we have.

Three months pregnant. By the New Year, Daniel would be a father again.

"Lil, I don't want this to be any harder on you and Phoebe than it has to be. You can have whatever you want: the house, money, whatever. I just don't want things to get ugly between us. Do you think we can do that?"

His voice was calm, soothing, the voice someone might use to bring a child out of a tantrum. Except Lily wasn't having a tantrum. Lily was watching her life implode.

"Lil, please. I know this is hard, and I'm sorry. I never meant for this to happen. I never wanted to hurt you. But I honestly think it'll be easier on both of us—and Phoebe—if we're able to keep things civilized. I'll take all the blame. You can petition me on the grounds of adultery. It only needs to be as difficult as we make it."

He had it all worked out: a petition for adultery, the quickest route to a clean divorce, leaving him free to marry the redhead before the ink had dried on their divorce decree.

"Part of me will always love you, Lil. Always. But surely you must know things haven't been great between us these past few years. I don't know . . . After all those miscarriages . . . I never felt like we'd just lost a baby. I always felt we'd lost a little piece of our marriage too."

The back of Lily's throat burned. She thought about her lost babies, those ghostly figures of children who would never take up their rightful place in the family yet never altogether disappear. "Why didn't you tell me sooner? If you wanted to be with her so much, why didn't you just leave me?"

Daniel hesitated. "I don't know. I wasn't sure, I suppose."

"You weren't sure about *what*?"

"I wasn't sure about anything. For God's sake, it's not a decision I've taken lightly. I didn't know until I got here—until Amy and I were living together—that things were going to work out between us."

It took a moment for Lily to understand what he meant. "You were *hedging your bets*? You came out here to *test the water*? And what were you going to do if it didn't work out? Come back to me? Pretend nothing had ever happened? Wait

until someone else came along? I can't *believe* your audacity, Daniel. I can't believe you could be so selfish, so calculating."

Lily watched Daniel's eyes flick up to the left, as they always did when he was in the wrong, the way his lips rolled inward when he was lost for words, the way his fingers rubbed against one another when he was agitated. And in that moment she hated him. She hated him for calling time on their marriage without so much as a warning. Hated him for not having had the courage to leave her until he'd already replaced her. Hated him for the biological injustice that he could start a whole new family. More than anything she hated him for the inequity of it all.

Lily released her hands from their grip on the stone wall, took a step backward, and began to walk away. Her legs felt as though they were no longer attached to her body, seemed to be moving independently of the rest of her. Her head felt light, as though it had been emptied of everything she thought she knew about her life. Just a single thought went around in her mind: that she needed to keep going, putting one foot in front of the other, and accept the fact that she didn't know where she was heading or where she might end up.

"Lil? Where are you going? You can't just leave. We need to talk."

Lily whipped her head around and looked directly into Daniel's eyes. "*I* can't just leave? You're the one doing the leaving, Daniel. You're the one who's shacked up in New York with a mistress half your age. You're the one who's about to become a father again at nearly fifty, with no thought at all for the daughter you've abandoned in London. You're pathetic, do you know that? You're pathetic and cowardly and a total bloody cliché. So do not tell me I can't leave. I didn't do this. *You* did it. And now you don't get to decide what happens next."

Chapter 54
Audrey

Sitting on a bench in Central Park, overlooking the boating lake, Audrey hoped that if she surrendered to the pain in her chest it might grant her a brief respite.

Cancer was like that, she'd discovered. It turned you into someone in a permanent state of negotiation, bargaining with the intruder inside your body. Audrey would find herself offering deals to it, anticipating their rejection, proposing new terms. But cancer was an unreliable business partner, constantly making ever greater demands for less favorable returns.

Right now, all Audrey wanted was to enjoy her first afternoon in New York: to walk around a park she had seen in so many photographs and films that visiting it now gave her an uncanny sense of déjà vu.

Next to her, Jess flicked through a guidebook with unintentional impatience, wanting to see things, do things, make the most of their time. Audrey would have been like that once too. She would have wanted to cram in as much sightseeing as possible, to tick off all the major attractions and fulfill a set of objectives. Now all she wanted was to sit quietly and soak up the atmosphere.

Dotted across the lake, boats were being rowed by young couples, enthusiastic dads, groups of laughing girls. As Audrey

looked out across the water, wondering if she dared risk embarking on the next stage of their walk, someone caught her eye hurrying along the path toward them. "Lily? Lily! We're over here."

As Lily raised her head and turned toward them, Audrey saw immediately the creased forehead, the red eyes, the pinched eyebrows. As Lily sat down on the bench next to her, Audrey could see she was trembling. "What is it? Whatever's the matter?"

Audrey listened in silence as Lily gabbled a story about Daniel and a redhead, about a pregnancy and a divorce, all the time wondering how it was possible that she could think herself so close to her daughter yet know so little about her life. "Why didn't you tell me there were problems between you and Daniel?"

There was a microscopic quiver in Lily's chin that Audrey last remembered seeing decades before in the wake of their double loss, accompanied by the muffled echo of restrained grief.

"He said he just needed some space. I thought everything would go back to normal once he was home."

Lily's voice flatlined, and she stared straight ahead as if gazing toward a future she didn't dare approach.

All this time Audrey had allowed herself to believe that Lily was strong, secure, unshakable. Five months earlier she'd moved in with Jess rather than Lily, to live with the daughter who needed her rather than the daughter whose life, she'd believed, was perfect. Now she felt as though she had failed them both.

With Jess sitting silently next to her, Audrey sensed something stir in the atmosphere, as if somewhere out to sea a hurricane was gathering pace and the winds on land were eddying in response.

Chapter 55
Jess

Jess sat unmoving as her mum held Lily's hand.

It had always been like this, for as long as she could remember. Lily, the good girl, who could do no wrong. Lily, the chosen one, who deserved the very best life had to offer. Lily, the innocent, to whom nothing bad should ever happen. Except she wasn't. And it had.

"Maybe it's karma, Lily." The words whispered their way through Jess's lips. Her heart knocked in her chest, warning her of what was to come, cautioning her that once the story was out in the world there was no way of erasing it from their family history.

Jess watched Lily raise her head from their mum's shoulder, watched her widen her bloodshot eyes, thin red lines streaking above her green irises like a pastoral sunset.

"What do you mean?"

"You know exactly what I mean." Jess tried to encourage some air into her lungs, willed her voice to stay strong.

Lily glanced at their mum as if she might hold the answer.

"What are you talking about, Jess? What karma? What could Lily possibly have done to deserve this?"

Perhaps it was the incredulous tone of her mum's voice. Perhaps it was Lily's self-righteous tears. Or perhaps it was

simply the change of scene. But suddenly decades of unspoken fury were erupting from deep within Jess where they had lain dormant for decades. "Stop pretending, Lily. Stop lying. You know what you did and so do I. I saw you. Don't pretend you don't remember. You know I saw you."

She watched Lily turn to their mum, saw the almost imperceptible shake of her head, watched the lines furrow across Lily's forehead as she turned back to her. "I don't know what you're talking about. What do you think you saw?"

And there it was, before Jess had a chance to stop it: the ticking bomb that had always been destined, one day, to explode. "I *saw* you! The day Zoe died I saw you coming out of her room. I saw the expression on your face. You were white as a sheet. It was so obvious something had happened in there but you wouldn't let me in, you barricaded yourself against the door, and I knew—I just *knew*—something terrible had happened. And then I got home from school and Dad told me Zoe had died that morning, and he said she'd died naturally in her sleep, but I knew what had happened. I knew it was you. I've always known it was you."

Chapter 56
Audrey

Beads of sweat trickled down Audrey's spine and pooled in the small of her back. Scenes she had packaged up so carefully and sealed in boxes many years ago ripped themselves open, the past fighting its way into the present. All this time, unbeknown to her, Jess had been rummaging inside those boxes like a child in a dress-up chest, discovering a version of family history that didn't quite fit but which she had been trying on for size all these years nonetheless.

Audrey gripped the wooden slats of the bench, her head vertiginous with memories, aware that she was tumbling down a rabbit hole and that there was nothing to break her fall.

It was all her fault. She should have been able to protect them, all three of them. But she hadn't, and this was the consequence of her failure: tales told to fill the gaping hole where the truth should have been.

Chapter 57
June 22, 1988

Audrey peeks around the edge of the curtain to see if there is any sign. Her eyes skim across the square from left to right, past empty benches, parked cars, magnolia trees that have long since shed their bloom.

The square is empty. No one is yet hurrying toward her front door.

She closes the curtain, careful not to let any glaring sunshine into the room. Even in her sleep, bright light seems to hurt Zoe's eyes.

Kneeling by her daughter's bed, Audrey watches her sleep and listens to her breathing, imploring herself to hear it differently.

She noticed it as soon as she woke up this morning from a fitful night on the camp bed in Zoe's room on which she has slept since her daughter came home from the hospital thirteen days ago. The change in Zoe's breathing: shallow, irregular, as though her lungs occasionally forget what job they're supposed to be doing. Edward has tried to reassure her, has tried to convince her that she is imagining it, but Audrey knows she is not.

Zoe's breaths murmur in and then out again, short and sharp, as though wary of loitering too long.

Finally the doorbell rings. When Audrey answers it and sees the home-care nurse standing in front of her she is unable to hold back her tears. As she allows her head to fall on the nurse's shoulder she does not know whether she is crying with relief that here at last is someone who can explain to her what is happening or shedding tears of dread that her worst fears are about to be confirmed.

After Grace, the home-care nurse, has examined Zoe, she asks Audrey and Edward to accompany her to the sitting room below. Grace suggests they all take a seat but Audrey refuses: to sit down might indicate that she intends to stay when all she really wants is to get back to Zoe.

"What can we do to make her more comfortable?" Edward's voice is calm, and even though his calmness is one of the things Audrey has always loved about him, today she finds it intolerable. Today she needs to hear her panic reflected back at her, needs to know she is not alone in her terror.

"You're doing everything you can, honestly. I know how upsetting it is seeing her in distress and not being able to stop it. Just be with her, talk to her, let her know you're there. Even right up to the end there's a chance she'll be able to hear you. But I should warn you now that this final stage can be quite protracted. You do need to prepare yourselves for that."

Audrey thinks about her little girl, upstairs alone, restless even in sleep. "What do you mean, *protracted*?"

There is a pause during which Grace smiles so kindly that Audrey fears she might cry.

"It's difficult to be precise. Sometimes it can be just a few hours. Sometimes this stage can last a few days. I know that's really hard to hear but I need you to be aware of what might

happen. We usually find that the better prepared parents are, the better they're able to cope."

Audrey reaches out for the back of the armchair to steady herself. The thought of Zoe struggling for breath for days to come clutches at her throat.

"Are you sure you wouldn't like me to find a hospital bed for Zoe? The nurses would take exceptional care of her and you could still stay with her the whole time. It might just take the pressure off you both."

She senses both Edward and Grace looking at her but does not raise her head to meet their gaze. She knows what they are thinking. It has been discussed already, at length, but nothing either of them says will make Audrey change her mind. "Absolutely not. I want to keep her here, at home. I want to look after her myself." She hears the determination—almost maniacal—in her voice but does not care what they think of her. She will not have anyone taking Zoe away.

"OK, I understand. You know you can call me anytime, day or night, and I'll come. And you've got the number of the hospital if you change your mind. In the meantime, use as much liquid morphine as you need to top up Zoe's medication and keep her comfortable, just not more than one oral syringe an hour. If you think she's still in too much pain, do talk to the doctor about increasing her dosage. But the best thing you can do for her now is to be with her and talk to her, let her know she's not alone. You're doing a wonderful job, both of you. Please don't forget that."

Grace picks up her bag from the arm of the chair and turns to leave. Audrey allows Edward to see the nurse to the front door as she makes her way back up the stairs, back to Zoe, already mourning the three or four minutes she has lost of the precious time she has left with her little girl.

*

Audrey walks into the kitchen where Edward is washing up. The girls got home from school half an hour ago and she has left Jess snuggled up in bed with Zoe, reading poems aloud even though Zoe is sleeping.

Ever since Grace left this morning, Audrey has been plagued by thoughts she cannot shake from her mind, thoughts she does not want to keep to herself but is nonetheless fearful of sharing.

She studies Edward's back as he stands at the sink. His hair is thinning on top, a depletion she is sure had not begun before the onset of Zoe's illness. "I can't bear to see her like this, Edward. What if Grace is right? What if it goes on for days?"

Edward turns around and offers her the kindness in his eyes. "We don't know that it will. We just have to be there for her. You heard Grace. That's all we can do."

He moves to walk past her, but as he reaches for the tea towel she grabs his soapy hand. "It's just . . . I was thinking . . . Those morphine doses are such an inexact science. No two ten-year-olds are the same. How do we know that what we're giving Zoe is enough to ease her pain as much as we possibly can?"

Edward frowns, and Audrey is unsure whether he is failing to follow what she is saying or simply choosing not to understand.

"We know because that's what the doctor told us to give her. I know how hard this is, but we just have to get through it, one hour at a time."

He pulls her into his arms and she knows he means to be comforting but Audrey does not want comfort. She frees herself from his embrace, walks over to the back door and looks out onto the garden that is overgrown with weeds after

months of neglect. "But *days*, Edward. We can't let this go on for days, can we? She's in so much pain, so much distress. We can't just sit by and do nothing, can we?"

"We're not doing nothing. We're with her. We're loving her. We're letting her know she's not alone."

Audrey thinks of Zoe upstairs, struggling for breath, and panic knocks inside her chest. "Is that true, though? Is that really as much as we can do?"

She turns around to find Edward staring at her, unblinking. "What do you mean?"

Audrey hesitates, still unsure whether she has the courage to say the words out loud. "Morphine isn't just for pain relief. It can do more than that . . ." Her voice trails off and she isn't brave enough to chase it back.

She watches Edward's expression shift—confusion to uncertainty, then a flash of recognition—and he glares at her with a look she has never seen before, something between disbelief and disappointment. "If you're saying what I think you're saying, then don't. Don't even think it, let alone say it. It's a dreadful thing even to consider."

There is such incredulity in his voice that Audrey cannot bear to look at him. She feels herself falter but then remembers Zoe upstairs, her breaths shortening, her life ebbing away one inhalation at a time. "But she's in pain, Edward. She's suffering. How can you bear to see her like that and do nothing?"

"Because I don't believe in playing God. Anything could happen—anything. The doctors don't know everything. She could get better, you just don't know. Miracles do happen. You hear about them all the time in the papers."

It is a line Edward has repeated again and again over the past fourteen months and Audrey cannot tell if he actually believes it or whether it is simply a verbal comfort blanket.

He has never been a particularly religious man but this belief in miracles—in the possibility of divine intervention against all the scientific and medical odds—has erected itself as an invisible wall between them.

No, Audrey wants to say, miracles don't happen all the time. The reason you read about them in the papers is because of how rare they are. "But you heard what the doctor said, you heard what Grace said. There isn't going to be an eleventh-hour reprieve. She's not going to get better, Edward. She's dying. Our little girl is going to die."

Her voice splinters, the words she has not dared say aloud before burning in the back of her throat, and there is a moment of terror that voicing them has somehow sealed Zoe's fate, like a spell in a fairy tale that cannot be undone.

"Stop it, Audrey, just stop it. You don't know that. You don't know what's going to happen. You might have given up hope but I haven't. I won't give up hope until there's nothing left to hope for. I can't believe you're even thinking like this, let alone talking about it. I will never give up on her, never. Now I'm going upstairs to be with Zoe. Don't follow me—I want to be on my own with her."

Edward's cheeks are blotchy as he turns and leaves. Left alone in the kitchen, Audrey sheds tears for the miracle she feels certain will never arrive.

Audrey has not slept all night. She has not wanted to sleep, has not wanted to miss a second of however much time Zoe has left. Instead, she has sat by Zoe's bed listening to her breathing, her ears attuned to every change, however small, like a bat vigilant to the sound of predators swooping through the darkness.

She knows that, in spite of Edward's belief in miracles, Grace is right—they have already passed the beginning of the

end. She does not know how long the end will be but she can sense its presence. Life is retreating from her daughter, leaving her gasping for air, her body restless and twitching, and there is nothing Audrey can do to make her better.

She runs her fingers along Zoe's forehead where once her hairline had been. It had been such beautiful hair, so thick and shiny, just like Jess's. Now all Audrey has left of Zoe's hair are photographs and the single envelope of locks that she keeps tucked away in a box at the back of her wardrobe, hidden from Edward, who thinks it macabre.

She leans over, kisses her daughter's bare scalp, breathes in a smell that she silently implores to be different: she wants it to be the sweet, fragrant, childlike scent of Zoe's first ten years, not this sour bitterness which seems to ooze from her pores as if the leukemia is leaking out through her skin.

From the kitchen two floors below Audrey hears a loud clatter and silently curses the disruption. It is probably Edward organizing the girls' breakfasts or emptying the dishwasher. She and Edward have not spoken since their disagreement yesterday afternoon. Audrey has kept vigil by Zoe's bed overnight while Edward has assumed the household responsibilities that had, not so long ago, been Audrey's domain. His belief in miracles has wedged itself between them and neither of them has the strength to close the gap.

She strokes Zoe's bare head, brushes her fingers across her forehead, over her temple, behind her ear, following the same path again and again, just as she has so many times throughout Zoe's childhood.

Stroke my hair to sleep, Mummy.

When she was little, Zoe would ask it almost every night as she clambered under the duvet, Jess in the bunk either above or below, the two of them taking turns each night as

to who would sleep on top. Often, in the morning, Audrey would find them curled up in the same bed, their limbs tangled, flesh pressed together as though—even seven, eight, nine years after their birth—their bodies still craved being entwined in a confined space. Audrey would sit or stand by the bed, stroking Jess or Zoe's hair, and sing to them both—"Somewhere Over the Rainbow," "Hush Little Baby," "My Favorite Things"—until her daughters' breathing deepened, lengthening into that heavy, satisfied sleep in which they would remain until morning.

Now when Audrey runs her fingers along Zoe's skin it is arid and unyielding, like writing paper puckered by dried tears.

Zoe's eyes are closed and Audrey tries to convince herself that her daughter is asleep and dreaming, even though she knows Zoe is in something much deeper than sleep.

Morning creeps around the edge of the curtains, creating a thin shaft of light on the tiny blue hummingbirds that decorate the wallpaper. The silence is punctuated by the short, shallow breaths that rattle through Zoe's body. They seem to serrate her throat on the way down, get caught somewhere between her lips and her lungs, forcing her to arch her neck as if trying to clear a safe passage for air to pass through. There is an invisible snag somewhere inside Zoe's windpipe that Audrey can neither see nor cure, but she hears it, feels it as though it is reverberating through her own body.

So many times she has wished she could swap places with Zoe. So many times she has sat by her daughter's bed, at home or in the hospital, and silently intoned the same incantation: *If I could give you my blood, I would. If I could swap your damaged cells for mine, I would do it in an instant.*

Now, as she watches the life receding from her daughter's body, one rasping breath at a time, she knows without a

shadow of a doubt that if she were given the chance to swap places with Zoe, she would not hesitate.

If I could give you my life, I would.

Audrey does not know which is worse: watching her little girl writhe in pain and being unable to help or wishing that her suffering would soon be over in spite of what that means.

As Zoe breathes in and the air catches in her throat, her fingers squeeze hard around Audrey's hand with a strength she did not know Zoe still possessed. For a brief, ephemeral moment, Audrey imagines that perhaps she is being granted the miracle Edward so fervently believes in. But when she looks at her daughter's face—sees the pinching around her closed eyes, the tensing of the muscles across her forehead, the jaw slack and mouth open—she understands that this is not the beginnings of a miracle.

She holds her daughter's hand as tightly as Zoe holds hers and waits for the convulsion to pass.

Clutching Zoe's hand, Audrey remembers the first time she held Zoe in her arms. She remembers Zoe's warm, sticky skin against hers, the flood of love so great it had temporarily washed away the unfinished pain that was yet to bring Jess into the world. During her pregnancy Audrey had worried that perhaps she would not experience the same intensity of feelings as she had with Lily, that perhaps there was a special bond reserved for firstborns, never to be replicated. But as soon as she had held Zoe against her chest—as soon as those tiny hands had clutched her little finger, as if holding on for dear life—she had understood that every new baby remade you as a mother.

Looking at Zoe now, it is impossible to comprehend that this small, frail ten-year-old is the same robust baby who had parted her newborn lips and cried out into the world, her voice

loud and muscular, exuding a confidence that seemed to say: *This is my life and I will make myself heard.* It is impossible to think that Zoe and Jess—two halves of the same soul who have been inseparable for a decade—are soon to be cleaved apart.

She strokes the back of Zoe's fingers, rubbing her thumb gently along skin so thin it is like touching bone.

She needs Zoe to know that she is there, that she would never leave her. Audrey understands that sitting here now, being with Zoe, is the most important thing she has ever done, the most important thing she will ever do. She could live to be a hundred and still there would be nothing more important than Zoe knowing that Audrey would never leave her side.

If I could give you my life, I would.

Something rattles in Zoe's throat and there is a spluttering sound as the muscles respond, an automatic reflex trying to clear the obstruction, but it is as if her body has forgotten what it needs to do and instead her neck twists to one side, her face contorted with pain or distress, Audrey does not know which. All she knows is that her daughter is suffering and that the face on the pillow no longer resembles that of her beautiful little girl.

It is then that she notices the full bottle of medicine by the bed, remembers Grace's words as she left the previous morning: *Sometimes this stage can last a few days. Use as much liquid morphine as you need to keep her comfortable.*

There is a moment's stillness during which Audrey is not conscious of making a decision. But the next thing she knows, she is watching one hand reach out toward the bedside table and pick up the plastic syringe, the other hand the bottle, watching herself fill the syringe to the top with clear liquid.

She slides a hand under Zoe's head, raising it a few inches

from the pillow, and slowly drops the liquid morphine onto Zoe's tongue, all the time whispering into her ear that she loves her, that she is there for her, that she will never, ever leave her side. She senses a change in the air, a tiny disturbance of light, but she is focused on what she is doing and does not allow her eyes to leave Zoe's face.

It seems to Audrey to be an eternity until the syringe is empty. But when, at last, it has all gone, she watches her hand reach for the bottle again, watches herself insert the syringe a second time, sucking up medicine until it is full.

She is aware of performing these movements but is not conscious of being in control of them. Again she lifts Zoe's head, again she administers the medicine onto Zoe's tongue, again she whispers the same recitation: *I love you, angel. I will always, always love you.* There is a gurgling sound in the back of Zoe's throat as though, in moving her head, Audrey has dislodged a small reservoir that has collected around her tonsils. She waits for it to pass, and once the second syringe is empty, Audrey fills and administers another and then another—too many to count—until there is nothing left in the bottle.

She puts the syringe back on the bedside table and is aware that the room is completely still. It is only when she feels that her cheeks are damp and her face is hot that she realizes she is crying.

She lifts the edge of the duvet and climbs into bed next to her daughter, wraps an arm around her, and holds her close, hoping the warmth of her body will seep into Zoe's skin. She rests her cheek against Zoe's, hugging her tight, breathing her in and filling her lungs, as if, in doing so, she is holding on to Zoe's life. She places the palm of her hand against Zoe's cheek, feels the thin sheen of skin where once plump flesh had been, feels the vibrations of air rattling in and out of Zoe's

lungs, but does not let go. She needs Zoe to know that she will never stop holding her, that she will never be without her. She sings softly into Zoe's ear, all the songs they have always loved—"Edelweis," "Castle on a Cloud," "Dream a Little Dream of Me"—the notes finding their way through a gap in her lips in spite of the narrowing of her throat and the tears flooding her cheeks. When there are no more songs to be sung, Audrey whispers into Zoe's ear about all the places they will go, all the things they will do, all the adventures they will have together in Zoe's dreams.

Audrey does not know how long they lie there. Time seems to bend and stretch. Zoe's breaths become longer, the gaps between them wider. Audrey breathes in time with her daughter, the two of them inhaling in unison as though sharing a single pair of lungs.

Zoe takes in a breath, holds it, lets it out again, and Audrey waits for the next one to come.

The seconds pass—three seconds, four—with no movement.

And then it comes: the slow, laborious inhalation.

Five seconds, six seconds, seven before the next breath. It is a pattern repeated so many times, the rhythm becomes almost hypnotic.

And then Zoe breathes out and Audrey waits for her chest to rise, for the almost imperceptible widening of her lips, for the air to be sucked in slowly as though it has all the time in the world.

Six seconds, seven.

Audrey waits, her own breath static in her chest.

Eight seconds, nine.

She closes her eyes, listening, silent.

Ten seconds, eleven.

It has been this long before, Audrey tells herself. There has been this great gap of time before.

Twelve seconds, thirteen.

She presses her face tighter against Zoe's, feels her tears slide onto her daughter's cheek.

Fourteen seconds, fifteen.

Audrey's arm tightens around Zoe's body.

Sixteen, seventeen.

She keeps hold of her, keeps her close, needing Zoe to know she is there.

Eighteen, nineteen.

Her lips caress Zoe's cheek.

Twenty, twenty-one.

She holds Zoe's face next to hers, tightly, fiercely.

Twenty-two, twenty-three.

She presses their bodies together, will not let her go.

Twenty-four, twenty-five.

Her throat tightens, her eyes sting.

Twenty-six, twenty-seven.

She clings to Zoe as though she may yet be able to fuse their bodies together, may yet be able to transfer her own life to her daughter.

Twenty-eight, twenty-nine.

The silence hurts Audrey's ears.

Thirty.

Audrey feels the air exit her own lungs, feels her chest collapse under the weight of her grief, feels something empty out of her that she knows will never return. She hears a sound emerge from her throat, something so raw it is as though it must be coming from someone else, something outside her, somewhere she cannot bear to go even though she knows she

is already there. Her throat burns, her eyes are hot with tears, her lips brushing over Zoe's skin, kissing every inch of her.

She presses her body to Zoe's, knowing that her daughter is no longer there but unable to let her go.

For minutes and then hours—long after Edward comes in, long after he has called the doctor, long after the doctor has written out the certificate to finalize a life so short-lived—Audrey lies next to her little girl, holding her tight, determined Zoe should know that Audrey would never leave her.

And for all the time Audrey lies there with Zoe—all the seconds that pass into minutes, and the minutes that pass into hours—the same single thought repeats silently in her mind, somewhere between a prayer and a lamentation.

If I could have given my life for you, I would.

Chapter 58

Audrey

Audrey opened her eyes and blinked her tears into the bright light of the afternoon sun, her head throbbing with remembrance.

She took a moment to get her bearings. A foreign city. Boaters on a lake. Water flanked by trees and buildings. And on either side of her, sitting on the bench, two sisters who had been estranged for over two decades because of the secret she had kept from them.

She thought back to the evening of Zoe's funeral: she and Edward sitting silently on the sofa, only a single table lamp illuminating the darkness, neither of them able to muster the energy to clear the plates of curling sandwiches and lipstick-marked paper cups that guests had left behind. Lily and Jess had been in bed already and Audrey had wished she could not be far behind but had known there was little point because for the ten days since Zoe's death sleep had been elusive and the only thing Audrey could now be sure of when she climbed under the duvet and shut her eyes was that she would be greeted by the memory of Zoe's body, encased in her arms, as the life had ebbed out of her.

She remembered glancing across to where Edward was sitting, staring straight ahead. She had felt guilt clawing at

her throat like rats in a cellar demanding to be let out, and eventually she had found the courage to tell him what she had done.

He had looked at her—unblinking, disbelieving—but she had seen the realization spread across his face like the tentative light of an early dawn.

How could you? How could you make that decision and not even tell me? She was our *little girl,* ours. *Not yours. It wasn't your decision to make. You had no right, Audrey, no right.*

His words had brimmed with rage and she had not known what to do to calm the tempest of his fury. But then he had turned to her and his voice, when he had next spoken, had been quiet, barely more than a whisper.

You killed *her, Audrey. You killed our little girl.*

His eyes had glimmered with anger but there had been something beyond that, something that had made Audrey flinch even though she did not, at first, understand why: he had looked at her not just with disbelief but with contempt.

She had placed a hand on his arm in the hope that they might begin to find their way back to one another but the violence with which he had shaken her off had made her recoil.

Don't touch me, Audrey. I mean it. I don't want you near me. How could you? How could you have done that? I will never, ever be able to forgive you.

I'm sorry. I'm so, so sorry. I never meant to hurt you. You know *that. The last thing I'd ever want is to hurt you or the girls. You* must *know that.*

He had turned to her then, his eyes stony, his voice wrapped in ice.

Do you know the worst thing? Zoe was bearing that pain—she was strong—but you were weak. You were too weak to bear the pain with her. What kind of mother does that make you? What kind of

mother can't look after their own child when they need them most? I'll never forgive you for what you've done. And I'll never forgive myself for having failed to stop you.

Just over twelve weeks later, when Audrey had run past the parked police cars and into the sitting room to find Jess hysterical and to be told what Edward had done, she had known immediately that she was to blame.

So many times during the intervening years she had spent sleepless nights thinking about how different their lives might have been had she never told Edward the truth, wondering whether he might still be alive, whether they might still be married, happy even. Whenever she had seen a newspaper report or watched a documentary about a child surviving cancer against the odds, she had heard Edward's allegations resounding in her ears until she had understood that there needed to be only the thinnest sliver of doubt between conviction and uncertainty for the guilt to slip in and consume you every single day of your life.

Sitting now on a bench in Central Park between her daughters, Audrey thought back to that morning in Zoe's room, administering those doses of morphine in an attempt to alleviate her daughter's suffering. She remembered how she had sensed a change in the air, a tiny disturbance of light, but had been too preoccupied to turn around and investigate. She thought about Jess's accusation and her hatred of Lily all these years, Jess's words hammering in her ears: *I saw you coming out of her room. I saw the expression on your face. You were white as a sheet. You barricaded yourself against the door, and I knew—I just* knew—*something terrible had happened.*

And all at once Audrey understood that decades of unspoken stories were like strata of ancient rock: layer upon layer of family secrets impacting on one another until the truth was

hidden so far beneath the surface that only the most committed could excavate it.

Audrey looked from left to right, from Lily to Jess.

"Lily didn't kill Zoe, Jess. It was me. I was the one who helped Zoe to die."

She turned to Lily and held her gaze even as she longed to look away. "But you already knew that, didn't you, Lily?"

Chapter 59

Lily

Lily felt the heat of her mum's understanding, felt a history she had long since buried begin to resurface.

For years she had speculated as to the cause of Jess's hostility but never once had she imagined that Jess had got the facts so very nearly right but all the key players wrong. All this time she had imagined that it was their dad's death Jess blamed her for, even though she had never been able to pinpoint why. Only now did Lily understand that Jess had plugged the gap in her knowledge with her own version of the truth. Because sometimes, Lily knew only too well, the only way to make sense of the incomprehensible was to tell yourself a story.

Lily raised her head to look at her mum, at her marbled, tear-stained cheeks and the bones jutting from her skin like mountains rising from the earth. As their eyes locked, she realized that the secret she had kept for almost thirty years was no longer hers alone.

Chapter 60

June 23, 1988

Lily is standing outside the door to the spare bedroom, hovering on the cusp of a decision. She has been told not to go inside but before she leaves for school she wants to say goodbye to Zoe. She knows how ill her little sister is, and ever since Zoe came home from the hospital two weeks ago, whenever Lily now leaves the house she fears that Zoe may not be there when she gets home.

Turning the door handle silently, Lily slips into the room, her breath held in her chest so as not to make a sound, fearful of disturbing Zoe should she still be sleeping. She sinks her bare toes noiselessly into the thick pile of the carpet, opens the door only enough for her body to squeeze through, careful not to bring too much light into the room. She knows that light can hurt Zoe's eyes, does not want to do anything that might unsettle her.

It is dark in the spare bedroom, only the faintest morning light visible around the edges of the closed curtains. She can just make out the shape of the blue hummingbirds that pattern the wallpaper around the window but everything else is in silhouette. The air is still and smells pungent—sharp and slightly sweet—like overripe fruit or an open bottle of vinegar.

She hears the crying before her eyes have adjusted to the darkness, before they have found the figure sitting on the bed: her mum's sobs are low and painful, a sound that seems to Lily to be filled not only with fear but with disbelief and a quiet fury that this should be happening. It is a sound that causes Lily's heart to knock against her chest, gently at first and then more insistently, until she fears her mum may hear it.

She holds the palm of her hand against her chest. She knows she should not be there but now that she is—unnoticed, unheard—she is too scared to leave in case she accidentally reveals her presence. She allows only the smallest stream of air in and out of her mouth, the shallowest of breaths she hopes will not betray her.

As her eyes adjust to the darkness Lily sees that her mum is giving Zoe some medicine. With one hand, she lifts Zoe's head from the pillow as gently as if she were handling a precious artifact in a museum. With the other, she drips medicine from a plastic syringe onto Zoe's tongue. Her mum is crying, low, mournful sobs, and whispering declarations of love into the darkness: "I love you, angel. I will always, always love you." Giving Zoe the syringe of medicine seems to take forever but when finally it is over, instead of putting the syringe back down, her mum picks up the bottle of morphine, fills the syringe again, and drops more medicine into Zoe's mouth.

Thoughts scramble to form an orderly queue in Lily's head. She wonders whether her mum has forgotten or whether she is too upset to remember the rules that Lily has heard her parents discuss so many times over the past few days: *When did you last give her some medicine? Remember, she's not allowed more than one syringe of morphine an hour.* She feels an urge to call out but the words stick in her throat and she realizes she does not know what she wants to say.

Lily watches in silence as her mum finishes dispensing the second batch of medicine and then administers a third. Her heart is hammering, her lungs tight with the limited supply of oxygen, but still she says nothing as her mum reaches for the bottle, again and again, giving Zoe more and more medicine, until she is holding the bottle almost upside down to fill the syringe with the last of the morphine.

Lily's skin prickles, her eyes straining in the semidarkness. Her brain scrabbles to find possible—better—solutions to the shadowy thoughts creeping through her mind, but however much she tries to settle on a different narrative, the same dark story rises up through the gloom.

Still Lily does not move as her mum gets into bed beside Zoe, wraps an arm around her, and holds on to her tightly. Her mum is still crying but she begins to sing through her tears and the sound is like nothing Lily has ever heard before: a sound so sad Lily knows she will remember it for as long as she lives. She tries to swallow her grief but instead tastes something bitter and metallic on her tongue and she knows it is the taste of fear.

She cannot stay in there any longer. She cannot stay because she knows—the truth of it clenching her heart in its fist—that what she has witnessed is all her fault. Her own words of eleven days ago come back to haunt her, echoing in her ears like a child's playground taunt: *It's inhumane. For goodness' sake, people do more for sick pets than they do for people. There must be something we can do. Please, Mum. Please stop it. You have to.*

Lily backs silently out of the room and onto the landing, closing the door quietly behind her. Her heart is still thundering in her chest, her cheeks hot, the air slowly—finally—escaping from her lungs. She feels tears in her eyes and she blinks them

away because she knows that if they begin to fall there will be no way of stopping them.

"What are you doing?"

Lily jumps around, startled, the silent terror of the last few minutes shattered by the sight of Jess, at the top of the stairs, staring at her.

There follows a stand-off between them, Jess demanding to go in and see Zoe, Lily knowing that she has to do everything in her power to stop her.

The alarm on Lily's digital watch beeps and she jerks her hand to turn it off, frantic that her mum shouldn't hear, that she shouldn't know she and Jess are loitering outside.

Lily holds her sister's gaze, willing Jess to turn and walk away. And when, eventually, Jess retreats and begins to go down the stairs, Lily knows she must follow close behind.

All the way to school Lily manages not to cry. She must not let Jess see that she is upset, must not let her know that there is already cause to be grieving. But when they reach the school gates—when she has safely deposited Jess in the junior school playground and rounded the corner to her own senior school—she walks up the stairs to the top-floor toilets that are always empty at this time and locks herself inside. There she allows the horror of the past thirty minutes to catch up with her in loud, lonely sobs that reverberate around the cubicle as if they will never be silenced.

Chapter 61
Jess

Jess's head reeled: a sense that the bench, her body, her feet were no longer anchored to the ground.

Her mum looked at her and Jess saw it in her eyes: an expression that tipped Jess's world onto a different axis, sent it spinning out of control.

And then there was a torrent of words, unstoppable and unrelenting, her mum talking and talking, confessing to something Jess didn't want to hear: something that undid the past and recast the present.

"You have to believe me, both of you. I did what I thought was best for Zoe."

Her mum dragged a tissue along her cheek and Jess turned to look at her, but it was as if she were staring at a stranger. "The best? How can you say that? How can that possibly have been the best for Zoe?"

There was hysteria in her voice, and passersby turned to stare but her words had a momentum of their own and Jess couldn't stop them.

Her mum reached out, tried to take her hand, but Jess yanked it away.

"She was going to die, Jess. There was nothing any of us could do to change that. We brought her home to die."

Her mum spoke softly but the words jabbed into Jess's chest. "Why didn't you tell me that at the time? Why did you all pretend that she was coming home because she was better? You should have told me the truth. She was *my twin*. I had a right to know."

Her mum began to weep again, and Jess turned her head away, felt the blood pounding in her ears. "What about Dad? Did he know? Did the two of you plan it together?"

Her mum coughed into her hand, wiped it on a tissue, shook her head. "Dad wasn't involved at all. He didn't know anything about it. I didn't tell him until after the funeral."

Pieces of a jigsaw Jess had never been able to complete began to slot into place. Hazy scenes from her childhood pulled into focus as if they had been waiting all these years to be restored. Coming in from the garden one day that summer—barefoot, unintentionally silent—hearing her parents hissing at one another in the kitchen, the words long since forgotten but the tone of animosity and contrition still audible in her ears. Her dad's changed demeanor that summer, his kindness and affection replaced by distant coldness, and Jess's belief that it must be her fault for reminding him of the daughter he had lost. The four of them having Sunday lunch, the kitchen silent save for the muted orchestra of cutlery against crockery, her mum reaching out a hand toward her dad's arm and him flinching, glaring at her and speaking with a ferocity Jess had never heard before: *Don't. Just don't.* All those nights her dad had failed to come home before Jess went to sleep, all those nights she had lain under the duvet, alone on the bottom bunk bed, believing her dad could no longer bear to be in the same house as her because he resented her for still being alive when her funny, brave, superior twin was dead.

"That's why Dad killed himself, isn't it? He couldn't bear what you'd done?"

Her mum nodded, and it was as though Jess could feel her family's foundations shifting beneath her. "Why didn't you tell me? Why did you let me think he didn't care about us when all along it was your fault he killed himself?" She was shouting now, her voice hot, her throat raw. "Why did you never tell me the truth? Why did you let me think Zoe might get better? Why didn't you let me say goodbye?"

Decades of confusion and grief swam in Jess's head until a single, lonely thought rose to the surface, a thought Jess had kept submerged for almost thirty years.

"All I ever wanted was to say goodbye."

Chapter 62
Audrey

As Jess staggered up from the bench, Audrey reached out a hand and heard her own plaintive cry: "Jess, please don't go." But Jess wrenched her arm away and ran along the path, back in the direction of the hotel. Audrey felt her legs prepare to follow but as she tried to raise herself to her feet, it was as though her muscles had dissolved and there was nothing solid to hold her up. Her eyes followed Jess through the park until she rounded a corner and disappeared.

She turned to Lily, a horde of questions lining her throat. "Why did you never say anything? Why did you never tell me that you'd seen what happened?"

Lily was fiddling with one of the shiny black buttons on her jacket, popping it through the hole and then doing it back up again. "I couldn't. I just couldn't."

"Why not? I can't bear to think of you having kept that to yourself all these years. It must have been torture for you." The thought of Lily alone with that burden of knowledge pressed down hard on Audrey's windpipe, squeezing the air from her lungs.

"Because I knew it would be worse for you if you found out I'd seen it all. I knew it would make it so much harder for you."

It took a moment for the lump in Audrey's throat to make space for her voice to find its way out. "You were fifteen, Lily. You shouldn't have had to deal with that all by yourself."

Lily shrugged, and there was something in the gesture that rolled back the decades to the weeks after Zoe's death, when Lily had demanded so little time and attention. Now Audrey couldn't understand why she had failed to see that Lily was perhaps the most disturbed of them all. "I'm sorry, Lily. I'm sorry for what you saw, and I'm sorry you've been alone with it all this time. Have you never told anyone?"

Audrey watched the slow rise and fall of Lily's ribs, wondering how she could love someone so much and yet know so little of what had troubled them for decades.

"No. But you don't need to apologize. It's not your fault I've kept it to myself. I couldn't say anything . . ." Lily shook her head, deep vertical grooves indenting the skin between her eyebrows.

"What is it? What were you going to say?"

Audrey kept watch on Lily's profile as she stared out across the boating lake into the distance as if looking back in time.

"I couldn't say anything because I was worried it was all my fault."

The words were almost a whisper, as if even now, after all this time, they still weren't quite ready to come out of hiding.

"What do you mean? How could it have been your fault?"

Lily didn't immediately reply. Audrey could hear squeals coming from somewhere on the lake but she didn't turn her head to look, didn't care about anyone else's joy or pain. She kept her eyes on Lily, searching for clues.

"Because of what I said in the kitchen that morning."

A single plump tear crept over Lily's bottom eyelid before trickling onto her cheek below.

"When? What did you say?"

Lily turned to her, her expression caught somewhere between a question and remorse. "In the kitchen, with you and Dad, a few days after Zoe came home from the hospital. It was a Sunday morning. You must remember?"

Audrey tried to rewind her memory in search of the conversation Lily might be referring to. "I'm sorry, darling, I honestly don't know what conversation you mean."

"You *must* remember. Zoe and Jess were still in bed but you, me, and Dad were up really early and you made me some hot chocolate and I got really upset about Zoe . . ." Lily's words trailed off and her eyes drifted across the park as if watching her voice disappear, unsure whether to chase it back.

"What, Lily? What did you say? I honestly don't remember."

There was a heartbeat of silence.

"I was really upset about Zoe. *Really* upset. I said that people treat pets better than humans. I begged you and Dad to do something. I begged you to put an end to her suffering—"

Lily stopped abruptly and Audrey felt the past lurch into the present. She remembered now. Sitting at the kitchen table, she and Edward flanking Lily, their arms around her shoulders. Lily had been hysterical and all Audrey had wanted was to stop her crying, soothe her distress. All she had really wanted, the memory squeezing her throat, was to calm Lily down so that she could return to Zoe's bedside.

"Sweetheart, we were all upset in those last few weeks. We all said things in the heat of the moment we didn't really mean. But nothing you said—nothing you did—contributed to my decision. I *promise* you. You are not in any way responsible for what I did."

"But I am. I must have been. I must have planted the seed."

Audrey shook her head, trying to slot all the new information into place. All these years Lily had blamed herself for Zoe's death because of a conversation Audrey hadn't even remembered. "You didn't, Lily. I promise you didn't. You mustn't think that, *please*." She took Lily's hand, felt the New York humidity between their clammy palms.

"What about Dad?" Lily's voice was low and flat as though she'd ironed all the creases before letting it out.

"What do you mean? What about Dad?"

"I heard you. After Zoe's funeral. I heard you tell Dad what you'd done. I know he was furious with you. And I can't help thinking . . ."

"What? What can't you help thinking?"

A slow trickle of tears fell down Lily's cheeks. Audrey smoothed her thumb over the back of Lily's hand, wondering whether she could ever soothe away a past that had, for so long, contaminated the present.

"I should have said something. I should have stopped you. Because if I had . . ."

"If you had what?"

Lily didn't speak for a few seconds and when she did, the words sounded small, far away, as though they belonged not to the forty-three-year-old woman sitting next to Audrey on a bench in Central Park but to the teenager who'd first thought them almost three decades before.

"If I'd stopped you then you wouldn't have needed to confess to Dad and he'd never have got so angry and maybe he'd still be alive today." The tears dropped, one after the other, onto the pale gray silk of Lily's skirt where they dilated into large, dark circles.

"Lily, Dad's death was *not* your fault. If anyone's responsible for Dad's suicide, it's me, not you. It was not your job

to stop me doing what I did. And it was certainly not your job to stop Dad doing what he did. You were fifteen, Lily. *Fifteen.* Two years younger than Phoebe is now. You were just a child. You are *not* responsible."

Audrey put her arms around Lily and held her tight, hoping that somehow, in the closeness of their embrace, Lily might find enough love to forgive herself. "I'm sorry, Lily. I'm so sorry I didn't do more to help you come to terms with it."

They sat holding one another as all the years of lonely guilt began to seep out through Lily's tears. As the sun beat down on them, Audrey wondered whether there might be a way for it to burn through the secrets that had poisoned her family for decades.

As they sat there, a single desire nudged its way into Audrey's thoughts: the possibility that perhaps it wasn't too late to rewrite this story with a different ending. "Lily, I know this is all still very raw, but do you think you could do something for me?"

Lily turned to her, mascara smudged across her mottled skin.

"Can you go and find Jess, talk to her, try to sort this out? It's all such a mess of misunderstandings. None of this ever needed to happen." The truth scorched Audrey's throat: all those wasted years because of a collection of tales told in lieu of the truth.

"But you need to talk to her too, Mum. You need to tell her your side of the story."

An image flashed into Audrey's mind: three little girls—Lily aged nine, the twins aged four—playing in the garden, the sun streaming through the leaves on the trees as Lily tried to teach her little sisters how to perform handstands. Zoe and Jess—their faces almost indistinguishable—placing their palms flat on the grass, kicking their legs into the air only to have

them tip straight back to earth. Frustration mounting until Lily took their ankles, lifted them up, delivered them their moment of assisted triumph. The twins returning to their feet and hugging their big sister, arms around her waist, and her taking their hands, forming a circle with them, dancing and singing. Audrey watching from the kitchen window knowing that of all the relationships her girls must cherish throughout their lives, those sibling bonds were the ones she hoped would see them through to the end of their days.

"I can do that later. But right now, all I want is for you two to start talking again, for you two . . ."

The thought got trapped, halfway formed: that there would come a time, very soon, when what mattered was not Audrey's relationship with her daughters but, in her absence, her daughters' relationship with each other.

"I just want you two to be sisters again. That's all I've ever wanted. Can you try and do that for me? Please?"

Chapter 63
Jess

Running into the lobby of the Plaza Hotel, her thoughts sprinting ahead of her, Jess heard a man's voice call her name. She turned to see who it was.

"Hey, Jess. Is everything all right?"

It took Jess a few moments to place him, not because she didn't recognize him but because she hadn't expected to see him there. She hadn't, in truth, expected to see him ever again.

"Ben? What are you doing here?"

"Do you mean here in New York or here at the Plaza? I've moved back here now—didn't your mom mention it? She was the catalyst, if I'm honest. I said I'd meet her for a quick drink this evening. Do you know where she is?"

Jess thought about her mum sitting in the park and about how, just a few minutes before, she had watched the past change before her eyes. And before she knew it was going to happen, she burst into tears.

"What's wrong? What's happened? Audrey's OK, isn't she?"

Jess managed to nod, her head heavy with confessions, uncertain what she was supposed to do with them all.

"So what's the matter?"

She felt Ben's hand on her shoulder, and suddenly the afternoon's events were spilling out of her mouth. As Ben

led her to a sofa in the corner of the lobby she told him about her terrible misunderstanding, her false accusation, the needless family rupture she had caused. He listened without interrupting as she described a twenty-eight-year estrangement that now made her feel physically sick with shame and regret. And what surprised Jess was not that she was pouring out her confession to a man she barely knew but how very easy it was to confide in him.

"So, you see, I've ruined my entire family because of a misunderstanding when I was ten years old. That's all it was—a misunderstanding. All this time I've been angry with Lily when she'd done nothing wrong."

Jess thought about batting away her mum's arm as it had reached out toward her. Her mum so frail where once she had been strong. This, the first afternoon of a trip that was supposed to have plugged the gap of her mum's disappointments, but had instead shattered what small pretense of stability they had left. She couldn't tell Ben about what her mum had done, however deep her desire to confide in someone: even in the heat of her anger, she knew it would be too great a betrayal.

"Don't be so hard on yourself. You were just a child. God, it's difficult enough making sense of life and death when you're an adult. You can't possibly be expected to understand it when you're ten. And losing a twin—I can't even begin to imagine how hard that must have been. It's only natural you'd want to find someone to blame."

"I'm not sure it's normal to hate your sister for nearly three decades because of something she didn't even do. Looking back now, I don't really understand how I let it happen."

Guilt nestled in the back of Jess's throat.

"Because you're human? Because we all make mistakes? Because dealing with grief is probably the hardest thing any

of us ever has to do? You wouldn't be the first person to cut yourself off from your family as a means of managing your pain, and I doubt very much you'll be the last."

Jess thought back to the night before Zoe died, lying in bed with her sister, reading aloud the poems of their childhood: "The King's Breakfast," "Binker," "Us Two." Jess's belief as she snuggled up beside Zoe that soon her twin would be better, soon the two of them would be sharing their bunk beds again, soon Zoe would return to school where Jess had spent the last year feeling as though half of her was missing, not wanting to make new friends because somehow that would acknowledge the possibility that Zoe might not return.

"I just can't believe they didn't let me say goodbye. Why they didn't let me tell her one last time that I loved her?" Her voice began to tear and she waited while it stitched itself back together. She thought about all those times she had recalled that final morning, filled with regret that she hadn't insisted on seeing Zoe before she left for school. "Knowing I could have said goodbye but wasn't given the chance . . . It feels like a whole new layer of grief. A whole new layer of anger." Jess reached into her bag, pulled out a tissue, dragged it under her eyes and across her cheek.

"Of course that's hard, Jess. Of course that's going to hurt. But you and Zoe—you must have said a thousand times that you loved each other. She'll have known what she meant to you. She'll have known without you needing to tell her one last time."

Ben's voice was calm and gentle, and Jess wished she could bottle it up, breathe it in, make herself feel it inside, but every time she closed her eyes, there it was: an image of her parents and Lily discussing the fact that Zoe was never going to get better and choosing not to tell her.

"It's not just that. It's all of it. If only Mum had told me that Zoe was coming home to die, I'd never have suspected Lily and I'd never have cut her out of my life. All of this could have been avoided if Mum and Dad had told me the truth. And I'm not sure how I begin to forgive my mum for that." Jess wound the damp tissue around her forefinger, watched the blood fill the flesh at her fingertip.

"I get that you're angry and upset. But ask yourself this: can you honestly say that your mum wasn't doing what she thought was for the best? When she decided not to tell you how ill Zoe was, wasn't she only trying to protect you?"

Jess folded the tissue into a crumpled square and flattened it between her palms. "But even if that's true, I still can't get away from the consequences of it. She's been lying to me for years, not just about this, about other stuff too . . ." Jess stopped herself, the truth about Zoe's death hovering in the wings, waiting to see if it was about to be called onstage. She glanced across at Ben, had an instinctive sense that he wouldn't judge her mum if she told him. But it was her mum's story to tell, not hers. "I don't know. It just feels as though everything I thought I knew about my mum has come undone. I feel like I don't even know who she is anymore."

"Of course you do. None of this has to change your relationship with her if you don't want it to. She's still the same person she was two hours ago. I totally understand that you're upset, but do you honestly think she meant to hurt you by not telling you? Haven't you ever done something you thought was for the best for your daughter but somehow, inadvertently, managed to upset her in the process?"

Jess thought about the fight she'd had with Mia in the car that morning, less than fifteen hours before but already feeling as though it belonged to a different lifetime. When she began

to speak again her voice was small and distant as though she were whispering from the far end of a long tunnel. "But it's not just how I feel about Mum. It's how I feel about Dad and Lily too. So much of what I thought I knew isn't actually true. And if everything about your past changes, where does that leave who you are in the present?"

"You're all the same people, Jess. You just need to make adjustments in the way you think about your family. It's what we all do, every single day, shifting the parameters, reshaping our expectations. It's just that this adjustment is a lot bigger than most."

Jess let Ben's words settle in her head, rubbing her fingers against her temples. "I just don't know how to forgive her for not telling me. I want to forgive her, I know I have to, that I'll regret it if I don't, but I'm just not sure I can." She blew her nose, shoved the crumpled tissue into her handbag, pulled out a fresh one.

She detected an expression on Ben's face that seemed strangely familiar: an expression of independence and self-sufficiency, like a crab's shell evolved over millennia to protect what was inside. It was an expression she recognized because she'd seen it herself so many times in the mirror.

And then Ben turned to her and it was as though she could see a decision click into place. "Forgiveness is a decision, Jess. I've done things I never imagined my daughter would forgive me for but over the past few weeks she's begun to let me back into her life. It's up to you whether you want to do the same for your mum. I'm not saying it'll be easy, but the decision is yours."

Ben's voice had ascended a semitone and Jess couldn't stop herself asking the question. "What happened? With your daughter?"

There was a fractional hesitation, Ben glancing at her, then away again quickly, and it was as though Jess could hear the acceleration of his heartbeat.

"I had a son, Zach. He was a great kid. Funny and smart and interested in the world. A kid full of curiosity. I know everyone thinks their kids are special but Zach really was different. He just had this way of making people around him feel good."

Jess watched in silence as Ben rested his elbows on his thighs, hands clasped together under his chin. She tuned out the white noise of other people's conversations, held on tight to her own memories and focused on Ben.

"Zach was ten when 9/11 happened. He'd been at school in Brooklyn when the Twin Towers were hit, saw from his classroom window smoke rising out of the buildings. He watched the second plane fly into the south tower, watched both towers tumble to the ground. I still can't imagine what that must have been like for a child—to see your city under attack, to understand that things you thought were solid and indestructible were weak and defenseless. We lost two of our best friends that day. Zach had known them all his life. It was such a surreal time—I don't think anyone who wasn't there can ever really understand. It was like being in a daze for weeks on end, a really bad dream you just couldn't wake from. There was so much confusion and anger and shock."

Ben sat stock-still, shoulders hunched high around his neck. Jess remained silent beside him, knowing that sometimes what stories needed more than anything was the space to find their way out into the world.

"Zach changed after that day. Everything changed, obviously, but Zach's whole personality was different. Everyone we knew had been affected by 9/11 in some way but . . . I don't know . . . Zach seemed to feel it more deeply than his

friends. It was as though the dust from all that debris had got under his skin, filtered into his bloodstream, become a part of who he was. He went from being a gregarious, life-loving kid to someone who was watchful, quiet, wistful. I'd always assumed he'd abhor violence and conflict, hate anything to do with war. I don't know. Maybe we should have seen the signs, clocked what he was thinking sooner. Maybe then we'd have stood a chance of stopping him."

Ben paused, ran his fingers through his hair, let his chin rest back on his clasped hands.

"He told us just before his eighteenth birthday that he was deferring his university place, joining the military, going to fight in Afghanistan. I can't really describe what a shock it was. Of all the kids in his class, Zach was the last person you'd think would do that. Nicole and I did everything we could to try and dissuade him. We pleaded with him, rationalized with him, showed him the videos and the stats and the *New York Times* articles. We got angry with him, got angry with each other, but he was resolute. He joined up, did his training, left for Kandahar the day after his nineteenth birthday."

Ben swallowed hard, his eyes flicking briefly toward Jess's face, and Jess knew where the story must be heading but she also knew she needed to let Ben tell it. That now he'd begun, she must let him finish.

"It was seven weeks later that we got a knock on the door. I was nagging Erin because she was going to be late for school, so Nicole went to answer it, assuming it would be the mailman. As soon as I heard her coffee cup smash on the hallway floor, I knew. It's weird. You've watched that scene so many times on TV, read about it in books, seen reports of it in the newspapers. It just felt unreal, as though we were characters in a film and this couldn't possibly be real life."

Jess heard her own intake of breath, felt the air suspended in her lungs, sensing there was more to come.

"It was an IED. Zach had been manning a checkpoint when a car had driven up with a single driver inside who'd detonated himself. Zach was the only casualty. Two army officers stood in our kitchen that morning telling us how proud we should be, how brave Zach was, how he'd done such a great service for his country, but all I could think about was what had gone through the head of that driver as he'd drawn up at the checkpoint, knowing what he was about to do. What kind of madness made him go through with it?"

Anger bled from Ben's voice and Jess placed the flat of her hand on his back. "I'm sorry, Ben. I'm so sorry. I can't imagine what that must have been like for you."

She watched him train his eyes on the floor, breathing deeply, as though he didn't yet trust himself to look her in the eye.

"You know the thing I find hardest about it? I don't understand now why I let him go. Why didn't I just lock him in a room until he'd got the stupid idea out of his system? I look back now and I think, What kind of a father lets his son walk out of the front door and into a senseless war?"

Ben's voice was low and tight, as though his vocal cords were being squeezed.

"He was eighteen, Ben. He wanted to make his own decision. That's what teenagers do. There's nothing you could have done to stop him."

"Isn't there? It doesn't feel like that now. Now it feels like I'd strap my body to his and never let him out of my sight if it meant he'd still be here."

Jess blinked hard against images of Zoe that final night and her regret that she had ever left her sister's side. "You have

nothing to feel guilty about, Ben. Nothing to seek forgiveness for." She thought about Lily standing outside Zoe's bedroom door that morning and her determination to stop Jess venturing inside. All these years she had hated herself for not doing more—for not pushing Lily aside and forcing her way in—as though perhaps, if she had, she might have been able to save her twin's life.

"But that's not the end of it. I wish to God it was, but it's not. You know how people say that tragedies either bring families closer together or tear them apart? I didn't just lose Zach in that explosion. I lost Erin and Nicole too. It was all my own fault. I pushed them away. They did all the things grieving families are supposed to do, but I just couldn't cope with it. I couldn't cope with their grief on top of my own. I left four months after the funeral and I didn't see Erin for five years. It's inexcusable, I know. There were phone calls, emails, cards, but that was it. But after the concert at the Albert Hall—after your mum told me how ill she was and still she got on that stage and sang—I realized I had to make things better. I couldn't waste any more time. When I first got back, I didn't have any hope that Erin might let me back in her life. I wasn't sure Nicole would even allow me to see her. I'm not suggesting for a second it's been easy, but we're getting there, slowly. Erin's beginning to forgive me, and I can honestly say it's the greatest gift I've ever had. And it's within your power to give your mum that forgiveness too. It's completely up to you."

Ben raised his head and turned to Jess, his face washed of all color. Jess let the story settle in her mind, let it adjust to being in the outside world.

"Do you know, I've not told that story to anyone in five years? Usually I run a mile if there's any chance of someone

finding out. But I suppose the reason I'm telling you now is that I want you to see that even when you're convinced relationships are beyond repair, there's always hope."

Jess thought about her mum and Lily in Central Park, no doubt discussing what a terrible mess her misunderstanding had made of their lives. She pulled at the cuticle of her little finger, watched the skin rip away from the nail, leaving behind a bright pink sore. "It's all very well me worrying about how I'm going to forgive my mum. But what about Lily forgiving me? How's she ever going to do that given the way I've treated her?"

"I know it's hard. I'm not saying it's going to be easy. But there's always a chance of reconciliation. You just have to be honest enough to want it and brave enough to pursue it."

They fell silent and Jess's eyes roamed the lobby until they settled on a figure she wasn't yet ready to see. "Shit, there's Lily. Do you think she's spotted me? I can't talk to her yet."

Ben followed her gaze to where Lily was standing by the staircase, scrolling through something on her phone. "Of course you can. The sooner you two start talking the sooner you can begin to repair the damage."

"Unless she really doesn't want to speak to me again."

"Well, you won't find out unless you try, will you?"

Jess looked again to where Lily was standing, her eyes narrowing with uncertainty, before turning back to Ben. "I really am sorry for dumping all this on you. You just caught me at a really bad time. I'm not always like this, honestly."

"Don't be silly. There's no need to apologize. I'm glad I happened to be here when you needed to vent."

There was a pause and Jess felt herself rush to speak before she knew what she was going to say. "You know I'm here with Mum for a few days? Maybe . . . I don't know . . .

maybe we could get a coffee or something before I head back? I can fill you in on the latest episode of my family drama." She gave a short, tentative laugh, felt heat flush her cheeks.

"I'd really like that. How about I give you a call here at the hotel tomorrow morning—around nine? We can make a plan then."

"That'd be great. And thank you—for listening, I mean, and for the wise advice. I'm sorry for sniveling all over your shoulder. The other guests here must think we're a couple in the midst of some awful breakup or something."

They smiled and said goodbye, and as Jess crossed the marble-floored lobby toward Lily, she tried to think of all the ways the members of her family might yet be able to forgive one another.

Chapter 64
Lily

Lily looked up in time to see Jess walking across the lobby toward her, to see her sister wipe the palms of her hands on the back of her jeans, to catch the hesitation before the question.

"Where's Mum?"

Their eyes met only briefly and Lily couldn't be sure which of them had looked away first.

"She wanted a bit of time by herself. She's walking back through the park. She wanted . . ." The words floundered in Lily's throat, choked by the strangeness of standing next to her sister, just the two of them, for the first time in decades. "Do you want to . . . get a drink or something?" She felt heat rise into her cheeks, was aware of the seconds stretching incalculably as she waited for Jess to reply.

Her sister glanced up just long enough for Lily to catch the relief—or was it doubt?—that skimmed across her face. Lily wasn't sufficiently schooled in Jess's expressions to be able to read it. But then Jess nodded, and before she had a chance to change her mind, Lily led the way into a room with wood-paneled walls, parquet flooring, and rose-petal lighting. The bar was busy and she headed for an empty table in the corner. She sat down, Jess opposite, feeling like a little

girl on a playdate, uncertain as to who should take the lead, which toys they should play with, which game should begin.

She thought about her mum's last words to her in the park: *I just want you two to be sisters again. Can you try and do that for me?*

As Lily tried to work out how to restart a conversation that had fallen silent years ago, she realized that there were so many ways to begin, yet no way of knowing which might lead to the right ending. "How are you feeling?" The question felt strange in Lily's mouth, as though her brain and her voice box had conspired to let it out without asking her first.

Jess glanced up at her—fleeting, furtive—then looked back down at the table, tearing at the corner of a paper napkin. "I'm not sure. Confused. Angry. Humiliated. Take your pick."

Neither spoke for a moment, a carousel of recent memories revolving in Lily's head: Daniel and the redhead and the new baby Lily would have given anything to be her own; the tone of Jess's hatred as she'd finally voiced an accusation so much wilder than anything Lily had ever imagined; her mum's expression as she'd turned to Lily, realizing that Lily had known all along.

"I just hate the fact that everyone else knew the truth about how Zoe died and I didn't. Why didn't you tell me?" Jess's voice was quiet, just the lightest ripple on the surface to hint at the rip current beneath.

Lily thought about all the times she'd yearned to confide in her sister. All those evenings in the office, staring at a computer screen in lieu of facing her memories. All those early mornings in the gym, pounding her feet on a treadmill in an effort to pummel thoughts from her head. All those nights lying awake next to Daniel, wishing she could creep downstairs and call Jess to describe the scene that had haunted her for years. Somewhere in Lily's mind there had always been a

parallel life, one in which she had told Jess the truth and, in doing so, had cemented a bond between them.

"When should I have told you? I couldn't have told you at the time: you were only ten. It was bad enough for me knowing and I was fifteen. It would have completely destroyed you. And by the time you were old enough to know, you weren't speaking to me anymore. I tried, Jess. I tried to have a relationship with you but you didn't want to know." Frustration spilled from Lily's voice and she stopped herself before the rift between them deepened.

"So you're saying that if I hadn't cut you out of my life, you'd have told me the truth?"

Lily was about to nod but then she replayed Jess's question, dug deeper for an answer. An image shuttered in her mind like the split-second opening of a camera lens: arriving home that day to the parked police car on the curb outside, her heart rising into her throat as she walked through the hallway and into the sitting room to find her mum and Jess locked in grief. A look on her mum's face not only of shock and horror but of something else too: fear wrapped in a guilt so thick that Lily couldn't imagine her mum ever being free of it.

"Honestly? I don't know. It wasn't my confession to make. And Mum obviously didn't want us to know or she'd have told us herself. And can you really blame her? Think what could have happened if anyone had found out."

"What's that got to do with you telling me? What do you think I'd have done if I'd known? Gone to the police? For God's sake, Lily, don't you credit me with any integrity at all? I've never told anyone what I thought you'd done. I'd have never put Mum in jeopardy like that."

"I'm not saying you would. I'm just saying it wasn't my story to tell."

They both fell silent. Lily thought about her mum in Central Park, wondering where she was, whether she was back at the hotel yet, feeling a stab of panic that she shouldn't have left her alone.

"Did you never tell anyone? Not even Daniel?"

Lily shook her head and looked down at the table, noticing how the grain of the wood rippled across its surface. There had been so many moments when she'd considered confiding in Daniel, but each time the fear of exposing her mum had stopped her. Now Lily wondered whether it had always been there in her marriage, wedged between them, whether any relationship could survive a secret like that.

Lily thought back to that morning in the school toilets—less than half an hour after watching her mum give Zoe the overdose—grieving for a death she wasn't yet supposed to know had happened. A death she had been convinced was all her fault. She had not known then that she would spend the next three decades striving for perfection as a means of smothering her guilt. She had not known that she would study with a feverish commitment to get the A-level grades needed for Oxford, or that throughout her three years at university she would make no lasting friendships, allow herself no romantic encounters. She had not known that she would immerse herself in her studies as a distraction from her thoughts, a tactic she would employ for many years to come, professional approbation filling the gaping void where her family should have been. She had presented a picture to the world of a life and a career so unblemished there had been days she had almost managed to believe it herself.

In lieu of anyone to confide in, Lily had shed the events of that summer like a snake shedding its skin, refashioning herself into someone new, someone good, someone other people

aspired to be. It was an impression of her life she had clung to as tightly as if it were a raft in the middle of an ocean. But the fear had always been there, sitting on her shoulder like a vexatious golem: the fear that at any moment the truth might be discovered. Countless times over the years she had imagined her mum confessing, imagined the police interviews, the trial, the prison sentence. So many times she had tried to imagine what she would say if questioned, whether she would confess to her part in it, whether she would acknowledge that she had sown the seed in her mum's mind. But this was one part of the scenario where her imagination always failed her.

"I couldn't. I knew that if I told anyone, I'd be putting Mum at risk. I couldn't do that to her. I couldn't do it to any of us." Lily felt a fissure opening up in her voice.

"So you've been trying to protect Mum all this time? That's why you didn't say anything? You just wanted to protect her?"

Lily was about to nod but a series of memories crept into her head: Zoe and Jess sitting cross-legged on the bottom bunk, painting each other's fingernails, brushing each other's hair, whispering into each other's ears. Zoe and Jess glancing at one another across the dinner table, silent communications indecipherable to all but the two of them. The way her sisters had finished each other's sentences, how they had laughed at the same jokes and cried at the same books, how they had always known that the other was in distress long before it had been voiced.

As she glanced across the table to where Jess was awaiting an answer, Lily glimpsed a shadow of the ten-year-old girl who had sat on the edge of the sofa, encased in their mum's arms, face contorting with grief as she was told of Zoe's death. She heard the sound of Jess sobbing into her pillow every night after Zoe had died. She remembered coming down to

breakfast each morning to the stippling of skin around Jess's eyes, recalled the months that Jess's face had seemed permanently mottled with grief. Lily had known what it was to lose a sister and she had always understood it was a bereavement from which she would never recover. But she had not lost a twin. And the incomprehensibility of Jess's grief made Lily shake her head. "Not just Mum. You, too. Because if you'd known the truth about Zoe's death, you'd have had to live with it. And you two were so close, I just couldn't imagine how you'd be able to do that."

Lily paused and it seemed to her that this was one of those moments when words were as delicate as eggshells and only the lightest tread ensured they wouldn't get broken. "But isn't that what you've been doing too, Jess? Isn't that why you never told Mum what you suspected me of doing? Because you knew it would devastate her. Weren't you just trying to protect her too?"

Chapter 65
Jess

Jess thought about all those times her belief in Lily's crime had strained at the leash, urging her toward disclosure. All the times she had dared imagine the relief at unburdening herself. But each time she had been silenced by the same single image: that of her mum's face crumpling with renewed grief. "Of course it was. I couldn't have done that to her."

Jess blinked and there it was: the image of Lily standing outside the door to the spare bedroom, arm twisted behind her, Jess so certain of the guilt on Lily's face. As she replayed the scene, watching it afresh, knowing what she now knew, she could see her misreading so clearly: how she had mistaken distress for anger, fear for panic, grief for guilt. And the effect of that replay—watching, frame by frame, the shift in perspective, the change in meaning—was disorienting, bewildering. For the first time Jess recognized the grave simplicity of her error of judgment: one emotion exchanged for another, a story invented to ward off a trauma she was not ready to face. All these years she had supplanted anger for mourning, had punished one sister for still being alive out of grief for the one who was not.

"I'm sorry, Lily. I really am truly sorry. I know that what

I've done is unforgivable. I wish you could know how much I hate myself for it. I wish you could know how sorry I am." She swallowed, the muscles in her throat conspiring against her. Ben's words echoed in her ears and she raised her head, looked directly at Lily, holding her gaze. "I'm sorry for cutting you off all this time. And I'm sorry for the impact it's had on you, on Mum, on all of us. I don't expect you ever to be able to forgive me but if there was any chance we could . . . I don't know . . . If there was any chance we could just not hate each other . . ." She faltered, words eluding her. She dropped her head, pulling at a loose thread on her blouse, winding it around and around her finger until it dug into her flesh.

"I've never hated you, Jess. Never. I've been angry with you. I've been bewildered by you. There've been times I've wanted to scream with frustration at you. But I've never hated you. You're my sister and I love you. I love you even when you're acting in ways I don't understand, even when I don't see you for years. I never stopped loving you."

Jess blinked and watched one tear, then another, drop onto the thighs of her jeans. It was only once she'd counted a dozen that she felt able to lift her head and find her voice. "I love you too, Lily. And I'm sorry. I'm so, so sorry."

They reached out and found one another's hands across the rosewood table, their eyes clouded with tears, and it was as though all the years of separation were slowly dissolving.

"I've got some tissues in my bag. Let me get them out."

Jess sniffed loudly as Lily burrowed in her bag and emerged with a packet of tissues, handing one to Jess. "Are you OK?"

Jess nodded, even though she wasn't quite sure what it meant anymore. "You?"

Lily smiled, and it was as if her sister were transforming

in front of her: no longer the monster Jess had spent almost thirty years imagining her to be, but a woman who had spent as long as Jess imprisoned by a secret she had felt compelled to keep for the protection of others.

"It's going to be OK, Jess. We can do this, I know we can."

Lily smiled at her again, and Jess wanted to reciprocate but there was still so much to be resolved. "What about Mum . . . ?"

"Do you think Mum's OK . . . ?"

Their questions collided and they each stopped abruptly, their eyes catching and releasing like a hook-and-eye fastening that couldn't quite hold.

"You go ahead. In what way?"

Jess paused, trying to untangle a knot of feelings, unsure whether she could work her way from the guilt at one end to absolution at the other. "When Zoe died I felt as though a part of me had died too, a part of me I knew I'd never get back. And I haven't. There's always been a part of me missing. And now, knowing what Mum did . . . I can't help feeling it was Mum who stole that part away from me and I don't know how to forgive her for it."

Fresh tears began to fall down Jess's cheeks and as she wiped them away, Lily began to speak.

"I know none of us can ever completely understand what it was like for you. I guess only another set of twins could. But however hard it is to accept, Zoe was going to die whatever Mum did. There's no changing that fact. And however conflicted you are with Mum right now, ask yourself what you'd have done in her position. What would you do if Mia was sick, if she was in that much pain, and you knew she wasn't going to get better? Are you honestly telling me, as a mother, that you wouldn't want to do something to put an

end to her suffering, however awful that thing was? Because I'd like to think that, if I could find the courage, I'd do the same for Phoebe."

Jess tried to imagine how her mum must have felt as she'd sat on Zoe's bed and given her the overdose. She tried to envisage what must have gone through her mind as she'd filled the syringe, as she'd administered the excess of morphine, as she'd watched her daughter die. She tried to imagine ever having to do that for Mia but her temples throbbed, resisting the image.

She thought back to that day, walking through the front door, knowing instinctively that Zoe was dead and yet hoping that, if only she could stand still long enough, perhaps she could stop time—reverse it, even—so that the future, when it arrived, might be different.

"Do you know what I find hardest? I can't even remember the last thing I said to Zoe. She was my twin sister and I can't recall my last words to her." Jess wiped at her tears, aware of having said something she hadn't been able to acknowledge to herself all these years.

"I know, Jess. I understand, really I do. But you can't undo the past. And things with Mum . . . well, they're different now, aren't they?"

Jess thought about her mum wandering alone around Central Park, nursing her disappointment that her longed-for trip to New York had gone so horribly wrong on its first day. She pictured the way her shoulder blades now jutted out from her clothes like stunted wings. She remembered her mum lying under the stiff hospital sheets in the ER less than two months before and how, in the split second after she'd swished back the curtain, the panic Jess had felt was not about seeing Mia

and Lily in the same room together but about seeing her mum so frail under the harsh strip lighting.

Jess allowed herself to imagine how lonely and isolated her mum must have been all this time, knowing that the only person in whom she had ever confided about Zoe's death had found her confession so intolerable that he hadn't been able to live with it.

Pulling at the soggy tissue between her fingers, she knew that a part of her would always wish things could have been different. She would always wish that she had been told about the severity of Zoe's illness and that she'd known the truth about her death. But most of all Jess wished, very simply, that Zoe had never got ill. And that was a wish, she admitted to herself for the first time, that hadn't been in anyone's control: not hers, not her mum's, not Lily's or their dad's. Not the doctors' or nurses' who had tried so valiantly to cure Zoe. Jess realized that she had spent all these years being angry with Lily because it was easier to feel anger than it was to feel grief.

She knew how easy it would be to allow her anger to find a new focus in her mum. But as she glanced toward the entrance and saw her mum standing hesitantly in the doorway, as though unsure whether she was yet ready to cross the threshold, Jess felt something shift inside her: her anger being edged to one side and, in its place, the acute sense of loss she had spent so many years smothering with fury.

Chapter 66
Audrey

Audrey scanned the room until she saw them in the far corner, sitting opposite one another at a round rosewood table. She stood completely still, watching Lily and Jess, wishing she could know what had already been said.

Hovering in the doorway, she felt all her regrets lining up behind her lips as if determined to take one final collective curtain call before it was too late. She watched her daughters, her breath unmoving in her chest, her lungs clinging to every last drop of air.

And then she saw it. She saw their hands reach across the table, saw them hold one another for the first time in years. It was a moment of complete stillness in which she felt she was watching their estrangement evaporate, like condensation rising from a frozen, sunlit lake. She caught an unmistakable glance of sympathy pass from Lily to Jess, a look that was received, accepted, reciprocated: such a simple exchange and yet one which made Audrey's lungs inflate.

This, Audrey thought, as she watched the tears trickle down Jess's cheeks, as she saw Lily reach into her bag to hand her sister a tissue, as she watched a conversation resume after decades of unnecessary silence: this was all she wanted. Seeing her daughters together, daring to hope that they might be

there for each other once she could no longer be there for either of them. For years it had seemed such an impossible dream. And yet here they were, engaging in something so unremarkable in the grand scheme of things—a conversation between sisters in a bar on a Saturday evening—yet it seemed to Audrey to be one of the most vital, precious things in the world.

Once upon a time Audrey had believed that her life was set on a clear path and that any diversion led to a complete derailment. Only now did she realize that those moments of change were not an ending but a beginning: a chance for a different kind of life, a different kind of journey, a different form of happiness.

She thought about the diary upstairs in her hotel room. All those dreams, all those ambitions. Throughout her adult life, she had packaged her desires into tidy little boxes, parceled them up, and stacked them neatly inside her head, never believing that she deserved any of them to come true. Now the only thing she wished was that she had found a little of her eleventh-hour courage sooner.

Standing in the doorway to the Rose Club in the Plaza Hotel, Audrey realized that nothing she had done over the past few months—not the choir, not the art class, not even the trip to New York—had really been about the fulfillment of those ambitions. They had all been just a framework on which to hang what really mattered: spending time with her family, and finding a way to bring them back together.

As a waiter stopped by her side and asked if he could be of any assistance, Audrey soaked up the sight of her daughters together and thought how strange it was that of all the things she had wished for on her sixteenth birthday, she had not known to include a moment like this.

She shook her head, knowing she needed to speak to Lily and Jess but feeling that theirs was a group she had not yet earned the right to join. She wanted to seek their forgiveness but was not yet ready for the possibility of rejection.

And then, just as she was contemplating going back to her room, rehearsing her apology once more and refining her explanation, giving the girls more time to accustom themselves to their own conversation before she intervened, Jess caught her eye, the two of them locking gazes for what seemed an eternity. She saw Jess turn to Lily, watched her say something, saw them both turn back to look at her in unison. She watched, her heart racing, as they stared at her. And then Lily raised a hand and beckoned her over.

For a moment Audrey's feet refused to move, as though they weren't yet ready to trust what her eyes were telling her. But then Lily waved again and Audrey saw on Jess's face what she thought might have been the most tentative nod in her direction.

Walking toward them, Audrey tried to remember all the things she wanted to say. As she reached the table, both girls held out their hands to her, and as Audrey took hold of them she felt the first flicker of hope that this might be a new beginning for all of them. Because she was certain now that a person's story didn't follow a straight narrative trajectory from birth to death. There were countless beginnings and endings, countless opportunities to start again. There were as many different beginnings to a life as someone was brave and kind enough to allow themselves.

Part Seven

November

Chapter 67
Jess

The sound was like water gurgling down a semi-clogged drain.

Jess sat in the dim light of the bedroom, listening to her mum's shallow, labored breaths.

Keep the room dark. Bright light will hurt her head, even behind closed eyes. That was what the nurse had said just over nine hours ago, shortly before Jess had telephoned Lily and suggested she and Phoebe come to Shepherd's Bush right away.

Behind her, Jess heard someone sniff. She reached out, took Mia's hand, squeezed gently. There were no words, Jess knew that. This was the moment language failed you.

Another breath rasped inside her mum's chest, came wheezing out through the small parting of her lips: sharp and sour, like fruit left to ripen too long in a bowl.

Jess glanced across the bed to where Lily and Phoebe were sitting on the far side, Lily's face pale and watchful as though she didn't dare blink for fear of missing the moment they all knew to be imminent.

She felt a hand rest on the back of her neck, felt newly familiar fingers stroke gently along her nape, turned, and met Ben's eyes just long enough to see the concern and affection in his expression.

A short, jagged breath made its way into her mum's lungs. It wouldn't be long. Jess knew that without needing to be

told. And the knowledge caused a wave of panic that had been ebbing and flowing throughout the night to rise into her throat with a need to mark the moment, to make this last sliver of time count for something.

She watched Mia kneel beside her, watched her daughter smooth her fingers across the papery skin of Audrey's forehead. Glancing sideways, she saw a lone tear trickle down Phoebe's cheek.

Jess took her mum's hand, stroked the back of it with the pad of her thumb, wanting her mum to know she was there, that they were all there. Leaning forward she whispered in her mum's ear, words of tenderness and gratitude that had, for so many years, remained unspoken: a torrent of love she hoped might seep into her mum's consciousness, to be heard and understood before it was too late.

Jess turned her head, caught Lily's eye, and nodded.

Chapter 68
Lily

Lily unscrewed the lid, inserted the syringe, and drew up the medicine inside. Slowly, carefully, one drop at a time, she dripped the liquid morphine onto her mum's tongue.

Her mum's lips closed, as if in slow motion, and then gradually opened again, the sound of her tongue peeling from the dry roof of her mouth echoing around the room.

Lily waited for the next breath to come but her mum lay there, inert, her jaw slack, lips parted, body unmoving.

And just at the point Lily thought the moment had arrived, her mum took in another short, jarring breath, her chest rising and holding on to the air as if her body knew how very precious every last atom was.

She brought her face close to her mum's, breathed in the sharp acetone odor on her breath as she kissed her forehead, knew from the last time, twenty-eight years ago, what that smell meant.

Lily rested her cheek against the back of her mum's hand, brought her lips to her mum's arid skin—skin she had kissed a thousand times before yet never with the significance with which she kissed it now—and felt the first of her tears begin to fall.

As another breath rattled in and out, Lily noticed the tiniest movement in her mum's mouth: a fractional upending of her lips.

A smile.

Her mum was smiling. Infinitesimal and yet, to Lily, momentous.

Chapter 69
Audrey

There is something bitter on her tongue. Something metallic and bitter as though her mouth is coated in mercury. It is a familiar taste but only recently so.

She manages to close her lips although her bottom jaw feels heavy and her head wants to sink back onto the pillow. But there is something hard underneath her skull. Something is holding her head at a distance higher than the pillow, causing her neck muscles to strain against the effort.

A hand. That's what it is. A hand.

She feels her tongue make contact with the roof of her mouth. It seems to stick there, spreading the strange flavor across her palate. For a moment she does not think she will be able to pull her tongue free but slowly, there it comes, and with it a loud sticking noise that seems to echo in her ears.

She breathes in and hears something rattle at the back of her throat. It is a noise she knows although she cannot place it. But she does not like it and wishes she was not hearing it. It is a noise that causes images to flash behind her closed eyes. Images of a darkened room, a small figure under a duvet, tiny blue hummingbirds, and waiting: waiting for something she knows will happen but wishes with all her heart would not. It is an image that squeezes something deep inside her

yet she does not know whether the feeling belongs to the past or the present.

Somebody is whispering into her ear. Their breath is soft, moist, reassuring, even though the words are slippery, unable to form shapes she recognizes. But it is a voice that warms the inside of her head, filling it with something familiar, something she wants more of even though she is not sure exactly what it is.

She breathes out and there is a sense of release in letting the air go.

She feels something warm being smoothed across her forehead, soft as a feather, brushing across her skin. And then a similar sensation on the back of her hand. She wonders if time has reversed, if she is a little girl again, back in the white wooden bed in the flat above the shop, recovering from scarlet fever, her mother keeping vigil by her side, feeding her sips of sugary drinks, singing her songs, stroking her hair.

She is filled, suddenly, with a sense that there is something she ought to do—something she needs to do—but hard as she tries, she cannot remember what it is. It is somewhere just out of reach, beyond her grasp, and yet she is sure it is there. And just as she is about to give up looking for it, she feels a trickle of air pass slowly through her lips, feels it suck the moisture out of her mouth on its way down her windpipe, feels her chest expand to make room for it, and there is a sense of relief that her body has found the answer.

Emerging out of the darkness, a scene filters into view behind her closed eyes.

It is a meadow, grasses high, variegated flowers in bloom. A cloudless sky, sun shining brightly, bathing the air in a hazy yellow hue. And beneath the blue sky and the burnished sun, in the middle of the meadow, four girls are dancing.

Lily, Jess, Mia, Phoebe. All of them children, all of them dancing, holding hands in a circle, daisy chains in their hair like woodland nymphs, their movements illuminated by an ethereal glow.

They are happy. They are all safe and they are all happy. She can see it in their smiles, in their laughter, in the clutching of their hands and the motion of their limbs.

And there, standing to one side of the meadow, is Zoe. Zoe is watching them dance and she, too, is smiling. All of her girls are smiling.

She feels something soft against her cheek, something soft and smooth and warm, and there is comfort in it, a comfort that goes beyond words. And the warmth seeps through her cheek and down her neck, across her shoulders, into her chest, weaving itself through her ribs until her whole body is infused with it.

Behind her closed eyes, she turns her head to follow the movement of her dancing girls, but the glare of the sun bathes the scene in a light too bright for her to penetrate. Too light, too bright for her to see her girls anymore.

She watches them disappear and whispers a silent goodbye.

Acknowledgments

Second novels are notoriously tricky beasts, and I owe thanks to an army of people who have encouraged and supported me over the past few years.

Thanks to my agent, Sheila Crowley, who always reassured me that she would stick by me until I found the book I was meant to write: we got there in the end! Thanks to all at Curtis Brown, particularly Abbie Greaves and Luke Speed.

Eternal thanks to my editor, Harriet Bourton, for believing in me and this book. You really are the very best of editors and it's no exaggeration to say that your creative input has been transformative. If this were an Oscar speech, I would say I was sharing the award with you.

To all at Orion who have been such passionate champions, guardians, and promoters of this novel: Poppy Stimpson in publicity and Katie Moss in marketing for their tireless creativity and boundless enthusiasm; Bethan Jones for guiding the book (and me) through the process; Susan Howe, Jessica Purdue, and Krystyna Kujawinska in the rights team for a fantastic lineup of foreign deals; Jen Wilson, Rachael Hum, and the whole sales team; Maggy Park, Dominic Smith, and, the fantastic sales reps; Paul Stark and Amber Bates in audio; Ruth Sharvell in production; Charlotte Abrams-Simpson for

the gorgeous cover; and the Orion bigwigs, Katie Espiner and Sarah Benton, for allowing me to be published by the best team in the business.

Enormous thanks to my American publisher, HarperCollins, for bringing the book to a US audience with such enthusiasm and passion, especially to Tessa Woodward and Elle Keck in editorial, Molly Waxman in marketing, Jessica Lyons in publicity, and Rachel Meyers in production editorial.

So many people in publishing and journalism have become friends over the past few years (and have often provided me with gainful employment). Thanks to Georgina Moore, Alison Barrow, Charlotte Heathcote, Lisa O'Kelly, Nina Pottell, and Sara-Jade Virtue: the profession is so much better for having you all in it. Sincere thanks, too, to Mari Evans for invaluable advice and encouragement when I was very much in need of it.

To the fellow writers whom I now have the privilege of calling friends: thanks to Amanda Jennings, Maggie O'Farrell, and Rachel Joyce.

Particular thanks to my wonderful friend and fellow novelist Lucy Atkins for being the person with whom I first discussed this novel and who helped shape it in so many crucial ways, not to mention being my first reader, and such an incisive one at that. Huge thanks, too, to Emilya Hall for invaluable notes on an early draft.

For both friendship and patience with my endless medical inquiries, thanks to Joanna Cannon and Adam Kay. Suffice it to say, any medical mistakes are mine.

To my brother and sister-in-law, Matthew and Sally Bush, for their early readings and reassurance that this book was "much better than your last."

Thanks to my step-dad, Jerry Bowler: for all the days I

have taken over your study, not to mention your unwavering belief that this book will be a success.

To my mum: thank you for your unstinting love, support, and encouragement; for your help with childcare when I've been on a deadline; for reading this novel *so* many times and doing such a great proofread; and for always making it clear that you would be proud of me whatever I did.

To my daughter, Aurelia, who pointed out that she can write a book in two days so why does it take Mummy two years? Thank you for your unbridled enthusiasm every time a new author endorsement came in, for your very honest feedback about various book jackets, and for taking so much pleasure in telling your friends that your mummy is a writer. Keep writing, angel, and I look forward to coming to *your* book launch one day.

And finally, to my husband, Adam. Being married to a writer is not easy, I know. The wild swings from optimism to despair (often on an hourly basis) would test the most patient of individuals. Luckily, you *are* the most patient of individuals, not to mention the most loving, supportive, and kind. You are a partner in the truest sense and I could not be more grateful for you. Thank you, with all my love.

About the Author

Hannah Beckerman worked as a television producer and commissioning editor for twelve years before becoming a full-time author, journalist, and broadcaster. She is a features writer and reviewer for *The Observer, The Guardian,* and the *FT Magazine,* appears regularly as a book critic on BBC Radio 2, and chairs literary events across the UK. Hannah lives in London with her husband and daughter.

You can connect with Hannah online:

hannahbeckerman.com
Twitter: @hannahbeckerman
Facebook: hannahbeckermanauthor
Instagram: hannahbeckermanauthor